D1105229

LEGEND
OF THE
STORM SNEEZER

KRISTIANA SFIRLEA

MONSTER IVY
PUBLISHING

To anyone who's waited for the perfect storm—
Here you go.

ENTRY 0

AUTHOR(S) INTERLUDE PART 1

Dear Reader Name Here _____,

May I call you Reader Name Here _____? Truth is, I don't know your name—though I'd like to! You don't know mine, either, but we can fix that. I'm Rose. Rosy. Rosebud. Thunder Rose. Bunch of other names I probably shouldn't put in print. I've been told my parents had no business giving me a one-syllable name 'cause it's misleading, like I'll be easy to manage or something. I like to think they gave it to me 'cause it's short and sweet. Like me!

Maybe you're wondering why a book called The Stormwatch Diaries: Legend of the Storm Sneezer *isn't starting with the words "Dear Diary." First off, that's a blah way to start a story ("Dear Blah" would've been better), and second, this isn't your typical diary. You, dear Reader Name Here _____, have stum-*

bled upon a time traveler's diary! Do you know what that means? It means there's only one author of this story—me— but while there's only ONE author, there's MORE than one of me. ~ Rose Skylar, 1526 A.S.

There's two! ~Rose Skylar, 1527 A.S.

Three. ~Rose Skylar, 1529 A.S.

Four! ~Rose Skylar, 1530 A.S.

And five. ~Rose Skylar, 1532 A.S.

It's not as complicated as it sounds. Promise! See, every time traveler needs a diary to keep track of their time traveling so that events happen in the right order, timelines don't tangle, worlds don't collide, and life as we know it doesn't become completely unwritten. That's why keeping a diary is so important—and why YOU'RE so important, Reader Name Here ____! Because the best way to remember a story is to tell it to someone who's never heard it before. And today, that's you! ~1526 A.S.

(Unless you're rereading this book. And we don't blame you if you are. It's a good book.) ~1527 A.S.

Ever wonder what it would be like if your future selves could comment on your diary while you're writing it? That's our job.

2

We're here to teach our youngest Little Me how to write her first traveler's diary and thus keep the fabric of Time from unraveling before our eyes. (No pressure, right?) Are you paying attention, Little Me, 1526? Good. **How to Write a Time Traveler's Diary, Lesson One:** *Side notes. Make 'em ALL CAPS and put them in parentheses.*

(LIKE THIS.)

Use them whenever you need to clarify something or make a clever observation. You'll be doing a lot of both. ~1529 A.S.

Should I be writing this down? ~1526 A.S.

What do you think we're doing, silly? ~1527 A.S.

How to Write a Time Traveler's Diary, Lesson Two: *Asterisks. When time passes between scenes, pop an asterisk.* ~1530 A.S.

What are those, for headaches? ~1526 A.S.

If only. ~1529 A.S.

*It's the little * symbol. They indicate a time lapse. Or, when you come across something in the story that Reader Name Here ____ might not know about, pop three asterisks (***) to break up the page and do a little explaining. We call those info-aster-isks.* ~1532 A.S.

*= Time lapse-asterisk. *** = Info-asterisks. Got it. Anything else? ~1526 A.S.

How to Write a Time Traveler's Diary, Lesson Three: Sometimes you have to look at the past to make sense of the present and prepare for the future. And this is where our story begins —in the past, when a girl of storms meets a boy of shadows and the friendship of legends is born ... ~1532 A.S.

... Is that my cue? That's my cue, isn't it? Sorry, I'm new at this "narrator" thing. Ahem. Flip the page, Reader Name Here ____, and get ready for a story that'll knock your socks off! ~1526 A.S.

Assuming you're wearing socks. It could be warm where you're reading. ~1529 A.S.

Or you could be wearing socks and shoes. ~1530 A.S.

Or you could be one of those weirdoes who wears shoes without socks, in which case we could just blow the whole foot off. ~1526 A.S.

How to Write a Time Traveler's Diary, Lesson Four: We do not DISMEMBER READER NAME HERE ____!!! ~1529 A.S.

Oops. ~1526 A.S.

Just—do what 1532 was doing. That was a very intriguing start. ~1530 A.S.

Fine, fine, fine. How'd it go again? Our story begins in the past, when a girl of storms meets a boy of shadows and the friendship of legends is born ... ~1526 A.S. (previously 1532 A.S. because that's time travel for you)

ENTRY 1

HELLO DARKNESS MY NEW FRIEND

Oh, the joys of being your own babysitter! Self-employment had never tasted so sweet. Yes, lack of pay was a slight disadvantage, but why would a girl be counting coins when she could be counting the steps from her house to the heart of a forbidden forest?

Of course, just because she was her own babysitter didn't mean she was alone strolling the backwoods of her family's estate. Rose was never alone, not with the little gray storm cloud following her wherever she went. Inside, outside, in the bathtub or in bed, there it was dripping raindrops like a runny nose. Lightning combed her curls till every strand was a live wire and the *thunder* ... well, like most uncomfortable noises, thunder picked the absolute worst times to crack. Her storm cloud was, without any competition, the biggest nuisance in the domain of Chunter Woods.

Gosh, she loved that thing.

"I'm a good babysitter, aren't I?" Rose asked her storm cloud. Stormy considered this, fluttering in thought, and patted her head affirmatively. Her hair poofed like a kernel of popcorn. "Thought so." She nodded in satisfaction.

She really *was* a good babysitter. Qualified in all babysitting necessities such as storytelling, how to open child safety locks, and—"Can we do that thing where you sock someone in the stomach when they're choking?"

Stormy swooped, ramming between her ribs with the force of a fist. Rose belly-flopped on the ground, supplies spilling out of her rucksack. "Good," she wheezed. "Good to know."

When her lungs filled with air again, Rose got up and recovered her fallen equipment. The best babysitters always come well-prepared! She'd packed chocolate bars and strawberries for sustenance, a wooden sword for protection—

(OH, DON'T LAUGH, WOODEN SWORDS CAN BE VERY THREATEN-ING. WHEN WAS THE LAST TIME YOU PULLED A HALF-INCH SPLINTER FROM YOUR SKIN?)

—and her scarlet umbrella, which served no purpose whatsoever except to twirl over her shoulder and bring out the color of her red and gray wings. Umbrellas were for indoor use where mothers preferred wet floors to soggy bread and rain-soaked tablecloths at dinner.

Given the choice, Momma would prefer her house bone-dry at all times, but particularly when she had company over, which was why she shooed Rose outside every Tuesday afternoon while she hosted her ladies' knitting club.

Rose shook out her feathers and reached for the final object from her rucksack. It was *Blackout's Tales*, the famous, eight-hundred-page anthology of Old World legends and the reason she was traipsing through the woods today, same as every Tuesday the past year. Do you know how many Tuesdays there are on a calendar? A lot. A *lotta* lot. And she and Stormy had spent every one of them following the example left behind by the greatest legend seeker to ever live.

Blackout was a man who devoted years to chasing down ancient scholars—

(OKAY, MAYBE NOT CHASING—THEY WERE PRETTY ANCIENT— BUT, LIKE, POWER-WALKING)

—to collect their stories of the Old World in the book that would earn him his name. And once *Blackout's Tales* was complete, Blackout dedicated the rest of his days to storytelling, traveling from realm to realm, regaling the masses with his life's work.

What Rose wouldn't have given to hear him speak and experience his trademark move firsthand.

See, the book earned him his name, but the feat at the end of recitals earned him his fame. When Blackout finished his stories, he would close the cover of *Blackout's Tales*, stand up from his storyteller's chair, and *sing*.

It was a lullaby laced with magic, one that swept his listeners into oblivion. And as they blacked out, Blackout himself would disappear from the crowd, exiting the town the way he did everything else: without a trace.

Ages had passed since Blackout's death, but his legends remained, and Rose was going to seal his legacy forever.

She was gonna prove that the legends of *Blackout's Tales* were true.

Sounds impressive, doesn't it? So dramatic. So purposeful! So utterly *impossible* for a nine-year-old angel without proper transportation. Wings only got you so far, and that was without her mother calling her home for dinner! But. Yes, *but*. There *was* a legend that could be found within an hour radius of her mother's voice: the will-o'-the-wisp—or *wispies*, she called them. Forest-dwelling tricksters appearing as little blue balls of light that lead hikers off their trails and sometimes over cliffs. Their playful giggles and beguiling light will enthrall just about anyone who crosses their path, but legend has it they have a particular fondness for lumberjacks.

Which was convenient since Rose had a back yard full of 'em.

In the middle of the forest at the end of her family's property lay the border between Pandrum, realm of artisan bread and bakery goods, and their neighbor Faberland, realm of carpentry and wooden novelties. They had more lumberjacks and janes than trees! She'd spy them frequently at the border, sawing away with occasional shouts of "timber!"

But the lumberjacks weren't there today. And if *they* weren't there, chances were the *wispies* wouldn't be, either.

"Gah!" she groaned and slumped to the ground. This was going nowhere! Think, think, *think*. What else did she know about wispies? According to legend, they aren't just interested in tricking lumberjacks or leading travelers to their dooms. If they like you enough, they'll lead you to their home, a place known as the Wishing Mist. Step into the Mist, and it'll taste you. If it likes the flavor, it'll swallow you whole. And when it spits you out, you'll have any wish your heart desires.

Eaten alive by a mist. Now *that* was the opposite of boring. Rose would gladly take being digested by a legend from *Blackout's Tales* over slowly dissolving in a stew of her own boredom. Stirred with her own bored stiff spoon. Dying a slow, painful, boring death of—

A deluge of water doused her curls. She shook her head, flinging raindrops right and left. "Thanks. I needed that."

She tilted her face, and Stormy twisted itself like a wet rag, wringing out a mini downpour. Rain washed the sweat from her forehead and filled her mouth with water. It tasted good and quenched her thirst, but sweet *magic*, what she wouldn't give for a glass of chocolate milk right now. Rich, creamy chocolate milk. In a world brimming with magic, why wasn't there such a thing as a chocolate dairy cow? Imagine: a whole herd of cows that only give chocolate milk! And when you first milk 'em and the milk's all warm, instant hot chocolate! Amazing. How had no one thought of this? She wished—

A bolt of lightning struck her tongue, and Rose swallowed compulsively. A pleasant buzz rippled through her body. She blinked the rain from her eyes and looked around.

There, peeking around a tree trunk, was a little blue ball of light.

Aha! When all else fails, wishful thinking does the trick!

(In retrospect, I wish I'd thought of that sooner.)

Months of waiting were about to pay off, so long as no one made any sudden moves or—

Above her, Stormy exploded with lightning, followed by a burst of bone-rattling thunder. "Shhh!" Rose hissed. "I know we're excited. Behave." She turned to the wispy. "Hi. I'm—"

"Follow me," it whispered, high-pitched and giggling, and raced off at light speed.

"—right behind you." If it was a chase the wispy wanted, then a chase it would get! Rose flexed her wings in pursuit, preparing for unexpected flight. No sneaky will-o'-the-wisp was gonna lead *her* over a cliff unawares! They spun through the woods, twisting and turning around shrubs, leapfrogging over fallen trees, and splashing through streams. She and her storm cloud were gaining. A few more feet and she could poke the wispy with her umbrella. Two feet now. One foot!

The blue ball of light took a sudden turn to the left, and Rose smacked headfirst into a tree trunk. She dropped to the ground in a heap of—what was the word? Discomba. Discom*baba*. *Discombobulation.*

(You don't need a dictionary for that one, Reader Name Here _____. Just bobble your head a bit, and you'll know exactly what it means.)

The wispy circled overhead, tittering. "Not this time, not this time! Next time, next time!" it promised and winked out of existence before her very eyes.

"Ugh!" Rose slammed her fist against the ground and glared up at the big, skull-crushing maple tree. "A real tree would come down here and apologize, you know." To be fair, the tree did *try* to make a noise, but it sounded less like an apology and more like ... snoring?

Rose squinted up. Up, up, up to where a blue flannel shirtsleeve dangled from the higher branches.

Cradled in the maple's ancient arms, someone was taking a nap.

She got to her feet, swaying from dizziness and indecision. Option 1) She could leave, go looking for the wispy again with 0.00001% chance of success.

The sleeper gave a loud, snuffling snore.

Or Option 2) If someone could saw logs like that in their sleep, they *had* to be a lumberjack. The flannel confirmed it. And if she woke up a lumberjack, the will-o'-the-wisp's favorite victim, maybe—just maybe—the wispy would come back!

Looking at Stormy from the corner of her eye, Rose smiled. A wink of lightning, and the storm cloud lifted from her head, growing bigger and bigger and bigger. In no time at all, her baby thunderhead was the size of a small house.

(Sniff; they grow up so fast.)

Stormy rose to the level of the sleeping lumberjack, blocking the sky completely. How could Dad not love this? He *hated* when she let her storm cloud off its leash, but how could you hate something so breathtaking?

It gave the signal. Three lightning bolts, two lightning bolts, one lightning bolt ...

BOOM!

13

Thunder roared like a cannon blast, scaring birds from branches and generally upsetting the wildlife, and Rose couldn't help but laugh along with it as a large lump came tumbling out of the maple tree. She dashed behind a tree trunk, still giggling. Stormy reverted to the size of a pillow and zoomed to muffle the noise. It covered her face like an enormous gray moustache, plugging her mouth and nose. Was this what she'd looked like as a baby when her first cry spat the storm cloud from her lungs in a great, gusty sneeze?

Behind them, the lump on the ground groaned deeply. Lumberjacks were *used* to falling out of trees, right? They wouldn't ... hold a grudge or anything?

She tightened her grip on her wooden sword and readied her umbrella. Something long and stretchy moved at her feet, winding around the tree trunk like a length of ribbon that had lost its spool. It spiraled up her legs, stealing around her waist. What *was* it? Black, velvety, softer than anything she'd ever felt. No name came to mind, but never fear! When all else fails—

(INCLUDING WISHFUL THINKING)

—the scientific method is an infallible fallback.

She would have to lick it.

The black matter rejected this idea the instant her tongue emerged. It went taut, yanking her off of her feet and turning her upside down. Chocolate bars, strawberries, and *Blackout's Tales* all tumbled out of her rucksack, bonking her head on their way to the ground.

"Let me go, let me go!" Wings beating frantically, Rose popped her umbrella like a shield and sliced her sword. "Let me g ... oh."

Her captor was most definitely a lumberjack, decked in flannel and towering over her with the height of a cliff and the width of a boulder. He was really old, too. Thirteen, maybe fourteen. Broad face, squat nose, eyebrows akin to fuzzy caterpillars—there was something wonderfully frightening about him. His hair was a mop, and blue eyes twinkled against dark skin like moons at nightfall.

She gaped at him from her upside-down vantage point, enthralled by her find and enthralled by those twinkling eyes. Moonstones, they were. Gems of frozen moonlight. She'd half a mind to scoop 'em out of their sockets and add them to her gem, button, and assorted shiny objects collection.

(*Finest collection this side of the multiverse.*)

As if reading her thoughts, the lumberjack's eyebrows rose, and his wings snapped open forcefully. Like he *needed* to look any bigger. His feathers were black and oddly blurry, shifting like shadows. From their tips flowed a braided strand of darkness that made up the lasso around her waist. With a flick of his wing, the lasso spun her upright, and she touched it with renewed fascination. That's what it was. A shadow!

It retracted suddenly, joining the darkness seeping from Shadow Boy's wings. His feathers became runaway inkblots, doubling, tripling, quadrupling in length, and he took to the air, blocking the sky as effectively as her storm cloud. The beat of his enormous shadow-wings whipped her curls like a wind tunnel, and Stormy struggled to maintain its molecules. The *size* of that wingspan! Just think of how fast he could fly. Faster than she could. Four times the speed would mean four times the distance. *Holy haloed hellhounds!* Are you thinking what she was thinking?

Shadow Boy hovered there, a harbinger of the flannel apocalypse and the solution to all her problems. She stared up at him with a look of sheer wonder.

"This is a withering glare," he informed her.

Rose nodded, blank and mesmerized. A moment or two floated by.

"You're supposed to wither."

"Oh! Oops. Should I—do you want me to get on my knees? Is that what I'm s'posta do? Or is it more of a droopy thing, like I hang my head and sorta—" She slumped forward, flopping her arms.

Shadow Boy sighed, and his shadow-wings receded. He landed on the ground with a resounding *thump*. "You don't find me threatening at all, do you?"

He was a Faberfrom for sure. His accent had all the

refinement of Aurialis mixed with the ruggedness of the realms on the Shell, and it was rich and sweet as maple butter.

"I'm not afraid of a lotta things I should be 'cause my head's not screwed on right." She wrinkled her nose. "Or that's what everyone's always telling me."

Shadow Boy plucked a twig idly from his shirt. "That's a lovely storm cloud you have. Is this the one that woke me? You have a mighty voice."

Stormy blushed a darker shade of gray, and Rose rocked bashfully on her heels. "Thanks. I like your shadows, too."

"Shadows and storms. Quite a pair, aren't they?"

She couldn't contain herself any longer. "Say, are you any good at stopping things from running into trees?"

"Hmm." He crossed his massive arms. "Can't say I have much experience as I'm usually running them through with an axe. But I bet I could learn."

"Good." She mimicked the tone her dad used when conducting knightly business, all brisk and stuffy like they'd run out of tissues. "I've got a proposition for you, Shadow Boy. See, I'm a legend seeker. I've been one for some time, actually, but today I suffered my first severe injury."

"By running into a tree, I'm guessing?"

"Yes."

"Hard?"

"Can't you see the bruise on my forehead?"

"Okay. That explains the signs of concussion."

"This is how I normally am!"

"Normal has nothing to do with it. Please, continue."

"What I'm *saying* is, I could use a guardian angel." She looked him up and down. An inch more in any direction, and he'd have a mountain range named in his honor. "You'd do."

"Guardian angel." Shadow Boy scratched his chin. "I suppose the hours are awful?"

"Just once a week! Around this time, but I can come later so you can finish your nap."

"Considerate. And we would meet here?"

"Yup." Say yes, say yes, *please*, say yes!

He gave a profound humph. "And what would I be paid with?"

Yeesh. She hadn't thought of that. There were five bronze kudos jingling in her piggybank back home. Five hours' worth of sermons on the importance of money management had borne her those coins. If she used them up, she'd have to go through another five hours of playtime persecution to gain them back! The very idea challenged the child endangerment laws of her realm.

Rose scooped up a strawberry and a square of chocolate from her spilled rucksack and dropped them in his hand. "These. You'll get paid in these."

Shadow Boy inspected the unusual currency and tested its legitimacy by tossing the pair into his mouth.

"Wait!" she cried, and he abruptly stopped chewing.

"That's not how you eat it! It isn't melted yet. Open your mouth. Wider. Wider. *Wider*. Perfect!"

A lightning bolt struck the square of chocolate on his tongue, melting it instantly.

"Okay, you can chew now. Go on, chew."

His mouth stayed open. So did his eyes.

"Chew." She grabbed his jaw and worked it up and down. His taste buds caught up with his brain, and Shadow Boy chewed vigorously. Swallowed. Licked his lips. He was quiet for a long time. "What's your name?"

"Rose," she said.

"Well, Thunder Rose"—he stooped, dusting off another strawberry and chocolate square from the ground —"you have yourself a guardian angel. Marek Knoxwind, at your service." Marek bowed, and shadows whisked from his wings, picking up her fallen *Blackout's Tales*. "Now, about this legend-seeking business," he said, flipping through the pages, "where would you like us to start?"

Rose grinned. Wishing Mist or no Wishing Mist, that wispy had given her something even better than a chocolate dairy cow. She'd like very much to thank it. "How's tracking down will-o'-the-wisps sound?"

Marek tossed the chocolate and strawberry into his mouth and opened wide.

ENTRY 2

THE GOOD OL' DAYS

"A m I your only friend in the worlds?"

They were trudging through the sludge of a swamp—

(WELL, MAREK TRUDGED—I TRUDGED IN SPIRIT WHILST PIGGYBACKING.)

—in search of the central figure from the *Blackout's Tales'* classic, "Legend of the Man-Eating Sponge."

"Four months we've known each other, and already you're the center of my universe?" he laughed.

It hadn't been an overly eventful four months, it's true. There was the instance with the three-footed jackalope and the burrow full of stolen carrot gold—

(NOT TO BE CONFUSED WITH KARAT GOLD. CARROT GOLD IS A

TYPE OF MAGICAL YELLOW CARROT THAT, WHEN EATEN, MAY BRING ABOUT A SLEW OF FINANCIAL SUCCESS.

HOW'S THAT FOR EATING YOUR VEGGIES?)

—which was worthy of a legend itself, but finding an *actual* legend from *Blackout's Tales*? No such luck.

"You don't talk about anybody else," Rose pointed out. Somewhere above, Stormy rumbled in agreement, its shape indiscernible in the fog.

"I live in Nomad's Doormat, where every traveler wipes their feet. Angels come and go as they please, and no one stays around for long."

"What about the orphanage? Do you have any friends there?"

Marek stepped in a hidden, swampy puddle and grimaced. "Yes. The janitor. He says he'll cut off my head and use my hair as a mop if I don't stop tracking mud on the floors. I'm friends with my lumber crew as well."

"I still can't *believe* they let you work as a lumberjack at fourteen," she huffed, admiring her muck-free boots from her elevated position between his wings. If this was what having a big brother was like, she could get used to it. "I don't care how big you are, those men are ten times your age in angel years! You could hurt yourself."

"Says the girl who has me hunting down a giant, man-eating sponge."

Rose squinted through the fog, scouring the scenery for the stony alcove the sponge is said to reside in. If they brushed against the wrong rock formation, the legendary sponge would suck them in, dissolve them, and wring out the bony bits. "What about hobbies? Do you have any hobbies?"

"Outside of you, you mean? I like to carve wood." The puddles on the ground rippled with the impact of heavy footsteps. Parting the mist ahead was a lumbering mass of mossy roots and seaweed. Shadow Boy's hand went to his belt. "That man-eating sponge may not be on today's itinerary, but what are your feelings on bog monsters?"

Apparently carving wasn't the only thing his knife was good for.

(DEPLOYING TIME LAPSE-ASTERISK IN THREE ... TWO ... ONE ...

BUCKLE UP, READER NAME HERE _____. WE'VE GOT A LOTTA TIME TO COVER.)

*

Rose gaped at her guardian angel. "You fell out of a tree."

Marek stood, brushing dirt and leaves from the seat of his pants. "Yes."

"It wasn't even my fault this time."

"True."

"You're afraid of squirrels?"

"Deathly."

*

"I brought something for you!" Rose plopped the gift-wrapped box proudly at Marek's feet.

He sat up from where he'd been snoozing against their maple tree's trunk. "For me?" Rubbing sleep from his eyes, he took off the box's lid. His look of dismay showed clear as day before clouding over with polite interest. "It's ... lovely." He held up the shapeless, holey, seasick green sweater with garish yellow polka dots.

Rose giggled, and Stormy slapped her a lightning-laced high five. "No, it's not—it's the ugliest sweater in the history of the worlds! It makes *knitting needles* wanna impale themselves! It's so absolutely, all-consumingly *hideous*, it can only be one thing." She leaned forward and yanked the knitted nightmare down to meet Marek's eyes. "It's the sweater from 'Legend of the Ugly Sweater Slayer.'"

"The one that's made from the mane of a murdered unicorn?" he said.

"Yes."

"The one that appears randomly as a gift in the homes of unsuspecting angels?"

"Uh-huh."

"The one that judges the purity of the wearer's thankfulness for the gift and, if it detects even a *hint* of ingratitude, will then proceed to strangle them to death?"

Rose nodded gleefully. "That's the one!"

Marek stared at the killer cardigan. "What do you want me to do with it?"

"Put it on, of course!" Duh. How else were they gonna know if it was truly the sweater from "Legend of the Ugly Sweater Slayer"?

He shrugged and slipped it on over his wide shoulders. Fiddled with the buttons. Went still.

Then he clutched at his throat.

Excitement and dread tightened in a chokehold around her own throat as Shadow Boy tore at the material around his neck. Rose rushed forward to help. She gripped the sweater by one of its holes and pulled the woolen weapon over his head. "Die, die, die!" she cried, stomping it into the ground. When it was suitably subdued, she turned to Marek with a grin that threatened to split her face in half. "It's real. Marek, it's real! We found a legend from *Blackout's Tales!*"

"Thunder, I ..." Marek massaged his throat. "I'm sorry. I don't like turtlenecks. Pulling them off—it's a reflex."

Her grin faded. "So, it wasn't trying to kill you?"

"Well, don't sound so happy about it. Where did you find the sweater, anyway?"

Rose sank dejectedly to the dirt. "Under some floorboards in my sister's room. I think it's one of her failed knitting projects, honestly. She's been going to Momma's knitting club every Tuesday for years, but I don't think it does her much good. Maybe I could help her if they'd let me join them—not that I wouldn't rather spend Tuesdays with you!" She bit her lip. "I just wish ... I wish they wanted me there."

Stormy dripped a raindrop on her nose, and she rubbed it away.

"Come on, Thunder." Marek fluffed his feathers, and his shadows pulled her bracingly to her feet. "We may not be a knitting club, but we *are* a legend-seeking club. And you are very much wanted here. We have work to do! I'm sure there's more murderous clothing just waiting to be sought out."

*

"I can't help but notice you're wearing a tutu," Marek observed.

"Yep! Got it on clearance at the market yesterday. The tailor said they couldn't get rid of it." Rose struggled to belt her wooden sword over the delightful poofs of her new skirt. "Can you believe it?"

"Hardly. But I thought we were going ghost hunting today?"

"We are!"

"Aren't you concerned that your present apparel may put you in peril?"

"You'd be amazed what a girl in a tutu can accomplish."

"You amaze me most days."

*

Marek was waiting for her by their maple tree, grinning like a court jester. "I do believe yesterday was someone's tenth anniversary of life." He produced a cupcake from behind his back, stuck with a pink candle. "Happy birthday, Thunder!"

Rose stared at the cupcake. Red velvet. Her favorite.

She burst into tears, hiding her face in her wings. Stormy slunk away to the highest branches of the tree, drizzling miserably.

Dropping to his knees, Marek immediately drew her in for a bear hug. "Shh, Thunder Rose, what's the matter? Did I get the wrong flavor?"

"He *hates* it!" she sobbed. "Why does he hate it so much?"

"I'm not sure." Shadow Boy patted her back comfortingly. "But if you give me a few less pronouns, I might be able to help."

"My dad hates Stormy." She pulled back, sniffling. "I rained all over my birthday party. I just got excited, but all the knights and dames from the Order were there, and Dad says I ruined it. He says Stormy's ugly and horrible and ruins *everything*."

"Oh, Thunder Rose." Shadows cupped her cheek, the soft velvet wiping her tears. "Listen to me, both of you." Marek gestured for Stormy, and it drifted shamefully from its perch. "You wouldn't believe it, but I pity your father. He hasn't a clue what he's missing out on, and if he did, I promise you he would never look at your storm cloud the same. It isn't ugly and horrible. It's beautiful and powerful and full of mischief. It's you, Rose. And the only thing you ruin is a bad day." He presented her with the cupcake. "Someday we're going to find you a place where everyone knows how to dance in the rain. Just you wait."

Rose smiled wetly, and lightning glinted off her teeth, setting her birthday candle aflame. One puff, and she wished Marek would be her best friend forever and ever.

*

Rose sat next to Marek beneath their maple tree and took a deep breath. "I know about your drinking problem."

He whipped his head around. "*Excuse* me?"

"I found the empty bottles in your rucksack. I'm staging an intervention."

"Rose, I'm a lumberjack. It can't be helped."

"Drinking maple syrup straight from the bottle is gonna kill you."

"Then I will die a happy death."

"At least lemme make you some pancakes to go with it!"

"Well, now you're just enabling."

*

"We're not friends anymore!" Rose hollered, stamping

her foot. She picked up her duffle bag, sat down on the other side of the tree, and sulked. Stormy blew a thunderous raspberry and joined her.

Marek, with wisdom beyond his fifteen years, gave her a few minutes before sitting down next to her. "Well, we had some good times, didn't we? A few laughs? A few near-death experiences? It was a good run."

"Go away." She shoved him as hard as she could.

(*Try shoving a boulder and see how far it moves.*)

"You're s'posta be on *my* side!" she said.

"I *am* on your side. Which is why I'm telling you that running away from home isn't the answer."

"I heard them talking. They said if I can't find a way to control Stormy, they're gonna send me to an asylum for unstable magic. I can't go there, Shadow Boy, I just *can't!*"

"You won't," Marek said firmly. "You're eleven, not thirteen—you aren't old enough to be committed. We have a few more years to figure out what to do, and when we do figure it out, you won't be running *from* something. You'll be running *towards* something."

Rose looked at him reproachfully and held up a solemn pinky. "Promise?"

He wrapped his finger around hers. "Pinky promise."

*

Rose twirled a curl mischievously around her finger. "Hey, Shadow Boy?"

Marek glanced at her suspiciously. "Ye-e-s?"

"Why did the tree tell the lumberjack to stop telling him jokes?"

"I don't know."

" 'Cause they were splitting his sides!"

"Why do I even bother?"

*

Rose sat with her back against the maple tree, *Blackout's Tales* in her lap. She bit into a chocolate-covered strawberry and almost spat it back out.

The fruit was sour, the chocolate bitter, without Marek there.

Three times. *Three times* he hadn't shown up at their meeting spot. In the years they'd known each other, he'd never missed more than a week. Was he sick? Break a leg? Did a tree fall on him, and he couldn't walk anymore?

Was he bored with being her guardian angel and decided to quit when she needed him most?

On cue, a burst of panicked lightning shot from her fingertips, singeing the forest floor. Stormy wasn't hanging above her anymore. It was ... well, it was ...

Rose breathed deeply, and thunder rattled in her chest. She and Stormy had done something—something too terrible for words—and as punishment, Dad had found a way to trap her storm cloud inside her body, and it was *killing* her.

(*METAPHORICALLY SPEAKING. THOUGH HAVING A STORM CLOUD TRAPPED INSIDE OF YOU PROBABLY ISN'T ON YOUR PHYSICIAN'S TOP 10 TIPS FOR HEALTHY LIVING.*)

But right now, Marek's absence hurt worse than the storm roiling beneath her skin, trapped and fighting to get out.

Had she lost both of her best friends at once? She knew where Stormy was—but where had Shadow Boy gone?

Being an eleven-year-old gumshoe has its challenges, but if there were two things Rose never said no to, it was a challenge and a mystery to solve. And nothing mattered more than solving the mystery of Marek's disappearance.

She began by sneaking out of bed one night and taking a trip to his orphanage. The matron answered the door, wearing a tired dressing gown and an even more tired scowl. When Rose asked to see Marek, she was told in no uncertain terms that there were no Marek Knoxwinds on the premises and to leave said premises immediately unless she wished to become an orphan herself, in which case she would never leave the premises *ever again*.

Rose was halfway to the road when the matron called after her, "What was it you wanted, had he been here? The boy."

Chin high, she turned around. "To adopt him."

The lumberjacks and janes weren't any better. "Marek Knoxwind?" Rose called up and down their favorite logging grounds on the border between Pandrum and Faberland. "Shadow-wings, drinks maple syrup straight from the bottle, poster boy of Chunker Munkers United? You *have* to remember him."

Most of them ignored her, drowning out her voice with their sawing, but one lumberjane slung her axe over her shoulder and sauntered over. "Listen, girl. We don't know any Marek Knoxwinds. And if we did"—she looked sternly down her nose—"we *forgot* him. I suggest you do the same."

Like heck she would.

But who else could she turn to for help? Enlisting family was out of the question. Suppose they *could* find Marek—hooray! However, they'd just as soon forbid her from seeing him, or press charges or something stupid.

Rose refused to introduce them for that very reason.

Actually, she hadn't introduced Marek to *anyone*.

Doubts grew like vines, itching like poison ivy. No one had ever seen him; no one had ever heard him speak. He laughed like he was real, he hugged like he was real, and yet ... "What if I made you up inside my head?" she whispered to the empty space beside her and held her head that wasn't screwed on right in her hands. Lightning from her trapped storm cloud crackled between her fingers.

Marek had asked her once what she wanted to be when she grew up, if she didn't have to follow in her father's footsteps. Her answer? *Professional legend seeker—*

(DUH.)

— and part-time ghost hunter.

(PART-TIME WAS A MUST. YOU JUST CAN'T MAKE A LIVING OFF THE DEAD.)

Now she had another occupation to add. *Time traveler.* That way, she could change everything back to the way it was supposed to be: chasing down legends from *Blackout's Tales* with her best friends at her side and above her head.

She belonged with them in a way she'd never belonged anywhere else. Not with Dad and his ironclad plans for her future, nor in Chunter Woods, a town that would gladly dispose of her and the problems she caused and cry "Good riddance!" Marek and Stormy were her safe place in a world that didn't understand the beauty of thunderstorms or the faith to believe that legends can be true.

Would she ever find a place like that again?

... And how long would it take to get there?

TWO HUNDRED YEARS LATER ...

(SLIGHT EXAGGERATION. YOU CAN CROSS OUT THE HUNDRED.)

ENTRY 3

MIND TRICKS

To: Rose Skylar
From: Your Past

I s it possible to talk to your future self?

Thirteen-year-old Rose Skylar pondered this question as she stared at the blank piece of paper in front of her. She popped a cucumber finger sandwich in her mouth, and the crunch seemed to echo in the empty bakery. Why wasn't Ottis back from the carriage yet? It's not nice to leave the birthday girl at a table all by herself.

In honor of her birthday—

(YES, READER NAME HERE _____. THIS IS ONE OF THOSE STORIES. THE ONES WHERE SOMETHING TERRIBLE AND WONDERFUL HAPPENS ON AN IMPORTANT BIRTHDAY. CAN'T BE HELPED IN THIS CASE, BUT IF YOU'RE TIRED OF THE CLICHÉ [AND I DON'T BLAME YOU IF YOU ARE], YOU CAN PRETEND TODAY IS SOMETHING ELSE. A BANK HOLIDAY, SAY.)

—Sir Ottis the Amiable—her knightly instructor, pseudo-uncle, and glorified babysitter from the Noble Guard—had skipped their daily sword-training session and taken them to her favorite place in town, Minni's Bakery. Minni's had one of those cutesy double meanings in that 1) Minni was the name of the owner, and 2) Every item on her menu was sold exclusively in miniature: mini quiches, mini muffins, mini bowls of custard. In Pandrum's endless supply of worlds-class bakeries, Minni's had managed to make a name for itself because who doesn't love pretending to be a giant devouring an entire pantry in seconds? On any normal day, the place would be packed.

("BUT IF MINNI'S IS SO POPULAR," YOU ASK, "THEN WHERE ARE ALL OF ITS HUNGRY PATRONS?" OH, JUST TAKING THEIR BUSINESS ELSEWHERE FOR THE NEXT HOUR OR SO TILL OUR BANQUET FOR TWO WAS OVER. OTTIS JOKED THAT HE'D BOUGHT THE PLACE OUT JUST FOR ME, WHICH IS NICER THAN SAYING THE BAKERY CLEARED OUT LIKE A STINK BOMB HAD GONE OFF WHEN HE MADE OUR RESERVATION.)

But birthdays—

(BANK HOLIDAYS.)

—are rarely normal days.

Brushing crumbs from the paper, Rose began her letter.

> *Dear Future Me,*
>
> *How are you? Alive, I hope, with all our limbs intact? (Or at least in functioning order.) Knowing us, probably not.*
>
> *Do you remember why I'm writing to you today? You were me once, but it's been a while. You might've forgotten. It's the 13th of the Eleventh Moon, 1525 A.S. My thirteenth birthday.*
>
> *(BANK HOLIDAY.)*
>
> *I'm the one who blows out the candles, but it's Dad who gets his biggest wish tonight. Everyone expects me to follow in his footsteps—WHY do Knight Commanders have to pass on their titles to their firstborn heirs?—but tonight it becomes official. I'll be knighted a Dame Commander-in-training in front of the entire Order.*
>
> *There's no going back after that. Once you're in, you're in for life.*
>
> *And I just ... I don't know if I'm ready for that. I don't think the Order is, either. They're afraid of me. Everyone's afraid of me since The Incident.*

She paused to glance around the bakery. Still empty.

Ottis was taking his sweet time retrieving her present from his carriage.

> *Sometimes I wonder if it would be better if I just went away. I know what Marek would say. He'd tell me to wait for him. But Marek isn't here anymore, is he? Maybe he never was. He didn't stop The Incident. He didn't stop Dad from trapping Stormy inside me afterward. Truth is, I don't have a guardian angel anymore, and no amount of missing him can bring him back. (Can it?)*
>
> *If being Dame Commander of Chunter Woods is my future, then I want to make the best of it. I guess my question for you is ... do we?*
>
> *Or do we find a way to change our future?*
>
> *Anyway, thanks for listening. I'm looking forward to the day I read this letter and know the answer. Until then ...*
>
> *With love from the past,*
> *Your Little Me*

"Who're ya writing to? Boyfriend? Dear Abbeline?"

Rose's head popped up. A man sat in the booth across from her. His eyes and wings were the color of mud, but the good sort of mud, the kind that's fun to squish your toes in after it rains. Shaggy, rust-brown hair crowned his head, and an expertly trimmed beard trailed the length of his jaw and up over his curling lip.

Someone was talking to her. Someone was actually, voluntarily talking to her!

(Stranger danger bells were going off in my head, don't worry. It's just when no one except family has purposefully talked to your face in two years, it's hard to brush off the only conversationalist to show up.)

She fumbled for words. "I, um—the future! I'm writing to my future self."

He snorted. "Didn't know they'd invented time travel yet." The mystery man's accent was Pandrum's pell-mell dialect slowed to a drawl. A Saxumite, then, from their friendly neighbor on the Shell, Saxum, the mining realm. An out-of-towner.

No wonder he wasn't afraid to talk to her. Word of The Incident couldn't have spread *that* far.

She grinned. "Oh, I'm not a time traveler." She patted the envelop that said *To: Rose Skylar, From: Your Past.* "I have to deliver this the old-fashioned way. Stuff it in a sock drawer and wait."

The man raised a rust-brown eyebrow. "And why d'ya wanna write to your future?"

Rose folded her letter neatly and stuffed it in the envelope. " 'Cause I might wanna change it."

"How come?"

Enough questions. "Can I interest you in a two-ounce glass of water?" she asked politely. Whatever this guy's game was, he needed to know who he was dealing with. Usually, her wild black hair was enough to alarm most angels because it reminded them of a thunderstorm.

(THERE WAS EVEN SOME BELIEF THAT MY STORM CLOUD HADN'T REALLY DISAPPEARED BUT WAS LIVING IN MY CURLS. I'D BEEN BLACKLISTED AT FIVE BEAUTY PARLORS AND COUNTING.)

But she could understand why her mystery man wasn't put off. It was the cheeks, really. Rose had what her sister fondly called a "strawberries and cream" complexion, which basically meant her cheeks were perpetually pink. And what cheeks they were, full and round and—"Cherubic!" Amber insisted, which is another word for "chubby in a way that incites much cheek-pinching." They, along with her sleepy gray eyes that *oozed* innocence, were the perfect disguise for a mischief-maker.

From the outside, no one would suspect she could pour a mean glass of water.

Rose served from the miniature pitcher and passed her hand over the minuscule glass, a small bolt of lightning shooting from her palm. Catching it in hand, she stirred the water into a sizzling frenzy. "We call this one *The Lightning Fizz*." She gulped it in a single go. Electricity tickled her insides and burst from her skin, looping up her arms and racing through her curls. Her hair poofed like a mad alchemist's.

That oughta show him not to mess with her!

The man leaned forward curiously. "Interesting. I heard you were Rose Skylar, girl o' storms. How'd your soul signia—

(*SOUL SIG·NI·A*
/sōl/ /'signēə/

NOUN

THE UNIQUE FORM AN INDIVIDUAL'S SOUL MAGIC TAKES
"THE GIRL'S SOUL SIGNIA WAS A LOVEABLE STORM CLOUD, REPRE-
SENTING THE CUTELY TEMPESTUOUS NATURE OF HER SOUL")

—get cheapened into a parlor trick?"

Ouch.

Deep in her chest, Stormy swelled with indignation. Rain pressed behind her eyes and lightning buzzed inside her fingertips, but she pushed the storm down with a shrug. "It's a long story. And my trainer's gonna be here any second, so whatever you came to say, you better say it fast. He won't like me talking to you."

The man's lips twisted in a sour smirk like there was a lemon wedge on his tongue. "Your trainer's that Noble Guard stiff, isn't he? Talks to himself, uniform's a bit tight around the middle? He's been outside measuring the wheels on your carriage for the past fifteen minutes."

That's what Ottis was doing? What, the wheels on a carriage were more interesting than her? All they did was go 'round and 'round and 'round. If Ottis thought *that* was entertainment, she'd make a point to talk in circles for the rest of the week. "He's a vigilant driver. Checking tire pressures and whatnot."

"Your wheels are made of wood."

Right. Time to cut to the chase.

(Ha! And if you skip to the next chapter, you can cut to the actual chase!

Except don't, 'cause that's cheating.)

"Who are you?"

The man examined a teaspoon no bigger than his pinky. "Think this is real silver?" He pocketed it without an answer and got up from the booth. "I'm just someone who can help you change your future, but if you've got it covered ..." He turned to leave, his cloak swishing at the hem. The fabric was so black and velvety, it reminded her of ... well, of shadows.

"Wait!" Rose said. "I, uh, I like your cloak." Compliments—the greatest stall tactic.

He stopped and revolved on the spot, arms and wings spread for her appraisal. "Tailor-made." The cloak was exceptional: black with rich white lining and laughably out of place amongst the pinks and doilies of Minni's Bakery. It was belted around his middle with a wide band and a fancy round buckle, and the sleeves had intricate swirls around the wrists. Like silver bracelets embedded in the fabric.

"What's on the sleeves?" She did love sparkly things. "Is that real silver or—"

"Rose!" Sir Ottis the Amiable was on his way to the table, clutching a long, thin package. He squeezed into the booth opposite her, eyes shining with a story to tell. "You won't *believe* what's happened. There I was getting your present out of the carriage when I noticed the wheels seemed uneven, giving the carriage a distinct tilt. Distinct, I say! So, I went ahead and measured each wheel, and— this is the part you won't believe—I think someone *stole* one of our wheels and replaced it with a smaller—"

Rose interrupted him with the nicest, phlegm-less clear of her throat she could muster and jerked her head towards the mystery man. "Um, Ottis? Aren't you gonna introduce yourself?"

Ottis laughed. "Rose, I've known you since you were a baby! Thirteen years ago to the day, your mother handed me a pink bundle of wrinkled skin and fluffy hair and said—"

"Not to me," she interrupted again.

(*It's necessary with Ottis. Anything softer than a*

"To *him*."

Ottis twisted in his seat. "Him, who?"

"Don't bother. I'll just be going," said the man, and Rose lunged out of her seat, grabbing his sleeve. "Don't even think about it, mister! You're staying right here till we get this sorted out." He stood tolerantly while she gestured wildly in his direction. "*Him*," she told Ottis. "The man standing right in front of you. Nice cloak, snazzy beard, looks like he's sucking on a lemon?"

The man offered a mocking wave with his wing. Ottis, for his part, was staring to the right of the man's nose as if seeing straight through him.

"Rose," he said after a protracted silence, "there's no one there."

Something tingled in her chest, and it wasn't lightning whispering to be let out. "Is this a joke?"

"Make no mistake, if this were a joke, your hair would be the punch line," the man chuckled. "Ah, I can see it now. A girl with a rat's nest on her head walks into a pub ..."

Her curls sparked in outrage. "My hair does not look like a—" The flash of electricity had reflected off the silver bracelets embedded in his sleeve. But they weren't bracelets. They were *letters*. A circle of letters stitched into the fabric with metallic thread, and they spelled a name that drained the color from her ever-pink cheeks. "That's not your cloak."

"Yeah?" he countered. "Says who?"

"It's not your name on it."

"I guess that makes it your cloak, too?" He rotated his wrist.

What in the *worlds*?

Rose touched the silver letters, tracing the circle of names that should always be stitched together:

Marek Knoxwind. Rose Skylar.

"Rose," Ottis said gently, approaching her with wings outstretched, "you're not thinking straight again. Let's go home so you can lie down and drink some water—but not in that order, of course!" He laughed nervously. "Definitely not in that order. That would be a choking hazard!" In one swift movement, his arms and feathers wrapped around her, tighter than a straitjacket. For a moment, she pretended it was a hug.

"Let me go!" She struggled against him, and the mystery man's sleeve slipped from her fingers. "No! Where did you get that cloak? *Where*?"

"I'll buy you a cloak, Rose. We'll go to every tailor in town, and I'll buy you one just like it. I promise!" Ottis pleaded.

She stilled in his grip. "Am I imagining you? For real?"

The mystery man tipped an imaginary hat—oh, *very*

clever—and slipped her letter to her future self into his pocket. "Be seeing you."

And he left her kicking, flailing, wings flapping savagely in the arms of her trainer. Ottis was stronger than her in all areas except one, but she couldn't hurt him like that, she *wouldn't* hurt him like that, she—

Lightning zigzagged across her body, burning Ottis and setting fire to the tablecloth. He cried out and released her, blowing on his feathers and plunging his hands inside the miniature water pitcher. They jammed in the small opening, and water sloshed over the flaming tablecloth as Ottis tried to shake them free.

"I'm sorry," Rose said. "I'm so, so sorry." Hungry flames scarfed down the remains of her birthday—

(OKAY, ENOUGH WITH THE BANK HOLIDAYS. YOU'LL JUST HAVE TO ACCEPT THAT IT WAS MY BIRTHDAY AND THAT'S THAT.)

—banquet, and she snatched Ottis's gift from the fire and bolted out of the bakery.

ENTRY 4

PUPPY LOVE

T he mystery man had a solid head start as they tore through town square, but while he was able to slip between the crowds unobserved, Rose had a special power he hadn't accounted for: the Curse of the Imaginary Bad Smell.

(WELL, WHAT ELSE DO YOU CALL IT WHEN EVERYONE DROPS WHAT THEY'RE DOING AND LEAVES WHENEVER THEY SEE YOU?)

It wafted through the throngs of shoppers, and angels hurtled away from her, clearing a direct path to him. Before long, the man had no choice but to abandon their foot chase and shoot into the sky. Rose unfurled her wings and flew after him, dodging past angels on their afternoon flutters. A few of them shrieked, plummeting at the sight of her.

The scenery below transformed from town to treetops. Like a grand old lady changing wigs, the woods had swapped its green leaves for the reds and yellows of autumn. Up ahead, the man dove into the sea of color, touching down in the forest.

Rose plunged after him and hit the ground running. The woods welcomed her as an old friend, and she slowed to a stop, leaning against an ancient tree. *She needed—to catch—her breath.* For a figment of her imagination, this guy was awfully spry! Maybe she could imagine him slower? Like a snail or a turtle or a great, big glob of molasses.

A familiar face leered around a tree trunk. "Looking for me?" asked the mystery man before he broke into a very un-molasses-like sprint.

"These aren't your woods!" Rose shouted, thundering after him. "This is my family's property!" Though technically speaking, if he *was* a figment of her imagination, what was hers could be considered his, too. He certainly knew the path well as they spun through the woods, twisting and turning around shrubs, leapfrogging over fallen trees, and splashing through streams—hang on. Was it just her, or was there a suspicious ring of déjà vu to this whole situation? Familiar, kinda like these trees. And if familiar trees led to a familiar bend in the path ahead, then Rose was putting an end to this chase.

The bend appeared. She stopped dead, breathing hard. "Why did you bring me here?"

The mystery man turned, flashing her that sour smirk. "Why don'tcha find out for yourself?" And waving her letter to the future, he winked out of existence before her very eyes.

Of course a figment of her imagination would lead to her and Marek's meeting spot. Of course their sacred maple was just around the corner. Of course there would be something waiting there for her. Or some*one*?

Heart pounding like the gavel of an impatient judge, she rounded the bend—

—and promptly dropped to the ground, skidded away on her bottom, and concealed herself behind a tree. A trickle of adrenaline cascaded down her back, turning her blood to fire and her skin to ice.

Something was waiting for her under the red canopy of maple leaves, but it wasn't Shadow Boy.

It was a hearse.

An asylum hearse. The medical crest on the side confirmed it.

(MAYBE WHERE YOU COME FROM, HEARSES ARE ONLY USED FOR CARTING AROUND DEAD FOLKS, NOT FOR TRANSPORTING NEW PATIENTS TO ASYLUMS FOR UNSTABLE MAGIC. "BUT WHY USE A HEARSE?" YOU ASK? GREAT QUESTION! IT'S THE BUILT-IN CONVENIENCE, MAINLY. IF A PATIENT'S BEING UNCOOPERATIVE, JUST TOSS 'EM IN THE CASKET. AND SHOULD SOMETHING GO TERRIBLY WRONG EN ROUTE TO THE ASYLUM, ALL THE DRIVER

Hunched behind the tree, Rose clutched Ottis's long, thin, birthday present to her heaving chest. She ripped off the wrapping—*please* let it be what she thought it was—and read the note that fell out:

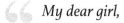

> *My dear girl,*
> *I saw you eyeing the cape rubies at the jeweler's stall and put in a special order with the blacksmith. A rose needs her kiss of thorns.*
> *Happy birthday!*
> *Fondly yours,*
> *Ottis*

She slid the stunning, double-edged sword from its sheathe. *Perfect.* It glistened with rubies, green leather vines lacing the handle for maximum grip, and its pommel was in the shape of a rose. Her kiss of thorns. Thorn Kisser. T.K. for short. A cheeky name for a cheeky blade destined for many cheeky deeds. She was gonna poke the bottoms of her worst adversaries with this sword!

"Thank you, Ottis," she whispered and, strapping the scabbard to her waist, slunk closer to the hearse. It looked empty. Abandoned. Hooked up to the carriage, a team of Sonorific Huskies (she could tell by their enormous ears) sprawled lazily on the ground, enjoying an afternoon nap.

Figment or not, the mystery man had brought her here for a purpose. "What do you think?" she murmured. "Do we check it out?" A wave of lightning rippled across her skin. "My thoughts exactly."

Ducking low, Rose tiptoed past the sleeping huskies. They didn't so much as stir—which was good, because one bark from those magic-enhanced lungs would burst her eardrums.

Safely out of the dogs' sight, she studied the name painted elegantly beneath the medical crest: Heartstone Asylum.

Heartstone Asylum?! They had the guts to name their prison for patients with unstable magic after the most sacred building in history? *Blackout's Tales*, page one: "Legend of Heartstone Asylum." Home of the Heartstone Eternal, Dimidia's own vessel—the vessel of a *god*—and now they were associating it with the terrors of a modern-day madhouse? It was—it was sacrilege!

Fuming, she crept to the back of the vehicle and peered through the rear window. Empty. She undid the latch and opened the door a crack. The carriage had all the usual features of a hearse: windows swallowed up by curtains, plush seating on either wall for loved ones to sit with their dead on the way to the burial ground. The casket was stationed on a catafalque bolted to the middle of the floor. Nothing to see here.

The casket gave a violent shake.

Eep! Eep, eep, *EEP!* Giggles and a shriek met in her

throat, clogging her scream, and thank Dimidia for that. Someone was in this hearse! Asylum escorts couldn't be far off.

"Okay. Okay." Rose patted herself calm and climbed into the carriage. She had to act fast! Open the casket, unbind the patient, arm them with all the coins she had in her pockets, and wish them a long and happy life on the run. Only ...

Only what if there was a reason this hearse was abandoned? What if Heartstone Asylum was transporting a *dead* patient, but then the patient came back as an enchanted corpse on the way to the cemetery, seeking revenge? And what if the driver heard it banging around and ditched the hearse, running for his sanity?

That did it. Rose hadn't run for her sanity a day in her life, and she wasn't about to start now. Wings shielding her eyes, she unlatched the casket and gripped the lid. On the count of three. *One ... two ...* three!

The lid opened, and something leaped at her face. Her *face!* It was huge and furry like a giant, horrible bat. She unsheathed T.K. in an instant. Lightning danced up the blade, ready to slice, dice, and sizzle whatever vile creature had decided to make its home inside a casket.

Rose peeked bravely through her feathers.

A Sonorific Husky puppy sat at her feet, head cocked quizzically at her. He was all legs and ears and gray and white fur. Also, he was wearing goggles. *Goggles.* Who puts *goggles* on a dog? They made his eyes look twice as big, which was beyond ridiculously the cutest thing ever.

"Hi!" Rose squeaked. "Oh my gosh, you're adorable, hello." She sheathed T.K. and reached tentatively for him. The puppy bumped her palm with his cold nose. Taking this as an invitation, she scratched behind his ears, and he flew into her chest with the force of a cuddly bowling ball.

"Whoa! Hi there, boy. Who locked you up inside that nasty ol' casket, huh? Aww, you're such a—s'cuse me, good sir!" The puppy was gnawing on the jewel-studded hilt of her sword. He stopped, tail wagging apologetically, and snuggled under her chin.

Warm and fuzzy and completely unafraid of being barbequed.

Lightning lathered anxiously beneath her skin, and she massaged it in slow, soothing patterns. "Shhh, Stormy. We'd *never* have an Incident with a puppy. Relax." She wrapped the puppy inside her cloak and stepped warily out of the carriage.

Dry leaves crunched. Rose whirled around, wings snapping to attention. Her spine tingled.

"Marek?" Dark shapes blurred at the corners of her vision, but here at the foot of their sacred maple, that wasn't unusual. Sometimes it felt like Shadow Boy was straining at the corners of her imagination, trying to get back to her.

It was a nice thought.

An icy breeze rustled the red maple leaves, playing

with her curls and biting her nose. The mystery man, whoever he was, *whatever* he was, had said he could help her change her future. But how was an empty asylum hearse and a puppy supposed to stop her from being knighted tonight and sealing her fate as her father's successor? Unless this was a trap somehow. And her begoggled bundle of fur was the bait.

One hand on her sword, the other hugging the puppy, Rose backed away from the hearse. The Sonorific Huskies stirred, vibrations from their yawns shaking the earth.

Better risk it.

She turned, running full speed down the path, crunching through a thousand fallen leaves that got in her way.

(AND MAYBE A FEW THAT HADN'T, BUT WHEN YOU SEE THAT PERFECT CRUNCHY LEAF, YOU GOTTA POUNCE. NATURE'S LAW.)

She still couldn't shake the feeling that the blurry shapes were following her home.

ENTRY 5

EAVESDROPPER'S LAMENT

The Skylar residence was modest compared to the families of other Knight or Dame Commanders, but then Chunter Woods wasn't the most—what's the word? The one that sounds like a sneeze? *Affluent.* Chunter Woods wasn't the most *affluent*—

(Bless you.)

—domain of Pandrum, and Rose liked it that way. Most days. Today, the fact that their largest gathering area was not a dining hall but a parlor room right by the entrance was making her life very inconvenient. Voices drifted from the closed door, meaning guests had arrived prematurely for her knighting/birthday party. Why do nobility always insist on showing up early to things? *Ugh.* They made sneaking stressful!

Rose bounded noiselessly up the stairs to her bedroom, careful not to wake the fuzzy stowaway sleeping in her cloak. She did a quick sweep of her room for chewable items and choking hazards (namely her gem, button, and assorted shiny objects collection), and laid the puppy on her bed.

What could she say to her parents to convince them to let her keep him? Probably not, *I found him in a casket in an abandoned hearse, I don't think he belongs to anybody.*

Why was he in that casket in the first place, anyway? What was an empty asylum hearse doing at her and Marek's meeting spot? Who was the mystery man? Was he really a figment of her imagination? Why did he have Marek's name on his sleeve? Why was *her* name on his sleeve? Why did he take her letter to her future self? Why, why—gah!

She flopped on her bed with a groan. Nothing got under her skin like the needling of an unsolved mystery. And solving mysteries was supposed to be her specialty!

Next to her, the puppy woke up and stretched, his yawn rattling her windowpane. Rose scratched him happily behind his enormous ears. "Listen, mister. I gotta go downstairs for a bit, but *no barking* while I'm gone, 'kay?" Even the bark of a Sonorific Husky *puppy* could put a crack in the house's foundation. "I'll check in on you soon."

She snuck down the stairs, opened the front door, and slammed it loudly, announcing her arrival to the rest of the house. Standing outside the parlor, she took a deep, cleansing breath. Straight face. No quips. Inside voice. Those were Dad's rules for interaction with the esteemed Knight and Dame Commanders of Pandrum's Order of the Rose.

(YES, I WAS NAMED AFTER THE ORDER. DAD'S IDEA. JUST HIS SUBTLE WAY OF SAYING, "EMBRACE YOUR FUTURE AS A DAME COMMANDER. YOU CAN'T ESCAPE IT IF YOU TRY.")

One day these scholarly men and women would be her colleagues, each ruling their designated domain of Pandrum in harmony.

Apparently, cracking jokes about receding hairlines is *not* the best way to cultivate friendly business relationships.

(PARTICULARLY IF THE HAIRLINE IN QUESTION IS A LADY'S.)

The doorknob turned before Rose could reach it. Momma slipped out of the parlor and closed the door firmly behind her. Her regal braid of dark hair was as tufted and fraying as an old rug—it only got that way when she was worrying about something. She'd stroke her braid over and over, an unsmoothed crease between her brows. Just like there was now. "We're having a discussion with Ottis about your Incident at the bakery today.

We want you to wait in the kitchen with your sister until we've finished."

Guilt pricked. Rose had almost forgotten about that. "Should I go change for my knighting first?"

"No, there—" Momma's falter was almost imperceptible, "there'll be time for that later. Go be with your sister."

Rose nodded glumly. A wing brushed her cheek, and she startled. Momma *never* touched her anymore. No one did. Not since The Incident.

"Rosy? Happy birthday, my sweet girl." Momma's feathers fell away, and she returned to the parlor.

Amber was sitting at the kitchen table, fiddling absently with her necklace and frowning at the bundle of holey material in her lap. She was knitting again. Always knitting. Rose admired her sister's sheer tenacity in mastering a skill that refused to be enslaved. She also admired Amber's blonde hair that swept smoothly across her shoulders and her beautiful brown eyes, the color of her namesake. Amber bore no resemblance whatsoever to either of their parents. That probably had something to do with her being adopted.

Rose pointed a finger at a demoralizing sight. "What are *those*?"

Amber placed the half-knitted scarf on the table to give Rose her full attention. "Cupcakes."

"What flavor?"

"Vanilla."

"Not red velvet?"

"Momma thought vanilla would be a more refined flavor to serve. Sorry." Amber's sympathetic smile took on a pearly sheen.

Rose rolled her eyes and pointedly ignored her sister's soul signia, the magical show of teeth that invited her to calm down and think rationally. That magic-infused smile was what had inspired Dad to pick Amber when they were choosing a baby to continue the Skylar legacy. Three years later, Rose was born, and the role of future Dame Commander switched inescapably to her little baby head ... and the storm cloud hanging over it.

Those were the rules—rules she would gladly break if given a diplomatic sledgehammer. She may have been the rightful heir by blood, but Amber was born to be a Dame Commander.

Grabbing a plate, Rose plopped a vanilla (*blegh*) cupcake on it and sat across from her sister. She folded her arms on the table, resting her chin on top, and glared at the offensive dessert. "I had an Incident at Minni's today."

Amber nodded. "That explains the discussion in the parlor."

"Dad's probably grilling Ottis within an inch of his life. It's not his fault." Though in Dad's eyes, it would be. Ottis was assigned to her after The Incident under the guise of *keeping her safe* and *training her to be a worthy dame.* Yeah, right. He was there to minimize public Incidents, and she knew it. "I wonder what they're saying." She glanced at Amber from the corner of her eye. "Maybe we could—"

"We are *not* going to crouch outside the door and listen." Amber picked up her knitting project dismissively.

"But they always bring you with them to important discussions! You're the voice of reason. The Order *adores* you. So why leave you out now? Aren't you curious?"

Her knitting needles scraped in irritation. "No."

Rose loved her big sissy, but sometimes she was just that: a big sissy. "Wouldja mind if I gave the eulogy at your curiosity's funeral? It lived a short and useless life, but I'm sure I can find something nice to say."

Amber put down the scarf. "My curiosity isn't dead. It's just—"

"—in a coma?"

Amber sucked agitatedly on the pendant around her neck. It was one of their sister necklaces: a silver key with a heart-shaped bow. *The key to each other's hearts.* They each had one.

"Of course I'm curious!" she blurted.

And so there they were, crouching outside the parlor with a plateful of cupcakes.

(AH, THE POWERS OF SISTER PERSUASION.)

61

The argument inside was reaching a crescendo.

"How could you do this to her?" Momma's hiss could be heard through the door, and was that a tremble in her voice? "She cares about you like you were her own *father!*"

"And a better one I might've been!" Ottis roared, and Rose choked on a cupcake. Amber waved her hands frantically to shush her. "I did this *because* I care about her. I care about her safety. I care about her *soul.* I care about them more than I care about your desire to keep your bloodline knighted!"

"That is no way to talk to the wife of your Knight Commander, Sir Ottis Nickelby!" Dad rebuked furiously.

"Don't try to pull rank on me, Tace Skylar. I have been with you through every bad decision you've made and every attempt to change the lot Dimidia has given you. I've offered every service I can to you, for your sake and for hers. We've tried, Tace!" Ottis laughed desperately. "We've tried. But Rose has unstable magic, and there's no hiding it anymore."

A tug on her sleeve. "We need to go," Amber whispered urgently, but Rose was rooted to the spot. *Unstable magic,* he said. *Unstable magic.* Those were supposed to disappear the day they trapped Stormy inside her.

"So, you called them." Dad sounded resigned.

"Better this than watching you come up with another perverse way to control her storm cloud." She'd never heard Ottis, with his gentle eyes and jolly girth, so angry in all her life.

"Enough!" Dad commanded. "She is supposed to be Dame Commander. What will our subjects say if my own *daughter* is taken to an asylum? Do you *want* my leadership questioned?"

That was the "a" word. They'd used the "a" word. They hadn't used the "a" word in the same sentence as her since —since—

"I understand how hard this must be for you, my lord, but legally Blackthorn Asylum must take her," said an unfamiliar voice. Calm. Professional. An asylum escort. "Your daughter turned thirteen today. She's of age."

A knock on the front door made Rose and Amber jump to their feet. Amber shoved the plate of cupcakes into Rose's hands. "Hide!"

Rose ducked behind the cloak tree at the corner of the entrance, hunkering down in the folds of fabric. She parted the cloaks a sliver.

Momma emerged from the parlor. "Amber! What are you doing here? I told you to stay in the kitchen."

"I was just answering the door, Momma," Amber said innocently. "I thought you didn't want to be disturbed."

Momma surveyed her shrewdly. "Thank you, but I'll get it." She opened the door, and Rose saw her sister take an immediate step back.

"Good evening, my lady." It was a woman speaking.

She had the clear, lilting voice of a wind chime that rang with surprising authority. An Aurial accent. "We are here to escort one Rose Skylar to a selected asylum under the lawful charge of the U.M.R. Act. The Unstable Magic Removal Act cites that—"

"I am fully aware of my daughter's rights," Momma told her curtly. "I was reminded of them not twenty minutes ago when escorts from *Blackthorn* Asylum came to my door. I'm sorry for the miscommunication, but they're already here to take her."

The woman tsked. "Trying to steal our prize patient, are they? Allow me to show them the documents that prove your daughter is meant to come with us. She deserves the finest care, after all, and there is none finer than that of Heartstone Asylum."

Heartstone Asylum? Abandoned-hearse-in-the-woods Heartstone Asylum?

Momma smoothed her wings and stepped aside. "Do come in. Tace?" she called. "We have more ... visitors."

The woman from Heartstone Asylum came into view, flanked by two orderlies. Lightning sparked from Rose's fingertips, and she stuffed them sizzling into her mouth. The brown-winged orderly was swagger personified, arms crossed, and the sleeves of his white cloak rolled back over muscular forearms. The blue-winged orderly was a hibernation-ready bear rearing on its hind legs. It was a wonder he'd even fit through the door!

Dad, Ottis, and the three representatives from Blackthorn Asylum appeared from the parlor and stopped short. Both asylum parties wore the customary white cloaks with hoods pulled up, but Blackthorn's seemed frayed and graying compared to the rich ivory texture and black lining of Heartstone's. The cloaks of Blackthorn were baggy and outdated; the cloaks of Heartstone were fitted, cinched at the waist with a wide band and fancy round buckle. The orderlies of either asylum wore surgical masks, but Blackthorn's had a yellowish tinge while Heartstone's were clean and bright.

"Good evening, Nigel," the woman from Heartstone greeted pleasantly.

The man from Blackthorn sighed. "Heartstone's taking another one, eh? Let's see it, then." He thumbed through the documents. "Signed by the man himself. We'll take our leave. My lords." Nigel and his orderlies bowed to Dad and Ottis. "My ladies." They bowed to Amber and Momma and, shaking their wings, exited the house without the kick of a single fuss.

Dad gaped at the closed door. "Your reputation must precede you. I'm sorry to say I've never heard of this Heartstone Asylum."

"I'll take that as a compliment. Our asylum specializes in"—the woman searched for the right word—"*privacy.* Our patients enjoy a new life far removed from society where any ... *misconduct* of the past is forgiven and forgotten. Those who are welcomed through our doors are shielded from prying eyes that may wish to see the misfortune of the patient's family made into a spectacle. Our confidentiality ensures that no such grievance takes place."

Dad weighed her words carefully. "I see."

"We knew this could happen eventually," Amber spoke up. "We should be grateful it's with an asylum that understands the importance of discretion. Thank you for maintaining my sister's dignity." She flashed them her magical smile, keeping everyone calm till Rose picked the perfect moment to escape.

The blue-winged orderly, the bear, was by far her biggest obstacle. Chunker Munkers United must've kicked him from their ranks and hired him out as a bouncer. If he threw his weight around in a literal sense, he'd be pouring maple syrup on the pancakes formerly known as his patients. How much did he charge for his services? He'd make a *heckuva* guardian angel.

The orderly pushed his hood off his forehead, and she noticed his eyes—his twinkling, moonstone blue eyes. Also, they were staring right at her.

Rose got the feeling he was smiling beneath his surgical mask as a small mountain dropped through her stomach, shredding all twenty-seven feet of her intestines to visceral ribbons.

Ding dong! Her moment had arrived. She knocked over the cloak tree with a war cry, lightning pulsing from every inch of her body, and the conversation snapped like a severed rope. Still whooping, Rose charged for the stairs, holding her plate of cupcakes above her head like a berserking waitress.

If he thought for one *second* that she was gonna make this easy on him, he had another thing coming.

She made it to her bedroom where her awaiting puppy scrambled to greet her. His cheeks were oddly bulging.

Amber shut the door behind them, twisting the lock. "You have a plan, don't you? I know that look in your eyes." She pulled Rose's duffle bag from the closet and packed a flurry of underwear and other essentials. "Grab anything else you want to bring, and quick!"

Books! Books were even more important than underwear. Rose tossed *Blackout's Tales* and a few other favorites into the duffel. She threw open a drawer to retrieve her gem, button, and assorted shiny objects collection, but the leather bag was empty. Empty! Aghast, she turned it upside down. A single gemstone clattered to the bottom of the drawer. "Where's my gem, button, and assorted shiny objects collection?" She looked at her puppy and his bulging cheeks. "What did you do?"

Sheepishly, he opened his mouth, and a torrent of slobbery gems, buttons, and shiny things spilled on the floor. "Little kleptomaniac!" She hurriedly scooped her saliva-slick collection into the bag.

(A COLLECTOR'S SECRET TO MAINTAINING BEAUTIFUL COLLEC-TIONS: SPIT-SHINING.

UNLESS YOU COLLECT STAMPS. EW.)

"Wait. My sister necklace. Where's my sister necklace?"

Someone pounded on the bedroom door. "Amber, open this door immediately!" Dad demanded.

Ignoring him, Amber undid the latch of her own necklace. "Take mine."

"No!" Rose pushed it back. A Stormy-sized lump lodged in her throat. "I don't want you to forget me."

Her sister rushed forward, breaking every rule of the house by cupping her face in her hands. Like, real skin-to-skin contact. Rose's muscles seized, but she couldn't bring herself to pull away. Not in a million years. "This is not goodbye, not forever. I *will* see you again. You're gonna be fine. I believe in you, Rosy."

Amber's magical smile calmed her thudding heart even as the door was being hammered to splinters. She thrust the puppy, duffel bag, and plate of cupcakes into Rose's arms and shoved her towards the window. "Now *go!*"

An ink bottle had upturned on the horizon, rivers of black streaking through the darkening blue. Perched on the windowsill, Rose turned to her sister one last time. "Amber ..." What could she say? What could she say that her sister didn't already know? "You're gonna be an amazing Dame Commander."

"Rosy?" Amber's eyes were wet. "So would you."

An axe buried its head in the bedroom door, cracking it down the middle. They were out of time. Wings spread, Rose launched from the windowsill and into the seeping night.

ENTRY 6

IF YOU GIVE A ROSE A CUPCAKE …

It's funny how when you start a day, you never really know where you'll end up before it's over.

Rose, for one, hadn't expected to be hiding in a casket. In an asylum hearse. With a plate of cupcakes on her stomach. T.K.'s hilt dug into her side, and her Sonorific Husky puppy slept in the crook of her arm. Darkness tucked her in like a blanket, and the puppy's chest rose in deep, steady breaths.

It was kinda relaxing.

Except her toes wriggled, and her muscles twitched, and either there were termites in this casket, or her curiosity was finally eating her alive. The darkness above her was branded with the memory of two moonstone blue eyes staring at her above a surgical mask.

She wasn't leaving this hearse until she had answers.

Time hobbled on. Rose bit the inside of her cheek to

keep a yawn in check. The puppy tucked his nose under her elbow, warm and cozy. His fur was unbearably soft. She petted him while he slept, and her hand snagged on something cool and bumpy around his neck.

The little kleptomaniac had nabbed her sister necklace.

"Oh, you beautiful boy," she whispered, clinging to the key pendant—identical to the one hanging around Amber's neck. Connecting them forever.

It made sense now. Why asylums use hearses and caskets to transport patients. It's the death of your old life. Whatever happened next, she wouldn't be the future Dame Commander of Chunter Woods. She wouldn't be part of the place she grew up in, the one that had never accepted her. What *would* she be when the casket opened?

One thing was certain. She was gonna be *alive*.

(SERIOUSLY, DON'T WORRY. THEY'D POKED AIR HOLES IN THE CASKET.)

*

The chatter of approaching voices roused her from a doze. The angels of Heartstone Asylum were boarding the hearse.

"I was quite certain she'd be waiting here. Pity," said one of the orderlies cheerfully—the big, bear-like one, if his deep voice was anything to go by.

"At least she has Beta," the woman with the lilting, Aurial accent replied. "He'll keep her safe until we find them."

"Yes, but who will keep the worlds safe from *them?*" He sounded far too pleased. "I knew the little rascal would be the perfect companion."

Cushions squeaked as the angels sat.

"Are you *sure* she recognized you?" the woman asked tentatively. "Two years is ... well, it isn't much in the scheme of a five-hundred-year lifespan, but it's a long time for a young girl."

The orderly rumbled a laugh. "Oh, she recognized me all right. She just isn't too happy with me at the mo'." Darn right she wasn't. "Like you said, two years is a long time. Mark my words, though, she'll show herself when she's ready."

"How can you be so sure?"

"Because I know my Rose, and she won't be able to resist. Until then"—Rose imagined him stretching back in his seat, hands tucked comfortably behind his head—"we wait."

A beat.

"For what?"

"Something unexpected. Something absurd. Something like—"

Rose slammed her boots on the lid of the casket, and it sprang open with an aggrieved squeal of the hinges. The woman's scream lasted five satisfying seconds, and the big orderly nodded musingly to himself. "That would do it."

The back door of the carriage swung open to reveal the second orderly, the swaggering one. "What the—?"

Sitting up in the casket, hair wild, eyes wilder, like an enchanted corpse returning from the grave ... you gotta admit, she had to look pretty impressive. The puppy, Beta, blinked sleepily behind his goggles and chewed reproachfully on her sleeve for disrupting his nap.

"So about this Heartstone Asylum," Rose said, propping her chin on a fist. "Do they use shock therapy? I've always wanted to try shock therapy." She examined her hand, ribbons of lightning weaving between her fingers. "Probably tickles."

The orderlies weren't wearing their surgical masks anymore, but they still had their hoods up. The dark lining shadowed their faces. She smiled at them.

"Rose, dear, we're—we're not here to hurt you," the woman stuttered.

"D'you think I'd be here if you were? Tell me about Heartstone Asylum. What's it like? What do you do there? Who signed the papers that made Blackthorn drop me like a hot potato?"

"Why tell ya when we're gonna show ya?" countered the swaggering orderly.

Rose cocked her head. "Because I don't have to go if I don't want to."

"Oh, really? You'll just blast your way outta here with that parlor trick?"

"What, this?" She snuffed Stormy's lightning from her fingers. "Gosh, no."

The orderly's gaze flicked to her scabbard. "The Rosebud's got thorns. Your sword, then? You'll hack us to pieces and be on your way?"

"No*pe*," she grinned, popping the *p*. "Wrong again. And if you don't start doing something interesting like telling me about Heartstone Asylum or licking your elbow, I'm leaving." She climbed out of the casket with her plate of undamaged cupcakes.

"Without magic?"

"Yes."

"Without your sword?"

She dipped her pinky in the frosting and sucked on it. "Uh-huh."

"How?"

Had this man no imagination? "Piece o' cake."

Rose lunged, slashing a cupcake beneath his hood like a dagger and—judging by his roar—smearing his eyes with frosting. He flailed in vanilla-flavored agony, and she dodged past him into the woods.

The moons were out, twelve in all, blue and brilliant, and getting closer by the day. The Eleventh was the closest and the brightest, taking its place of honor in the sky according to the lunar calendar, but in less than two months, all twelve moons would eclipse, and the new year would begin. How did asylums celebrate Moonsfrost Eve? Did patients still dress up like lunatics and have candy pelted at them from windows? Did everyone still gather at midnight to watch the moons become one giant orb, showering the world with frozen moonlight?

(THERE. THAT DIDN'T NEED AN INFO-ASTERISK EXPLANATION, DID IT, READER NAME HERE ____? DRESSING UP IN COSTUMES TO GET CANDY, LOOKING UP AT A BIG BALL IN THE SKY TO CELE-BRATE THE NEW YEAR—SURELY YOU HAVE SIMILAR TRADITIONS IN YOUR OWN CULTURE?)

A second pair of footsteps joined her.

"A food fight," said the big orderly. "You always did have a taste for subtlety."

She stopped abruptly, spinning a cupcake in hand. "How 'bout you taste this!" Twisting blindly, she mashed it in his face. He laughed in her ear.

"You should put your confidence where your mouth is." He plucked a cupcake from her plate and rammed it gleefully up her nose. Rose stiffened with that horrible, conflicting desire to scream and belly laugh all at once, gobs of cake plopping into her open mouth. She snorted frosting.

A scuffle ensued over the remaining ammunition. When the plate was empty, Rose hurled it away as hard as she could. It shattered against a tree trunk.

"Hey. Hey, Thunder, look at me."

Heaving with exertion, she stared mulishly at the broken pieces on the ground. Two frosting-coated fingers lifted her chin.

And there he was, caterpillar eyebrows and all. He was older, significantly cakier, and familiar as her own reflection. "Hi," she managed weakly.

"Hi yourself," said Marek Knoxwind, signature smile in tow.

ENTRY 7

HEADBUTTS AND HEADLOCKS

Marek stood there, gunked in frosting, happy shadows misting from his wings.

He was solid. Real.

Rose lowered her head and charged, pummeling him in the stomach with the intention of breaking his non-imaginary ribs. He eked out an *oomph* and braced her shoulders, not pushing her away, but holding her in place. She pounded and punched, and sweet *magic* it felt like beating a brick wall with her bare knuckles, and why, oh, why would anyone pick a fight with a brick wall?

Panting, she dropped her fists. "You left me. For *years*. No note, no explanation, just poof! Here one Tuesday, gone the next. Do you have any idea how worried I was about you? How much I missed—" Her voice cracked. She patched it quickly. "I thought you were gone for good."

"Like Stormy?"

How *dare* he! Rose stormed him with another head-butt, which he caught and swung around in a headlock. It took an insulting lack of effort. "Stormy isn't gone!" she grunted, struggling in his grip. "Stormy would *never* leave me! Just 'cause you can't always see it doesn't mean it isn't there!"

Shadow Boy patted her back with the same arm he was using to nearly strangle her. "Precisely."

And what was *that* supposed to mean?

"I never left you, Rose. Abandon my post as your guardian angel? Banish the thought! And if you stop trying to pulverize my ribs for the next ten seconds, I can explain how."

Marek released her from his headlock. She faced him, curiosity pacifying her desire to launch another full-frontal assault. Unbuckling his white asylum uniform, he took the cloak off and reversed it so that the dark, inner lining was on the outside. He slipped it back on, and recognition burst like fireworks.

It was the cloak! The same exact cloak as the mystery man's, down to the names embedded in the sleeves. Except this one was tailor-made to Shadow Boy's large frame.

He dipped into his pocket and pulled out something shiny. A silver teaspoon, like the one the mystery man had stolen from Minni's! "What does silver do to the strongest magical properties?" Arm raised for effect, he tapped the spoon against the cuff of his sleeve.

And his entire body vanished. Just like the mystery man.

A figure flitted at the corner of her eye, and Rose whipped around. Marek reappeared at her elbow.

"It disrupts them." He pocketed the silverware. "This is called a Corner Cloak. One side is used as an asylum uniform, but flip it inside out and *ta-da!* No one can see or hear you. The only way to catch someone wearing a Corner Cloak is out of the corner of your eye, but when you turn to get a better look—they're gone. Nifty, isn't it?"

Yes, yes, it was, nifty to the point that she was going to explore it fiber by fiber once her bottom lip quit its wobbling. "So, all this time ... you were hiding from me? I came every week, searched every place I could think of, and you were hiding from me? I missed you so much, and you were *hiding* from me?" Marek reached for her, and she threw her hands up to stop him. "Don't touch!" Lightning spurted from her wrists like a punctured vein. "Marek, I—" Had she ever admitted it out loud before? "I have unstable magic."

"Thunder ..." He reached as if to slap her a double high five but stopped short, the rumor of an inch separating their skin. His hands dwarfed her own. The lines on his palms read like words, translating into a childhood tongue of scrapes and bumps and chipped baby teeth. *Protector*, they said. *Security blanket.* "So do I."

79

What? Well, no wonder the matron at his orphanage and the lumberjacks had pretended he didn't exist! No one wants to be associated with someone who has unstable magic. "Why didn't you tell me? I coulda helped you." She would've made sure he *never* felt as alone and unwanted as she had.

"But you did. Unstable magic didn't matter with you and Stormy, and that mattered more than anything to me. I kept it a secret from everyone else ... until I had an Incident with my lumber crew. That's how I ended up at Heartstone Asylum. It changed my future." Marek pulled her crinkled letter to her future self from his pocket. "It can change yours, too. Do you remember the promise I made you? I promised that if you ever had to leave home, you wouldn't be running *from* something. You'd be running *towards* something. A place where everyone knows how to dance in the rain. Heartstone Asylum is that place. Trust me."

Did she? Did she still trust him with the same unwavering faith she'd had in him since she was nine? "And they let you come every Tuesday to keep an eye on me?"

"I wasn't alone. The man and woman you met back at the hearse were with me as well. You've had more guardian angels than you'd know what to do with."

That would explain the blurry shapes that frequented their sacred maple. "But why couldn't you tell me you were here?" she demanded. How could he have stood there while she waited for him, cried for him, wondered if he was ever even real?

Marek took her shoulders, and she jolted.

(IN THE NON-ELECTRICAL SENSE.)

All this physical contact—she wasn't used to it. "Think about it," he said. "I was committed to Heartstone Asylum when you were eleven. Why couldn't I take you with me?"

Gradually, screechingly, her train of thought was syncing to his tracks. How long had it been since they were of one mind? They could use some oiling. "The asylum age restriction. You had to wait till I was thirteen."

"Exactly. And why didn't I reveal myself earlier?"

"Because I'd have said, 'To Saturnity with the age restriction!' and followed you home, made friends with your doormat, and refused to leave."

Marek nodded, pleased with her deduction. "And how could I have kept you when legally you weren't allowed to be there for another two years? Your father would have gone poking, Heartstone Asylum would've had an inquiry, and if there's one thing Heartstone Asylum hates, it's an inquiry."

Rose picked up his sleeve and inspected the names stitched into the fabric.

Rose Skylar. Marek Knoxwind.

"Is this how I'm seeing you now? Because my name's been stitched on with—" she lifted the sleeve and licked the metallic lettering. Her tongue zinged. "—definitely magic thread? The man at the bakery had my name stitched into his cloak, too, and he disappeared right in front of me just like you did. And he used that silver teaspoon!"

"Ah, yes," said Marek. "The invisible man, switching the wheels to distract Sir Ottis, leading you to the hearse to buy us time. We needed you to cause an Incident proportionate to someone calling the authorities. Then, when they dispatched local asylum transportation, we'd be ready to intercept. What did you think of our little performance?"

Rose clapped enthusiastically.

(HEY, CREDIT WHERE CREDIT'S DUE. THEY'D HALF-CONVINCED ME I WAS CRAZY. WHICH, LET'S BE HONEST, ISN'T MUCH OF A STRETCH. IF EVERYONE HAD TURNED OUT TO BE A FIGMENT OF MY IMAGINATION, I'D HAVE HAPPILY INVITED THEM ALL TO AN IMAGINARY TEA PARTY. UNLESS THAT'S CONSIDERED OFFENSIVE IN IMAGINARY CIRCLES.)

"Bravo! Standing ovation! Who played the mystery man? I'd like his autograph."

"He'll be thrilled. Once he's finished removing the frosting from his eyes, that is."

Her clapping tapered to a halt. "Oops."

"Malachy Thaynwood can hold a grudge like none other, but not with you." A shadow poked her side. "He likes you too much. Thinks you're clever. He and Cade— the lady you met back at the hearse—have watched you grow up, and they can't wait to meet you properly. So, what do you say?" Shadows swirled hopefully from Marek's wings, delivering her letter back into her hands. "Can we be your new future?"

The shadows twisted together in the shape of a hand, reaching out.

Rose took it, darkness entwining her fingers.

*

They walked back to the hearse, bumping wings companionably.

"Your feathers looked different," Rose said. "When you were at my house, I didn't recognize them. They weren't all blurry and shadowy. Just regular-looking."

"You mean like this?" The velvety darkness retracted into his feathers, leaving them midnight blue and smooth.

"Yeah! How'd you do that?"

"Little trick I picked up at Heartstone. You'll learn a few yourself about controlling your soul signia."

Malachy Thaynwood was standing at the back of the hearse, still wiping his face clean with a cloth. He looked up at their approach, eyes red, puffy, and glowering.

"There's something I need to do," she murmured and walked over to her mystery man.

He caught sight of her own frosted face, and his lips quirked imperceptibly. "Well?"

Dazzling him with her most winning smile, she took the corner of her sleeve and wiped a smear of frosting from his cheek. "Missed a spot."

ENTRY 8

LIVE FREE OR DIET HARD

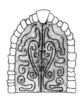

C adence "Cade" Locklear worked as an escort and nurse at Heartstone Asylum. A young woman in her early one hundred and thirties, she had fair skin, black-and-white checkered wings, and an aura imbued with a certain degree of sophistication that began with her elaborate updo and ended with her stiletto heels.

(FOOTWEAR THAT INDUBITABLY DOUBLES AS WEAPONS OF IMPALEMENT.)

Her hair was worth a second mention—not just because it looked like one of those incredible fisherman's knots that no one can untie, but because it was purple. That's right. *Purple.* A lovely shade of lavender, to be exact.

"You almost never get to see purple in a rainbow,"

Rose told her. "It's the dimmest rim. I like seeing it on your head."

Cade smiled. It was all of her most charming features summed up in a slight overbite and pearly white teeth. "And I like seeing a storm cloud on yours."

They acted like they'd known her for years, Cade and Malachy. And according to Marek, they had. All those Tuesdays sitting under the maple tree, thinking she was alone and forgotten about when all the while she was being planned for and watched over ...

She hadn't picked her nose, had she?

(AND DON'T EVEN MENTION MY ATTEMPTS TO PATENT A NEW, MIXED MAGICAL ARTS MOVE. THAT SQUIRREL WAS NEVER THE SAME.)

Best not think about it.

"What was this li'l guy doing in a casket when I got here?" Rose nuzzled the puppy in her lap. "Afraid he'd loot your valuables when you weren't looking?"

Marek mussed Beta's ears affectionately. "Us and any town within a five-mile radius. Beta is a master escape artist, but home is where he hides his treasures. He's going to make someone a fine, faithful companion one day. Or today, if you like him." Shadow Boy winked. "He's a welcoming present."

Puppy? *Her* puppy? A puppy for her? Puppy! Puppy. Puppy, puppy, puppy, puppy—

Her excitement was sparking in a very literal sense, and she put Beta on the seat, scooting him a safe distance away. "Do you keep a lotta dogs at Heartstone Asylum?"

"We do," said Cade. "We believe that canine affection is therapeutic for our patients, and, when trained properly, Sonorific Huskies make excellent service dogs." She produced a small service vest and fastened it around Beta's wriggling body. "He's still getting used to his vest, but this provides a protective shield against most forms of magic. Don't be afraid to play with him. You won't hurt him."

Nervous lightning jumped from Rose's skin. Crackling head to foot, she inched over to Beta—small, trusting Beta —and a waft of memory-smell collided with her senses.

Memories, as you know, take the form of all different senses: memory-sight, memory-taste, memory-sound. And when one memory-sense links to another, which links to another, which links to another, it forms a reliving so vivid it could be time travel. For a split second, she was eleven years old again, tasting the smell of burning meat, ears packed with screams as dense as cotton. She could see the fractured lightning scars across dark, bruising skin.

She remembered thinking how beautiful scars could be.

Rose immediately pulled her hand away, but shadows

nudged it back. "He'll be fine," Marek assured her. The shadows pressed down, and her lightning-laced fingers cupped the puppy's head.

No burning meat.

No horrified screaming.

Beta blinked his magnified eyes at her, unimpressed.

"Oh!" Rose returned the puppy readily to her lap. "I can't think of any asylums that have service dogs. Heartstone does things differently, doesn't it? How come I've never heard of you before?"

"There are reasons Heartstone Asylum is so private," Marek said, "and we're going to tell you all about them. But not yet. And we can't tell you *why* we can't tell you yet, either. Just trust me. Would I take you someplace boring?"

Rose leaned her head against the window with a sigh. "Fine. But can I at least have a location?"

"Of course." He smiled obligingly. "Heartstone Asylum is located in the Petrified Forest."

(DEPLOYING INFO-ASTERISKS IN THREE … TWO … ONE …)

* * *

About a hundred years ago, there was a legendary war known as the War o' the Wargs. It was a standoff between an army of angels and an army of magical, horse-sized, talking wolves. A vicious, bloody conflict, it hung the world in balance as the two armies raged against each other, one in the name of peace, the other in the name of pandemonium.

And it all began with a simple argument over nutrition.

Wargs, you see, have an *interesting* diet, to say the least. Their food pyramid consists of meat, berries, and pure, raw screams. Which isn't nearly as terrible as it sounds. Screaming can be as much fun as laughing, and often the two go hand-in-hand, warming a Warg's heart as well as his belly. It was this line of thinking that led the Wargs to create the most popular spectator sport of the time: Warg riding. The monthly tournaments were veritable feasts for the giant wolves as they attempted to buck their angel riders to the screams and cheers of a packed arena.

A fabulous arrangement any way you looked at it.

But a thousand good things can be brought to an end by a single bad, and after a killer Warg gang sprang up in the Saxum mountains, the leaders of the realms decided it would be wise to restrict interaction between Wargs and angels. They banned Warg-riding tournaments and with them, the endless supply of friends and food the Wargs had grown to rely on.

And Wargs ... they're just not themselves when they're hungry.

Initially, their goal was to convince the angelic communities to have Warg-riding tournaments reinstated. To head up their crusade, the Wargs enlisted the help of, amazingly, an *angel*—an infamous Warg rider known as the Sinner. He identified with the plight of his canine friends and took up their cause, doing everything in his power to persuade the leaders of the realms to lift their ban on Warg-riding tournaments.

But what set out as a simple campaign quickly turned violent when the Sinner and his pack were met with intense discrimination from their once-friends. Fights broke out—riots and raids, and as the towns screamed with terror, the Wargs' aching bellies began to fill. They started to believe the words the angels were saying about them, that they were barbaric beasts with no morals, and deserved to be locked away or eradicated.

And so, in their pursuit to feed their appetite for screams, that is what they became.

They attacked town after town, city after city, any place that had rejected their appeals to have Warg-riding tournaments reinstated, feasting on their terrified screams. The Wargs hailed the Sinner as their great general, the one who would conquer every inch of land and put Wargs in charge of it all, but very soon, the angel side of the conflict had a champion of their own, a man they christened the Saint.

Clever, weren't they?

The Sinner and the Saint battled for half a decade before facing each other in the heart of a remote forest where the stuff of legend was born. It was Moonsfrost Eve, 1425 A.S. No one knows quite what happened that night the War o' the Wargs ended, just that the armies which entered the forest never came out again. Their bodies were gone. Dead or alive, it didn't matter. Their fates were a secret known only to the trees; a secret so terrible it had turned their bark and leaves to stone.

The Petrified Forest is hallowed ground, despised and revered, and avoided at all costs. Until some genius decided to build an asylum smack dab in the middle of it, apparently.

No, Marek wasn't taking her someplace boring at all.

* * *

"Close your eyes. I want you to take it all in at once," Marek said.

The journey was over. There was the rattle of a gate being opened, and the hearse jerked forward on its wheels. Blindly, Rose searched under the catafalque's skirt where she'd stashed her duffel bag and grabbed onto Marek's sleeve. He led her down the carriage steps and stood her in the cool night, rotating her shoulders slightly. "Okay. You can open."

She blinked. Hugged her duffel a little tighter. Blinked again. "It's ... it's ... " She spun, drinking in the landscape like a drowning man. "Whoa."

"It is rather *whoa*, isn't it?"

They were standing in an iron-fenced courtyard
surrounded by trees made entirely of stone. And here,
seeming to pulse with the very life the Petrified Forest had

lost the final night of the War, was Heartstone Asylum. An enormous manor of aging majesty, it boasted cobblestone walls snared with vines, arched windows, a crescent-shaped lake curling around its side, and a looming tower crowned with battlements.

"That's where we live." Marek nodded up.

Poking from the center of the manor, the tower looked like a giant lollypop clutched in the fist of a possessive five-year-old. "The Lollypop Tower?"

Malachy snorted, hopping down from the hearse's driver seat. "That's one name for it. Think patients would be more docile if they got a lollypop afterward?"

"Don't be cruel," Cade reproached. "You know it's a simple matter of asylum regulations. Aldric despises the practice."

Rose had absolutely no idea what they were talking about.

"You know what else Ace despises? Being kept up past his bedtime. You'd best get going." Malachy left to put the dogs in the kennels, and Rose followed Cade and Marek to the asylum's black double doors. Cade reached for the handles. The doors gave a sleepy groan, but even her movement couldn't disguise the fact that they'd opened of their own accord.

"Everyone is asleep," she whispered and slipped her graceful figure through the opening.

Gone were the visions of cold white walls and padded cells. The foyer of Heartstone Asylum was cozy and symmetrical with fireplaces on either side and a lovely assortment of furniture. The ceiling was high and domed. Straight ahead were twin staircases that led to the upper floor and bowed around the opening to the lower. It was a friendly foyer, warm and welcoming and—

The doors behind Rose closed without assistance.

Also, very, very off, now that you mention it. The air was still as a corpse. Could houses hold their breath? If so, this one was probably blue in the face—were houses in the habit of having faces and, you know, lungs.

Something flashed at the corner of her eye, and Rose turned. That footstool hadn't been there before. Had it? "Are you the only ones here who have Corner Cloaks?"

"Not ... necessarily," Cade said. "Why do you ask?"

" 'Cause I saw something move outta the corner of my eye."

"Oh, that's just—" She shook her head. "Never mind. You'll know soon enough. Marek is going to take you to meet our proprietor."

Marek offered Rose the crook of his elbow. "Shall we?"

Wait. She was getting careless with all this physical stuff. *Dangerously* careless. What was the system her parents had given her? No skin-on-skin contact and something about layers?

(NOT THAT THEY EVER USED IT. EASIER NOT TO TOUCH AT ALL.)

With his cloak and flannel shirt beneath it, Marek's

skin was separated from hers by at least two layers of fabric. Add in her long-sleeved shirt and cloak, and that would be four. Four was a happy number. Four had friends.

She looped her arm through his.

"Rose." Cade had a pained look on her face. "Perhaps we should straighten you up a bit before you go?"

Rose touched her frosting-caked cheeks and grinned. "This is an asylum. I'm sure your proprietor has seen worse than a food fight."

"Yes," Cade ceded, "but you only get one first impression, dear. Why not make it the best it can be?"

It was such an Amber thing to say that Rose rolled her eyes and acquiesced. Cade took this as permission to whip out a handkerchief and begin scrubbing her face. She stiffened. A single layer of flimsy fabric was all that separated their skin. One was a lonely number. One didn't have any friends.

Cade must've noticed her discomfort because the torture was over within seconds. "There. Much better. Of course, a change of clothes would be preferable, but—"

"But it would be rude to keep Aldric waiting." Marek looped his other arm through Cade's so that the three of them formed a jaunty semicircle. "Relax. He's going to like her as much as we do." He patted her hand.

Cade gave a breathy laugh. "Well, of course he will. What a silly thought!" Disentangling herself, she picked up Rose's duffle bag. "I'll just take this upstairs for you.

Good luck!" She dusted a residual fleck of frosting from Rose's nose and hurried away, stiletto heels *click-clicking* up the stairs.

"Aren't those shoes kinda impractical for her line of work?" Rose said as Marek took a right down a dimly-lit hallway.

"Try telling her that," he said quietly. "Cade's a miracle worker. She could save the worlds without breaking a heel. Don't let her worry you, though. Fussing is just her way of saying she wants everything to be perfect now that you're finally here." He went to pat her hand as he'd done with Cade, and Rose yanked away on reflex.

"Sorry," she whispered, mortified. "Sorry, I just—" Lightning flashed from her skin, and she backed away further.

Soft, tangible shadows wrapped around her, ambassadors of Marek's hugs, and her storm cloud calmed inside her. "What happened, Thunder? What happened to Stormy?" The compassion in his gaze was a scalpel that would have her spilling her guts in seconds.

Rose looked anywhere but him.

"You can tell me."

Was it just her, or were the walls getting closer when she wasn't watching?

"But if you don't want to, that's okay, too." His shadows patted her cheeks and withdrew. "We have an expert on magic studies here. He wants to meet with you tomorrow. You don't have to tell him what happened, either, but it might help him find a way to free Stormy. Would you like to talk to him?"

Well, dead ends aren't dead ends till you give 'em a good kick with your foot, she always said. "I guess it couldn't hurt."

"*Hurt* ... " The word hissed through the hallway like a snake.

"Ah," Marek murmured. "Forgot to mention. Best keep your voice down in—"

Phantom footsteps rushed past them, and Rose squeaked in alarm. Up ahead, a girl's voice shouted, "*Watch where you're going, Carrot Top! Ugh, you spilled ink all over me!*"

There was a vengeful crack like a whip. "*Ouch!*" a boy echoed petulantly. "*That* hurt, *Seph! A drop of ink is no excuse to give me splinters!*"

"What was *that*? Who were they?" Rose spun in circles. "Where'd they go?"

Marek resumed walking. "They didn't go anywhere. That was just the hallway remembering."

Shadows pressed against the small of her back, encouraging her to keep up. "That's a dumb answer."

"You want a better one? It's waiting for you right behind that door." He pointed to the end of the hallway at a door labeled *Office*. "And at this time of night, it's probably wearing fluffy slippers."

ENTRY 9

BANANA SHAKES

Answers, slippered or otherwise, were not waiting for Rose when she arrived.

The empty office was robed with regality from the cherry wood desk with a luscious fruit bowl and imposing high back chair, to the burgundy walls, each bearing the crest of Heartstone Asylum: a shield crisscrossed by two machete swords with a polished stone heart at its center. Affixed behind the desk was a sprawling map of their world, Shaolandir.

(SOUNDS LIKE "CHANDELIER.")

It was peppered with red dots like a bad case of halo pox. Spread out on the broad canvas, the landmasses resembled a turtle swimming around the globe. The

Islands of Salfair made up the four legs, Aurialis its head, and the realms Saxum, Pandrum, and Faberland the shell.

She took a seat in front of the desk and counted the map's red dots. Were they locations of patients, past and present? Potential vacationing spots? She gave a pondering hum.

The office hummed back.

"Come again?" she asked politely.

The hum was louder this time, unlike any sound a vocal cord could make. It was like—like—have you ever stroked the rim of a wineglass and heard it sing? *That's* what it sounded like. Singing wineglasses. Only there wasn't a wineglass in sight.

The melody bounced from wall to wall, crest to crest, blade to blade as four pairs of machete swords wrested free of their wall mounts and twirled elegantly to the floor. They turned to her with synchronized bows and proceeded to confirm what she'd suspected all along:

This asylum had magic in its bones.

And the proof was in the singing machetes performing an impromptu line dance up and down the office floor, blades clashing to the beat.

"What do you think of my machetes?" At the left of the desk, a tall man stood in the doorway of an adjoining room, carefully positioned so that his face was cast in shadow. It had an impressively mysterious effect.

Rose was standing up on her chair, bouncing to the

music. "They're the most choreographed machetes I've ever seen!"

The machetes beamed with pride. Their song clanged to a close, and with coordinated hops, they reattached to their wall mounts, humming contently.

"I'm glad you like them." The man stepped into the light, and she sat down hard. With a title like "proprietor," she was expecting a wizened old man wearing spectacles and grooming a long, white beard.

(And don't say you weren't, either, Reader Name Here _____.)

But the proprietor of Heartstone Asylum was a man no older than Malachy—early to mid-two-hundreds—with a curtain of black hair past his chin and a dramatically barbered beard accentuating his high cheekbones. The feathers of his wings were like rows of knives, steely gray and pointed, but his eyes, similar in color, were kind.

He carried a tray of hot chocolate to the desk, his noble bearing offset by the pair of fluffy slippers on his feet. "Allow me," he said and poured her a mug. "My name is Aldric Ragnar, and I am sorry we're meeting under these circumstances. Oftentimes I'll ask myself, under what circumstances would I like to be meeting you and every patient who walks through the doors of Heartstone Asylum? Ask me, and I will tell you that more than anything, I wish I could meet you in a world where 'asylum' means what it was meant to mean. Sanctuary. Refuge. A safe place to live and grow and learn. Despite what you've heard about other asylums, this is the standard to which Heartstone is held. We are here to offer you asylum in the truest sense of the word." Ragnar held out the mug of hot chocolate.

Rose accepted it. "Is that why you named it Heartstone Asylum? Because that's what the original Heartstone Asylum was. A safe place for anyone who needed it. It was Dimidia's home."

"A good namesake, isn't it? Not everyone recognizes the significance. You're familiar with *Blackout's Tales*, then?"

"My favorite book."

"Mine as well! Now"—he rifled through a desk drawer —"here is an itinerary of a typical week at Heartstone. We've found that the best ways to manage unstable magic are, among other things, engaging in the creative arts, physical activity, and studying the underlying causes of your condition itself."

She scanned the schedule in disbelief. Nature walks, music class, art therapy, magic studies, self-defense —"*Umbrella* making?"

Ragnar smiled. "With your arrival, I hear this may be of particular use in days to come. We sell them in markets and at festivals for a small profit."

She choked on her hot chocolate. A host of angels who could kill/maim/seriously injure with a stray thought gathered together in close quarters making *umbrellas*? Where was the shock therapy? The lobotomies? The straitjackets? "How are you not all *dead*?"

"We take precautions. The patients here are partitioned into intimate groups—teams, you could say. Each team is assigned a nurse and an orderly who are in charge of their well-being. For you and Marek, that would be Nurse Locklear and Master Thaynwood. But nurses, orderlies, they would hardly be enough to allow patients the freedom we offer without endangering the whole asylum. So, the asylum itself lends a hand."

"With magic," Rose said.

"With magic," he agreed. "You'll see it take many forms within these walls. The asylum's number one priority is to protect patients from all harm. You're safe here. In fact, there isn't a safer place for you in all the—"

Ragnar's speech was interrupted by a scream, a hiss, and the chime of breaking glass from the other room. He winced.

A girl with disheveled hair and dark circles under her eyes poked her head around the door of the adjoining room. "We got the dimensions wrong. I'm not sure it's going to fit through the window, but—" her thought dropped off as she took in Rose's appearance. "Good lords, her *hair*!"

Rose twisted a curl. Lightning spiraled up the strands. "Shocking, isn't it?"

"Excuse me a moment. Terribly sorry," Ragnar murmured and hastened to the other room.

The girl spared a longing glance at the fruit bowl and closed the door.

Sipping her hot chocolate, Rose sidled closer to the sounds of chaos. More hissing, more breaking glass, more shrieking, and a woman's voice cutting through the clamor, "We could've used more hands, Aldric!"

"I told you," Ragnar said, straining with exertion, "they're occupied with our newest patient. Now *grab that rope!*"

Rose pressed her ear against the door. It cracked open, and a sliver of moss green eyes squinted appraisingly at her.

Someone found her more interesting than whatever monster was trashing the other room? Why, she'd take that as a compliment!

Hi, Rose mouthed, waving. She motioned for the girl to wait and dashed to the fruit bowl. "You looked hungry," she whispered, presenting a banana. "I'm Rose."

The door opened wider. The girl clasped the other end of the fruit. "Sephone," she said. "Persephone Darrow."

Rose shook the banana gladly. "Nice to meet you."

Sephone had the silky russet complexion and cutlass-sharp features of Salfair's Southwestern sea-farers. Her wings were a camouflage blend of browns and greens, and her hair was dark and wavy. There was a notch in her upper lip, an old scar like a nick in a blade that had fought something stronger than itself and won. Judging by her squint, Sephone was either in desperate need of glasses or lived in a perpetual state of distrust towards the world.

She looked over her shoulder to check that everything was under control in the other room. A vase flew over her head and smashed against the wall, raining glass shards. Shrugging, Sephone unpeeled her snack. "Thanks, New Girl. I needed this."

"Don't mention it." There was an enraged hiss, and a humongous tail lashed against the door. "You should probably get back to that."

Sephone regarded her suspiciously. "You're not going to ask about it?"

"And spoil the surprise? Nah. Enjoy the banana. Good source of potassium." Rose nudged the door shut on her bewildered, banana-eating face.

Venturing back to the fruit bowl, she chose a speckled plum and was sucking on its pit by the time Ragnar returned, hurriedly straightening his wrinkled attire. A thin strip of red grazed his cheek. He cleared his throat and sat. "Apologies for the interruption. Where were we?"

"I *believe* you were telling me all about the safety of Heartstone Asylum." She picked a tooth idly. "Isn't that right?"

Ragnar grimaced, resting his forehead against steepled fingers. "I was afraid it was that. I suppose you're going to ask what was happening in the other room just now?"

There was only one thing that could curb her curiosity's insatiable appetite: the taste of a challenge.

"No." Rose gave her sweetest smile. "Marek says there are reasons Heartstone Asylum is so private, but that you'll explain it all sooner or later."

The question was, could she figure it out before they got the chance?

Challenge accepted.

ENTRY 10

THE POWER OF THE WITCHING HOUR

R ose stared at the alcove, where a spiral staircase wound its way up to the top of the Lollypop Tower. She turned to Marek. "You're telling me that this staircase may or may not start shaking like an earthquake and break our kneecaps based on its *mood*? What kind of asylum is this?"

"An insane one," Marek said cheerfully. "Ragnar told you how the asylum goes out of its way to protect patients from getting hurt? Well, the asylum doesn't like what the tower was originally designed for, and sometimes it forgets that we don't use it for its intended purpose. Hence the possessed staircase."

"And what was its intended purpose?"

"I'll show you." Marek bounced a few times, loosening his muscles for a run.

"Can't you just float us up on a shadow blanket? Save our kneecaps the trouble?"

"And deny you the experience? Hardly. Mine turned a brilliant shade of maroon the first time. It's a rite of passage." And with that, he lowered his shoulders and charged the stairs like a grizzly bear.

A little *warning* wouldn't hurt. Rose stampeded in his wake, flapping her wings for speed. This staircase was wound tighter than her curls! Dang, she could've used some stretching. By the time the door came into view, her legs were tight and searing. Almost there, almost there, almost there! "I think we're gonna make—"

Marek body-slammed the door just as the steps beneath her feet started jiggling like upset gelatin. Rose leaped. "Timber!" she screamed, slamming into Shadow Boy's legs. They sprawled across the threshold of her new home.

"Why do I have the feeling that things are about to get much noisier around here?" Cade remarked, hands on hips, from above.

"Sorry." Rose grinned. Pulling herself up, she braced against the wall and was met with something weirdly squishy, like the walls were ... cushioned. "Oh."

The Lollypop Tower was the asylum's solitary confinement. Except not, because it was retrofitted with a small kitchen, eating area, and den all mingled together. The wall in front of the dining table had been knocked out completely and replaced with a prodigious window wall, which gave the space a wide, very *un*confined feel.

Cade whisked Rose around on a tour. "The tower *insists* on creating a carefree ambiance with the décor," she said, indicating the abundant supply of bunny-themed pictures and knick-knacks. Happy bunnies, hopping bunnies, bunnies eating carrots, bunnies, bunnies everywhere. "Though I do wish it could settle on something more sophisticated than *bunny* rabbits. It does switch occasionally. When one of us is feeling strongly about something, the tower can't help but sympathize with our mood."

To the right was a hallway no longer than Rose if she stretched across the floor. It led to three tightly wedged bedrooms and a bathroom. Cramped. The whole place was cramped. For a tower designed to confine patients to their own company, Rose had never felt less alone in all her life.

She loved it.

But three bedrooms, four angels ... that left one *teensy* little math problem. "Where do I stay?"

Marek stood on a chair from the dining table and pulled a rope ladder from a hatch in the ceiling. "The tower cooked up something extra special for you. Go check it out."

"I'll put some tea on, and when you come back down, you can tell us all about your talk with Master Ragnar, all right? I—I assume all went well?" Cade had the decency to not wring her hands out loud.

"Oh, yes! He told me all about Heartstone Asylum." Rose hid her smile against a ladder wrung. "You have some interesting activities"—like monster-wrangling —"around here. I'm excited to try them. Be down in a few."

Have you ever had an attic bedroom? They're adorable. The ceilings are low, the close proximity of the bed, dresser, and closet means you can pretend the floor is made of lava and hop around a built-in obstacle course, and looking out that single window makes you feel like you're on top of the world.

Laughing, Rose face-planted on her bed, narrowly missing the cupcake *someone* had stationed on her pillow. Red velvet. Her favorite.

She took a frosting-thick bite and rolled on her back. Above her hung a remarkable piece of craftsmanship. A mobile, it was. Tremendous in size and detail with curved rosewood beams and whimsical carvings up the wazoo. She nudged it with her toe and watched the figures spin like a merry-go-round. Thunderclouds with clinking lightning bolts. A miniature book with *Blackout's Tales* scrawled across its cover. A trio of strawberries dripping with chocolate. Each painstakingly carved and painted down to the tiniest seed.

It had Marek's fingerprints all over it.

Rose sat up straight. She'd witnessed firsthand how

long it took him to crank out carvings of this caliber. A whole *mobile's* worth of them, well, it would've taken about two years.

He really had been planning for her all along.

(NO, THOSE ARE YOUR EYES GETTING ALL ITCHY, WATERY.)

*

Sleep that night was a restless affair. Rose curled up in the attic's window seat, munching on the last of her red velvet cupcake and enjoying the panorama of the Petrified Forest. It was midnight, and her letter to her future self was open at her side. "I guess we changed our future after all, huh?" What kind of future would it be now? Full of mysteries and adventure and friendship? "Whoever you are, Future Me, I can't wait to meet you."

She tucked the letter under her pillow and went back to the window. Pockets of moonlight lit the stone trees with a bluish glow, and wind howled through the motionless branches.

Rose rested her head against the cool pane.

*

2:00 AM.

Moonlight was a beautiful thing. It drifted through the trees like a cartographer tracing his maps, sweeping back and forth as it inched closer to the asylum. Blue light blurred at the edges of the forest.

Rose rubbed her sleepy eyes.

*

3:00 AM.

Nocturnal creatures had gone to bed, early birds had yet to rise. Night and day were in limbo. It was the Witching Hour, the time of night when ghosts are said to walk—

(*FLOAT?*)

—the earth.

There was a book by Warden "Wraith Warder" Carlyle called *I Look Like I've Seen a Ghost: Memoirs of a Ghost Hunter*, and it proposed a theory about the Witching Hour. According to ol' Wraith Warder, the reason the moons have a tendency to disappear around 3:00 AM is because ghosts, drawing their paramagical energy from moonlight, have spent the better half of the night sucking them dry. As the moons grow darker, the ghosts grow brighter till the clock chimes three, and the moons give up the last of their light to the departed spirits below, allowing them to interact with the land of the living once more.

Rose unpacked her copy of *I Look Like I've Seen a Ghost: Memoirs of a Ghost Hunter* from her duffle bag—

(Never leave home, no matter how unexpectedly, without a good book on ghost hunting.)

—and reread the section like a bedtime story. Outside, moonslit shapes wreathed the asylum's iron-fenced courtyard.

There wasn't a moon in the sky.

*

By 4:00 AM, Rose was certain of several things:

1) Her imaginary best friend was not actually imaginary.

2) He'd just committed her to an asylum.

3) The asylum was in the middle of a stone forest where hundreds of soldiers had died mysterious deaths.

4) That forest was most *definitely* haunted.

ENTRY 11

AUTHOR(S) INTERLUDE PART 2

Knock, knock. Anybody home? Haven't heard from you guys in a while ... are you still there? ~1526 A.S.

How to Write a Time Traveler's Diary, Lesson Five: NEVER interrupt on a cliffhanger! Reader Name Here ____ probably hates you right now. ~1529 A.S.

Little Me, we don't just interrupt for interrupting's sake. It's always to impart some useful bit of instruction or information. ~1530 A.S.

(Mostly.) ~1527 A.S.

Sorry. I just wanted to see how you thought I was doing. Compared to your diaries, I mean. ~1526 A.S.

Well, you know what they say about comparing yourself to others ... ~1532 A.S.

Yeah. But I'm not. ~1526 A.S.

Good point! ~1530 A.S.

Just tell me—am I doing this right? Am I including all the right details? Is Reader Name Here ____ asking all the right questions? ~1526 A.S.

Like why did your best friend commit you to a haunted asylum? ~1527 A.S.

And does Heartstone Asylum know that it's haunted? ~1532 A.S.

And what secrets is Heartstone hiding that Marek isn't telling you about? ~1530 A.S.

And finally, WHY—for a time traveler's diary—does there seem to be a suspicious lack of time travel? ~1529 A.S.

That's a lot of questions. ~1526 A.S.

How to Write a Time Traveler's Diary, Lesson Six: *Time is the iron that smooths question marks into exclamation points.*

The more questions, the more excitement when you find the answers. ~1532 A.S.

See, 1526? That means you're doing great! Just wait till you're an old pro like me. ~1527 A.S.

You've been doing this a year. ~1529 A.S.

Wait till you're a young pro like me. ~1527 A.S.

So, my job is to iron question marks into exclamation points? Hmm. Well, I am good at irony—how different can ironing be, really? ~1526 A.S.

They're both the opposite of wrinkly! You'll be fine. We believe in you, Little Me. Right, everyone? ~1530 A.S.

Yes! ~1527 A.S.

Absolutely. ~1532 A.S.

Rah-rah. ~1529 A.S.

ENTRY 12

THE MYSTERIOUS BENEFACTRESS

The next morning, Marek led Rose, along with Malachy, Cade, and Beta, around the asylum with the air of an all-knowing tour guide. "Now, we've seen the Foyer of Moving Furniture, walked the Remembrance Hall, had breakfast in the Dining Hall of Giggling Walls, and you saw the Office's machete spectacular last night, but *here* is the pride and joy of Heartstone Asylum."

They came upon a door with a plaque that read:

The Topsy-Turvy Library
Because bookworms need exercise, too.

Rose opened the door—and her world turned upside down.

It was an obstacle course. A *library* obstacle course.

Bookcases hung from the tall ceiling like bats in a cave, encircled by rope bridges for readers to walk while they perused the shelves. Each shelf was its own island in a sea of challenges. To get from one to another involved various means of transportation such as zip lines, chain rings, swinging ropes, and climbing nets. Platforms jutted from the walls as starting points for the obstacle course, but while the library itself was wide and spacious, it wasn't enough to allow indoor flight. No, to get to the platforms, you had to rock-climb the walls.

Readers whizzed, flailing and straining, overhead, books tucked under their arms or between their teeth. The ground level was littered with exhausted library patrons slumping in chairs or across tables.

Cade pried Beta's leash from Rose's wonderstruck hand. "Go find something you like. But do stretch first. You can pull a muscle finding a good book to read."

*

Rose observed the Topsy-Turvy Library from her perch on the Bookshelf Island of How-To. *Topsy-turvy.* Now there's an accurate description. The whole room was literally turned on its head. Even the bookshelves were hanging upside down from the ceiling, held in place by some gravity-defying magic. Dousing the library in sunlight was a chapel window that took up a third of the central wall. In front of it sat a plump armchair, as red and velvety as her favorite cupcake, on a rounded dais. A storyteller's chair.

Did they have story hour at Heartstone Asylum? Rose *loved* stories. Loved telling them even more. Nothing beat the stillness of an audience entranced by the words of a good book. She could almost hear it now ...

No storyteller sat on the red velvet armchair, but silence, quick and clean as a trial at the guillotines, had befallen the library just the same.

(*AND IN A LIBRARY DESIGNED TO EXERCISE BOTH BODY AND MIND, THE QUIET RULE IS SO RARELY OBSERVED.*)

Its source was the five battered-looking angels that had entered the door.

Giant snake wrangling must be a real gut punch. Sephone looked no less exhausted than the night before, and her teammates weren't faring any better. Two of them looked about a century past their adventuring days, but whether their stiff gait was from giant snake wrangling or arthritis, it was hard to tell. Angels rushed to push back chairs and offer their seats to the newcomers. Some shook the team's hands and gingerly patted their backs, but the fivesome shooed away the attention and chose a table at the back of the library.

"Trying to unravel the mystery of Elektra Waverly's team?" said a scratchy, aging voice behind Rose. "They cause quite a stir, don't they?"

She perked up. Whoever was talking to her sounded old. An "I've seen many things in my day" kind of old. An "I'm a treasure trove of ancient secrets" kind of old. If she turned around and he had a long, white beard, she knew she'd struck gold.

Rose turned. The man's ivory beard was so long he'd braided the end and tucked it into his belt. "Hard to unravel a mystery without any clues," she said casually. "Who are they?"

"Patients, same as you and I. Well, not all of them." He pointed to a woman with pale skin and spunky red spikes of hair. "*That* is Elektra Waverly—or Nurse Waverly, as you should call her—and her son, Aiden, the team's orderly."

"*He's* their orderly?" That boy wasn't much older than her!

"He may be a mere fourteen years, but he can be quite *persuasive* when he needs to. You'll see."

"So, what do they do? Nurse Waverly's team, I mean." Did he know about the giant snake wrangling?

"Well, the truth is"—the man leaned in conspiratorially—"no one knows. They train separately from us during self-defense classes and some magic exercises. They'll disappear for days, sometimes weeks, and come back looking tired and bruised. Their work is a mystery, but I know what they are." He beckoned her closer, covering the side of his mouth with his wing. "They're *heroes*."

Rose scratched her nose. "Heroes? Heroes of what?"

"Something grand! Something dangerous! Something only Master Ragnar knows about."

"And no one's ever thought to *ask*?"

"Ask?" the old man spluttered. "Why in the worlds would we *ask*? We have a very unique situation here, my dear girl. Aldric Ragnar offers us a life unlike any other asylum. I won't question the methods he uses to keep us that way, and you'll find few other patients who will." He puffed out his chest, beard billowing with indignation. "We trust our proprietor implicitly."

"But if you *did* ask, do you think he'd tell you?"

The beard deflated ruefully. "Yes. I know he would. I've seen it happen. There's a twin brother and sister, Zephyr and Cascada Delmar, who are old friends of mine —and I mean *properly* old. They have to be in their four hundred and twenties now! They love that Sephone girl like she was their own, and when she started disappearing for stretches of time and coming back with all those bruises, they wanted to know what sort of trouble she was getting into. And can you believe what they did? They went right up to Master Ragnar's office and—and *asked* him about it! Next thing you know, they're—they're"—the old man had a fearful look in his eye—"well, look at them!"

He pointed to the two oldest members of Elektra Waverly's team, the ones with stark-white wings, graying hair, and wrinkled ebony skin, who walked stiffly from their table to strike up a conversation with Marek, Cade, and Malachy.

"I respect whatever service Nurse Waverly and her team are doing for us, but if that's what comes of asking questions, I want no part of it! Angels our age have no business playing hero. I'm going to participate in *age-appropriate* activities," the old man huffed and, taking hold of a zip line's anchor, zipped away with legs akimbo.

Sigh. So much for the beard of wisdom. He should've picked up a book on how to shave.

Rose glanced back over at Elektra's team and found two members missing. Sephone and Aiden had ditched the table and were swinging across chain rings on the other side of the obstacle course. And they were headed straight for the Bookshelf Island of How-To.

Ohh, Dimidia was smiling on her today! Rose clambered up the inverted bookcase and watched their approach between the shelves. Aiden Waverly—fourteen years old and already an orderly. She'd like to take a peek at those credentials. Nothing about him screamed *deadly* or *intimidating.* He was tall, but not too tall. Lean, but not too lean. His warm brown skin harkened to a darker heritage on his father's side, but his crop of carrot-top curls and cinnamon freckles were all adorably his mother's.

Then there was the question of his wardrobe. Orderlies wore stiff white shirts tucked into dark work pants with belts. Aiden's top half was the customary shirt, but his bottom half was a pair of unreasonably baggy khakis. Keeping close pace with Sephone, his pants ballooned like mini parachutes with every leap.

They landed on the rope bridge, and Sephone began fervidly searching the How-To titles on the other side of Rose's bookshelf. "G, g, g, we need *g*."

"What's the point of investigating during the day if they only come out at night?" Aiden asked in a low voice.

"Because the asylum won't let *us* out at night, so this is our only alternative. We can still look for clues. They might even be easier to find in daylight."

"But why do you think they're coming so close to the asylum? They've never done it before," Aiden said. "And did you see, it was *both* armies? The Saint's angels and the Sinner's Wargs. I thought they hated each other. That's what the War o' the Wargs was all about, right? So why were they together? What do you think they want?"

Rose held her breath. Her nose tickled fiercely.

"I asked Ragnar, but he just said not to worry about it. Of *course*. Till he calls us in mid-crisis to clean up the mess." Sephone's reply was tinged with bitterness. "Which is why we're worrying about it *now* instead of *then*."

Aiden hesitated. "You sound ..."

"Tired? Because that's what I am. I'm *tired*." She sagged against the bookcase, scratching absently at the scar in her lip. "It's been a really long week."

"This should cheer you up." He pulled a book off the shelf. Its title? *How to Hunt Ghosts Without Becoming One.*

(A CHARMING READ WITH THE SLIGHT DISADVANTAGE IN THAT THE AUTHOR HIMSELF IS A GHOST, CALLING INTO QUESTION THE CREDIBILITY OF HIS GUIDE AS A WHOLE.)

Rose couldn't resist. She pursed her lips and blew a tunnel of air between the shelves. It tickled the backs of their necks, and Sephone and Aiden jumped, looking over their shoulders. They grinned at their own skittishness, all traces of exhaustion forgotten.

Rose shook her head from behind her bookcase observatory. For two heroes about to embark on solving a mystery, they didn't have a clue what they were doing. They needed what all heroes need: a mysterious benefactress to help them along the way. Someone who could swap the questionable *How to Hunt Ghosts Without Becoming One* with her own copy of Wraith Warder's reliable *I Look Like I've Seen a Ghost: Memoirs of a Ghost Hunter* without them noticing.

And maybe—just maybe—if she helped them hunt these ghostly armies from the War o' the Wargs who died inexplicable deaths, she'd uncover what it was about Heartstone Asylum that Marek wasn't telling her.

ENTRY 13

TWO ARE BETTER THAN ONE

I t was a windless day of crystal-clear skies and warm autumn sunshine—ideal conditions for hunting ghosts.

(NO, REALLY! DAYTIME GHOST HUNTING AND NIGHTTIME GHOST HUNTING REQUIRE COMPLETELY DIFFERENT ATMOSPHERES. DAYTIME MEANS THE LACK OF WIND HELPS DIFFERENTIATE BETWEEN A GENTLE BREEZE AND GHOST BREATH, CLEAR SKIES ILLUMINATE ECTOPLASM STAINS, AND THE WARMTH OF THE SUN AIDS IN IDENTIFYING COLD SPOTS.)

It was good, for once, that a certain storm cloud wasn't around to give the climate a makeover.

Ragnar paced in front of the patients gathered in the courtyard, listing the rules of the nature walk like he was addressing a legion of soldiers. Given the nature of the

Petrified Forest and its history, Rose couldn't blame him for being cautious, but that didn't stop her ears from tuning in and out and in and out till his instructions went something like:

Tying shoelaces—in sight of—team's—walking sticks—are not weapons—to avoid—three-leaved—plant-eaters—so be—not—careful—with them.

Duly noted.

She wasn't the only one with attention problems. Three rows behind, Sephone and Aiden were sneaking glances at Wraith Warder's *I Look Like I've Seen a Ghost: Memoirs of a Ghost Hunter* and whispering. They both carried rucksacks heavy with ghost tracking equipment—

(SALT, A GHOST HUNTING MUST, HADN'T MADE IT ON THEIR LIST OF ESSENTIALS, BUT SOMEONE MADE SURE TO SLIP A SALT SHAKER INTO EACH OF THEIR PACKS.)

—and their faces radiated barely-contained excitement.

Everything was coming up roses.

"And on that note, let us now fill our lungs with fresh air and enjoy the beauty of nature. Onward!" Ragnar led the march into the Petrified Forest. Teams clustered together, each with a nurse, orderly, and obedient Sonorific Husky to care for their patients. Rose was in charge of Beta—or was it the other way around?—and she noticed almost everyone was ogling his goggles. He held

125

his head high and kept up on his chubby paws, oblivious. She loved that pup so much it hurt.

"That rucksack is a bit hefty for a nature walk, don't you think?" Marek commented.

Rose hoisted her pack, filled with its own supply of ghost tracking equipment, further up her shoulders. "I'm on a very important mission."

"Oh?" Cade said.

"I'm on the hunt for the perfect pet rock."

"O-oh?" she faltered. "Is that, erm, quite a *selective* process?"

"Absolutely! You need all the proper tools—shoe brushes, magnifying glass, exfoliants—to tell what sort of temperament it has. Wouldn't want to bring home an ornery pet rock, would you? It's all in the fracture lines, really. You can read 'em like palms. Smooth surfaces are actually a sign of foul-temperament, but it's what's on the inside that counts the most. That's why geodes make the best pets."

Cade shot Marek a *she can't be serious* look.

Marek raised both eyebrows. *Yes, she can.*

Up ahead, Malachy had fallen in step with Ragnar. "I hear someone was throwing quite a hissy fit in your office the other night."

Ragnar stopped dead in his tracks. He studied Malachy, stroking his artfully trimmed beard as he did so. Malachy mirrored his actions, eyes narrowed in assessment.

"What you are witnessing is this year's three hundred and seventeenth Battle of the Beards," Marek whispered in Rose's ear. "It's a daily ritual and not to be disturbed."

"And *I* see that, once again, you've chosen to sharpen your wit rather than razor this morning." Ragnar stole a furtive glance at Rose. She got the feeling he was going to tell Malachy about the giant snake in his office and didn't want her eavesdropping. "Walk with me," he said, and they took a fork in the path, hiking along in their identical, steel-toed boots.

Marek watched them go.

"You can catch up with them if you want," she told him. He was curious, too, but unlike her, *he* was allowed in on the secrets of Heartstone Asylum.

"Are you sure?"

"Sure, I'm sure. Cade and Beta will keep me company. You go on."

Two distracted. One more to go.

"I'm gonna check through that patch of rocks over there, is that okay?" she asked Cade.

"Yes," Cade said, "but remember to—"

"Keep in sight of—team's—walking sticks—are not weapons—to—avoid—three-leaved—plant-eaters. Yes, I remember."

Now Cade's *she can't be serious* look was aimed directly at her. Rose grinned. "I'll be careful. I'm just looking at rocks."

"I hope you find a suitable pet, dear. If I can offer any assistance ..."

"Thanks, but I'll let you know if I find any worth introducing."

Beta, it turned out, had a keen nose for ectoplasm.

(No surprise there. Most animals have an acute sense of paramagical activity.)

Rose had searched through five piles of rocks to no avail when he dropped a stone coated with a crusty white substance at her feet. She scrubbed it with a shoe brush and examined it through her magnifying glass. "I think you've got something here, boy." A sprinkle of salt that sizzled on contact confirmed her suspicions. "Atta boy, Beta! That's an ectoplasm stain, all right. Can you find more?"

Beta wagged his tail obligingly. Within minutes, Rose had five ectoplasm-stained rocks for pets. "It's a trail, Bates. Now, all we need to do is shake our purple-haired nurse, follow it, and make sure our heroic beneficiaries pick it up as well." She looked around. "Where are they, anyway?"

Two fire hazard redheads and a brunette were sidling up to Cade.

"Hey, Momma," Aiden said loudly. "I heard Master Ragnar put you and Nurse Locklear in charge of the Moonsfrost Eve celebration again."

Cade and Elektra stiffened like someone had dropped ice cubes down their backs. Then they smiled and said things like, "Yes, won't that be fun," and "Aldric does enjoy seeing us work together," but their body language told a different story.

Sephone and Aiden had their own nurse to get rid of, and they were bringing their A-game.

"You probably haven't thought about it much since it's still a month and a half away," Sephone added, "but after last year's glitter explosion, have you decided what to do for decorations?"

Cha-ching. Hear that? They just bought themselves an hour of uninterrupted freedom. Way to go, Team Hero!

Still, an hour was a bit of a time crunch for what they had to do. "Let's give them a boost, shall we?" Rose whispered to Beta and lobbed an ectoplasm-stained rock at the back of Aiden's head.

"Hey! What the—whoa." Aiden picked up the rock. "Seph, look at this! Is that—?"

"Dried ectoplasm." Sephone whipped out *I Look Like I've Seen a Ghost: Memoirs of a Ghost Hunter* and rifled through the pages. "White, crusty, it matches the description, but ... well, it could be bird poop for all we know."

"You want to hold it?"

"No, you're doing fine. Here, this says the best way to identify dried ectoplasm is to use—salt! We forgot the salt!"

Rose was *probably* enjoying this more than she should've. Probably.

"There's got to be something else we can use." Aiden threw open his rucksack. "What else does it say?"

"It says most animals have a keen nose for paramagical substances, especially canines. Wraith Warder took his dog Spookie with him everywhere." Sephone snapped the book shut. "That settles it, then. Take a good, long sniff and tell me what you think."

"You know it doesn't work like that. Besides, like you said, it could be bird poop."

"Fine," she grumbled, opening her rucksack, "let's just look in our bags and see ..." A saltshaker appeared in her hand. "That wasn't there before."

Aiden dropped his rucksack and tore through its contents. "I have one, too!"

"I didn't pack them. Did you?"

"No! They were just there. Like the book."

They looked at each other in awe.

This, it should be noted, was incredibly satisfying.

"Someone out there really wants us investigating these ghosts," Sephone mused. "Let's not disappoint them."

*

Day or night, the Petrified Forest was a work of art. The trees had been at the peak of their season when they turned to stone. Sunlight filtered through the splayed, unmoving leaves, scattering diamond patterns across the forest floor.

Rose brushed aside a leafy fern to scoop up a white-flecked rock at the base of a tree. Why had the trees been petrified and nothing else? Not the moss or grass or bushes. She shoe-shined the speckled rock and sprinkled it with salt. No sizzle. It wasn't stained with ectoplasm. Rose took a closer look at the white spots with her magnifying glass and laughed.

It was a plum! A speckled plum like the one she'd eaten in Ragnar's office, except this one was made of stone. "These must be some sort of plum trees."

But if the legend was correct and the Petrified Forest had really turned to stone on the night of Moonsfrost Eve, 1425 A.S., it would've been winter. "Magical plum trees, then." Only trees of the Magicae genus produced fruit all year long.

Did that have something to do with why they were the only plants of the Petrified Forest to turn to stone? Because they were magical? *Hmm.* "Think I found my pet rock," she said to Beta, but he wasn't listening. His back was arched, his ears were pricked, and if he could growl without shattering her eardrums, he would have. "What is it, boy? Whatcha got?"

Her pup pointed his nose at a grove of trees straight ahead. It was the darkest, densest part of the forest yet. Trunks leaned inward, and branches knotted together like a gangly group hug.

Or a séance.

This was it. This was where the ghost tracks stopped. "Good work, Bates." Rose scratched his stiff neck. Salt and shoe brushes are all well and good for *tracking* ghosts, but walking into what could be the heart of a haunting? It was time to break out the heavy artillery.

She reached into her rucksack and pulled out a pair of sterling silver butter knives.

(WHAT? SILVER IS THE NUMBER ONE DISRUPTER OF MAGICAL AND PARAMAGICAL PROPERTIES. DOESN'T MATTER WHAT FORM IT'S IN. BUTTER KNIFE OR SWORD, THEY'RE BOTH JUST AS EFFECTIVE. THOUGH IF T.K. HADN'T BEEN CONFISCATED FROM ME UPON MY ARRIVAL AT HEARTSTONE ...)

"All right, boy." She scraped her knives together like a murderous butter churner. "Let's do this."

One step into the tenebrous grove and her breath caught in her throat. *Cold.* One giant cold spot. Some think cold spots are the portals through which ghosts enter the living world, but Wraith Warder was of a different opinion. He believed that cold spots were the ghosts themselves, forever stuck on this side of eternity, too weak to manifest fully on account of energy-sucking sunlight or despair.

So, when you look at it that way, she was walking through a giant throng of unseen spirits.

"S'cuse me, pardon me, watch your toes." Rose paused

in front of a large plum tree. Its trunk, weatherworn and smooth, had been carved with a morbid poem:

How terrible to not be fed
To taste for bread
But can't: you're dead

A neighboring tree shared similar sentiments:

How terrible to be alone
To wish for home
With aching bones

And another:

Help!
We're trapped!
Please, take us back

She touched their chilling laments. "What happened to you?"

Bushes rustled from behind. Rose whirled around, wings unfurling. Her breath came out in misty plumes, and she twirled the butter knives in hand. Sparks of lightning danced up the blades. "Whoever you are, whatever you are, you can come out. I'm not gonna hurt you."

A shadowy silhouette emerged. It was *huge*. It was

hideous. It was—"And what were you going to do?" Marek asked. "Butter me up?"

"Mar*ek*," she groaned.

Hands in his pockets, he strolled over. " 'Looking for a pet rock' my foot. Admit it, you're ghost hunting without me."

"I figured 'haunted forest' would fall under the category of 'Mysterious Mysteries of Heartstone Asylum That You Won't Tell Me About.' "

"Only slightly. I was going to surprise you, but the ghosts don't usually come out till the end of the month when the moons are full. How'd you find out about them?"

"They came to the edge of the courtyard last night. I saw them from my window."

"*Really*? They should never be that close to the asylum. Ragnar has an arrangement with them. Patients aren't even supposed to know they *exist*."

"Something worth investigating?"

"Do you even have to ask?"

Rose armed Marek with a butter knife.

ENTRY 14

ONE STEP AHEAD FROM BEHIND

Marek read the miserable poetry etched in the stone trees. His expression was somber. "What do you suppose this place is?"

"I was hoping you'd tell me," Rose said.

He rubbed his thick arms against the cold of the haunted grove. "I've never been this far into the forest before. Ragnar doesn't let his patients just wander about. It's a miracle we were able to slip away when we did, and we weren't the only ones."

"Sephone and Aiden?"

"How did you guess?"

"I've been giving them a little help with their ghost hunting. 'Course they don't *know* I've been giving them help. After all, they're he-he—*heroes*," she sneezed. "Ugh, it's cold in here. Anyways, you know heroes won't accept help unless it comes from some cryptic source. Think that might even be in the Heroes Handbook." Beta snuffled the ground and tugged Rose to another ghost-inscribed tree. "Those two would find this place a lot faster if they had a dog with them. I noticed they're the only team that doesn't have one. How come?"

"Oh, that." Marek smiled. "Can't have too many canines under the same roof."

"What's that s'posta mean?"

"It means you should test Aiden's patience at your earliest convenience and see."

They continued deeper into the ghosts' abode. Have you ever heard someone talk about something that's nice and easy to do, and they call it "a walk in the park"? Well, they should change the phrase to "a walk through a haunted forest in daylight." Uncannily muted from sound and sun, the grove inspired a sense of otherworldly calmness and contemplation.

"You know," Marek said, "I had no idea that walking through the heart of a haunting would be so peacef—" A pebble covered in sticky, opalescent goo bounced off his forehead and slimed down his nose.

"What was—" A stone leaf, coated in fresh ectoplasm, slapped Rose's cheek like a starfish.

"On second thought, I think we may have overstayed our welcome," he murmured, and his shadows flared instinctively to absorb the impact of a hundred, gooey projectiles.

Evidently, the ghosts were tired of being walked over.

"Sorry!" Marek shouted over the dull whumps and thumps of rocks hitting the canopy of darkness. "So sorry to disturb you." The objects rained harder. "We're leaving right now."

"A midday manifestation!" Rose exclaimed. "Do you know how incredible this is? We're witnessing one of the rarest phenomena in paramagical investigation! And now ... we're going to be slimed. Slimed and concussed."

"Thunder, how much do you trust me?"

" 'Bout as far as you can throw me."

"That's pretty far."

"I know. So, what's the plan?"

"It's simple, really." He picked Beta off the ground and tucked him under his arm. Shadows siphoned from his wings and spun a cocoon of absolute darkness around them. "Close your eyes and *run*."

Rose had faith in Marek, sure. But now it was blind faith. Her feet were pounding the ground, and she couldn't see an inch in front of her face. The dark had a fluffy texture that kept her tight at Marek's side while a hardened shell of shadows deflected the ghosts' endless ammunition. It was like being inside a giant chocolate truffle of darkness. They ran till she felt sunlight on her eyelids, and Marek collapsed to the ground, wheezing. She tripped over his crumpled form, and they rolled on their backs, laughing with what little breath they had left.

He lifted Beta onto his stomach. The pup seemed to have enjoyed the chase. "How are you?" he asked Rose.

"Hungry for chocolate truffles."

"I have that effect sometimes."

She propped up on her elbows and froze. "Marek," she said, "where did you take us?"

That was a rhetorical question. Surrounded by headstones and wrought iron railing, it was quite obvious they'd barreled headfirst into a graveyard. Plum trees spread thinly throughout the grave markers, which bore no names, and the fence that encompassed them ended in a rocky formation with a great, gaping hole at its center.

A cave.

Marek got up slowly. "I believe we've found our ghosties' final resting place. Shall we look around?"

Their first stop was the fence, topped with solid iron pickets. Iron is nearly as effective as silver when dealing with ghosts, and this stuff was heavy duty. It was the same sort of fencing that guarded Heartstone's courtyard where the ghosts had congregated the night before. They weren't able to pass through the iron barrier there, and Rose doubted they'd be able to pass through the iron barrier here, either. "Marek, the ghosts are free to roam wherever they want so long as it's in the forest, right? Ragnar put up a fence around Heartstone and told them to stay far away, but they can still do whatever they want?"

"That does seem to be the arrangement, yes."

She rattled the sturdy railing. "Then why have they been banned from their own graveyard?"

They walked in silence, searching for signs of para-magical activity, but by unspoken agreement, their course was set for the black mouth of the cave.

"Question Two," Marek said. "If these are truly the Sinner and the Saint's armies from the War o' the Wargs, the soldiers who disappeared without a trace, the stuff of legend never to be seen again ... who buried them?"

They stood outside the cave, peering down its murky esophagus to the depths of its dark belly. Beta backed up, sandwiched between their legs.

"Should we?" Rose ventured and was answered by a piercing scream.

"Nope," said Marek, and a swathe of shadows swooped her off her feet and deposited her in the high branches of a tree. He clambered after her, Beta slung over his shoulder. They crouched in the fork of the tree and watched as Sephone and Aiden stumbled into the graveyard, dripping with ectoplasm and hollering like the dead.

"Ew, ew, ew," Sephone chanted, yanking gooey sticks out of her hair. A nearby bush pulled itself out of the ground, waddled over on its roots, and tugged on the hem of her shirt. Sephone offered a rare smile and wiped her face on its absorbent leaves. She patted the bush kindly, and it wandered back to its spot, settling into the ground once more. Whatever her soul signia was, Sephone clearly loved nature. "Aiden, how did you offend the ghosts so much?"

"Me?" he cried indignantly. "All I did was compliment the rhythm of their tercets. I thought we were bonding!"

"Poets don't bond over each other's work. They bond over critiquing it. You told me that."

"You're right," Aiden growled. "You're right." He stomped over to the graveyard's archway, cupped his hands over his mouth, and yelled, "Your composition is good, but your assonance stinks!"

A blob of ectoplasm hit him square in the face. Sephone laughed.

Without realizing it, they were tracing Rose and Marek's steps around the graveyard, making similar observations, and always, always moving towards the cave. When they stopped in front of it, they were silent, gazing into the fathomless dark.

"Aiden," said Sephone, "what are your thoughts on spelunking?"

Aiden shrugged. "Oh, you know, bit hard on the knees, too many liabilities, and who likes changing into a wetsuit?"

"You have no idea what spelunking is, do you?"

"I'm a poet, not a dictionary."

"It's cave exploration." She grabbed his wrist. "C'mon."

He dug his heels in. "Do we *have* to?"

"Just say it with me. Spe-*lunn*-king. Let it roll off your tongue."

"Spe-*lunn*-king." Aiden fought a grudging smile.

"See? If that's how fun it is to say, imagine how much more fun it'll be to do!"

"It could be a trick."

"Pessimism is *my* forte, not yours. I'm the cynic. You're the melodramatic dreamer. When we pool our resources, we become a well-balanced realist, and that's what we bring to the table. It's what we're good at. So, let's go be cynically optimistic together." She tugged firmly on his wrist. Aiden wasn't budging. She sighed. "Fine. Forget what I said. Remember when you told me you wanted to try your hand at epic poetry but didn't have the inspiration for it? I think you'll find all sorts of ideas exploring the damp recesses of a haunted cave. Doesn't that sound like an epic poem just waiting to happen?"

Aiden's countenance brightened. "Seph, that's a great idea!" he said and headed straight for the cave.

"Oh, the things a writer will do for inspiration," Rose heard Sephone mutter and followed after him.

Marek pressed a finger to his lips and dropped from their perch, landing on a blanket of shadow-feathers that muffled his fall. Rose did likewise, and they crept to the entrance of the cave. Beta would set neither paw nor tail in it, so Marek held him in the crook of his arm. The pup snuggled fearfully under his chin. What was *with* him? He'd been fearless in the face of ghosts and other paramagical activity. Why should a cave be any different?

Up ahead, Sephone and Aiden stumbled through the

141

fathomless dark, but Marek could fathom it just fine. He steered them around puddles and stalagmites, sticking close to the cave walls. For vertigo's sake, she clutched his flannel sleeve and kept her eyes shut, letting Shadow Boy do the leading. Then they halted, and he whispered, "Open up." So, she did.

Rose gasped. Instantly, shadows filled her mouth to mute the sound.

(*THAT USED TO BE STORMY'S JOB.*)

She looked at Marek, his face lifted with pleasure, eyes aglow in the bluish-green light, and decided to forgive him his shadow-gag. The tunnel of fathomless dark had opened into a cavern, the ceiling of which was dotted with thousands of glowworms. It was a starry night sky of bioluminescence.

Marek pulled her to the wall of the cavern behind a row of stalagmites. With the light of the glowworms filling the cave, they would have to blend in with the scenery. A cloak of shadows descended on Rose, leaving two eyeholes for her to see Sephone and Aiden in the center of the cavern.

"This is beautiful," Aiden breathed, mouth open, staring up at the ceiling.

"It's a bunch of worms with glowing butts," Sephone retorted. "You're getting distracted."

They snooped around the cave, rolling rocks in their hands, rereading portions of *I Look Like I've Seen a Ghost: Memoirs of a Ghost Hunter* by the dim, bluish-green glow, and completely missing the massive, animal shape pacing the outer rim of the cavern. It passed by Rose and Marek's hiding spot, and suddenly she was grateful for the shadow-gag that silenced her mouth. The shape prowled around her heroic beneficiaries, its circles getting smaller and smaller with every loop. Lightning sparked on her fingertips. She would help Sephone and Aiden get away if the creature was threatened by their presence, but she wouldn't hurt it. This cave was someone's home, and they were trespassing.

"Hey, I want to try something." Aiden tapped Sephone's arm. "Watch this." Cupping a hand over his mouth, he shouted, "*Hello!*" It echoed threefold, bouncing off the ceiling's teething stalactites.

"Good afternoon." The voice that answered was deep and deliciously smooth, like caramel. It came as if from all directions, but Rose and Marek could see the exact location of the creature's skulking form. "So nice of you to drop by unannounced, but unless you're selling cookies, I'm afraid I don't take kindly to solicitors."

Team Hero whipped this way and that, trying to find the shape in the shadows. "We're not solicitors!" Aiden yipped. He cleared his throat. "I mean—"

"We're not solicitors," Sephone repeated forcefully. "We're investigating some abnormal behavioral patterns from our resident ghosts. Any pertinent information you can offer would be appreciated."

"And what makes you think *I* would help *you*?" The creature peeled himself from the darkness and into the glowworms' unearthly light. He was the size of a large pony with skin clinging to ragged bone and matted patches of fur, the color of which might once have matched his dulcet caramel voice.

Rose pulled the shadow-gag from her mouth. "*Look* at him."

"I know," Marek murmured sadly. "He looks starved."

Aiden had clearly lost the use of his vocal cords while Sephone maintained her rigid composure for a whole five seconds before belting out a scream.

The giant wolf smiled, licking his lips with relish. "Thank you. I haven't eaten a scream like that in over a decade. It doesn't show, does it?" He scratched a clump of fur from his balding ear.

"You—what—" Sephone attempted to form a coherent sentence. "Who are you?"

"You've found a half-dead Warg in the center of the forest where the final battle of the War o' the Wargs took place, and you want to know who I am?" He shook his head pityingly. "Investigator may not be the profession for you."

"No one survived that battle," Aiden spoke at last.

The Warg chuckled deep from his throat. "And who told you that, I wonder."

"If you truly are a survivor, then you can answer so many questions!" Aiden said excitedly. "Like what happened that night, what made the trees turn to stone, who buried the bodies—"

"The only questions you should be asking," the Warg growled, "are how soundproof are these walls? Will anyone hear you screaming?"

He stalked towards them, hackles raised, and Sephone grabbed her friend's wrist, squeezing. "Aiden ..." A shudder ran through Aiden's body, and an animalistic snarl gathered behind his teeth.

The Warg stopped and sagged. "You won't win this fight, little hound. Leave. The screams of the dying are far too bitter for my taste."

Aiden nodded and started pulling Sephone away from the cavern of glowworms, but she yanked back. "Is there nothing you can tell us about the ghosts?" she asked the Warg. "You must know *something*. You fought in the same war together. Half of them were your friends, the other half were your enemies. You must have *some* idea what they're up to."

The giant wolf sighed and sat on his haunches. "I'm not the one you should be asking. Your proprietor made the agreement with the ghosts, and if they're going back on his terms, then Aldric Ragnar has reason to be concerned. They want something. And for all your sakes, he'd better be prepared to give it."

"But—" Sephone began, and Aiden clapped a hand over her mouth.

"Thank you!" he called to the Warg, dragging Sephone down the tunnel. "You've been very helpful! And you've given me a great idea for a poem!"

The Warg laughed to himself as they hurried away. He stretched out on his forepaws and yawned, showing magnificently sharp canines. "And now," he said, "to deal with the other interlopers."

ENTRY 15

SCREAMING FOR LUNCH

"Wargonna die," Rose whispered.

(HEE. WARGONNA. GET IT? CAN'T LEAVE THAT GALLOWS HUMOR HANGING.)

The shadows fell away. She and Marek stood up from their hiding spot. One step towards the giant wolf and Beta scrabbled at Marek's arms like his tail had caught fire. Marek tied his leash to a stalagmite, and they approached the Warg in the middle of the cave. Up close, his size was remarkable. Beneath his tattered coat, his skin was pockmarked with old teeth punctures.

"There is really only one way to begin this conversation." Marek looked at Rose out of the corner of his eye and winked.

They plugged their ears and screamed.

Glowworms dropped like falling stars. Rose wrung her lungs of every last cubit of air, and when they finally gave out, Marek wiped his mouth on his sleeve and said, "How'd that taste?"

The Warg closed his eyes and licked his lips as if to recapture the flavor. "Smooth base, strong volume, subtle hints of laughter. A proper entrée if I've ever had one. And it's been some time since I've had one."

Marek stuck out a hand to shake his paw. "I'm Marek."

"And I'm Rose." The Warg's paw was equal parts fuzzy and calloused in her hand. His claws were long enough to graze her wrist. "We're patients up at Heartstone. Who are you, apart from a half-dead survivor of the War o' the Wargs?"

The giant wolf flicked his tail in amusement. "Most know me as Grave Dancer. But you may call me Silas."

Marek gave a gentlemanly bow.

(PICTURE A BEAR WEARING A TUXEDO.)

"Pleased to make your acquaintance, Silas. You have a beautiful home." He admired the ceiling for a moment. "Well, best be off!" He hooked Rose by the arm, leading her away. She let him.

"Wait!" Silas barked. His note of plea was quickly replaced by a more dignified tone. "Going so soon?"

"But of course. We've trespassed far too long as it is. It'd be rude to stay any longer without being invited."

"But don't you have pesky questions that need answering?"

Marek unwound Beta's leash from the stalagmite. "First, you expect us to continue intruding on your home without being welcomed, and now you think we're going to demand answers to questions you don't want asked? Just what do you take us for?"

Silas considered this. "My guests," he decided. "I'd offer you refreshments, but unfortunately they've stagnated. Bring me the visually-impaired pup. I won't hurt him."

Rose picked Beta up, and he wriggled frantically in her arms. "Sorry," she grunted. "He's not usually this skittish."

"Have *you* ever met someone ten times your size before?" Silas lowered himself to the ground, ears forward in a friendly gesture, and emitted a gentle whine. Beta padded cautiously towards him, tail down, ears flat against his head. He sniffed the enormous canine. Silas bumped his nose and snapped playfully at the band of his goggles. Immediately, Beta's ears and tail inflated like kites caught in the breeze, and he rolled on his back, batting at Silas's whiskers.

"You're part of Malachy's pack, are you not?" The Warg inhaled deeply. "I can smell him on you."

"You know Malachy?" Rose said.

"He brings me a steak every now and then and tells me what a good boy I am."

"So Heartstone knows that you live here?" Marek said, bemused.

Evidently, Shadow Boy wasn't privy to *all* of Heartstone's secrets.

Silas snorted. "They're the ones who appointed me guardian of this miserable graveyard."

Marek spread out a shadow-blanket, and they took seats on the cavern floor. "It must be a hard job, keeping ghosts out of their own graveyard," Rose said. "Why'd they pick you?"

"Isn't it obvious? Or don't they teach you about Wargs anymore?" Silas laid his great head on his paws. "No, I suppose they wouldn't after the War. We're practically extinct. They're more likely to dedicate their studies to exotic jellyfish."

"Wait." A scrap of thought floated in her memory. "Wait, I think I remember Wraith Warder saying something about Wargs once. That you have a special connection with the paramagical world. 'Acute sensitivity' or something?"

"Well, I should think so, considering Wraith Warder was a Warg."

Rose's jaw dropped. "Wraith Warder? *The* Wraith Warder? *I Look Like I've Seen a Ghost: Memoirs of a Ghost Hunter*, Wraith Warder?"

"The very same."

"But—but Spookie! He had a *dog*!"

Silas smiled the way all wolves do: with lots of teeth.

"And Wargs can't have pets? Warden Carlyle is one of our greatest celebrities, I assure you. Wargs do indeed have acute sensitivity to the paramagical world—and command over it, if we choose.

"They say Dimidia created Wargs to be spirit guides to the dead. Necromancy is in our blood. We know the gateways, the pathways, the rituals. During the War, we would call whole fleets of fallen brothers and sisters to our aid. For a time, of course. And a price." He licked the old teeth marks that canvassed his skin. "Wraith Warder, however, did not approve of such practices. He labeled it for what it was: a perversion of our sacred duty as spirit guides."

"Is he still alive?" Rose asked. "Wraith Warder. 'Cause I can think of a few stuck ghosts he could help." And a book for him to pawtograph. Wraith Warder. A *Warg*. Who'da thunk it?

"Last I heard, he went into hiding during the War. That was a hundred years ago. I'd venture to say that if he were alive, he'd have paid the Petrified Forest a visit by now. A haunting of this magnitude would have drawn his attention decades ago."

So much for the pawtograph.

"Do the ghosts here get along?" Marek said. "The Saint's angels and the Sinner's Wargs. During the War, they were enemies. And whether they killed each other in the end or something *else* did—"

"I will not answer questions about the Battle of the Petrified Forest," Silas cut him off calmly, "but I will say this: death is the great unifier. Whatever differences they might have had while they were alive have been settled in their afterlife."

"And what about you? Do you get along with the ghosts?"

"I'm not here to get along with them."

"Then why *are* you here?" Rose wondered. "You don't keep them in check or they wouldn't be getting so close to the asylum. Instead, you're the 'Beware of Dog' sign on a graveyard fence. Why aren't the ghosts allowed to visit their own graves?"

Silas awarded her that toothy smile. "You're operating under the assumption that I've been assigned my title as guardian to keep something *out* of this graveyard. Not once have you considered the option that I might be here to keep something else *in*."

ENTRY 16

BLACK (BOARD) MAGIC

You'd think after walking through a haunted forest and meeting a real live Warg, nothing could twist Rose's stomach in knots.

And yet here she was waiting for her first lesson in Magic Studies with her stomach pretending it was a rubber band ball, equal parts knotted and bouncy.

The unicorns weren't helping any. Drawings and paintings of the mystical pony (in varying degrees of artistic talent) plastered the homeroom of Magic Studies, and a giant stuffed animal unicorn hung, wings spread, above the blackboard. It made the Lollypop Tower's choice of abundant bunny décor look positively restrained.

A teacher obsessed with unicorns couldn't be *that* scary to talk to after class. Could he?

Rose craned around in her seat. The patients in attendance were overflowing. "So, what's this teacher like?" she asked Malachy, who sat next to her in the front row. "It's standing room only. He must be really good."

Malachy scoffed. "He's not the *worst* teacher I've ever heard, put it that way. Half the time I can't stand him, swaggering around like he's the smartest guy in the room. *Pfft.* Not much tact, either. Made three patients cry last month alone. They don't get his sense of humor, see. Still, they keep coming."

Rose pulled at her sister necklace, the key scraping against its chain. *Zrrt, zrrt, zrrt, zrrt.* A day apart, and she was already picking up Amber's nervous habits. "Malachy?"

"Yup?"

"Can you stay with me when I talk to him?"

His lips tipped upwards a smidge. "Yeah, sweetheart, I can stay."

Whew.

"Welp," Malachy slapped his knees and stood, "best get started." He sauntered over to the blackboard. "Mornin', class."

"Good morning, Master M!" came the enthusiastic response.

Malachy was the teacher of Magic Studies. Well, somebody could've *mentioned* that!

"Now, we have a new patient with us today, and you know what that means," he said, scribbling on the blackboard.

There was a universal groan that sounded like *eff-pum*. Rose wasn't familiar with the curse, but it must've meant something awful.

"F-PUM. The Fundamental Principle of Unstable Magic." Malachy underlined the words with his chalk.

Or that.

"It's always good to start with a visual so, Rose, why don't you come up here a minute?" He fished out a pair of glasses from his desk. "First thing you'll need is a change of perspective. With these on, you can do more than just sense magic. You can *see* it, too. These kinds of glasses played a huge role in helping us diagnose the cause of unstable magic. Put 'em on, and I'll show ya how."

Malachy held out the ordinary-looking glasses. The class of patients had gone deathly still. What were they waiting for?

Rose tipped the glasses onto her nose.

And screamed.

The world was gray and translucent through the lenses save for the rows and rows of skeletons filling the seats, jaws gaping with laughter. They weren't your typical skeletons, all dull and white. Their bones came in every shade of gray and green, brown and hazel, violet and blue, and they *glowed*. Glowed from the marrow with magic.

Rose looked to Malachy, or rather to the burnished bronze skeleton that matched the color of his eyes, the windows to his—"Am I seeing your *souls*?"

Malachy spread his glowing wing bones wide. "Souls make magic. This is where the magic happens."

"Yours is pretty. Kinda like mud reflecting sunlight."

"I've been called worse. Now take a peek at my head and tell me whatcha see." He bent his luminescent skull.

Rose inspected it. "There's a wall—like white fire—between the front of your skull and the back. It's bright. I can see it through the bone."

"Good." Malachy removed her glasses, and his non-skeletal face rapidly came into focus. "You can sit down." He began drawing on the blackboard.

Rose took her seat next to Marek and nudged him with her elbow. "Malachy likes unicorns?"

"It's the only thing he can draw," he explained. "This is Corny."

"You can say that again."

"This is Corny," Malachy announced, stepping away from an equestrian-esque image on the blackboard. "Corny is a unicorn with unstable magic. One day his friend Doodle drops by for a visit." He drew a stick figure with a scribbled frown next to the unicorn. "Doodle is having a bad day. His dog got run over by an eraser, and Corny feels terrible for him. Don'tcha, Corny?" Malachy rapped his knuckles on the blackboard. A second later, Corny the Unicorn snorted chalk dust and shook his scrawling mane.

Magic blackboard. Malachy taught in *style*.

"There he is, consoling his friend, doing good

things"—the unicorn wrapped a wing around the stick figure's spindly shoulders—"when suddenly, his magic pulls away from his control and—BAM!"

Rose jumped. An explosion of rainbows burst from the unicorn, one after the other, and Corny pawed the two-dimensional ground in surprise. Doodle, however, crossed his undefined arms in a classic stance of displeasure and promptly left the blackboard.

"Doodle's dog just died, and all Corny can think about are rainbows. Doodle thinks he's being insensitive, but really, Corny just can't control his magic. Or can he? Why did this exchange take place?" Malachy raised an eyebrow at the class.

"F-PUM," they sighed again.

"The Fundamental Principle of Unstable Magic." Malachy erased Corny and replaced him with a large circle. He drew a line down its middle, cutting it in half like a watermelon, and wrote *Sub.* and *Con.* on the opposing sides. Above it, he wrote:

Soul — Mind — Body

"Soul signias are a byproduct of—you guessed it—your soul. It's magic taking whatever form best represents who you are and what you're like. Think of your mind like a kitchen sink and your soul's a faucet that's always on, pouring magic into the basin. When ya use your soul signia, it's like your mind pulls the drain plug, flooding your body with magic and emptying the sink. But there's a catch. The faucet never turns off. Not when the sink's empty, not when the sink's full. Your soul never *stops* producing magic. So, what does your mind do when it doesn't have any room left? Easy." He tapped the part of the diagram's circle labeled *Sub*. "It dumps the magic into your subconscious.

"Your subconscious can hold infinite amounts of magic, and once it's there, it comes under your subconscious's influence. Ever been dreaming and notice your magic is more powerful than anything you can do while you're awake? Well, there you have it. In dreams, you have access to unlimited power. But what would happen if unlimited power invaded limited space?" Licking his thumb, Malachy smudged the line that separated *Sub.* from *Con.* on his diagram and knocked on the blackboard. The circle exploded, painting the board with chalky brain matter. "That wall of white fire you saw in my head, Rose? That's a dam that keeps your mind's magic and your subconscious mind's magic from intruding on each other's territory. Without it, we'd be scraping our brains off the walls."

Rose waved her hand in the air. "But what's the Fundamental Principle of Unstable Magic?"

"That," Malachy replied, "is when the dam has a leak."

*

The Fundamental Principle of Unstable Magic?

It isn't unstable.

It's magic that obeys your conscious and *sub*conscious mind.

After the lesson, patients filed quickly from the room. For all their enthusiasm about Malachy as a teacher, none of them seemed to want to stay and talk with him after class, which made Rose want to stay and talk with him even more. No one should feel unapproachable.

"So, what didja think of the lesson?" Malachy asked, wiping down the blackboard.

"I think you know your stuff." She boosted herself onto his desk and picked up the paperweight next to his inkbottle. It was a rainbow-haired unicorn sitting on a cupcake made with colorful sprinkles to match the pony's mane. "And all these tokens of appreciation from your students mean you must do a good job."

"That's not what I asked."

"You just told me that every bad thing my storm cloud's ever done is 'cause subconsciously I wanted them to happen. I'm being nice."

Malachy chuckled and sat at his desk. He steepled his fingers the same way Ragnar had the night before. Except Malachy was also leaning dangerously on the back legs of his chair, which kinda ruined the scholarly effect. "Just 'cause your magic listens to your subconscious doesn't mean your subconscious is evil. Take Corny and Doodle. Corny wasn't trying to make Doodle feel worse by shoving cheery rainbows down his throat. He wanted to make Doodle feel better, and unicorn ideology states that rainbows can fix anything, so that's what his subconscious made him do."

"Doesn't change anything, though." Rose rolled the unicorn cupcake paperweight in her hand. "Doodle's still mad at him."

"True. But you'll learn that motives play a big role in *controlling* unstable magic. First, though, let's talk about your storm cloud. Take me from goddess of thunder to parlor trick and everything in between."

She pressed the unicorn's horn with a fingertip. "Well—

(*EDITING STORIES IS SUCH A PAIN. IT'S LIKE A TOWER OF BLOCKS. HOW MUCH CAN YOU TAKE AWAY BEFORE THE WHOLE THING FALLS IN ON ITSELF?*)

—my dad knew I had unstable magic before I did. I was s'posta be Dame Commander of Chunter Woods when I grew up, but he knew that wasn't gonna happen from an asylum cell, so he started coming up with ideas to get rid of my soul signia. He found a witch doctor who did this thing where ... it's hard to describe, but he sorta cut off my soul's circulation so it would stop making magic? Tied it up, basically. In knots."

"In knots," Malachy repeated. "Your *soul*? Well, this I

gotta see." He popped on the magic-seeing glasses. The front legs of his chair slammed against the floor.

Rose chewed her lip. "That bad, huh?"

Something slow and deadly crept into Malachy's tone. "They did this to stop your magic?"

"Yeah. It was s'posta cut it *all* off but"—deep inside, Stormy gave a reassuring hum, and lightning sparked from her fingertips—"still got my parlor trick! Anyway, that's what happened." She forced a tight smile. Beads of sweat tickled her hairline. Nothing more to say, right?

The viper in Malachy's voice retreated. "How'd they do it?"

"Do what?"

"Tie your soul in knots."

"Oh. Well, they had to take it out first."

"Take it *out*? Of your body? With what?"

Rose pressed the tip of the unicorn paperweight so hard it left a dent in her finger. She didn't want to talk about this anymore. She didn't want to tell him the details of that horrific procedure and what it was like to have her soul removed from her body. She didn't want the memories escaping her subconscious like her magic apparently was. "They just did."

"All right. All right, that's a start." Malachy stared at the paperweight she was playing with. "You wanna know what my favorite unicorn in this whole classroom is? That paperweight right there."

"This one?" She giggled. "With the cupcake and the sprinkles and everything?"

"Yup. My favorite unicorn." He tapped his desk. "Tell ya what. You hold onto it till I find a way to fix your soul signia. It'll be my security deposit."

"Really?"

"Well, we already have a history of cupcakes between us, don't we?"

"Yeah." Rose kicked his chair with a smile. "We do."

ENTRY 17

NEWSPAPER BLUES

To: Rose Skylar
From: Your Future

R ose had ambitious plans for her first week at Heartstone Asylum. Day One set the bar sky-high, but she had a list of things to keep her momentum going. There was a masterpiece to be painted with water-colors in art therapy, a ukulele to be tried in music class, her first umbrella to craft, and mark her words, they were *gonna* figure out what Heartstone was hiding in the Petri-fied Forest's graveyard!

It was shaping up to be one heckuva week.

And then Day Two came, and reality slapped her in the face with a newspaper. A literal one.

SKYLAR HEIR SENT TO ASYLUM: ADOPTED DAUGHTER KNIGHTED INSTEAD! read the headline. They'd made front-page news. An artist had drawn a beautiful charcoal depiction of Amber bowed at her father's feet, the flat of his sword resting on her shoulder. Whoever the artist was, they'd captured her essence down to the wave of her hair and the solemn crease of her brow. Amber looked every bit the nobility she was, by blood or not. Dad's expression was more peaceful than Rose had ever seen, and Momma's smile in the background was all softness and wisdom. This was the Skylar name prevailing against the odds. This was a family cutting ties with the past and reaching for tomorrow. Reaching for a future that she wasn't part of.

The finality of the image was jarring. Her fate was sealed in the walls of an asylum. There was no going home. There was no seeing her family again.

Rose didn't feel like doing much that week.

*

"Duckies in galoshes, eh?" Marek plopped beside her with enough force to make the Lollypop Tower's comfiest couch creak. "Tough day?"

The Lollypop Tower had changed its décor to sympathize with her mood. Gone were the blissful bunny rabbits, replaced with pictures of ducklings wearing red raincoats and matching boots, covering their heads with their tiny wings as rain bashed them from above.

She sunk deeper into the couch and shrugged.

"There are so many things I have to remember to do

now that you're here," Marek continued cheerfully. "I have to feed you, take you for walks, kick you off the good furniture—it's like having a new pet. Given the circumstances, I may be persuaded to skip the walks and allow you to stay on the couch. However, as a responsible pet owner, I cannot in good conscience let you starve." He eyed the fruit bowl on the coffee table meaningfully.

Her stomach rumbled. When *was* the last time she'd eaten? She picked up a plum and took a reluctant bite. The explosion of sweet, zingy juice in her mouth demanded she take another. And another.

"Good, aren't they?"

Rose nodded. "Tastes magical." Her voice was hoarse from disuse.

"They are! Scalplums, they're called. Ragnar always keeps a supply in honor of the Petrified Forest. It's made up of Scalpo trees."

She was right. The forest's trees *were* magical. Wiping juice from her chin, she asked, "What do scalplums do, magic-wise?"

"Oh, it's nothing," Marek said dismissively. "Whoever eats the fruit becomes intensely ticklish, that's all." He raised his eyebrows.

"Marek, don't—!"

Too late.

They say to know one's enemy is to know their ticklish spots, and Marek knew hers too well. His shadows were relentless, nibbling her sides up and down like a congregation of church mice. Worse, a wisp of darkness targeted the sensitive spot under her chin, and she fell off the couch, writhing with laughter.

"I'll stop on one condition!" he called over her gasping giggles. "Say you'll attend Poetry Night!"

"*Poetry* Night?" she shrieked.

"You've missed every activity this week! Poetry Night would be good for your health!"

"Okay! Okay, I will!" Mercifully, the shadows ceased. "*Poetry* Night?" she wheezed, clutching her aching abdomen.

(*IS THERE ANY BETTER WORKOUT THAN A LAUGHTER WORKOUT?*)

"Yes. All you have to do is sit there, and if you hate it, just say the word, and we'll leave."

"... but *Poetry Night*?"

"Trust me."

*

Poetry Night was hosted in the Calm Room, also known as the Fishbowl, both of which were accurate monikers. It was a dome-shaped room of intimate size located beneath the asylum's small lake, and the walls were made of water. Beautiful, glistening water that splished and sploshed a serene melody. *Calm*, it sang, if the burbles could be translated. *Keep calm, little fishies. You're safe in your fishbowl, aren't you?*

Rose skimmed her hand over the water like a skipping stone. Her fingers came back wet, but the integrity of the water-wall was unaffected. Sunlight sifted through the waves above, casting mesmerizing shapes across the couches and podium set up for the evening's poetry reading.

Her eyes followed the shifting motif, but the room's hypnotic blue hue was making her drowsy. Marek guided her to a long couch at the back. Cade sat at one end and Malachy at the other, squeezing Rose and Marek in between. The cozy proximity was nice till Cade crossed her legs and bumped her knee accidentally. Then all Rose could do was keep very still and try not to think about what would happen if a stray bolt of lightning touched the water.

(*It wouldn't be the first time I fried an entire lake.*)

"So, you like poetry?" she asked Cade, who was sorting a neat stack of parchments on her lap.

"Oh, yes." Cade pulled a quill from her bun and took out a parchment that looked suspiciously like a list of supplies for the Moonsfrost Eve celebration. "A very cultured interest."

"Why, Miss Rose!" Aldric Ragnar, it seemed, had a cultured interest in poetry as well. "It's so good of you to attend tonight's activity," he said, without an ounce of sarcasm. No judgment from having missed the rest of the week. "Would the four of you care to join me at the front?"

"Thanks, but uh"—Malachy cleared his throat—"it's kind of a *back-row* seat day."

"Ah, I see. Then I bid you an enjoyable evening." He bowed and leaned into Malachy as he passed, whispering, "She doesn't snore, does she? Do remind her about the last patient who snored."

"See," Malachy turned to Rose, "artists aren't too appreciative when someone takes a nap while their creative genius is being presented. Something about their life's work being scorned. Throw in a little unstable magic, and the last guy who snored during Poetry Night went from 'go jump in a lake' to 'get thrown in a lake' in ten seconds flat." He chuckled fiendishly. "Aiden had fun that day, huh? Thought we'd never get the smell of wet dog out."

Rose was gonna make that boy squeal his secret the *moment* opportunity knocked on her door. "For the record, I don't snore. And off the record, I—what's Aiden doing up there?" Mr. Baggy Pants Redhead himself was dusting off the podium and setting up a pile of poetry books next to a tall glass of water, smiling proudly as he did so.

"This is his event. Came up with it 'bout a year ago and got a pretty steady following."

Rose assessed Aiden's crisp, button-down shirt stamped with Heartstone's emblem, marking him as an orderly. "Is it only the angels in charge that can host events, or can patients, too?"

"Why?" Malachy asked. "You got an idea?"

A red velvet storyteller's chair in the Topsy-Turvy Library said she might. "Maybe."

Cade surfaced from her listomania. "Rose, that's wonderful! We'll talk with Master Ragnar straight after the performance."

Aiden stood at the podium and coughed politely into his fist. "Good evening." When the room didn't settle, he tried with more volume. "*Good evening!*" The water-walls picked up the echo and tossed it like a boomerang, silencing the chatter. "Thank you for joining us tonight for our celebration of the poetical muse. Our first reader has chosen from a selection of poetry concerning the plight of the angelical post-war condition, including his original poem entitled 'Peacetime Passivity.' "

Mediocre clapping ushered the first reader to the podium, and Rose clamped her jaws on a yawn. "Angels come for this?" she said in an undertone.

"No," Marek assured her. "They come for the magic trick."

"What magic trick?"

"Close your eyes and count to thirty."

One. Two. Three. The guy reading had a voice like a foghorn. *Four. Five. Six.* He droned on. *Seven. Eight. Nine.*

And on. *Ten. Eleven. Twelve.* And on. *Thirteen. Fourteen. Fifteen.* Had this man no concept of the word "inflection"? *Sixteen. Seventeen. Eighteen.* Even the Fishbowl was crying with boredom. *Nineteen. Twenty. Twenty-one.* Splish. *Twenty-two. Twenty-three. Twenty-four.* Splosh. *Twenty-five. Twenty-six. Twenty-seven.* Splish.

Twenty-eight. Twenty-nine ...

Spl ... splo ... shhh.

*

"Thunder, wake up." No. "You're not going to want to miss this." Yes, she would. "You really wouldn't." She was sleeping. Sleep trumped all. "Thunder Rose, are you ignoring me?" Obviously. "Fine. Suit yourself, but you're going to miss Aiden's reading."

Rose cracked one eye open. "Is he any good?"

"Aiden's poetry is a *fascinating* expose on the underappreciated life of a sidekick." Marek smiled. "His delivery alone is worth waking up for."

All around her, the back row audience was righting themselves in their seats, rubbing sleep from their eyes and drool from their chins. The final reader stepped down from the podium, and Aiden bounded to take his place.

"That was the most heartfelt rendition of 'My Joy's Demise' I've heard since *last* month's meeting. Fifth time's the charm!" His listeners laughed appreciatively. "Thank you, everyone, for coming tonight. I thought we'd close the meeting with the debut of my newest poem I call 'Ode to the Sidekick.' I dedicate this poem to my good friend Sephone Darrow who, for—ahem—*personal* reasons, has decided not to join us this evening."

Aiden bowed his head till his chin touched his chest, gripping the sides of the podium. His head snapped up dramatically, and in a throaty voice, he cried:

> *"Hero, hero, listen clear, oh*
> *You think you've got it bad.*
> *But Chosen Ones have all the fun*
> *When you've lived the life we've had*

> *Just a kick to the side—sounds easy as pie!*
> *We thought that first as well*
> *But the list of sides we must supply*
> *Drag our egos straight through hell*

> *We take your side when no one else will listen to your plans*
> *And step aside for you to greet your thousand adoring fans*
> *We're your left side and your right side since you can't see past*
> *your nose*
> *And don't forget the backside—we're the butt of all your jokes!"*

Rose chuckled along with the rest of the back row, but her nose was really starting to itch. Was she allergic to something in here? She rubbed her offended olfactory system.

"Upside, downside, blindside
Villains love to take us captive
A thorn in one side, a stitch in the other
This job is really unattractive"

The insides of her nostrils felt like they were being tickled with a wing feather. Rose held a finger under her nose to stave off the inevitable.

"So hero, hero, listen clear, oh
Don't—"

"ACHOO!"

Inside that tiny, water-walled room, it was the snot heard 'round the worlds. All eyes turned to her. Rose bit her lip sheepishly. *Sorry,* she mouthed. Aiden stared at her, his face quite slack. He stepped down from the podium, and she pressed back in her seat. Now might be a good time to tell him that throwing an electrically-charged girl into a lake was a bad, bad idea, no matter how much she'd insulted his poetry.

He drifted down the aisle, reciting vacantly as he went:

"So hero, hero, listen clear, oh
Don't kick your underdog

We're at your side, we're on your side
Come hail or sleet or fog"

The audience leaped to a standing ovation. Aiden pushed past them in a dream. He was a poet scorned and out for blood.

Cade touched Rose's shoulder "Malachy and I are going to find Master Ragnar to discuss your interest in hosting an activity. We'll be right back."

They had to do that *now*?! Why were they abandoning her to a death-by-poet demise?

(*I'M HOPING FOR A POETIC DEATH, IT'S TRUE, BUT NOT ANYTIME SOON!*)

Why weren't they trying to save her? Why were they *smiling*?

Aiden stopped at their couch and knelt—actually *knelt* —at her feet. "Fair shield-maiden of rosy cheeks, smile of pearls, eyes of thunder, and hair of ... that ... which ... " At a loss for a flattering description, he got up and said, "Sephone wasn't kidding. Your hair really does make me want to grab a hairbrush and run for the hills."

Oh. So, he *wasn't* going to throw her into a water wall for disrupting his poetry. "Best not run too fast in those pants," she teased, covering her relief. "Nice to meet you, Aiden."

His eyes widened. "You know my name?"

Oops. "By your reputation, of course. I'm—"

"Rose, fairest of the flowers." Aiden was on his knees again. "Long have we awaited this blossom of hope, heralded by night's great Shadow, to be welcomed into our brethren and find the sanctity of aggregation therein."

"Uh ... what'd he just say?" she asked Marek out of the corner of her mouth.

"He says welcome to the family, and he's glad I told them about you," Marek translated.

"Oh! Well, thank you."

Aiden stood up, shoving his hands shyly into his sagging pockets. "So, what did you think of Poetry Night?"

"It was ..."

(I HAD A SUDDEN APPRECIATION FOR HIS LACK OF WORDS WHILST DESCRIBING MY HAIR.)

"... refreshing," she decided. Like a good, long nap.

"Refreshing, indeed!" Ragnar appeared with Cade and Malachy and clapped Aiden on the back. "It seems Poetry Night has inspired Rose to try hosting her own Heartstone activity." He looked at her expectantly. "What did you have in mind?"

*

Juice pouches and snack mix. Stories read by candlelight. A giant bedsheet and Shadow Boy's shadow puppets. Story Hour at Heartstone Asylum was going to be a smashing hit!

Rose lay on her bed, elbows tucked behind her head, plotting her big debut. She nudged Marek's mobile with her toe and watched the figures spin. All those memories hanging above, guarding her while she slept. There was room for more figures on the beams; Marek had made sure of it. Room for more memories. Heartstone was full of warmth and friends and cozy mysteries. It was everything she could want for a future.

She could belong here.

Rose turned to the newspaper clipping of Amber's knighting in plain view on the dresser. She took it from its place of honor and pressed it reverently to her lips. Then she tucked it under her pillow, right next to the letter to her future self. Well, right next to where the letter to her future self *should've* been.

Rose felt around. Where did it ...? She tossed her pillow to the floor and ripped back the sheets. Nothing. Down on her knees, curls mopping up dust bunnies, she searched under her bed. Like a little dragon hoarding its treasure, Beta was snoozing atop his own collection of gems, buttons, and assorted shiny objects. Since the newspaper incident, Malachy had been "forgetting" to take him back to the kennels at night, and the puppy slept contently under her bed. She reached around him and his nest of stolen goods and spotted an envelope in the far corner. Recovering her letter from the lair of the dust bunnies, Rose wiped a smudge from the words *To: Rose Skylar, From: Your Past* on the envelope.

Except it didn't say *To: Rose Skylar, From: Your Past*

It said *To: Rose Skylar, From: Your Future*

ENTRY 18

AUTHOR(S) INTERLUDE PART 3

It's about TIME! Time for some time travel, am I right?
~1529 A.S.

I'm squealing. Is anyone else squealing?! ~1527 A.S.

*I'm squealing! This is where it happens. This is where the story
begins FOR REAL. You can feel it, can't you? The tension? Gah,
I can't wait for the scene where—*
~1530 A.S.

*HOOOOLD IT!!! What happened to 'we don't interrupt for
interrupting's sake' and 'we only interrupt to impart useful
information' and 'DON'T INTERRUPT ON A CLIFFHANG-
ER'?!* ~1526 A.S.

Don't kid yourself, Little Me. We know better. You honestly

think we're not gonna interrupt when things get interesting?
~1529 A.S.

Pointless commentary is one of the many services we offer.
~1532 A.S.

Listen up, Reader Name Here ____. If it's between sleep and reading right now, break out the toothpicks and prop those eyelids open. You're gonna wanna be awake for what happens next. ~1529 A.S.

There are hauntings! ~1527 A.S.

And grave robbing! ~1530 A.S.

And don't forget the big plot twist at the end of Entry 29! Or the other big plot twist in—
~1532 A.S.

How to Write a Time Traveler's Diary, Lesson Seven: DON'T TELL READER NAME HERE ____ WHEN THE PLOT TWISTS ARE! ~1526 A.S.

Hey, you don't make up the lessons yet! We teach you, not vice versa. ~1529 A.S.

Oh, really? Thanks to you, Reader Name Here ____ is just gonna skip ahead to the plot twists and spoil them! ~1526 A.S.

No, they ... oh. They are, aren't they? ~1527 A.S.

Oops. ~1530 A.S.

Don't do it, okay, Reader Name Here _____? Please. Let me tell the story. I promise, it will be so worth it if you just let it unfold like it's supposed to and don't sneak ahead. ~1526 A.S.

They're still thinking about it. ~1527 A.S.

Forget what they said, Reader Name Here _____! A few years from now, they'll be talking your ears off in their own diaries, but today it's you and me. This is our moment. Don't spoil it by reading ahead. Trust me. If we're gonna do a series together, you have to be able to trust me. ~1526 A.S.

(Still thinking about it.) ~1527 A.S.

ENTRY 19

WITH LOVE, YOUR FUTURE ME

"Marek!" Rose hollered. She threw open the hatch of her bedroom floor. "Marek, get up here!"

He appeared at the foot of the ladder, slavering an alarming amount of toothpaste around his mouth. "I'm bruffing my teeff," he explained and disappeared from view.

She gave a cry of frustration and paced her room. A minute passed. What, was he flossing, too? *Marek!*

"I'm coming, I'm coming!"

"I coulda been *dying*," Rose hissed as he pulled himself into the attic. "There coulda been a *spider.*"

"What did you expect? I was foaming at the mouth. Now, what's this about?"

She pushed the letter into his hands. "It's this—look at this—this note I found when I was looking for my letter to my future self—you know, the one I wrote on my birthday? Anyway, I put it under my pillow, and now it's gone, and I can't find it anywhere, and then I looked under my bed and saw this! This!"

Marek scanned the envelope. "A letter from ... your future? Well, what does it say?"

"I don't know! Everything's shaking. My hands, my eyes—will you read it to me?"

He slit open the envelope with surprisingly steady fingers and began the letter inside:

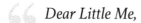 *Dear Little Me,*

Wow. Wowowowowowowow—WOW! I can't believe I'm finally writing this. I can't believe you're finally reading this. (Actually, Marek's reading, isn't he? Hi, Shadow Boy!) I can't believe this is your first taste of time travel.

This is gonna be a lot to take in, but hang with me, okay? Do you remember when we were little—even littler than you, Little Me—and we had that list of things we wanted to be when we grew up? Professional legend seeker, part-time ghost hunter, and time traveler?

Sometimes childhood dreams are more accurate than you'd expect.

I won't explain everything now, though I will soon. (From your perspective, anyway.) In the meantime, there's something you need to know. Before the year ends, Heartstone Asylum will be in danger. No, I won't tell you what from or how to stop it. That's not how this works.

I may know your future and everything in it, but it's your job to live it.

However, I will say this: most answers are all around you, right at the tips of your fingers ... and occasionally your toes.

When you're ready, write to me. I love hearing from the past, and I'm always willing to help. Don't worry about what's coming. Take it one mystery at a time, and remember—your future's got your back!

Love,

Your Future Me

Rose crawled onto her bed and collapsed. Her head was spinning, her thoughts were spinning, the figures on her mobile were spinning. 'Round and 'round they went, first the chocolate-covered strawberries, then the thunderclouds with lightning bolts, then the miniature *Blackout's Tales*, then the coffin—

She sat bolt upright.

Most answers are all around you, right at the tips of your fingers ... and occasionally your toes.

The coffin hadn't been there before. It was a lovely carving, stained chestnut brown with two spades dangling from the bottom. The scale-to-detail ratio was incredible. "Marek, did you make this?"

He rubbed a thumb over the remarkable craftsman-ship. "It looks like something I would make, but ... I didn't." He sank heavily onto her bed. "At least not *yet*."

They sat in silence.

"Thunder?"

"Yes?"

"I think we might grow up to be time travelers."

Rose laughed. It came out half-strangled and slippery with hysterics. "I think you might be right." She touched the miniature spades again. Her lips quirked with mischief. "It's not a bad idea, you know."

His lips twitched in response. "I know."

"Digging up the graveyard would be a foolproof way to figure out what Heartstone is hiding there."

"I've been thinking that for a while myself."

She twisted her fingers through her curls, processing their next move. "We'll need spades, of course. Real-size spades."

"There's a gardening shed out back. I can pick the lock with my shadows."

"We'd have to go at night, or else someone would miss us. Night means ghosts." She hopped off the bed and went to her dresser. "I've got salt, silver, and a handheld mirror, plus half of Beta's stolen jewelry collection has traces of silver and iron. I also have—" Her thought froze. Tenta-tively, Rose opened her top drawer and withdrew a small leather pouch containing the rarest of her gemstone collection. She beckoned Marek closer and poured the contents into his palm. Three balls of frozen moonlight clinked like marbles. Shadow Boy's eyes, as blue and twinkling as the moonstones themselves, lit up.

She lifted her head with pride. "Moonsfrost Eve, 1523. I risked life, limb, and twenty welts to get those."

He cradled them reverentially. "You don't say."

"Ghosts use energy from the moons to manifest, but their manifestations are burned by moonlight. Kinda ironic, isn't it?" Covering her skin with her sleeve—

(THE LAYER RULE GAVE ME SOME PEACE OF MIND, BUT ONLY ONE LAYER STILL MADE ME NERVOUS.)

—she closed his hand over the precious stones. "You keep those. They could get us out of a tight spot."

"There's only one problem." He tugged on the latch to her window.

"*Curfew*," Rose groaned. "We're patients. Even if we asked nicely, the asylum wouldn't let us out in a million—"

The window slammed open, letting in a shivery breeze.

Marek clapped his meaty hands together, the sound like a cannon shot in a canyon. "That settles it, then." He pulled the drawer to her stash of butter knives and handed her one. "Let's see what our future has in store for us, shall we?"

The evening sky was ready for bed, moons tucked under a blanket of clouds and stars brushed to a glow. Its yawns were heard throughout the forest, whistling through stone branches and harmonizing with the owls perched in the trees. A fitting atmosphere, wouldn't you say, given the task at hand?

Newsflash: spooky atmospheres are *not* conducive to successful grave raids.

First, there was the garden shed. Marek picked the lock easily enough, but without moonlight, the inside was pitch black. Which meant Rose had no way of seeing the rake on the floor and thus no way of avoiding the handle whacking her hard in the nose when she stepped on it. And then no way of clobbering Marek with the pointy end when he laughed generously in her face.

Marek was in charge of navigating the darkness to the graveyard, but even with his natural intuition, the going was slow, and the nighttime noises weren't helping any. Rose gripped Beta's leash in one hand and her spade in the other, waiting for the whispers of wind to prove far more ghostly. But by a quarter past eleven, neither the Sinner and his army of Wargs nor the Saint and his army of angels had materialized into anything more than faint shimmers in the distance.

And Marek still hadn't found the graveyard.

"Follow the path to the fork," he muttered under his

breath, "make a right off the trail, another right at the broken branch, go straight till the moss-covered boulder, another left and ... yes! The graveyard should be just around the bend!" They followed the curve of his imaginary trail, and Marek pulled up short. "Ah," he said. "The other left."

Instead of a graveyard, it was the ruins of a small cottage. The cottage was related to the asylum—even its state of dishevelment couldn't mask the family resemblance: cobblestone walls, arched windows, an iron-fenced yard. Like the architect had fallen in love with Heartstone Asylum's grand exterior and built a smaller version for his house.

"What is this place?" Rose asked.

"Master Ragnar didn't always live in the asylum. He had a house built out here so he could keep watch over Heartstone and the forest simultaneously. In fact," Marek said, pushing on the rickety gate, "he even installed a special spyglass to scope out the surroundings. I bet we could use it to find the graveyard. Come on."

Once upon a time, the cottage might've been a dream home—

(MINUS THE WHOLE 'LOCATED IN A HAUNTED FOREST' BIT. TALK ABOUT A REALTOR'S NIGHTMARE, AND THAT'S WITHOUT THE GHOSTS.)

—but age hadn't been its downfall. Age doesn't

186

knock doors off their hinges or shatter windows from the inside out. Age doesn't blow holes in walls of stone, split foundations in two, and discard roofs as easily as a hat. Age wasn't the reason Ragnar's old home was in shambles.

Rose rested her chin on the handle of her spade, admiring the sheer destruction. "What happened to it?"

Marek heaved the half-hinged door out of the way. "Disgruntled patient."

"A patient did this?" She ran her hands over the wounded masonry. How could a structure still be upright with so many holes in its walls? Incredible.

She smiled. Standing in the ruins of a magic-wrecked house, she'd never been more at home in her life. If this was the level of damage control they were used to at Heartstone, surely they could handle her storm cloud and all its baggage. Maybe it was time to tell them about The Incident.

Almost time.

Darkness evaporated from Marek's wings and entered the cottage, performing a safety check of the archways and floorboards. "All good," he said, and they went inside. Rose felt a firm tug on the leash. Beta, ears low and hackles raised, stood resolutely at the threshold, refusing entry. "What's wrong, boy?"

Marek looked around. "He must be sensing the ghosts."

She crouched by the Sonorific Husky puppy's rigid

form and scratched his ears. "It's okay, Bates. We're fenced in by iron. No ghosts here."

Beta cocked his head at her as if to say, *Yes, well, we're all entitled to our own opinions, but this is what I think of yours.* And he bared his teeth and growled. The ruins shook with the vibrations of his magic-enhanced vocal cords. Chunks of plaster fell from the ceiling, and Marek huddled Rose under an umbrella of shadows. The floor split widely down the middle, and she hurtled to Marek's side, clutching his cloak. Raining dust and chips of stone, the walls swayed like a slow dance.

With a dreamy sigh, they stilled.

Beta wagged his tail once, *Don't say I didn't warn you,* and hopped over the threshold to join them.

"Well," Marek said bracingly, "at least he didn't bark."

The interior of the cottage was humble, opening to a basic living room and kitchen with a bedroom to the left. An inch of dust had accumulated on the floor, swirling in plumes around their feet. Rose coughed, covering her face with her wings. In the kitchen, cupboards had been smashed to splinters, the table and chairs were in a dozen pieces stacked like firewood, and an entire set of broken dishes had been swept into the corner.

The living room wasn't much better. All furniture was dismantled and piled against the crumbling walls. The primary window had been pulverized, its flowing curtains shredded like a hundred-year-old death shroud. Positioned in front of it, miraculously unharmed, was a spyglass attached to a swivel stand. "That's the one." Marek pressed his eye to the glass and, after a few moments of swiveling, stepped back, triumphant. "He has a wing's eye view of the graveyard from here. Coincidence or convenient proximity?"

Rose checked the spyglass herself. The graveyard was kitty-corner to the cottage, less than a minute's walk. "Convenient proximity." She tried to unclip the spyglass from its stand and felt a small lever at its base. "What's this do—whoa!" The crystal-clear image diverged into four kaleidoscope reflections of the graveyard, expanding and contracting. She spun the glass to the haunted grove just a stone's throw from the graveyard. Shimmering shapes drifted in and out of view, a bustle of paramagical activity.

"Marek, this isn't a spyglass. It's a specterglass! The kaleidoscope captures the reflection of ghosts in their un-manifested state. It's just like the one in *Blackout's Tales*— you know, 'Legend of the Ghost Who Lost His Eyepiece'?" Rose stopped. "Marek," she said slowly, "this isn't *the* specterglass from 'Legend of the Ghost Who Lost His Eyepiece.' Is it?"

Marek looked her full in the face. "And whatever gave you that idea?"

"Suspicion. Intuition. My investigative constitution."

"So, you're saying that if Ragnar somehow managed to find an actual, legendary object from *Blackout's Tales*, you think he'd stash it in the ruins of a collapsing cottage in the middle of a haunted forest on asylum property?"

"Well, it's a *specterglass*, isn't it?" She tossed her curls importantly. "Only specters can move specterglasses. Maybe this is as far as the ghost would carry it."

Even in the half-dark, Marek's smile was unmistakable. "After all these years, do you still believe the legends of *Blackout's Tales* are true?"

Rose raised an eyebrow. "Do you?" He held her gaze steadily and didn't answer. She loved this song and dance. "What year was Heartstone Asylum built?"

"It was founded a hundred years ago."

"I didn't ask when it was founded. I asked when it was *built*."

His smile widened. A good bear knows when a trap's been laid. Shadow Boy kept his silence.

"I'm going to figure it out, you know," she said. "Why Sephone was wrangling a giant snake my first night here. Why Elektra's team are treated like heroes. What Ragnar has you doing behind the scenes of Heartstone Asylum's cuddly exterior."

He laughed warmly, dispelling the frigid cold creeping through the broken window. "Frankly, I'd be disappointed if you didn't."

"Then why can't you just *tell* me?"

"It's not so much a matter of *can't* as of *won't*. If I told you now, I'd be robbing Ragnar of his pleasure, and you of all angels can sympathize with the pain of having one's thunder stolen."

Stormy vibrated her bones from within. That she could. "And when will *he* tell me?"

"As soon as you prove that you're cut out for the job."

"Do you think I'm cut out for it?"

Marek shook his head in amusement. "Thunder Rose, you're the blueprint."

An icy sensation raced up her arm, and Rose let go of the specterglass. Cold. Burning cold. Legend has it that the surface of a specterglass drops in temperature when ghosts are near. "Uh-oh." She breathed warm breath on the glass and pressed her eye to the lens. A quartet of pulsing kaleidoscope images confirmed the worst: the iron fence protecting the cottage was ringed with the ghosts of angelic soldiers and giant wolves. She backed away. "They've got us surrounded. We need to get outta here before they manifest."

Beta, sensing her urgency, made a beeline for the half-hinged door, which swung shut suddenly. The house's framework trembled.

A well-timed breeze lifted the shredded curtains. They reached for her like drowning fingers, and Rose collided with Marek's back.

(*FOUR LAYERS, MIND YOU.*)

Their wings pressed together, his spine locking with

hers in the ever-strategic "I've got your back, you've got mine, now what?" formation, and Beta wound between their legs.

"There's something I should probably tell you about this cottage," Marek admitted. Great plumes of dust rose from the floorboards. Beta sneezed and rubbed his goggles against Marek's pant leg. "It's been said that the patient who destroyed this place might've done Ragnar a favor because, well, despite the iron fence, he always felt that the cottage was ... inhabited. By something large." The dust was beginning to settle. "And angry." Enormous paw prints littered the floor. "And not altogether living."

Sweat trickled down her back. "You brought me to a haunted house on purpose, didn't you?"

Delicately, ever so delicately, the stand of the specter-glass inched its way towards them.

"I thought it'd be a bonding experience."

Rose glanced up at him from the corner of her eye. "I missed you," she said and caught the violently spinning specterglass thrust at her by an unseen force.

She looked through the lens in time to see four psychedelic jaws lunging for her throat.

ENTRY 20

GHOST AND MIRRORS

I n case you've never experienced it yourself, having an un-manifested ghost jump through you is comparable to taking a bucket of ice water to the face. The reaction is quite similar as well.

Rose shrieked like an alarm clock, springing from foot to foot and rubbing her arms in frenzical motions.

"Good evening," Marek addressed the ghost while she flailed. "My name is Marek Knoxwind, and this is my good friend, Rose Skylar, prodigy of interpretive dance. May we inquire your name?"

Shards of broken window quivered on the floor, and the walls began to quake. A snarling voice replied, "I am the terror that stalks in the night. I am the scab that is ripped off before healing. I—am—*Gormonger!*" The ghost flickered into existence, a giant wolf with ivory fur stained crimson around the muzzle and torso. He flickered out as quickly as he'd come. "*Gormonger!*" roared the Warg, and his feeble manifestation returned, dim and rippling around the edges. His chest, burly and blood-soaked, heaved with spectral strain.

"T-t-trouble multitasking?" Rose's teeth still chattered with cold.

The ghost Warg let loose an explosive growl, the act of which caused him to disperse into a thousand particles of light. Chair legs ejected from the piles of broken furniture and hurtled towards their heads. Marek batted them away with his shadows, and Beta caught one with his teeth, shaking it furiously. The broken furniture ceased its attack.

"And there's PLENTY more where that came from!" boomed Gormonger's disembodied voice.

"Oh, yeah?" Rose challenged, hands on hips. "Why don't you say that to my face!"

The giant wolf materialized within a foot of her nose, huffing angry ghost breath. It smelled surprisingly of fresh, clean snow.

"Go on," she taunted.

Gormonger opened his jaws, but all he managed was a wordless snarl. He disappeared, and Rose ducked behind a shield of shadows as a two-legged footstool shot for her jugular. "That's what I thought," she whispered to Marek. "The iron fence outside is sucking up his energy. He can only do one thing at a time. Try to get him talking."

"Good thinking." Marek dodged a slashed-up couch

cushion. "You're one of the Sinner's Wargs, aren't you?" he asked the ghost. "Died in the Battle of the Petrified Forest? The rest of your pack is outside enjoying the lay of the land. What made you choose to spend your afterlife in a cottage surrounded by iron? You may be dead, but it can't be good for your health."

"TRICKED!" Gormonger bellowed, rattling the window frames. "I was TRICKED! They said to hide in the cottage while it was being built so I could haunt its owner —make him REGRET! They didn't say anything about the FENCE! They didn't say I'd be TRAPPED! They wanted to get rid of me. My own BROTHERS and SISTERS!" He broke off in a long, mournful howl.

"But why? Why would they do that?"

"They had a list," he whimpered. "I bark too much, I howl too much, I eat too much, I'm too aggressive, I talk five decibels louder than their ears can handle, I fight too much, I'm messy—"

"Oh, come now," Marek interrupted. "Look at this cottage! You keep everything swept and stacked."

"Yes, I do. I put everything back in its place. Wanna know why?" A blur of ghost light sped across the room and dove into a stack of broken furniture. It erupted in a shower of stuffing and splinters. "So, I can tear it all down again." Gormonger's outline appeared, held together by little more than threads of gossamer. Rose sidled up to Marek, clutching the butter knife in her pocket. Beta crowded inside the forest of their legs.

"They said I liked breaking things too much. HYPOCRITES! It's stupid. They're all stupid. During the War, they LIKED who I was. They LIKED that I broke things—skulls, skin, bones. They didn't care if I was MESSY. They didn't care if I was LOUD. My voice was the ONLY one that could carry across the battlefield! I kept them ALIVE! Now we're dead, and they can't stand an ETERNITY of me because they think I'm the scum that gives Wargs a bad name and STARTED the War in the first place. And you know WHAT?" Details filled Gormonger's outline: eyes and fur and sharp, sharp teeth. He forced his next words, fighting to maintain his wavering manifestation, "They're probably right."

His canines took on the hardened gleam of a full-on manifestation, and Gormonger pounced. A yip and a spurt of ectoplasm, and Rose was wiping her silver butter knife clean on her sleeve. "So that's how it went down, huh? You're a hopeless case, so they made you prisoner here." The ghost Warg swiped at her thigh with a paw the size of a dinner plate, and she jabbed him again with her knife. "Well, we might be able to help with that."

Without a full-on manifestation, he couldn't truly hurt them. And the only time he could be truly hurt was during a full-on manifestation. Gormonger had gotten himself into quite the pickle, and judging by the sour look on his face, he was chewing on it.

He dissolved into nothing and growled, "HOW? How can a pup and her sitter help me?"

"With this." Marek pulled the hand mirror out of his cloak pocket.

The ghost Warg howled with laughter. "A MIRROR? Swap one lousy prison for another? You must be BARKING!"

"Not our native tongue." A convoy of dish shards catapulted from the kitchen. Marek's shadows swept them away without concern. "Enough defense," he said under his breath and tapped the specterglass. "Tell me when I'm getting close."

Gormonger sensed a shift in tactic. Rose looked through the specterglass, sorting through the swelling, subdividing images, and found him crouching in the corner of the room. "Right corner!" she yelled, and Marek descended on the ghost, waving his mirror like a fly swatter. Gormonger dodged away and out of frame. Rose swiveled around. "Where'd he—?"

An ice-cold whisper in her ear. "Boo."

Gormonger dissipated, dazzling through the kaleidoscope images and jumping in and out of manifestation faster than she could blink. He bounced around the room in untraceable patterns, appearing randomly in his unmanifested state one moment and disappearing to the reality outside the specterglass the next. Following him was impossible.

Rose stepped back from the specterglass. Gormonger manifested above a stack of broken furniture. Marek swung his mirror—and missed by a long shot. The ghost was already behind him, tongue lolling with savage amusement. He was getting cocky. Cocky was good. Cocky meant mistakes. She just had to catch him in one. "Okay, okay, uh ..." Beta poked his head through her legs. His neck was arched, and his nose pointed straight like a compass, trained on a sight invisible to the naked eye. He snapped to the left.

"Left!" Rose shouted, and Marek's mirror missed Gormonger by a furs-breadth. Beta pointed north. "Up! Right! Noon! South!" Shadow Boy pirouetted like a lumberjack in a tutu. "Nine o'clock! Four! On your—" Pure instinct guided Marek's hand as he turned to his left and shot a glittering moonstone off his thumb, striking Gormonger square in his fully-manifested forehead. The ghost stumbled backwards, a smoking hole between his eyes, and collapsed. Bluish light pulsed from the open wound.

Marek approached him pityingly.

"Is this what you came for? To punish me for all I've done?" the Warg snarled weakly.

"Punish you?" Marek caught Rose's eye. "Oh, we're going to do something much worse than that."

"Much, much worse," she agreed.

He crouched by Gormonger and smoothed a hand across the Warg's ghostly cheek. Icicles clung to his glove on contact. "We're going to rehabilitate you." And the mirror came down like a gavel.

Outside, an army of spectral spectators, both angel soldier and Warg, had formed a circle around the iron fence. Rose took a headcount and inventoried their ghost fighting ammunition. Butter knives weren't gonna cut it.

(YOU KNOW, 'CAUSE THEY'RE REALLY DULL.)

Marek held the hand mirror high above his head. "We've captured your greatest nuisance, the one you took such great pains to shut up in this cottage. If you don't allow us safe passage to the graveyard, I will break this mirror and unleash Gormonger into your territory."

They walked safely to the graveyard through a sea of parted spirits.

Beta marched happily to the mouth of Silas's cave, tail wagging in anticipation. Rose nodded wordlessly to Marek, and together they opened their mouths and screamed a scream of the bloody murder variety.

A pair of flickering candlelight eyes appeared in the depths of the cave. "I don't recall ordering a midnight snack," remarked the caramel-furred Warg, absently licking his chops.

"We have a favor to ask," Marek said.

Silas's tail flicked with interest. "Oh?"

"Silas … dear Grave Dancer … guardian of the cemetery ..." Rose knelt on the handle of her spade like a dame on her sword. "We request permission to dig up your graveyard."

ENTRY 21

THE GRAVE ROBBERS

"Put your back into it."

Skrrt. Skrrt. Skrrt.

"Work those muscles!"

Skrrt. Skrrt. Skrrt.

"My grandmother could dig faster than you, and she was missing three toes and a dewclaw."

Marek wiped a muddy rivulet of sweat from his cheek and straightened. "Would *you* like to dig the graves?"

Silas rolled on his side, smirking. "Who do you think dug them in the first place?"

"I don't s'pose you could just tell us what's in them, then?" Rose hopped madly on her shovel. Beta dug enthusiastically at her feet, heaping a useless mound of dirt inside the grave.

"And keep you from building your moral character?"

The Warg rested his head on his gigantic paws. "I think not."

Marek climbed out of the partly dug grave and fished around the rucksack for a pouch of water. A glint of mirror and an angry set of teeth flashed from the bag, and Silas sat up. "What have you got in there?" He nosed into the rucksack and retrieved the hand mirror in which Gormonger was trapped, snapping furiously from inside the reflection.

Upon seeing Silas's face, the ghost Warg became positively rabid, foaming and pawing and gnawing at the corners of the mirror. Gormonger stepped back, chest heaving, and frosted his side of the mirror with his ghostly breath. Then, with a single claw he wrote what could be read backwards:

GRAVE DANCER! You lowdown, traitoring, filthy son of a—

"I fail to see how that is an insult," Silas said. "I know perfectly well what my mother is, and the fact that it is being *used* as an insult is, itself, quite insulting." He nosed the mirror back into the bag and looked seriously at Marek. "I don't know what you plan on doing with that mongrel, but I suggest you find a more permanent housing situation. If he somehow breaks the locks of his cage and enters the mirror world, there's no telling the trouble he'll cause. Think of your Cade."

"Cade?" Rose repeated worriedly. "Why Cade? I mean, I know she likes looking in the mirror ..."

"It's more than that," Marek told her. "Cade's soul signia allows her to *mirror hop*, if you will. The world inside mirrors is a second home to her."

"A home she wouldn't want invaded by a *monstrous ghost*," Silas emphasized.

Outside the iron fence, several ghost Wargs from the Sinner's pack and a few of the Saint's angelic soldiers had drifted over to investigate. They frowned at Rose and Marek with vague suspicion. Then their gaze alighted on Silas with all the annoyance and expectancy of a rent collector with an overdue tenant.

She cocked her head at the ghosts. "Why're they looking at you like that?"

"They are impatient for many things," Silas answered. "Things they've expected to happen by now. My death, for one."

She lowered her voice. "Do you know why they're coming so close to the asylum?"

"Like I said, they are impatient for many things. They're not happy with Ragnar's presence in the forest. Whatever contract they made at the beginning is dissolving."

"Do they want him to leave?"

"No." The Warg's battered whiskers twitched. "*They* want to leave." He scratched a patch of his mangy coat and stood. "Much as I enjoy watching you break your backs for the sake of a mystery, it *is* rather exhausting. I think I'll view the rest from the comfort of my cave."

Rose studied the bedraggled Warg as he slunk between gravestones. "Do you get the feeling that he's leaving because he's tired or because he doesn't want to stick around for whatever we find at the bottom of these graves?"

"Only one way to find out." Marek jumped back into the rectangular hole.

*

Dig, dig, dig, diggity, dig. They'd dug over five feet. The soil was moist, and her mouth was parched. Marek had gone to fetch water since Rose couldn't pull herself out of a hole that was now deeper than she was tall. She lay on her back, staring up at the night sky and contemplating the merits of being buried alive. Cut down on funeral costs? Check. Satisfy curiosity of life as an earthworm? Also check. Overall ease and comfort of death? Poor.

She sat up, sweeping dirt from her clothes. Beta gnawed on an impenetrable stone root poking through the ground. Marek had been gone longer than necessary to find a water pouch.

"Marek?" She jumped, head bobbing above the surface. "Marek, are you there?"

No answer. If he was snoozing against a tree trunk, she'd kill him.

Rose lunged at the ledge of the rectangular hole. Straining, wingspan scraping the edges of the grave, she clutched at the graveside grass above, pulling herself out clump by clump.

Zombies made this look *easy*.

"Marek!" The cemetery was still and empty. Lightning sparked on her fingertips. "Marek, where—?" A shape dropped from the tree branches, landing heavily beside her, and she screamed. Gloved fingers trapped the clamor to her lips. "Just me," Marek whispered. "I want to show you something."

A cyclone of shadows whisked her into the high branches of the tree. Marek perched beside her, pointing to a cluster of bright, blurry figures in the haunted grove next to the graveyard. "What does it look like they're doing?"

She cupped a hand over her eyes. There were Wargs and angels, and angels riding Wargs, and bucking and —"It looks like they're having a Warg-riding tournament!"

He leaned back against the tree trunk and folded his arms, pleased. "How about that, huh? The whole War started because angels banned Warg-tournaments out of fear. That fear turned to hate turned to *years* of bloodshed, and yet this is how they spend their afterlife. Doing the thing that made them friends in the first place."

Rose stretched as far as the branch would hold her. "D'you think that's the Sinner?" The ghostly angel gripping the ruff of the ghost Warg's back certainly looked impressive. Until the Warg gave a mighty rear, flinging the angel into the air. A cheer from another world rippled through the trees like the wind.

"I wouldn't bet on it. They say the Sinner was the only angel to never lose a match."

Shadows picked her up and deposited her back in the grave below. A moment later, Marek joined her with the water pouch.

"It's nifty, isn't it?" Rose said, resuming their excavation. "You hear all the stories about the Sinner and the Saint and the War o' the Wargs, and you start forgetting those things actually happened. But here we are surrounded by the *actual* spirits of the *actual* soldiers of the *actual* War o' the Wargs, in a graveyard digging up their *actual* bones." She frowned. "At least, I think that's what we're digging up. I still don't understand why the ghosts aren't allowed to visit their own graves."

"Silas said he wasn't hired to keep something out. He was hired to keep something *in*. Maybe Ragnar is afraid the ghosts would reanimate their bones if they came in contact with them?" Marek suggested.

"Well, maybe—" *Thunk*. Her spade hit something solid beneath the earth. "Maybe we should see for ourselves."

Unearthing the coffin took less than five minutes, but it felt longer than the entire excavation process put together. Marek gripped the lid of the coffin, thought better of it, and boosted himself out of the grave with his shadows, taking Rose and Beta with him. A tendril stayed behind, lodged beneath the coffin lid like a crowbar.

"All right." He tucked Beta under his arm and Rose under his wing for a game plan huddle. "We don't know what's going to be in that coffin. We may need to run. We may need to fight. We have to be prepared for any scenario. Are you with me?"

She gave a sharp nod. Beta licked his nose.

"Good." Marek focused on his shadow-bar. "On the count of three."

Rose covered her eyes with waffle-crossed fingers.

"One."

Waffle-crossed fingers only succeed in making one hungry for waffles. She put them down.

"Two."

How nasty could it be, really? The soldiers died a hundred years ago. They'd just be bits of black, shriveled skin clinging to old bones ... all stretched and sunken around the eyeholes ... with strands of musty hair falling out of a desiccated scalp ...

"Two-and-a-half."

Just get it over with!

"Three!" The shadow-bar flexed, snapping the coffin open with a groan of rotting wood.

.....

.....

.....

.....

"I—I don't get it."

The coffin did not contain the withering corpse of a long-dead soldier.

In fact, it contained nothing at all.

A deep-throated chuckle echoed from the mouth of Silas's cave, and a pair of flickering candlelight eyes snuffed out.

*

"Empty."

Footsteps fell in the otherwise quiet forest.

"*Empty.*"

A stone twig crunched underfoot.

"Empty!"

"It may have escaped your notice, Thunder," Marek said, "but saying 'empty' every few seconds for the rest of the night isn't going to change what we found."

"But why *empty?*" Rose exploded. "Why put a guardian in charge of an empty graveyard? Was it a trick, a ploy, a distraction? Was there something hidden in the graves that someone already stole? Should we tell Master Ragnar?" That wasn't the most appealing option. They could get in big trouble if he found out the asylum had let them out after curfew.

"Elektra's team is who he'd call if there was an issue. So long as a certain *mysterious benefactress* makes sure Sephone and Aiden dig up the empty graves first, they can be the ones to let Master Ragnar know if the bones aren't where they're supposed to be."

"Can I ask you something?" she said. "This might fall under 'Mysterious Mysteries of Heartstone Asylum That You Won't Tell Me About,' but ... why is Elektra's team treated differently than ours? Patients think they're *heroes*. They walk into a room, and everyone practically falls at their feet. If both our teams are part of whatever Ragnar has you doing behind the scenes, then why does no one treat you, Malachy, or Cade like that?"

Marek mulled over his answer. "Simply put, Elektra's team is in charge of saving the day. We, on the other hand, are in charge of saving the night. Everybody notices who saves them when the sun is shining. They take for granted the ones that keep them safe while they sleep."

"Future Me said the asylum is gonna be in danger soon. Which d'you think'll need saving then—the day or the night?"

"Maybe both."

When they found their way back to the asylum, Marek

directed them to Aiden's second-level window, where they propped the spades and poured graveyard dirt from their boots on the sill.

"That should be enough to get their wheels turning," Rose whispered.

"Poor, rusty things," Marek agreed.

They flew to the top of the Lollypop Tower, and she ducked through her open window, Beta in her arms. Marek retained the rucksack and the mirror with its unsavory occupant. "Get some sleep, won't you? Remember what your future said: *Take it one mystery at a time.* We'll think more in the morning. This was fun, wasn't it?" He winked and flew down to his own room.

It *was* fun. Felt just like their good ol' days of legend seeking. In other words, everything felt right with the worlds.

The letter from her future self was where Rose had left it on the dresser. Sitting on the floor, she scooped Beta into her lap and read it again. "Hard to fault someone for not giving more than they promised, but couldn't I have slipped another clue in here?" Sighing, she kissed her puppy between his goggles and went to brush her teeth.

Beta was lying on his back when Rose returned, tongue lolling blissfully from his mouth like he'd had a five-minute belly rub. "What are you so happy about?" She stepped over his tail to grab the letter from her dresser.

Her fingers froze inches from the parchment. The letter had been flipped over, and on the back was written:

> *P.S. Choosing a story for Story Hour? It'll be from* Blackout's Tales, *obviously. Personally—and this is just a suggestion from little old me to young little you—I'd say, pick the one that breaks your heart.*

The ink was still wet.

ENTRY 22

CANCELED: BAD WEATHER

The time was set. The snacks were prepared. The giant bedsheet hung proudly from the upside-down ceiling in the Topsy-Turvy Library. Story Hour was poised for success! Rose had even heard patients chatting animatedly about Heartstone's newest activity, and it drove her to practice her story three times a night: first to herself, then to Beta, and then to a mirror whose wolfish occupant frosted the surface with hateful reviews on her elocution. Part of Gormonger's rehabilitation was learning to express criticism without tearing someone down. Problem was, he *liked* tearing things down. A lot.

But by the night before her debut, even Gormonger's critique was limited to *Speak louder—*

(*Like he could HEAR through the mirror.*)

—and bite some noses. No one will have the guts to boo you off stage.

All in all, Rose's confidence was rather buoyed.

It lost some of its buoyancy the next morning when she woke with a thunderous cough. And by thunderous, she meant *thunderous*. Her first waking minutes were spent face-smushed in her pillow to stifle the noise.

Someone knocked on the hatch to her room, and she managed a deep, cough-less breath. "Come in."

Cade's purple head appeared. "Are you all right, dear? You sound a little hoarse."

"I've been practicing a lot." Yeah, that's all it was. Too much practice.

Cade climbed into the attic and saw the open *Blackout's Tales* on the dresser. "You enjoy that book, don't you? I remember loving those stories when I was your age. I still love them, of course. I just see them through different eyes now."

She folded herself neatly on the edge of Rose's bed. "You know, I'm very supportive of what you're doing today. Settling into this new situation can be painful, but you're taking a big step forward. We are all very proud of you, and we—" Cade broke off, faltering, and smoothed an imaginary crease from her nurse's uniform. "Well, despite the circumstances it took to bring you here, we're very happy to have you with us. I hope you know that." Her hand on the bedspread opened tentatively, an offer of reassurance.

Cade wasn't afraid to hold her bare hand.

It was the smallest gesture, yet it moved a mountain of resistance. For a single moment, Rose would've broken the layer rule outright and taken Cade's hand, but a storm of coughing seized her lungs.

"Are you sick?" Cade reached instantly for her forehead, and Rose flinched away from her touch.

"No, not sick." Not today. She *couldn't* be. "Just a tickle."

"Give the practice a rest. You don't want to strain your voice for tonight." Cade swept lightly to her feet. "Marek's made us breakfast. Why don't we join him downstairs?"

The table was set with plates of pancakes smothered in maple syrup. Rose sat opposite Cade and Marek while Malachy leaned against the Lollypop Tower's window wall, sipping his morning coffee and pondering the blue sky outdoors. "It's funny. I coulda sworn I heard thunder this morning."

Ducking her head, Rose shoveled pancakes into her mouth and almost spat them back out.

Marek noticed her reaction. "Taste okay? I've been experimenting with cinnamon."

She nodded and gulped. "They're delicious." Or they would be if her taste buds weren't polluted by the flavor of ozone. What was *happening*? Rose brought a napkin to her lips but swiftly changed trajectory when her eyes and nose begin to water.

"Are you sure you're all right?" Cade's delicate brows furrowed.

"I'm fine. Just allergies or something." *Or something.*

It was all downhill from there.

Umbrella making was their first activity of the day, and by mid workshop, Rose's eyes were streaming, her ears itched, her nose dripped, her throat was raw from holding back coughs, her voice was a rasp, and everything she touched gave a *pop* of static shock.

This wasn't a cold. "Stormy, whatever you're doing, *cut it out!*" she hissed, massaging her chest. Somewhere inside, her storm cloud quivered.

In the assembly line of umbrellas, she was in charge of attaching the shafts to the curved handles. It was mindless work and the finishing touch of the umbrella, which was satisfying even as she wiped her drippy nose. When the umbrella was finished, she'd snap it shut, tie it with a band, and deposit it in the umbrella stand by her chair.

There was a lull in the assembly line, and Rose stopped to stroke her current creation. How long had it been since she'd held an umbrella? Growing up, one was practically an extension of her arm. That first time she'd reached for the umbrella stand by her bed and found it empty ... it was the day after her fateful visit to the witch doctor. In celebration of her vanquished storm cloud, Dad henceforth banned all umbrellas from the house.

(WHICH WAS SILLY BECAUSE NATURAL THUNDERSTORMS STILL HAPPEN, AND ANGELS LOOK AT YOU FUNNY WHEN YOU'RE

Nowadays, she'd give anything for the chance to be soaked by a storm.

Her storm.

Just like that, her symptoms vanished. No runny nose, no hacking cough, no taste of ozone. Rose froze mid-reach for her next umbrella, every hair follicle of her body standing on end.

An Incident. An Incident to end all Incidents (except, perhaps, *The* Incident) was about to happen. How'd she know? Well, you don't get to have a storm cloud living inside you and *not* recognize the calm before a storm.

Heartstone could handle unstable magic—just yesterday Zephyr Delmar from Elektra's team caused a tornado in the Dining Hall with his windy soul signia, and they *still* hadn't finished cleaning the mashed potatoes off the ceiling—but this was different. Mashed potatoes never killed anyone. Lightning bolts had. Rose had seconds, *seconds*, to evacuate this room with its wide-open space and many innocent bystanders, and she couldn't move a muscle.

Cade was across from her, cutting lengths of waterproof fabric into triangles. Rose barely had to catch her eye, and her nurse was at her side. "A breath of fresh air, shall we?" She discreetly guided Rose, still clutching an umbrella, from her chair. Cade's hand brushed the place between her wings, and Rose recoiled. "Don't touch."

Cade waited until they were in the hallway. "Tell me what's happening, Rose."

Something was wrong. Something was very, *very* wrong. A pressure descended on her head, squeezing from all angles, and Rose clutched her skull. "Solitary confinement," she ground out. "You need to take me to solitary confinement. *Now.*"

"Heartstone Asylum doesn't have a solitary confinement. That's what the Lollypop Tower used to be, remember?"

"Then take me there! Take me somewhere small, lock me up, and *stay away!*"

"Rose, you have to tell me what's wrong."

Rose paced back and forth, wringing the umbrella in her hands. Cade touched her shoulder, and she jerked away, wings flaring. "Don't *touch!*"

"I'm a nurse, Rose," Cade said with gentle firmness. "I can help."

Rose stopped pacing. She closed her eyes, willing her shoulders to relax. "Okay," she said. "Okay." And she bolted down the corridor like the lightning vibrating under her skin.

She rubbed her chest as she ran. "Shh, shh, what's wrong, Stormy? What's wrong?" Her storm cloud spasmed inside her, expanding and contracting wildly. A shudder of electricity surged through her hair. It shot from a hundred different curls, little bolts of lightning as small and sharp as throwing knives. They struck the walls of the corridor, leaving charred black fissures in the stone.

Six seconds later, her lungs convulsed with thunder, and she staggered against the wall, heaving. Six seconds between lightning and thunder. The worst wasn't on her yet. Wheezing, Rose set off down another hallway, losing Cade completely. Rain began pouring from eyes, ears, mouth, and nose, splashing on the closed umbrella she hugged to her chest.

Three seconds now.

"What's wrong? What's wrong?" Rose demanded feverishly. "Are you okay? Stormy, tell me!"

"*Tell* ..." The word hissed like a snake crawling through the walls.

She'd stumbled into the Remembrance Hall.

"*We have to tell them,*" a familiar voice echoed in the hallway's memory. "*What if the graves aren't supposed to be empty? What if something got out?*"

Sephone cut Aiden's whining with a serrated retort. "*And what's Ragnar going to do if that happens? Call us. So, let's just skip the formality and do what we're going to have to do anyway and fix the problem ourselves.*"

"*You have a point.*"

"*Spears* are *my specialty.*"

Using her umbrella as a cane, Rose hobbled around the hallway's corner and collapsed against the wall. The best thing to do when you can't find a storm shelter? Make yourself as small as possible, and take refuge in an umbrella. She popped hers open, drew her knees up, and waited for the storm to pass. "It's okay. You're okay. We're okay." Rose wrapped her arms around her chest, the closest she could get to hugging the storm cloud within.

One second.

*

Beta found her rocking beneath a smoking, tattered umbrella amid a battlefield of scorched walls and fractured flagstones. He nosed his way under the hood and stationed himself at her side like a sentry. Rose didn't even have the strength to pet him.

A pair of heels clicked slow, measured steps on the broken floor. The umbrella tilted back. Cade crouched at eye-level, concern and relief vying for the vanguard of her expression. "Hey. Hey, it's okay. We found you. There's nothing to cry about."

Rose wiped her cheeks with the back of her hand and laughed, a harsh, crackling noise. "Not tears," she croaked. Her clothes were drenched. Puffy eyes, burning nose, dribbling mouth—the ears were the worst, trickling water down her neck. She was sitting in a puddle. "Rain."

Confusion did funny things to Cade's face, but it was still the prettiest face Rose ever did see, overbite and everything. She imagined that pretty face swollen and purple and ravaged by lightning burns. "Back," Rose thundered.

(METAPHORICALLY SPEAKING. THE LITERAL WOULD FOLLOW.)

"Get back!"

Mercifully, Cade did as she was told. Rose coughed so hard the walls shook, and her eardrums threatened to burst from the close-quartered volume. She couldn't breathe. *She couldn't breathe.*

The edges of her vision were fuzzy. Dark. She slumped on her side, cheek pressed against the cold floor.

Shadows brushed the hair from her face, and Marek was there, easing her head into his lap. "Easy, Rose. *Breathe.*" Cade was on her hands and knees beside him, and Malachy stooped over their shoulders, pushing his magic-seeing glasses up the bridge of his nose. All three of them wore pairs of shiny, industrial-grade gloves. Rose felt their cool, slippery texture when Marek put his hands on her bare arms, pressing her wings against her sides.

"Don't!" She jerked in his hold. "No touch! *No touch!*"

"Hold her still!" Malachy ordered. He was concentrating hard behind his glasses. "I need to see this."

Memories of another time—of her father and the witch doctor restraining her in a cave, running a blade that cut deeper than flesh and bone across her skin—triggered her muscles' reflexes, and Rose thrashed violently.

"Shhh, shhh, it's okay." Cade leaned across her torso, holding her legs together. "It's okay, Rosy, it's okay."

Rosy. Amber's nickname. Rose sucked in slivers of air. "*Amber.* I want—my sissy. I wanna—go—home. *Please.*" She banged her fist against the floor. "Please."

Marek bent low, whispering meaningless things into her hair. Rose clung to his soft baritone, the sound of comfort and sweet darkness. Why wasn't Stormy soothed by his voice? If anything, it stirred more powerfully, straining for him like it was—

Rose sneezed a great, gusty sneeze and a wet, gray mist ejected from her mouth. The cloud took shape, fluffing out its water molecules like a handkerchief freed from a pocket. It seemed to notice the girl on the floor, barely conscious, and zoomed eagerly for her face, pressing against her cheek like a damp kiss.

Rose touched her soul signia with the tips of her fingers. "Hi," she whispered with the last of her breath, "Hi, you."

Her eyes rolled to the back of her head, and the world went dark and stormless.

*

Sensations were the first to creep into her consciousness. The feel of the Lollypop Tower's comfiest couch beneath her. Warm, dry pajamas. A puppy snuggled against her thigh. Stormy's soft, damp kiss against her forehead.

Sounds came next. A rustle of pages. The gentle scrape of Marek's carving knife. The bunny-eared clock on the coffee table chiming a time that was well into the evening.

"Story Hour," Rose groaned. Her throat was raw.

"It's all right," Cade soothed. She sounded close enough to touch. "We're going to reschedule."

"First time we had to cancel an indoor event due to bad weather," Malachy added, and Rose smiled weakly. Her storm cloud shifted against her forehead, cool and comforting, and she opened her eyes.

There was no storm cloud.

Rose sat bolt upright, and the cold compress tumbled off her forehead. "Where is it? Where's Stormy?" Her chest felt hollow, much too hollow to be housing her storm cloud, but deep inside, there was a feeble flutter. That wasn't right. It *couldn't* be. It was so … so *small*. "What are you doing back in here?" she asked softly. "You were *out*. You were free." She looked to Cade sitting on the edge of the couch and Marek whittling at her feet and Malachy in the armchair, balancing a stack of enormous, leather-bound books on the armrest. "You saw it, didn't you?"

The tower's portrayal of playful bunnies had been washed away by a stream of bucktooth beavers chewing nervously on their nails. "We saw it," Marek said.

Cade reinstated the compress to Rose's forehead, and

the flinch at personal contact was automatic. Her purple-haired nurse was unperturbed. "You won't hurt me. Look at the gloves, see? Electric eel skin."

Clever.

Rose lay back down, and Beta nestled under her arm. "Stormy's inside me again. What happened?"

Malachy chewed on a thumbnail. "It was only free for a few seconds. The moment you passed out, it sucked right back in."

"You were watching me with those glasses. Did you see something?"

"I did." He thumped his pile of books. "And I've got a pretty decent idea as to what's going on with your soul signia."

Hope lurched with the storm cloud inside her. "What is it?"

Malachy hesitated, hunching forward in his chair. "The thing is ..." He tried again. "Ya see, the thing is ... look who's awake!" Beta yawned and shook out his ears. "Why don't we take him outside, you and me. You can help me run the dogs through their exercises, and I'll tell you what I know. Sound good?"

Nope. That didn't sound good at all.

ENTRY 23

HUGS AS A WEAPON

Malachy had a way with dogs.

They scampered around him like puppies, tails wagging, eager to chase the chew toys he kept in a satchel slung over his shoulder. He chucked a handful across the asylum's iron-fenced courtyard, and the Sonorific Huskies pelted after the balls and bones. Soon autumn would be hanging up its hiking boots in favor of snowshoes, and time outdoors would be limited.

Malachy tossed a bone in a wide arc, and Beta sprung into the air to catch it. Already he was less the lanky pup Rose had met in the hearse and more like the stocky, full-grown huskies around him. But he was still the smallest. "Where did Beta come from? I don't see any pups here his age. Did you buy him somewhere?"

"Ace—uh, Master Ragnar, got him half-price off a breeder on account of his eye condition. Dog can't see the side of a barn if it smacked him in the nose, but Cade fixed him up with a pair of those goggles, and he's good as new," Malachy said.

"Cade made his goggles?"

"Sure did. She's got a knack for inventions—like those magic-proof vests the dogs wear. Part of the reason Ragnar offered her a job at Heartstone is 'cause she can fix just about anything she puts her mind to, and he doesn't mind damaged goods."

Rose smiled as Beta plowed into the pack of huskies vying for his bone. "I don't mind damaged goods, either. Not one bit."

"Yeah?" Malachy glanced at her. "Why's that?"

"Because they know what it means to not be wanted." Beta trotted over, victorious, and dropped the bone at her feet. She scuffed the fur between his ears. "And look how happy he is now that he's loved."

Damaged goods. Call it coincidence that Malachy decided to pick up their discussion about her magic just then. "D'you remember everything I told ya about your mind being a kitchen sink and your soul's the spout pouring magic into it?"

"And how, when you use your soul signia, it's like pulling the plug to empty the sink. I remember."

"Apple for the teacher." Malachy smirked, patting himself on the back. "Then I told ya about the subconscious and how it stores any extra magic your mind doesn't have room for."

"Exactly. And that's where unstable magic comes from: subconscious magic leaking through the dam between your mind and your subconscious mind, right?"

"Very good! So, if your conscious mind's like a kitchen sink that can get full, let's imagine your subconscious is a bathtub with infinite space. All the runoff from the sink goes into the tub. Now, your soul's the faucet pouring magic, but like ya told me before, those knots in your soul have tied off the circulation, stopped the magic. Your mind, the sink, is empty. Your soul, the faucet, is off. That means that any magic you have access to right now is the trickle from the infinite bathtub, your subconscious."

Rose looked at the lightning curling around her fingers. "So, that's why Stormy's stuck inside me? That li'l trickle isn't enough for my soul signia to manifest outside my body."

"Nope." Malachy eyed her magic keenly. "And I wouldn't do that if I were you."

The rings of lightning vanished. "Why?"

He gave a sigh that longed for his magic blackboard. "So, ya've got this bathtub with the *capacity* to store infinite magic, but that doesn't mean it *has* infinite magic. Most angels acquire an impressive stockpile over the years, but we're talking *centuries*. Centuries of runoff magic filling up the tub, and Rosebud, you've—you haven't been around that long."

Rose stuffed her hands deep into her pockets, where a certain unicorn cupcake paperweight made its home. She took it everywhere with her. Not that she'd tell *Malachy* that. "What are you saying?"

Malachy wiped his hands dry of the slobbery chew toys and turned to her. "I'm saying, that storm attack of yours? That was the last bit of magic draining from your subconscious. Couple more uses, and it's over. No parlor trick, no nothing. You'll be completely empty of magic."

Last time someone told Rose she'd be empty of magic, it was Dad standing outside a cave with a rope in his hands. He'd said it with the same note of finality, and Stormy had shrunk against her, cold and clammy. Only this time it was on the inside.

But Malachy wasn't Dad. He was younger and rougher and scruff-bearded, and his eyes crinkled at the corners when he smiled. "The only way to save your soul signia," he said, "is to take the knots out of your soul and get the circulation going again. And our best shot at doing that depends on you telling me *exactly* how they removed your soul from your body and put the knots there in the first place."

Malachy was gruff, and he liked unicorns. He snorted milk when she told jokes at breakfast, and his sarcasm knew no bounds. Their relationship had started with a cupcake to the face, and he was asking her to trust him with the most painful memory in her possession. "I ..." Could she do it? For Stormy's sake? "I will. Soon. I promise."

"Okay," he said simply and passed her a handful of

doggie treats. "You'll like this next part. I usually have them practicing on a dummy, but this is much better."

"What are we doing?"

"Drills. Hugging-drills to be specific." He was dead serious.

"*Hugging* ... drills?"

(TRY SAYING THAT WITH A STRAIGHT FACE.)

Malachy raised a contrary eyebrow. "As service dogs of Heartstone Asylum, this is one of the most important commands in their arsenal. Don't believe me?" He blew a complicated note on a whistle that looked like the bottom half of a dog bone. The huskies immediately lined up in a horizontal formation. "And—hug!"

The first dog barreled towards Rose and threw massive paws on her shoulders. She stumbled back, laughing and clinging to him. He licked her ear and snarfed a treat from her open palm, then bounded away for the next dog to have its turn. Puppy love's a miracle drug, but there were dual properties at work in the husky hug: it was both immensely comforting and completely overpowering, an ideal combo for dealing with a hysterical asylum patient.

But Rose would happily give into hysterics if it meant cuddling these loveable lugs. She nuzzled cheeks with her current hugger—Nuka, her name was—and let her go with a sigh. "I miss hugging."

Malachy was quiet. Rose glanced at him sidelong. "I'll

have you know, my hugs were something of a legend back in Chunter Woods. I was *this close* to having a mixed magical arts move named after me."

He snorted. "Now there's something I'd like to see."

"Well, I wouldn't use it on *you*. And risk getting skewered like a pincushion? You're pricklier than a cactus. Malachy the Cacti."

"Cacti is plural. That doesn't make any sense."

"It doesn't have to if it rhymes."

"Fine. Then your *curls* look like *squirrels*."

Okay, now he was *begging* for a mixed magical arts hug. Rose stood on tiptoe, reaching up—and with a sleight of hand, plucked a dog treat from his ear. "What's this? A dangerous place to be keeping a doggie biscuit." She bit her lip mischievously, waggling her eyebrows, and dropped a fistful of dog treats down the back of his cloak.

Malachy sprang into action, cursing and tearing at his back while Rose danced out of reach, chanting, "Hug, hug, hug!" The pack of huskies charged, tackling their trainer to the ground and snuffling through his cloak with inquisitive snouts. Malachy drowned in a rolling sea of paws, laughing and wrestling and gasping for air. Rose stood aside, fluffing her feathers in a job well done. She could watch this for *hours*. Or at least until something more interesting came along.

And come it did, slinking outside the iron courtyard, as dim as the evening star.

It shouldn't be here. It was too early. There was still a

rim of orange and pink on the horizon. "Malachy? Malachy, I think we have a visitor."

He strained to look where Rose was pointing and when he saw what she saw, he blew a sharp, shrill note on his dog whistle. The dogs were off him in an instant. Malachy got up slowly, like a predator drawing up to its fullest height. He approached the courtyard fence with Rose and the huskies trailing compulsively behind. Knuckles tight, Malachy gripped the fence rail and leaned over, nose-to-nose with the ghost Warg on the other side. "I don't know what you think you're doing over here, but you put that tail between your legs, and you march back into that forest right now. That's an order."

Heartstone's service dogs recognized his tone. Their tails were down, ears flat in obedience. They studied the ghost Warg with a mixture of curiosity, vigilance, and reproach for not responding to their alpha. The ghost Warg maintained Malachy's gaze, a silent power struggle. Malachy put his whistle to his lips, and the sound he made was a wind's scream and a wolf's howl all in one. Gradually, the ghost's head and tail lowered. It glanced at the asylum one last time and swept around, disappearing into the Petrified Forest.

"That was a quiet one," Rose remarked. Gormonger's chatter was *incessant*. Her evenings were cluttered with the squeaky sounds of conversation scribbled on a fogged-up mirror. "Maybe it's that whistle. Did Marek make it for you?"

"What, this?" Malachy rolled the whistle between his fingers. "Nah. I've had it for years." He jerked his head towards the retreating ghost. "How much ya know 'bout them?"

"A little here, a little there." She smiled at him. Knowledge was like a secret stash of candy. Everyone was always asking where she got the chocolate smears around her mouth. "I know the Petrified Forest is haunted by the dead soldiers of the War o' the Wargs. I also know Master Ragnar has a deal with them and that they're breaking it by coming this close to the asylum. They want something from him."

Malachy squinted, appraising her. "What else do ya know?"

"Oh"—Rose rocked innocently on the balls of her feet—"more than I should."

ENTRY 24

THE HEARTBREAKER'S BROKEN HEART

B ut not as much as she'd like.

The mystery of the empty graves haunted her almost as much as the ghost Warg she faithfully spent her free-time with. "I overheard Sephone and Aiden in the Remembrance Hall," Rose told Marek as they waited, haunted mirror between them, for Gormonger to finish writing his essay on the woes of his puphood. "Team Hero doesn't know why the graves are empty, either. But they're gonna try and figure it out." Hopefully, their *mysterious benefactress* and her guardian angel would be able to help with that.

Weeks passed without Incidents—or as without Incidents as an asylum for unstable magic can be.

(What's the occasional exploding glue pot in arts and

Snow blanketed the grounds, and icicles hung from the stone trees like fangs. Rose spent five minutes every morning just looking out her window and admiring the frozen landscape. It was like something out of a storybook, like something from *Blackout's Tales*. "Legend of the View from My Asylum Window," that's what she'd call it. The beauty of the forest almost took the sting out of the fact that she was no closer to figuring out what had turned the trees to stone than she was the empty graves. Or why the ghosts lurked at the corners of the courtyard every night as if waiting for something.

Or how to save Stormy. The smallest unintentional spark made Rose's stomach clench—when would it be her last? She was exempt from all magic-based exercises on the schedule as well as anything that could be potentially magic-inducing.

(LIKE SELF-DEFENSE CLASS WITH ALL THE FUN PUNCHING BAGS. GRRR.)

What did she do with all that extra time? Made umbrellas, basically. Lots of 'em. Rose didn't even need an assembly line. She'd compiled a list of all asylum residents and their favorite colors with the goal of presenting a tailor-made umbrella to each and every one of them. Who knew? One day they might come in handy.

Her letter from the future remained tucked under her pillow. Rose hadn't written back yet. Every time she tried, the thousand and one questions cramped her fingers, and she gave up. She couldn't even ask why her future self had recommended she read a depressing legend—the *"one that breaks your heart"*—for Story Hour. Which, by the way, had been rescheduled for the day before Moonsfrost Eve, a full month after her failed first attempt.

"Before the year ends, Heartstone Asylum will be in danger." That's what her future self had promised. No helpful hints, no suggestions. The new year would begin on Moonsfrost Day, and all they knew was something bad was gonna happen before then.

Rose just prayed it would wait till after Story Hour.

*

Staring down a Topsy-Turvy Library full of angels was intimidating. Sitting on what was essentially a giant red velvet cupcake helped.

Upon Rose's request, Cade had draped an off-white blanket over the back of her red velvet storyteller's chair to represent the cream cheese frosting, and the combination was delicious. The chair angled left on the dais so she could see the bedsheet on which Marek's shadow puppets would soon be wreaking havoc. He was above her in the

235

obstacle course hemisphere of the library, making sure the strings on the bedsheet were tied securely to the upside-down bookcases. Smiling down at her, he tapped the side of his nose. *"You're clever,"* he was saying. *"You've got this."*

Rose thumped her chest twice and pointed to him. *"So, have you."*

Patients made themselves comfortable in their chairs while nurses and orderlies passed out snacks, little sweet rolls shaped like hearts, and coated in a gray glaze. No self-respecting Story Hour was complete without edible visuals! Cade finished with her basket of rolls and joined Malachy, Ragnar, and Elektra's team in the front row. Amber's smile might've calmed the lightning crackling on Rose's tongue, but Cade's gave her the strength to bite it.

Sitting between the elderly twins Zephyr and Cascada Delmar was Sephone, staring into space with a thoughtful scowl. Cascada—or *Miss Cassie*, Rose had heard her called —tucked a piece of Sephone's dark hair fondly behind her ear and whispered something to her. Sephone's expression tightened, then loosened; she nodded and turned her attention to Rose's chair and the bedsheet, her scowl now one of mild interest.

Sephone's scowls had an impressive range of settings.

Aiden sat next to his spiky redheaded mother, who sat stiffly next to Cade, comparing notes for the Moonsfrost Eve celebration. He looked furtively from his mom to Sephone and darted over to Rose's chair without their notice. Leaning over the arm, Aiden whispered, "Lubricate the vocal cords every fifteenth sentence and breathe from the diaphragm. You'll do great!" He smiled a bright, freckly smile and darted back to his chair, baggy pants sagging dangerously.

The lights dimmed. Marek lit the lamp behind the bedsheet and gave her a thumbs up.

Show time.

Rose took a sweet roll and held it up for effect. "This represents something very special: the Heartstone Eternal. In the Old World, two thousand years ago, this was the vessel the god Dimidia utilized to reside within the universe he had created.

"In the beginning, this Heart was made of flesh, and it pumped the world full of the life and magic of Dimidia himself. An extraordinary manor—or *asylum*, they called it—was built to house the Heart Eternal, and angels were welcome there anytime. Dimidia's asylum was a safe place for all who entered it. There were rooms to stay in and food to eat, and the Heartbeat Eternal could be heard on every floor. They say the asylum breathed magic, and that magic kept the Heart safe. But not forever."

Rose raised the heartstone sweet roll above her head. "Break it," she instructed, and her audience obeyed. Gray glaze cracked, oozing red jelly filling. "Do you know what happens when you break the heart of a god?" She licked a trail of jelly from the side of her hand and smiled. "You break the world in two."

Such drama! Such stakes! Such a great place to make her audience wait while she found her spot in *Blackout's Tales*.

Flip, flip, the rustle of pages—Rose paused on "Legend of the Perilous Fishing Trip" and the illustration of the Leviathan, an enormous water snake, looming over a fishing boat. Hoo-*ee!* Imagine trying to stuff *that* through a window. She snuck a glance at Sephone and briskly skimmed ahead to her legend of choice. "Tonight, we'll be reading 'Legend of the Two Worlds.' "

Apart from Malachy, Ragnar, and the rest of the front row, there was no obvious recognition from her listeners. Silly angels. Didn't they know where alchemists and historians first got the idea to explore the possibility of multiple worlds? Any clue what the abbreviations P.M. (pre-multiverse) and A.S. (after separation) meant when chronicling the past? Had they *never* wondered about the origins of their existence? "It all began with the first guardian angel, a man named Caelix ...

"Caelix was both proprietor and protector of Dimidia's asylum. He alone knew the location of the Heart Eternal and spent most of his days in that inner sanctum, guarding and worshipping in the presence of the god. Caelix was an orphan boy when the Heart was first made, and Dimidia appointed him specially as its guardian. It was all Caelix had, and he rarely left its side.

"Years passed, centuries, and Caelix watched thousands upon thousands of angels enter the asylum of Dimidia, lost and alone, only to leave with backs straight and footsteps as sure as a mountain lion's." Their hearts were changed by the Heart Eternal. They found rest in its home. Angels left there knowing where they belonged and who they belonged to. "And Caelix watched it all with jealous longing."

Marek crouched at the corner of the bedsheet, a steady stream of shadows misting from his wings, taking shape on the canvas. His shadow puppets played out the scenes as Rose spoke them; there was no delay between her words and the lively silhouettes swirling on the sheet. It was like their brains were connected, like his shadows were the mental images of her thoughts.

And they hadn't even *practiced*.

Robe flowing, chin tilted at an aggravated angle, Shadow-Caelix scrutinized the hundreds of little shadow-figures scurrying like ants into a shadow-building—which held an uncanny resemblance to the outline of Heartstone Asylum. "The Heart was Caelix's family, the only thing he'd ever truly loved. But if he looked deep into his own heart, there were times he still felt like an orphan. When Caelix saw the changes taking place in the angels around him, he was angry. They stayed for *weeks*. He spent every *day* with the god! Why wasn't he changed like they were? Why wasn't he satisfied? Why, on the darkest nights with his knees bent at Dimidia's altar, did he still feel like he didn't belong?"

Caelix, Caelix ... this was the part where Rose wanted to reach in and hug him through the pages. "Caelix wanted answers, but the Heart spoke a language he couldn't understand. So he came up with his own solution."

Marek's shadows danced and whorled, shifting into the shape of a man chiseling a pillar of stone. The pillar became a statue of an angel with outstretched wings. Caelix had made something like himself, a body for Dimidia that he could speak to. "He took the sacred Heart, placed it inside the statue's chest, and waited. The Heart Eternal contained the source of all magic. It gave life to the asylum, its home. It gave life to every angel who entered. It would give life to this statue."

But nothing happened. Shadow-Caelix tore his hair, and frustration bled to desperation. " 'If a heart of flesh won't bring to life a body of stone,' he reasoned, 'then I'll make a heart that can.' "

And he knew just how to do it.

"Once every seven years, Caelix would take a pilgrimage to a place known as the Forgotten Thicket, exile of the Wingless Ones." Fallen angels. Literally—wo-o-oh ... *splat*. Enemies of Dimidia, they were stripped of their wings and banished with a curse to remind them where they stood with their god: the hearts that beat inside their chests were made of stone. Heartstones.

(SEE WHERE THIS IS GOING, READER NAME HERE _____? OF COURSE, YOU DO. YOU'RE NOT THE IDIOT ABOUT TO CURSE THE

On behalf of Dimidia, Caelix would visit the Wingless Ones on the seventh day of the seventh year to offer them terms of peace. When they refused (and they *always* refused), he was to leave them to their misery, as were his instructions. "And on the seventh day of the seventh year, Caelix went to the Wingless Ones, as he had done for endless multiples of seven. Only this time, he did not bring with him peace but a sword."

The scene on the bedsheet depicted a shadowy massacre. Caelix struck like a python, stabbing and slaying till the final Wingless One lay lifeless on the ground. He flew above the slaughter, wings spread wide in victory. "When he had killed them all, Caelix bottled the Curse of the Wingless Ones and returned to the Heart Eternal. He knelt at the altar, prayed, and poured the curse out like an offering.

"Darkness fell on the noonday sky, and thunder shook the ground"—if only she could've added her own sound effects! But Marek's shadow puppets did a marvelous impression of the asylum being swallowed by a cloud of shadows and storms—"and Caelix held the Heart to his chest, trembling, as it became a living stone."

The darkness lifted. The storm ceased. Caelix got off his knees and carried the Heartstone Eternal to his statue, placing it lovingly inside its chest. He prayed. *Oh,* how he prayed. He knelt at the statue's feet, eyes closed, breaking his back in reverence, and imagined the euphoria he would feel when the statue reached down and touched his shoulder. None of his actions were unjustifiable to Caelix when he envisioned the god he serviced day after day leaning down and whispering words, *real* words, into his ear, telling him the truth, offering to change him the way Dimidia changed all others who came to his home.

But the moment never came. The Heartstone was alive, but its body remained lifeless.

"Caelix looked at the statue with the Heartstone beating futilely inside its chest, and he saw himself, lifeless and empty with a heart beyond healing." This was it. This was the catalyst. A man desperate for change, encasing himself in stone. "And he tore the Heartstone out of its prison and broke it over Dimidia's altar."

She felt it. Really. Rose could feel Dimidia's heartbreak. She felt the love and the pity and the compassion and the loss, and it broke her own heart in two. "When the Heartstone broke, the power of creation was exposed, ripping the Old World apart at its seams. In its place stood two parallel worlds in a universe that was now a multiverse." Shaolandir and Saturnity—that's what they were called. Two duplicate worlds, one with magic, the other without. "And with this act, the presence of Dimidia was removed from all of creation."

*

It was a short ending. Snappy, like Blackout didn't want to dwell on it for too long and thus forgot to answer some important questions like A) Where did Dimidia go? B) What happened to the Heartstone after it was broken? C) Who ended up in Saturnity, a world without magic? And most of all D) WHAT HAPPENED TO CAELIX?!

(HERE'S A FUN FACT FOR YOU: LOOSE THREADS ARE THE BANE OF MY EXISTENCE. I'LL RIP STRINGS OFF MY CLOTHES LIKE THEY THREATENED TO STRANGLE MY MOTHER.)

Her audience, however, didn't share her dissatisfaction. Patients came up to congratulate her and to express their interest in Story Hour becoming a staple of Heartstone Asylum's monthly schedule. Many of them had their handmade umbrellas twirling at their sides. Rose said "Aw, shucks" so many times she'd be mumbling it in her sleep for weeks. *Time to get up, Rose.* Aw, shucks. *You left the lamp on, Rose.* Aw, shucks. *You slept-walked into the bathtub again, Rose.* Aw, shucks.

In the end, it was just her, Marek, Malachy, and Cade cleaning up while everyone else headed off to Magic Meditation. Yet *another* activity she couldn't participate in till they found a way to save Stormy.

(DON'T SAY "IF." DON'T EVEN THINK IT.)

They worked in companionable silence, putting away

chairs and sweeping up crumbs.

"You know," she said, refolding the blanket on the back of her storyteller's chair, "they had a name for Dimidia's home after the worlds split. Heartstone Asylum, they called it. Our asylum's namesake. Fitting, don'tcha think?"

"I suppose." Cade's tone betrayed nothing.

Rose grinned.

"So why that one, huh?" Malachy wheeled on her suddenly. "Why'd ya pick 'Legend of the Two Worlds' for your *grand debut*." His fingers fluttered mockingly. The look on his face said he was sucking on a lemon or some equally acidic thought.

Apparently, the silence hadn't been *entirely* companionable.

"I told myself it was a good idea." She shrugged. "Why? You didn't like it?"

"Oh, ya told it great. It's just ..."

Spit it out, Malachy. You're killing your enamel!

"... I think it's the stupidest story ever written, and it had no business making it into *Blackout's Tales*, that's all."

"*Malachy!*" Cade said sharply.

"Oh, well, if that's all," Marek laughed, and Rose pumped her fist in a victory dance.

"See *that*," she crowed, "*that* is the sign of a good story. You weren't just, 'Meh, it was okay. I could take it or leave it.' You got fired up inside. It made you *feel* something. So, c'mon!" She hopped on her storyteller's chair, landing in a

245

crisscross applesauce position. "Discuss. What didja hate about it?"

"An excellent question!" Marek abandoned his attempts to take down the bedsheet and sat studiously against her chair on the lip of the dais, arms hanging off his knees. They might've been posing for a family portrait.

Malachy took one look at their expectant faces and sighed, reluctantly pulling up a chair. "My problem is, the whole thing's Caelix's fault, right? No question. He's responsible for breaking the Heartstone, he's responsible for splitting the worlds in two—but. *But.* As much as this was his fault, there were at least four key points in the story where Dimidia could've salvaged the whole mess.

"For starters, this 'god of all creation' is supposedly all-powerful and all-knowing ... if that's the case, why would he appoint *Caelix* as the Heart's guardian angel if he knew Caelix was gonna destroy it in the end? And second, couldn't he have *stopped* Caelix from going to the Forgotten Thicket and taking the curse in the first place? If the Heart embodies the power of Dimidia, it does a really lousy job of it. But the real kicker is, why couldn't Dimidia just give Caelix what he wanted? The guy was bending over backwards for him! Couldn't this *kind* and *benevolent* god just bring the statue to life and put Caelix out of his misery?"

Rose took a breath to answer, but Malachy wasn't done. "I mean, here's a god who supposedly wants to 'be involved with his creation' so he sticks a Heart on the planet and claims that it will give everyone access to their Maker. Now you've got thousands of angels flocking to this asylum and believing that if they stay there, listening to the 'Heartbeat Eternal,' they'll be changed into their higher, better selves. They think they have a real relationship with this god, and they float away believing in goodness and trusting that this great Presence is around them, shaping and protecting their lives.

"But the one man—the *one man* who actually has access to the god, the one that spends the most time with him and who literally holds his Heart in his hands—this man calls Dimidia's bluff. He's the first one to ask Dimidia to have a real, active presence in his life with a real, face-to-face relationship, and what does the god do?" Malachy looked them dead in the eye. "*Nothing.*"

Well. Talk about a touchy subject. Was this the tirade her future self had in mind when she helped Rose pick "Legend of the Two Worlds" for Story Hour?

"You asked why Dimidia didn't just *give* Caelix what he wanted," she said slowly. "Maybe it wouldn't have been enough. Maybe a statue wasn't what he needed. Maybe— maybe giving in to what Caelix *thought* was best would've stopped Dimidia from giving him what was *actually* best. If you've read *Blackout's Tales* and believe the stories," *And I know you do*, was what she didn't add, "then you know Dimidia would never have settled for anything less. Guess Caelix just wasn't willing to wait for it." Rose rested her cheek on her fist. "Wish we knew what happened to him."

Malachy laughed. It wasn't a nice sound. "I'll tell ya one thing, sweetheart: he either spent the rest of his life trying to make up for his mistakes, or he ended it."

"Malachy," Cade said warningly.

"What? I'm just telling her the truth. Some things you don't come back from."

"Maybe," Rose mused. "But I don't think Dimidia gave up on Caelix. Whatever happened afterwards, I think the god found him again."

"Those rose-tinted glasses came built-in with the name, didn't they? You break someone's heart, they don't come back for you."

"You said there were four points where Dimidia could've changed the story," Marek cut in. "You only told us three."

"The fourth's easy. Why a heart? Why come down in something so breakable? He could've chosen a boulder or a temple. Instead, he went with a flimsy internal organ. Where's the logic in that?"

Marek got up, stretching like the answer was at the tip of his fingers. "Well, that's easy. It's symbolism. You can't have a relationship with a boulder. Dimidia chose to come as something vulnerable to show how much he cared." He clapped Malachy's shoulder as he passed. "I'm going to pack up the bedsheet, and then I think we're done in here."

"Wait!" Rose blurted. "Don't. I have one more story to tell."

ENTRY 25

AN ORDER OF FRIED DUCK SOUP, PLEASE, WITH A SIDE OF RETRIBUTION

W hat was she doing?
        What was she doing?
What was she doing?

"Once upon a time ..." Rose wavered. Dang that *Blackout's Tales* for tugging on her heartstrings!

("Is it anatomically possible for a heart to have strings?" you ask? All right, fussbudget, do you want to check the expiration date on my poetic license? Is that what you want?)

She hated strings! Hated them! "Once upon a time ... there was a little girl with a storm cloud that followed her wherever she went."

Marek's eyes were on her, but shadows melted from his wings, taking form on the bedsheet. A swirling silhouette appeared, small and girlish, twirling an umbrella over her shoulder. Her hair was as wild as the storm cloud hanging over her head.

"Angels would see it from a distance and feel sorry for the girl. But soon they watched her playful skip and the way she tilted her head back and laughed when the storm cloud poured rain on her face, and they realized: this cloud wasn't a curse. It was the girl's soul signia, a soul of storms.

"The cloud was always doing something—raining when she was bored, rumbling when she was hungry, glinting lightning off her teeth when she smiled. It was how the girl expressed herself. It spoke for her even when she didn't know what to say.

"Stormy had been with her since she was born. Her parents told her the story, how scared they were when her first sneeze spit out a gust of gray mist and how funny it was when the cloud settled over her head like an old granny wig." That, along with Marek's shadow impression of a bouncing, storm-haired baby, was *supposed* to make them smile. Tough crowd.

"Her father was a Knight Commander, and it was the girl's birthright to one day take his place. But even then, her parents were worried that her soul signia would cause problems. They worried when their toddler ran through the parlor, soaking the rugs with rain and sending the nursemaid skidding." Amber would pretend to disapprove, as older sisters should, but she loved Rose's indoor slip-and-slides. "They worried when knights and ambassadors had to carry umbrellas in the house and watch that their beards weren't singed by stray lightning bolts." The bedsheet was alive with the shadows of flying nursemaids and the smoking moustaches of high-topped diplomats. "They worried because their daughter had unstable magic, and angels were beginning to notice.

"Her parents could only avert suspicion for so long. Incidents with the girl's storm cloud were becoming more and more frequent, and if they couldn't find a way to control it, she would be taken to an asylum for unstable magic the moment she turned thirteen, and the Skylar legacy of Knight and Dame Commanders would end with her. Something had to be done."

Rose took a deep breath. Was she gonna do it? Was she really gonna tell them? "And then came *The* Incident.

"It all began when the king and queen of Aurialis visited Chunter Woods, Pandrum—humble, little Chunter Woods, Pandrum—to discuss the possibility of an alliance through marriage."

Not for Rose! Yuck. For *Amber*. The royal family was convinced that their son, Crown Prince Tristan, was perfect for her, and when they combined the proposal with a profitable trade agreement, could their parents really refuse?

Yes. Yes, they could. And here's why: kingdoms were outdated. Monarchies were caput. Nobody likes putting the power of an entire realm into the hands of one (usually corrupt) royal family. The realms on the Shell ixnayed the practice ages ago when the first Knight and Dame Commanders overthrew the government and set up Orders to take its place. Nowadays, Aurialis, the self-proclaimed head of Shaolandir's turtle-shaped land-masses, was the only true monarchy left.

And Rose's parents wanted her sister to marry into it. In Chunter Woods, Pandrum, where the word "princess" was the type of insult your own mother would smack you for using. And they thought Amber should become one. For a *trade agreement*.

"When the royal family arrived," Rose continued her story, "the girl's sister was sent outside with Prince Tristan for a walk around the duck pond while the grown-ups talked. The girl and her storm cloud tagged along from a distance, chaperoning with her father's most trusted knight."

Sir Ottis the Amiable, not yet promoted to full-time babysitter, still managed to make time for Rose and teaching her all he knew about being a knight. Her pseudo-uncle was a comfort—even his nonstop chatter, like insects buzzing on a warm summer day. Ottis was kind to her before The Incident, when she was an honored Dame Commander-to-be, and afterward, when ... you know. Gosh, she missed him.

"The knight and the girl sat under a tree by the pond, feeding stale bread to the duckies and watching the prince and her sister walk in circles. The knight began to talk—

his favorite pastime—and once he'd settled into a long, drawn-out story from his childhood, which the girl had heard at *least* eight times, she seized an opportunity. She propped a nearby log next to the rambling knight, spreading curly moss over the top to look like hair, and crept away."

How many times had Ottis fallen for the log-and-moss routine? It didn't hurt that his eyes glazed over when he was telling a story, and he rarely checked to see if his audience was awake and listening.

"The girl wasn't content watching the prince and her sister," Rose explained. "She wanted to hear what they were saying." She and Stormy had dodged behind a tree and waited for Amber and the prince to pass. Her sister carried herself with poise and grace, and the prince was no less regal. They had talked mildly of the weather and Pandrum cuisine until slowly their conversation shifted towards politics.

Rose narrated their conversation exactly as she remembered it. " 'Pandrum is very different from Aurialis,' Prince Tristan admitted as they walked. 'Being a prince isn't like being the daughter of a Knight Commander.' 'How so?' the girl's sister asked. 'In Pandrum, you live with your subjects,' he said. 'Your lives mix together. In a kingdom, a prince must live *above* his subjects. How else will they know whom to follow?' He stopped her gently, brushing a lock of hair behind her ear. 'Do you understand what I mean?' 'No. I don't think I do,' the girl's sister replied, pushing him politely away.' "

For the first time in her story, Rose's throat clogged, but Marek's shadow puppets waited for no one. It was like he knew what happened next, like he could read her mind. "They stood by the pond, staring at each other, the ducks quacking pleasantly in the background. And the prince leaned forward and said, 'It means that because there are *seven* rulers of Pandrum and only *one* ruler of Aurialis, you are one-*seventh* the worth of a real princess. My parents have no right marrying me to you unless they give me six more just like you.' He kneed her in the stomach, and she doubled over. 'Now bow down before I make you bow so low you'll never get off the ground again.' "

In the scene on the bedsheet, a storm of thunder, lightning, and sisterly fury burst from the cover of the tree. Marek, no doubt recalling his own experience with her headbutts, winced as Rose's shadow-self pummeled the prince in the stomach. He fell backwards into the pond. Like a set of fangs, Stormy's lightning split the water, a current of electricity rippling across the top. "And ... the duckies weren't quacking anymore."

Aren't bad memories supposed to be a blur? She remembered everything with astonishing clarity. The *smell* ... fried duck soup mixed with something far more pungent. The screams—first Amber's, then hers, then Ottis's, all in surprisingly similar pitches. Tristan's body floating to the surface, his dark skin a mosaic of purple bruises and blistering burns that looked like lightning trees. The strength Rose didn't know she had to pull him out of the water.

"The prince lived," she said quickly. "He was scarred for life and unfit for the crown, but he survived. The king and queen were furious, of course. But when they saw the prince's disfigurement, it was the girl they couldn't stand to look at. Talk of The Incident spread faster than halo pox, and her father knew the time had come for drastic measures. Her storm cloud had to be stopped no matter what the cost."

Deep inside her, Stormy squirmed with discomfort. It didn't like this next part. Well, neither did she, but they'd already come this far. No turning back now. "One day, the girl's father told her they were going for a carriage ride. It took three days before they arrived in the neighborhood of nowhere at all. He led her to the mouth of a cave. There was a rope in his hands. Cupping her face, the rope scratching her cheeks, he said, 'I'm doing this for your own good.' And he knocked her unconscious."

Seeing the shadow-man on the bedsheet strike a violent blow to the shadow-girl should've stirred the familiar panic, but it was better this way, telling the story like a chapter from *Blackout's Tales*. Her audience was scooting on the edge of their seats, but she was soaring on wings of detachment.

"When the girl woke up, she was on the floor of the cave, her arms and legs tied up with the rope. Her father was there, talking with a witch doctor who looked more like a caveman. Only instead of a club, he carried a very big scythe. He claimed it was stolen from the Angel of Death himself because it had the power to separate body from soul."

Rose's pulse hammered at her throat. She was honed in on the bedsheet where Marek's shadow puppets acted out her words in perfect unison. His intuition was *insane*. "They began with a small cut on her foot. She started thrashing, and they held her down, the blade digging deeper, but it wasn't cutting her skin. It was cutting *beyond* her skin. All of a sudden, the girl saw her body on the table, but she wasn't in it anymore."

That out-of-body experience wasn't unlike the one she was having right now. Her little shadow-self on the bedsheet was living through the memory of her nightmare, but Rose was just a storyteller sitting in a storyteller's chair, relaying relevant details. The effect was strangely liberating.

She told them all about Dad and the witch doctor's dilemma, how they'd taken the soul out of the girl's body, but they didn't know how to stop it from producing magic. Then there was the time constraint. The longer her spirit lingered outside her corpse, the harder it would be to reconnect the two. In a last-ditch resort, the witch doctor managed to grab her soul like a pair of shoelaces and knotted her up good. Circulation was cut off and *bam*—no more soul magic. No more soul signia. No more Stormy.

"And that was that," Rose said. "Or so they thought." Her parlor trick came as a *shock*—

(*See what I did there?*)

—but after all his efforts, Dad refused to believe that the storm cloud living inside her would be an issue. It was hidden, wasn't it? Out of sight, out of mind. "He'd solved the problem of her unstable magic. He'd protected his legacy, and now nothing could stop the girl from being knighted his official successor on her thirteenth birthday. Nothing except maybe asylum transportation crashing the party. But after everything her father had done to keep her out of an asylum ... really, what were the chances of that?"

The shadow puppets on the bedsheet took a bow and dispersed. The story was over. There was no applause. Rose finally peeled her eyes off the sheet and faced her audience.

The library was quiet.

"I just thought you should know," she said. "What Stormy's capable of. What *I'm* capable of. And why"—she swallowed hard—"why we might not be able to save my storm cloud. Unless you can steal a scythe from the Angel of Death, the knots in my soul are staying put. I won't have magic anymore. I know that's gonna botch up your plans for bringing me here, but—"

"Thunder, stop." Marek's wings were steaming shadows. "I know you think we have some grand scheme going on behind the scenes, but we didn't bring you here *for* something. We brought you here for *you*. You haven't botched up our plans because our plans were to have you here with us. To be part of our team, magic or not."

"That is absolutely right," Cade agreed fervently. "Isn't it, Malachy?"

They looked expectantly at him.

"Yeah," Malachy said. "Right."

ENTRY 26

THE NEAR FUTURE

I t was time.

Rose sat at her dresser, quill in hand, staring at a page with three words on it:

 *Dear Future Me,*

She couldn't put this off any longer. Tomorrow was Moonsfrost Eve. Last day of the year. Last day for her future's prediction about the asylum being in danger to come true. It was imperative, yes, *imperative*—

(SUCH AN IMPORTANT-SOUNDING WORD, ISN'T IT? IMPORTANT, LIKE EATING FRUIT. IT'S IMPERATIVE YOU EAT YOUR PEARS.)

—that she contact her older self and see what she was

willing to share about the coming threat and how to prepare for it.

Words for her letter rested on the tip of her tongue. She pinched said tongue with her fingers and tugged. "Why won' 'oo 'ome off?"

Maybe company would help. Rose pulled out Gormonger's haunted mirror. His side was frosted solid. Either someone was sulking ... or up to something.

She fogged her side of the glass and wrote, *Hey! Everything okay in there?* Waited a moment. *Helloooo?*

Ghostly paws scraped away the frost, and Gormonger's ethereal snout appeared, flecked with its usual bloodstains. He looked bored.

Where were you a second ago? she asked.

The ghost Warg huffed at her suspicion. His icy breath clouded the mirror, and he scribbled with a claw what could be read backwards: *I'm trapped in a mirror. Where do you THINK, Bedhead?*

His favorite nickname for her. *Well, why was the glass frosted so thick? I couldn't see you.*

Can't I have a little privacy? Or is that not part of your THERAPY program? Besides, our session isn't for another hour. Didn't know you'd want to chat. He wiped his side of the conversation away with his tail and cocked his head impatiently for her reply.

I need your opinion on something. Rose tapped the glass absently. *Is there any reason you can think of that something bad would happen to the asylum tomorrow? It's Moonsfrost Eve, 1525 A.S.*

That's the hundredth anniversary of the Battle of the Petrified Forest where we all DIED. Gormonger pointed out. *ONE HUNDRED YEARS. DEAD.*

Was she supposed to wish him a happy deathday or offer condolences?

(GHOST ETIQUETTE IS A DYING COURTESY.)

Are the ghosts planning on celebrating this, um, special occasion any particular way?

He snorted snowflakes. *How should I know? They locked me up in a COTTAGE. I didn't exactly get an INVITATION.*

"Maybe that's what I should ask about in my letter, then," Rose mused out loud.

Who are you writing to? Gormonger loosed a fang-toothed grin at her surprise. *I'm getting GOOD at reading LIPS.*

Good to know. *I'm writing to someone who thinks the asylum might be in danger. I need to ask the right questions, but all the words are stuck on the tip of my tongue.* She showed him her tongue. *See?*

His luminescent fur flickered slyly. *This "SOMEONE." They wouldn't happen to be your pen pally SELF from the FUTURE, would they?*

Rose sucked her tongue in with a *lurp*. "How'd you know about that?"

His own tongue lolled smugly. *Like I said, I'm getting GOOD at reading LIPS. You've been putting this letter off forever. What's the problem? Almost two months at an asylum and you have NOTHING to write about?*

Nothing to write about? She could fill a book!

(*Perhaps one of the exact dimensions you're holding.*)

No, that's not it. It's the whole "writing to the future" thing. It scares me a little. What if I don't like what's gonna happen? She wiped the mirror with her sleeve and went on. *I always thought I was good at talking to myself, but now I don't know what to say. I have to get this letter right, or I won't be prepared to help the asylum from what's coming.*

Gormonger started a reply, paused, licked it away, and started again. *Look, your future already knows EVERY- THING. Future Bedhead is trying to HELP you. So, don't worry so much about getting the WORDS right. Just ramble about nothing, and it'll mean something.* He considered this profound statement and nodded, pleased with himself.

Rose smiled. *Like me and Marek do with you?*

The ghost Warg puffed indignantly. *Absolutely NOT! This is PUPNAP! Unlawful IMPRISONMENT! And when I get out of here, I won't miss you ONE BIT!* He made a show of swiping the message away with his paw. *But we're still on for tonight, right?* he added.

She gave the mirror an extra-long kiss. "Thanks, Gor." And picked up her quill.

Rose threw open the hatch of her bedroom floor and nearly collided with Shadow Boy's head. He'd managed to climb the attic's rope ladder carrying two plates of cheese on toast and a bowl of dried fruit. The strain on his face suggested he might've regretted this decision.

"Snacks!" Marek declared unnecessarily, and the dishes wobbled.

"Cheesy, gooey heaven, thank you!" Rose snagged a bite of toast and placed it back into Marek's precarious care. "Now, let's go to your room."

The plates rattled in protest. "But you said we were doing Gor's session in *your* room today. Do you know how hard it is to balance two plates and a bowl while climbing a rope ladder one-handed?"

"Yes, it's very impressive. And now we're going to your room."

"But—"

"I wrote back," Rose said. That shut him up. "And I thought we should give my room a little privacy in case *someone* wants to answer."

Marek sighed, adjusting his grip on the dishware. "My room it is."

*

Gormonger wasn't exactly in a sharing mood.

HOW do you expect me to want to talk about my first Warg-riding competition AT A TIME LIKE THIS?! Future Bedhead could be UPSTAIRS right now writing a letter and— wait, was that a twitch? Did you hear something, and you're not telling me? SPILL!

"This is going nowhere," Rose groaned, banging her head against Marek's bedpost.

It takes time to write a letter, even for a time traveler, Marek wrote back patiently. *Time we're trying to pass by talking about your first Warg-riding competition. We have to wait one way or another. Can't we at least make it interesting?*

Gormonger bared his teeth in a soundless growl. *Fine. My first Warg-riding tournament was nice. There was music and dancing and screams by the BUCKETLOAD. I've never eaten better than at a Warg-riding tournament. Not even during the War.*

Marek caught Rose's eye. Gormonger had never mentioned the War before.

When the competition started, he continued, *I saw five angels get BUCKED to the HEAVENS. The betting was hot in the Wargs' favor. And then along came the Sinner, and all bets were off. The angels knew they'd won.*

"What?" Rose gestured for the hand mirror, and Marek gave it to her. *You knew the Sinner before the War?*

'Course I did. He was the GREATEST Warg rider of all time. Rode me once or twice. Never did beat him, but no shame in that. No one could beat the SINNER. Gormonger brushed his side clean. Rose readied a breath to write her reply, but

the ghost Warg clouded the glass for another message. *The Sinner loved Warg-riding tournaments as much as WE did. That's why we made him our leader when we tried to have Warg-riding tournaments reinstated after your kind BANNED them. Then the War started, but we STILL put our FAITH in him. We were STARVING, and he swore he'd win the War and put Wargs in charge so that we'd never go hungry again. Our mistake was thinking he'd win for anyone but HIMSELF.*

Wait. Was he *actually* opening up to them? Rose fogged the mirror so fast she saw spots. *What do you mean?*

I mean, it's UNFAIR! Gormonger exploded. Spectral saliva dripped from his fangs, and his fur blazed ivory fire. *We chose the Sinner for the same reason the angels chose their SAINT. He had the smarts, the drive, and no matter how much he paraded around like he owned the place, he NEVER underestimated ANYONE. Especially the Saint.* When the mirror ran out of room, Gormonger washed it clean with his tongue and kept going. *They had this weird respect for each other. It's like they ENJOYED fighting. They got their KICKS from testing each other's WITS. That's all they were ever in it for: THEMSELVES.*

Now they were getting somewhere! *What makes you say—*

Because they ABANDONED US! The mirror squeaked with Gormonger's aggressive scribbles. Words overlapped, and Rose wiped her side of the conversation away to read his impatient response. *We came BACK! We DIED following their orders, and we came BACK to finish them. We missed our*

window into ETERNITY for them, and what did they do?
They found PEACE! They MOVED ON! Our own LEADERS!
He broke off in a noiseless howl.

Marek scratched his nose meaningfully. Rose rubbed
hers in agreement. They were on the verge of what those
in the business would call ... a *breakthrough*.

And now we're STUCK here because—wait, what was
that? Was that a signal? Was there a thump upstairs? Do you
two KNOW something you're not TELLING ME?!

We'll let you know if we hear anything. Promise. Rose
drew a smiley-face for reassurance. It didn't help.

Enough sharing. I'm bored. Want to play tic-tac-toe? He
looked past them around Marek's room. *Hey, where's that*
dumb pup with the goggles? Isn't he usually with you?

"Beta!" Rose exclaimed. "I forgot him upstairs! He's
sleeping under my bed."

Well, go GET him then! Gormonger wasn't kidding
about the lip-reading. *If you do, maybe it'll jog some*
DRAMATIC memory from my puphood I can share.

"You just want an excuse for us to check and see if
Future Me left a letter."

And you don't? he countered.

Excellent point. "Fine. We'll go get Beta."

Yes, yes, YES! Gormonger did a happy dance in the
mirror. He was still chasing his tail in circles when Marek
tucked him under his flannel shirt and crept for the door.

Up in her bedroom, Beta was lying in the middle of

the floor, paws up and tongue out, panting like he'd had the belly rub of a lifetime.

Just like last time.

Marek glanced at Rose.

Rose glanced at Marek.

He made a beeline for the mobile hanging above her bed, and she bulleted for the dresser. "Here!" Marek stopped the spinning mobile on a brand-new carving: four hands piled one on top of the other in a show of team spirit.

"And here!" Rose brandished the letter exultantly.

 *Dear Little Me,*

Thank you for writing back! I remember how unsure I was about writing to me, but I'm glad you did. The future isn't as scary as it seems once you're living it. Trust yourself on this.

Now, in your letter, you asked a good question. "Does the ghosts' one-hundredth deathday have anything to do with why the asylum will be in danger?" I have a good answer. But why settle for good? Isn't there better? Isn't there best?

Here's what I suggest. You asked me a good question. I'm gonna answer that question with a better question. Then you can answer that question with the best question of all, and when you find the answer, all your other questions will be tucked in bed and put to rest. Sound comfy?

You read "Legend of the Two Worlds" for Story Hour (excellent choice, by the way). My question for you is, how did Caelix bottle the Curse of the Wingless Ones?

You'll find the answer in the Topsy-Turvy Library. 10:30. Tonight.

Prepare for any scenario.

Love,

Your Future Me

ENTRY 27

FOUR ARE BETTER THAN TWO

P repare for any scenario.

Rose rummaged around the floor of her wardrobe for her bag of ghost warding supplies. Courtesy of their frequent nighttime visits to Silas, it was distressingly light. "Contingency plan!" She switched her rummaging to under the bed and stuffed the bag full of iron-and silver-laced jewelry from Beta's nest of pilfered treasure.

The pup looked at her reproachfully from under his goggles.

She took Amber's key pendant from its place of honor around her neck and looped it around Beta's as collateral. "You keep this safe for me till we get back, okay?" Rose kissed his nose and jumped to her feet. "Cloaks! We need cloaks." She tore savagely through her wardrobe. "Where *is* it? It should be right at the back! Marek, I can't find my cloak."

"We'll look for it later. Don't worry, I'll get you sorted." Marek opened her bedroom window, which the asylum had yet to lock since their first escapade with the empty graves. "Follow me."

Shadow Boy's version of "getting sorted" involved lending her his own cloak. All thirty-six extra inches of it. Rose stood there, drowning in pools of fabric with too-big wing holes letting in a nasty draft, and all he could say between muffles of laughter was, "All right there, short stuff?"

She folded her swaddled arms. "I can't *walk*."

Marek pulled her arms apart and folded the sleeves back five times each. "I have a belt for that." He reached into the back of his closet and withdrew a fitted black cloak with rich white lining, a wide band and buckle, and silver bracelets of names embedded in the sleeves.

His Corner Cloak.

He took the band, belted it around her middle, and tucked the cloak's too-long edges into her waist. "Better?"

Rose wiggled a now visible foot. "Better. But what are you gonna wear?"

"Like you said." Marek slipped the Corner Cloak from its hanger and folded it over his arm. "Prepare for any scenario."

*

Even with Marek invisible to all but the few whose names were stitched into his sleeves, why risk walking through hallways at a time when half the asylum was still awake? And should they reach the library unseen, who would want to make an entrance by *walking through the front door?* How pedestrian! How mundane.

Rose warmed herself with these thoughts as she and Marek stood in a foot of snow, peeking through the Topsy-Turvy Library's chapel window. The interior was dimly lit and without a hint of movement. "See anything?"

"Nope. You?"

"Nuh-uh."

Their breath fogged the glass.

"It's kind of a random question, isn't it?" she said. "'How did Caelix bottle the Curse of the Wingless Ones.' The legend doesn't say. It just says Caelix bottled it—it never says *how*. Where are we gonna find the answer in the library?" In a book other than *Blackout's Tales*?

"Let's say we find out." Marek pushed on a compartment of the expansive window. As always, the asylum was all too gracious about opening entries that were otherwise locked. He patted the glass appreciatively and helped Rose inside.

The upswing in temperature thawed her cheeks but not her nerves. What had her Future Me meant by prepare for any scenario? What terrible thing could be waiting for them here? She stayed by the window, analyzing the empty space. A few hours ago, they'd been putting the room back together after Story Hour. What had changed since then? The tables and chairs were in their natural positions. The lamps were turned low. And the focus of the room, her magnificent storyteller's chair exulted on the dais ...

The chair was facing the wrong way.

It should've been facing inwards, towards an audience, not outwards, towards the window. Marek broke away to patrol the outer rim of the library, and Rose moved to the middle of the room. She looked up. The bookcases were as they should be, hanging like bats from the floor-which-was-the-ceiling. The obstacle course spanned the entire upper hemisphere: ropes and chain rings, zip lines, and climbing nets connecting bookshelf island to bookshelf island.

Something flashed at the corner of her eye. Rose spotted a rope swaying in what could be a gentle breeze—if they'd left the window open, that is.

Huh. Now there's a theory to test. She chose a section of the rock-climbing wall on the far side of the room and focused directly on it. Not left, not right. Straight ahead.

Blurry shapes loomed at the corner of her vision.

"Mar-ek," Rose sang softly. "There's someone else he-re." She switched to her regular voice. "And I *think* they're wearing Corner Cloa—"

A pair of figures dropped from the ceiling, flinging their magical cloaks aside and landing in two impressive crouches. Rose squeaked, hopping back a step. Wings splayed, the figures straightened—

"A-*ha!*" Aiden cried, pointing an incriminating finger at Rose's face.

Sephone's frown lines were a connect-the-dots scowl of surprise, disbelief, and accusation. "*You,*" she breathed.

There's only one appropriate response to such a statement. "*Me,*" said Rose.

"You?" Sephone repeated. "*You're* the one behind all this? You gave us the ghost-hunting book? You put salt in our packs? You left the spades outside the window? *New Girl?*" She was breathing hard, and her silky russet complexion took on a darker, more rugged texture. Greenish veins pulsed beneath her strange, rough skin, popping through with her anger. Forget *veins*—they looked like *vines.*

"Deep breath, Seph." Aiden put a hand on her shoulder. Sephone smacked it away, and he yipped, sucking what seemed to be splinters from his skin. Hitting him had a calming effect on her. The vines retreated; her complexion softened, becoming smooth.

"Why?" Sephone asked bluntly. "Why were you helping us? And wipe that silly grin off your face."

Rose couldn't help herself. All those weeks helping her heroic beneficiaries behind the scenes, watching them bicker and work in sync, wanting to get to know them ... this was like meeting them face-to-face for the very first time. "I helped you because you needed help. We're both trying to solve the same mystery. The ghosts and the empty graves."

"You should have come right out and told us. Why the theatrics? I get enough of that from him!" Sephone jabbed Aiden with her thumb. "And if you're so *theatrical*, why the lousy entrance? I was expecting something a little more glamorous than *climbing through a window*."

"Better than the front door. And which would you have listened to? The new girl offering her expertise on ghost hunting or a mysterious benefactress leaving clues around every corner?"

Sephone's feathers ruffled irritably.

"Hence, your mysterious benefac—" Rose sneezed mid-bow "—tress. Is it dusty in here, or is it just me?"

"Just you. And you did this all by yourself?"

"Well ..." Sephone and Aiden couldn't see Marek skulking behind them, wearing his Corner Cloak. They couldn't hear him lumbering closer, a smile expanding under his hood. "Maybe not *all* by myself."

"BOO!" Marek boomed, ripping off his cloak.

Scaring the socks off of someone in an asylum for unstable magic is a gusty play. Wings flaring, Aiden let out a snarl too deep for his voice, and Rose swore his fingernails lengthened. Sephone's vines were back, lashing from her wrists at their surprise attacker, but Marek only laughed, swatting them away with his shadows.

"*Marek!*" Sephone was murderous. "I should've known you'd be in on this. How much have you told her? Oh, I am *so* telling Ragnar. But not until we get some answers." She folded her arms, thin green vines knotting them together. "How did Caelix bottle the Curse of the Wingless Ones?"

Rose blinked. "What?"

Sephone closed her eyes as if they were the drainpipes of her patience. "I *said*, how did Caelix bottle the Curse of the Wingless Ones? The question! What's the answer?"

"You're s'posta tell me!"

She flung her arms apart, the vines snapping like harp strings. "You wrote the note! You asked us how Caelix bottled the Curse of the Wingless Ones and told us to meet you here at ten-thirty for the answer!"

Rose found a use for her goldfish impersonation.

(OPPORTUNITIES DON'T COME AS OFTEN AS YOU'D THINK. JUST MOMENTS LIKE THESE AND AT PUBS WITH FISH TANKS.)

"I didn't write that note. I did everything else, Sephone, *everything*, but that one—that wasn't me."

"Actually," said a voice from the storyteller's chair, "that isn't *technically* true."

The chair that was facing the wrong way. Someone was sitting in it. Their legs draped over the armrest. "You know, sitting on this chair, I can't help feeling I'm sitting on top of something *very* important." A giggle. "That's gonna be funny in a bit." Slowly, a head of curls peered over the back. "How's that for an entrance, Seph?"

It was a girl, eighteen or nineteen, just a few years shy of entering that indeterminable age between twenty-five and a hundred and fifty. Heavy lids graced her with a sleepy countenance, but her gray eyes were laughing and alive with secrets. Wild black curls tickled her chubby— sorry, *cherubic*—cheeks, completing the picture of playful innocence.

Rose recognized the disguise. It was the look of an accomplished mischief-maker.

It was *her* disguise.

In fact, she might go so far as to say ... as to say it was ... "Who are you?"

"*What* are you?" Sephone added incredulously.

"*How* are you?" Aiden gulped.

Marek was silent.

" 'Who are you?' " the girl reiterated, propping her chin musingly on the back of the armchair. "That's a great question to ask yourself. Very introspective." She swept to her feet and stepped down from the dais. In one hand was an ancient tome. In the other, a familiar umbrella. "Who do you think you are?"

Rose held her gaze for a long time. It was like looking in a mirror. A six-years-older mirror. When she smiled, they smiled as one. "I'm you."

The girl nodded, pleased with her deduction, and addressed Sephone's question next. " '*What* are you?' I'm a time traveler. A Paradox, to be specific. It's my occupation." She grinned at Rose. "We get to bounce around time helping ourselves solve mysteries, prevent disasters, fight evil, and write really, *really* funny books. I'll tell you all about it later. Or earlier. I did that bit a few years ago."

Rose studied her older self. Paradox. Rose. Rosadox?

Rosadox winked. "It's a good name. But to answer your last question, '*How* are you?' On a pretty tight schedule, actually. I've got this timed to the second, and I know it works out perfect—obviously—but we should really get started. How did Caelix bottle the Curse of the Wingless Ones? I promised answers, and I deliver." She thumped her book of considerable and yellowing pages onto a nearby table. "*Cooking Up a Scare: The Necromancer's Guide to Undead Recipes.* They take their secrets to the grave." Her eyebrows waggled.

"So, I marked a few pages for you." She thumbed through the ghoulicious cookbook. Several pages fluttered to the floor, and she stuffed them back in. "Those could be important. Um, so check the sections on curses and bodily apparitions, and read them with the end of 'Legend of the Two Worlds.' You'll see how Caelix bottled the curse. It might answer a few other questions, too. And careful while you read 'cause this thing is falling to pieces. It's not even the original! You wouldn't think so looking at it, but it's actually the third edition. Maybe even the one Caelix himself used. But see, that's the thing about not having the original. Some things—notes, sentences, *important* things—get lost in transcript. Later editions might not have them." Rosadox's eyeballs bounced meaningfully from Sephone to Aiden to Marek. "Know what I'm saying?"

"What?" Rose tugged on Marek's sleeve. "What am I saying?"

He cleared his throat, speaking for the first time in minutes. "She's saying that the original of a book might have something that later editions are missing. Like a cook's notes."

"*Or an anthologist's commentary.*" Sephone linked gazes with Marek. They didn't break the connection.

"What? What am I missing here?" Rose looked to her future self for backup, but she just blinked innocently, her sleepy, gray eyes laughing louder. Great. Rose was being left out by *herself*. That wasn't even *fair*.

"Thanks for the information. We'll take it from here." Sephone made a decisive grab for the undead recipe book, and Rosadox clamped down on her wrist.

Rose was shocked—shocked that Sephone wasn't shocked.

(*ELECTRICALLY SPEAKING.*)

Full skin-on-skin contact! And her future self didn't bat an eye.

"Ah-bah-bah," Rosadox chided, holding Sephone in place. "Little Me, what's the newest carving on our mobile?"

"Four hands. One on top of the other," Rose said.

"Exactly. Team spirit!" Rosadox patted Sephone's wrist, trying to pry the book from her grasp. "The four of you are gonna work together on this."

Sephone yanked back. "That's not how this works."

Rosadox tugged, and pages fell like brittle autumn leaves. "Says who?"

"Says the preventing disasters and fighting evil you were talking about. Aiden and I will handle it, okay? That's our job," Sephone grunted. "No offense or anything, but you're still New Girl. You're part of Malachy's team. The B-Team. The backup. Let the heroes do the hard work."

Rose and her older self sneezed at precisely the same moment, and Sephone snatched the book free, toting it in success.

"Dirty play," Rosadox sniffed, wiping her nose on her sleeve. She hooked her umbrella on the back of a chair and leaped for the book. Sephone held her hostage higher.

"Seph!" Rosadox hopped indignantly, flapping her wings.

(DOES NO ONE PINCH ME ON BIRTHDAYS ANYMORE? I COULD SURE USE THOSE INCHES!)

"Look at me, Seph! Hey, look at me." She cupped Sephone's face with both hands. There was something in the gesture, familiarity and affection, and Sephone's normally squinty eyes went wide. The book lowered.

"Listen to me," Rosadox spoke gently. "I don't care who told you that you were destined for greatness or that the fate of the world is in your hands. Want me to let you in on a li'l secret?" She leaned closer. "You are not the Chosen One. You are Persephone Darrow, and you are a valuable member of a team who loves you for so much more than your strengths. The weight of the world does *not* rest on your shoulders, and whoever put it there was dead wrong. Chosen One, Schmozen One. We do this together. Got it?"

Sephone's bottom lip wobbled once, and her scowl hardened, cementing it in place. She nodded imperceptibly.

"Remember that tomorrow." Rosadox glanced in Rose's direction.

Dare she ask ... "Why?"

" 'Cause she's gonna do something very stupid." She looked directly at Rose. "And you're gonna help her." Releasing Sephone, she murmured, "Give us a sec?" Sephone nodded again, mutely, and dragged Aiden away by his sleeve.

Rose moved closer to Marek, shadowed in the concave of his wing. Feathers brushed her arm. Rosadox rocked on her heels, beaming at them.

Marek's face was frozen, a sculpted look of concentration he'd been wearing since her future self's debut. He regarded her closely, detailing her every move like she was an exotic deep-sea fish he'd caught and plopped in a fishbowl for observation.

Rosadox was silent, rocking, and beaming. And then, "Hey, Shadow Boy," and Marek's expression thawed to a smile.

"He's worried about you," she explained to Rose. "Wants to make sure we turn out okay." She stepped up to him, a pebble staring up at a mountain. "You're doing an amazing job with me, Marek. You're the best guardian angel a girl could ask for. The maple syrup to my pancakes. My rock." Rosadox stood on tiptoe and pulled on his shoulders. He tilted his head obligingly, and she scrunched her nose, wiggling it against his. "Usually, the one in my shoe," she added.

There were three things Rose was painfully aware of in that moment. One: she was talking to a Paradox of herself from six years in the future. Two: by nineteen, skin-to-skin contact would be second nature to her. And three: her future self did not have a storm cloud hovering overhead.

Rosadox read her mind. Or remembered what she'd been thinking in Rose's shoes. Either way. "Chin up, buttercup," she said, flicking her chin. "How's the nose?"

Rose rubbed it. "Itchy."

"Sephone and Aiden'll do that to you. It's the hero-complex. We've got a bit of an allergy to it. Take this." She offered a hanky with their initials on it. "You're gonna need it."

Rose took the handkerchief between pinched fingers and held it up to eye level. She fluttered it like a little ghost. Was this germy? Can you *get* germs from your future self?

"Of course not. You can sneeze on me all you'd like." Rosadox unhooked her umbrella from the back of the chair. "And you! Why aren't you carrying one of these, Little Me? What happened to preparing for any scenario?"

Stormy, frail and precious, inflated hopefully inside Rose's chest. "But I thought ..."

"Prepare for any scenario!" Rosadox insisted, tapping Rose's nose with the tip of the umbrella. "Remember that." She glanced over at Sephone and Aiden. "Which reminds me, you need to remember *all* of this. 'Cause they're not gonna remember any of it.

"Two of us talking to ourselves, interacting with ourselves—it's unnatural. A wound in Time. So, Time cauterizes the wound by making everyone else forget what they've seen. Don't worry, they assimilate quickly. Sephone and Aiden will take everything they learned from me, and their memories will file it away as fact. Just don't ask them how they know what they know. Their brains are telling them not to think about it, so they'll only get frustrated. We call these little episodes ... well, what would *you* call them?" she asked Rose. "You're the one who comes up with the name."

"Oh! Uh, how about Stolen Moments?"

"Stolen Moments it is! And only you remember them."

That was plural. She was looking at both of them.

"Marek, too?" Rose clarified.

"Of course, Marek, too! That's how we work." Rosadox twisted something on her wrist. It looked kinda like a tattered old shoelace, but the way she was smiling at it, it could've been a bracelet of jewels. "We're a couple of gumshoes with our laces tied together. Where one goes, the other's gonna follow. I'll explain it more later."

"Or earlier."

"Now you're getting it!" Rosadox turned to Marek. "So, Ragnar's out for about twenty minutes. You know what you have to do?"

He nodded. "Go to his office, take a peek, get out."

Rose was more than out of the loop. She was in another geometrical shape altogether. "Wait, Ragnar's office? What are we going there for?"

"Something you'll like," he promised.

"*Love*," Rosadox corrected.

"We're going to read a chapter out of the original *Blackout's Tales*."

If someone were to peek their head inside the Remembrance Hall at eleven o'clock that night, they would have seen a young asylum patient walking alone, chattering animatedly to herself under her breath. This someone would probably have shrugged and carried on their way, leaving Rose and the three angels wearing Corner Cloaks undisturbed.

They reached the door of Ragnar's office. Marek, Sephone, and Aiden pulled off their Corner Cloaks and switched them to the white, visible side.

"I'll pick the lock," Sephone said, and a pair of needle-sharp twigs appeared in her hands.

"That won't be necessary." Marek looked up and gave the ceiling his most endearing smile. "Please and thank you?"

There was a click, and the office door swung open.

"How'd you do that?" Aiden gaped.

Marek tapped his nose and slipped into the office.

As promised, the room was empty. Two windows let in shafts of moonlight. The cherry wood desk and high back chair were ominous shapes in the semi-dark, and the crisscrossed machetes hung quietly in their crests on the walls. Best not to set off the singing, if they could help it.

Except for the sprawling world map behind the desk, the office was tastefully bare. Not even a bookshelf. Where would Ragnar keep a precious—

(PRICELESS, SOMETHING *I* WOULD PLUCK AN EYEBALL FOR)

—collector's item like the original *Blackout's Tales*?

It *better* not be stuffed under a loose floorboard.

Rose stood aside, waiting for her companions to reveal its location. They tiptoed to the door at the far left of the room, and this time it opened without Marek breathing a word. She stroked the doorframe gratefully with her wing as she passed inside.

The door led to Ragnar's living quarters, if they could be called that. There was hardly more than a narrow, four-poster bed draped with burgundy curtains and a small kitchenette with a table for two wedged in the corner. A bowl of scalplums sat in the middle. So, this was where Ragnar moved after the patient destroyed his cottage in the forest. Even with an angry Gormonger haunting it, the cottage was a king's palace compared to *this*.

But there was a remnant of former glory. At the side of the bed was an elegant floor mirror, and at the foot, a resplendent white pedestal. On it, encased in glass, a gargantuan book lay open.

Rose approached it reverently. "It's ... it's ..." Scribbled side notes—

(NOT THAT THERE'S *ANYTHING* WRONG WITH SIDE NOTES.)

—were stuffed between lines and scrawled across the bottom of the pages. Some at the top, too. An ungainly arrow crossed the border, pointing to the continued thought, and careless ink drops blotted out several words. There were doodles in the margins. "Kinda sloppy."

Sephone scoffed. "That's one word for it. Blackout ruined his own book. I mean, who puts *doodles* in the margins?"

"I like them," Marek said. He lifted the glass case off the book and set it carefully on the floor. "Though I would prefer full-page illustrations."

"No way. Then everyone would skip ahead to look at the pictures, and what if they saw something that spoiled the story? Dumb idea."

Rose tuned them out. It was just her and the book now. Her and the *original Blackout's Tales*. Sparks of lightning danced on her tongue. She reached for it—were there violins playing in the background? There should be violins playing in the background.

Fingers brushed the ancient pages—

Rose retracted her hand abruptly. Something had flickered in the corner of her vision. There! By the mirror.

No one was wearing their Corner Cloaks.

Better hurry this up before something *else* hurried it for them. "Sephone, do you have the undead cookbook? She said to read the end of the legend with the pages she marked."

The looks on Sephone and Aiden's faces suggested a frying pan had mistaken their heads for eggs. Aiden shook his, dazed. "Who said?"

"Oh." Oops. Forgot about the memory thing. "Uh, me."

"You talk about yourself as a third party?"

(*Now that doesn't sound like me at all, does it, Reader Name Here _____?*)

"Mostly in writing."

"Whatever." Sephone brushed the conversation away impatiently. "Find 'Legend of the Two Worlds,' and I'll read the pages from the cookbook of death. Why'd you mark them with envelopes, anyway?"

Envelopes? Ah. Clever, Rosadox. *Very* clever. "Those are her next clues!"

Aiden shook his head again, a dog with water stuck in his ears. "Whose clues?"

"Me again."

"You left clues for yourself?"

"I'm complicated like that."

"Can we *shut up* about the clues?" Sephone snapped. "Just take the envelopes."

She shoved them into Rose's hands hard enough to leave a paper cut. Sheesh. Rosadox wasn't kidding about the irritability linked to the memory issues with Stolen Moments. Or maybe it was just Sephone.

"It's just Sephone," Rosadox would say. Amazing how she could imagine what her older self was saying years before the thought entered her head. Amazingly complicated.

Rose slit the top of the first envelope and, with Marek peering surreptitiously over her shoulder, read the note inside:

> *Dear Little Me,*
>
> *I would've given this to you earlier, but I didn't want you getting ahead of yourself—seeing as how I'm already there. You asked a good question, "Does the ghosts' one-hundredth deathday have anything to do with why the asylum will be in danger?" I answered with a better question, "How did Caelix bottle the Curse of the Wingless Ones?"*

Soon it'll be time for you to ask the best question of all. I've enclosed it in the next envelope. Once you've read it, you'll know who to ask. But DON'T read the question until you've finished "Legend of the Two Worlds" and the pages I marked in the cookbook. I repeat: DON'T READ THE QUESTION!!!

No worries, really. You won't have the time.

Love,

Rosadox

P.S. Check the mirror, won't you?

"Done jogging your memory?" Sephone rubbed her temples as if hers had been through a workout as well. "The first section you marked is about revenants."

"Didn't Wraith Warder hunt one of those, once?" said Marek.

"Yeah. Once. And it was the slowest chapter of the book," Aiden complained. "Revenants lead a *really* boring afterlife. Shuffle, mumble, stink ... don't you just cut their heads off and it's over? They're basically zombies."

"No, they're not," Sephone retorted. "Zombies are corpses animated with magic. They don't have any willpower. The book calls revenants the 'bodily apparitions of ghosts.' They're corpses animated by *spirits*. They think for themselves, but their bodies are falling apart, hence the shuffling and the mumbling and the stinking."

Well, gold star to Seph.

"They're also your most basic undead recipe," she continued, skimming the page with her finger. "Beginner's stuff. Anyone with an alchemy set could summon them. Easy to summon, easy to kill. And once they're dead again, they're dead for good." Sephone flipped to the next section and went silent. Lips moving with the words, her frown deepened. "This part is a warning about curses. Apparently, it's a bad idea to bring back anything that's died under a curse."

"Why?" Rose asked.

"Most of them have a failsafe built-in. In case someone tries to get rid of a curse by dying and bringing themselves back, the curse triples in power. Their whole body is contaminated, the blood especially. Anything magical it comes in contact with contracts the curse."

Pieces clipped together like links on a chain. "That's how he did it, then, isn't it?" Rose said. "That's how Caelix bottled the Curse of the Wingless Ones. He killed the Wingless Ones, brought them back as revenants, and bottled their blood."

"Then he poured it over the Heart Eternal, and it contracted the curse. It turned to stone," Marek concluded.

Aiden snagged a scalplum from the fruit bowl on the table and took a massive bite. "Aren't we supposed to read the end of the legend?" He smiled at Rose, a driblet of juice dripping down his chin. "Will the storyteller do the honors?"

Gliding through the pages of the original *Blackout's Tales*, she found "Legend of the Two Worlds" and read the last part of the story out loud. Caelix returning to the manor. Caelix pouring the Curse of the Wingless Ones over the Heart Eternal, turning it to stone. Caelix smashing the Heartstone on the altar, breaking the world in two.

And there, at the end of everything, a note from Blackout himself:

> *Not a very satisfying ending, is it? So many unanswered questions.*
>
> *The whereabouts of Caelix is a popular one, but he's probably off dying of embarrassment somewhere. Why? Here's a tip: if you're staking the fate of an entire world on a recipe, get it from the cook's mouth, all right? That's the thing about family recipes. Grammy's Famous Sugar Dusted Angel Wings gets written down and passed around and written down and passed around for generations. Maybe the ingredients stay the same, but all the little quirks—"add a pinch of cinnamon," "says it makes a dozen, actually makes three"—get lost along the way, and then what happens? Well, if you're Caelix, man without a backup plan, you find out that the recipe you used to cook up some revenants and bottle the Curse of the Wingless Ones comes with*

a caveat. Or it would've, if you'd gotten your recipe from the original cookbook instead of some hand-me-down third edition.

It's a simple matter of expiration dates. Hand-me-down recipe says that revenants are good till their second death. Original recipe agrees but also notes that product regains freshness once every hundred years.

Moral of the story? Be careful what you cook ... or you might end up like Caelix with a horde of the undead rising from their graves every century, calling for his blood.

Rose looked up from the book. Marek, Sephone, and Aiden were as still and serious as grave monuments. It would be very wrong to smile right now. Very, very wrong.

Her bottom lip betrayed her, and she sucked it in, chewing it into submission. "You know, none of you seems very surprised that Blackout has insider information about the legends he collected. I mean, these sorts of details ... these don't come from research. They come from personal experience with something."

"Personal experience?" Sephone folded her arms contemptuously. "Blackout got his legends from old folks whose minds were half gone. They're just stories. That's all he was. A storyteller."

A storyteller, yes. But he was so much more. This book was proof. "He told stories, and his stories were true. He heard the legends, and he wrote them down, and he made a book. And then he used that book to hunt them down." Rose flipped the pages of the original *Blackout's Tales*, rife with Blackout's ink-splattered commentary. "And he found them."

Sephone's vines were back, winding around her wrists in a quiet panic. "And how do you figure that?"

This was gonna be good. "We just read a legend about a host of cursed angels who died and were brought back as revenants. Their blood was so toxic, Caelix could bottle it and anything magical he poured it on turned to stone." Rose paused, smiling. She lunged at Aiden and tickled his side. Yelping, he dropped his half-eaten scalplum into her open palm.

"The scalplum," she said, holding it up for display. "Magical tickle fruit of the Scalpo tree. Which, incidentally, is what the *entire* Petrified Forest is made of. We're in a forest of magical trees that mysteriously turned to stone in a battle on Moonsfrost Eve, which, as of tomorrow night, will have taken place one hundred years ago exactly. The same number of years legend says a horde of the undead is allowed to return from the grave. And you're scared silly."

There it was again, Rosadox's voice in her head. *"C'mon. You've been holding this in for ages. Make it sizzle!"* "Heartstone Asylum isn't named after the original Heartstone Asylum, is it? It *is* the original Heartstone Asylum. *That's* what you guys are doing behind the scenes. You know the legends from *Blackout's Tales* are true because you're bona fide legend seekers hunting them down yourselves!"

Bam! How's *that* for sizzle? Like frying bacon on her fingertips.

(INNER STORM CLOUDS DO HAVE THEIR USES.)

Blood drained from Sephone and Aiden's faces, and they visibly began to shake. O-*kay*, that was a little dramatic. They had to know she'd figure it out eventually. It wasn't the end of the worlds.

Aiden raised a trembling finger, pointing behind Rose. "G-g-g—"

Marek rubbed a hand down his face. "Who let the dog out?"

"GHOST!"

P.S. Check the mirror, won't you?

Rose yanked Gormonger's mirror out of their ghost-warding supply bag. The glass was empty.

She turned to face his wolfish grin beaming from Ragnar's floor-length mirror. "*Gor!*" she hissed. "What are you doing here? How'd you get out?"

He picked his teeth with a ghostly claw, then wrote on the glass, *With SKILL, emphasis on the KILL. Before you get your whiskers in a twist, fog up the corner of that mirror you're holding. Next to the smooch you gave me earlier.*

Rose obliged. Her breath drew out the hours-old

imprint of her kiss. And next to it, an identical pair of fresh kissy lips. "What the—? Who did this? *Who* kissed you?"

Gormonger's wolfish grin widened. *Jealous?*

"Nobody kisses my Warg ghostie but me. *Nobody.*"

Well, it WAS you. I'm here under your orders. Maybe not for another six YEARS, but still.

"*I* sent you? And you remember? But I thought—"

Perks of the dead. The whole Paradox MIND WIPE doesn't work on us. Anyway, Future Bedhead said you might have a question for me. Something about the BEST question of all?

The other envelope. Finally! But didn't Rosadox also say something about having to—

"Wait," said Aiden. "I hear something."

Sephone listened at the door to Ragnar's office. "Someone's coming. Everyone *quiet.*"

"I'm so sorry to trouble you this late at night, Cadence," Ragnar's voice came from the other room. "I'm sure you're preoccupied with tomorrow's festivities, but you were the first one I thought to call. I know the mirror world is something of a specialty of yours."

"What seems to be the problem?" Cade asked.

His voice lowered considerably. "Patients have complained of seeing a giant, ghostly *wolf* lurking in their mirrors."

Rose pulled a face at the giant, ghostly *wolf* lurking in the mirror.

"It's probably nothing, of course," Ragnar continued.

"The ghosts couldn't get past our defenses if they tried. However ..."

"You'd like me to use my soul signia to investigate just the same?"

"Again, it's probably nothing. But for our peace of mind, yes. If you would be so kind? I know kindness is something I can rely on in you."

Cade gave a musical laugh. "No need for flattery. It would be my pleasure."

"What unusual pleasures you have, Nurse Locklear," Ragnar returned warmly. "Come. We'll find you some ghost wards, just in case, and you may use the mirror in my quarters."

Rose whirled on Gormonger. "Don't you scare her, Gor! Don't even—"

The ghost Warg feigned a gasp. *Have you looked in a mirror lately? You have an ENORMOUS pimple on your nose!*

"What?" She checked automatically. "Where?"

He grinned evilly. *Sorry. My mistake. I was just thinking about ... breakouts.*

ENTRY 29

THE FREE SPIRIT

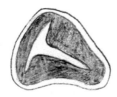

P icture this a sec:

It's slow-mo. Dramatic music in the background. Snowflakes falling. Four angels, side-by-side, striding through a stone forest. Their wrists, their necks, their ankles, their fingers are *covered* with silver jewelry. They're calm. Cooler than cukes. A girl tosses her curls in a spectral breeze. The other spins a chain-link necklace. Around them, ghosts veer out of their path, shielding their eyes. Every step clinks with bling.

Breathtaking, isn't it?

"We look like Wraith Warder raided a jewelry shop," Sephone grumbled.

Aiden pulled at a chain around his neck. "Hey, isn't this my mom's necklace?"

Marek twisted a sparkly ring on his pinky. "Beta has eclectic taste."

"I can't believe you made us climb out the window," Rose said to Sephone. "I thought they weren't *glamorous* enough for you?"

"And I can't believe you have a pet *ghost*," Sephone retorted. "Where are we taking it?"

"He's not a pet. And we're taking him somewhere safe."

Gormonger couldn't stay in the mirror world, not with Cade poking around. The cottage was a cruel prison—taking him back there would smash any trust they'd built to smithereens. That left only one option.

Sephone and Aiden halted when they saw the graveyard. "Are you *insane*?" she hissed. "Do you know what lives in that cave?"

"Is it something dreadful? If it is, I shall fetch the exterminator," came a smooth, caramel voice. Silas appeared at the entrance. Weeks of feeding had done him good. His fur was growing back in a glossy coat, and his ribs weren't half as noticeable.

Rose waved. "Hiya, Silas!"

"You have a pet *Warg*, too?" Sephone groaned.

"Still not a pet," Rose muttered.

Marek led them into the graveyard. "We have another favor to ask." He pulled out Gormonger's mirror.

"No," Silas said flatly. "Absolutely not. I told you to get rid of that abomination."

"But Cade's in trouble!" Rose insisted.

"Then you should have listened to me when you had the chance."

Marek looked to Rose, and they took a breath in unison. "Puh-leeeeeeeeee—" They climbed to a harmonious shriek.

Sephone and Aiden covered their ears, and Silas winced. Then he rolled the flavor around his tongue. "Hm. Pleasantly sour. You two should whine more often." He huffed in defeat. "One night and one night only. I am not a babysitter. I will not babysit your problems. Is that clear?"

"As glass," said Marek and punched the mirror without ceremony.

"FREEEEEE!" A streak of light burst from the shards, taking the shape of a translucent white wolf slightly smaller than the average warhorse. "I'm free, I'm free, I'm free!" Gormonger spun in circles, bouncing front to back on his paws in what had to be the Warg version of cartwheels. "Thank you, thank you, thank you!" He romped around Marek and dodged past the jewelry defenses to lick his cheek.

"Cold!" Shadow Boy brushed ice flakes from his skin.

"Free, free, free!" Gormonger chomped at Rose's curls, and she shook her head, flinging icicles. "Oh, Bedhead, I'm FREE!"

"Yes," she laughed. "You're very free. Now about this question I'm s'posta to ask you." She pulled the note out of her future self's envelope. "The 'best question of—"

"FREEEEEE!" Gormonger howled and took off at light speed. The iron fence contained him within the graveyard, but he shot around the perimeter, a blur of swirling snow and ghost light knocking down gravestones.

"Oh, he'll—he'll fix those. It's kinda his thing. Knock stuff down, put it back up."

"Yes," Silas sighed, watching the meticulous dismantlement of his graveyard. "I'm aware." He sat back on his haunches. "So, you're working with the she-alpha and her little hound now, are you?"

"Apologies," said Marek. "This is Sephone and Aiden."

Sephone eyed the Warg carefully. "And you're Silas."

Silas snapped his tail, and she flinched. "Grave Dancer, if you please."

"Why'd they name you Grave Dancer?" Aiden asked.

The Warg gave a toothy smile. "If you're lucky, you'll never find out. And what brings *you* here? More pesky questions, I'm sure?"

"Well, since we're here and you're not trying to eat us, maybe a few," said Sephone. "If that's okay."

"She has manners! Will wonders never cease?" Silas turned his back on her. "We may continue this conversation out of the elements. Do come in. You're invited this time."

His cave offered a welcome change in temperature. In an effort to look at ease, Sephone sat cross-legged on the ground several feet from the Warg. She yanked Aiden down next to her.

Silas stretched out on his forepaws, and Marek settled in the curve of his body, leaning against him. Team Hero's eyes widened. Rose made herself comfortable on Silas's back (fur had to count for, like, five layers, right?), and their eyeballs bugged.

"We, um"—Sephone cleared her throat—"we've come across some new information that's changed our opinion of your graveyard. At first, we thought this was the ghosts' graveyard and that it was *their* bodies that were supposed to be here. But now we're not so sure."

Rose chewed casually on one of Silas's ears. Hopefully, he didn't mind, but it was priceless seeing the looks on Sephone and Aiden's faces.

"And so, uh—and so," Aiden stammered, "we were wondering if you could tell us the, um, the nature of the bodies buried—"

"Beating around the bush does little to improve my opinion of you," Silas said simply. "Ask me your question and ask it directly."

Now he was talking Sephone's language. "Is this the graveyard of the Wingless Ones?"

The Warg's back vibrated with laughter. "You finally figured it out! Not a day too soon, either. And here I was thinking I'd have to improvise."

Marek shifted against him. "What do you mean?"

"Do you know why the graves are empty?" Aiden questioned.

"Of course I do," Silas answered. "I'm the one who emptied them."

Sephone was on her feet, feathers puffed and vines snapping from her wrists. "You *emptied* them? Where are the bodies? Do you know what those things *are*? They're revenants! Cursed revenants! Their blood turns whole *forests* to stone! They come back every hundred years—"

"Which in our case is tomorrow night, yes," Silas interrupted smoothly. "Hence the reason I need your help." He was looking at Marek, and his ears flicked Rose's chin. "I hope that I've earned enough of your trust to at least listen to what I have to say."

Rose scooted down his back so she could see his furry face. "We're listening."

"Well, *we're* not! We're going to tell Ragnar about this *right now*." Sephone pulled Aiden up by the wrist.

"Not so fast, PUPS!" Gormonger growled, materializing in the mouth of the cave. "Just whose side are you on, Grave Dancer?"

"The side of justice, Gormonger," Silas replied.

"And here I thought you were a lowdown, traitoring, filthy son of a—"

"So you've said."

"You can't scare us. We have *these!*" Aiden swung a necklace like a pair of nunchucks.

"Aww, did da whittle boy waid his mommy's jewelry box?" Gormonger sneered. "I'm a Sinner's Warg, PUP. I've picked my teeth with bones bigger than your THIGH. You think a little SILVER is gonna stop me?"

"No," Marek chuckled. "But a moonstone might."

Gormonger glared at him.

Silas gave a sharp yip. "Ahem. Sephone, Aiden, you may go if you please. Tell Ragnar everything you know. But what would you say if I told you your proprietor has more secrets to keep than he knows what to do with?"

Sephone stiffened. "I have my issues with Ragnar, but I still trust his word over a Warg's." But she wasn't moving.

"I'm not asking for your trust. All I'm asking, for the safety of the asylum, is that you wait until tomorrow evening to tell him."

Marek nudged Rose's foot. "You've been awfully quiet. What are you thinking?"

(You've been wondering the same thing, haven't you, Reader Name Here _____? It's not like your narrator to be so coy. Totally intentional, by the way.)

"I'm thinking ..." she played with Silas's soft ruff. "What do you want us to do tomorrow?"

"Spend the evening in the library. Don't leave it for a second. Wait for the signal." His tail brushed her leg. "Then don't be afraid to cry wolf."

"What's the signal?"

"Oh, you'll know it when you hear it."

"*Stop*," Sephone snarled. "Just stop. This is stupid! I

don't care *what* you call it, you're asking us to trust you. To put the fate of the entire asylum in your hands—paws —*whatever*. Why would we do that?"

Silas looked her in her ever-squinty eyes. "Because I may be the only one you *can* trust."

Ooh. Who knew Silas was fluent in hero-speak?

"Fine." Sephone crossed her arms. "Then I want a down payment. Tell us where you hid the bodies, and we will consider your—"

"*Hush!*" Silas growled.

"*Excuse* me? You big—mmph!" Aiden's hand covered Sephone's mouth.

"Shh. I hear it, too. Someone's coming. Quick! Change cloaks!" Aiden wriggled to put on the invisible side of his Corner Cloak.

"No time." Silas shook Rose off his back. "All of you, hide!"

Marek herded them behind a cluster of stalagmites and threw up a wall of shadows with his wings. "Trust me. This is for your own good." And he stuffed each of their mouths with a shadow-gag. Sephone protested, but the gags *did* mute the sound of their breathing.

"Gormonger, it would be best if you made yourself scarce. Please, don't allow your emotions to dictate your actions," Silas told the ghost Warg, and shadows plugged Rose's nose to hide her snort. He did realize this was *Gormonger* he was talking to? "Be still. Be silent. Making them aware of your presence could ruin everything."

"Is that what you're saying?" Gormonger's rumble became a roar. "That all I do is RUIN THINGS?"

"No, I—we don't have time for this. Just behave. The conversation I'm about to have is more delicate than your ego, and I can't afford any complications."

"You don't tell me what to do, GRAVE DANCER!"

"I'm not telling. I'm asking. Please?"

Gormonger grumbled something, and Rose peeked around the shadow-wall to see him burst into a thousand particles of light. Marek pulled her back.

Silence. Then—footsteps crunching in snow. Then—

"Good evening, Grave Dancer." That was Ragnar's voice. *Someone* was having a busy night. "I hope we're not interrupting anything. Did I hear voices?"

"But of course," Silas replied. "You know how I enjoy the sound of my own company."

"Brought you a steak, big guy." *Malachy?* What was Malachy doing here? "Happy Moonsfrost and all. Say, you're looking pretty fit."

"Yes. An infestation of little nuisances has been to my benefit."

Hey! Who's he calling little?

"We can spring for some mouse traps if you need 'em."

"I prefer to play with my food, thank you. And what brings you to my cave this evening? I assume you've come to ensure all security protocols are in place for tomorrow? I assure you they are. The bodies are under full protection, and all safety measures have been taken to prevent any harm from coming to the asylum and its patients." Somehow, Rose got the feeling he was looking in their direction. "Everything should go exactly as planned, and if there is any trouble at all, I will inform you immediately."

"You have our gratitude, Silas," Ragnar said quietly.

"An opportunity to choose justice, to protect as I should have during the War?" Silas said. "It is you who have mine."

There was a respectful silence concluded by a *fump* that sounded suspiciously like a gravestone being knocked over.

"What was that noise?" Ragnar's voice retreated as he moved to the mouth of the cave.

"Another one of my nuisances, no doubt. They've taken to tipping over gravestones."

"Yeesh," Malachy drawled. "Must be bigger than you said."

"You have no idea."

"Take care of yourself, Grave Dancer. We'll check in on you day after tomorrow."

"Thank you for the steak."

For a while, the only sound in the cave was chewing. Finally, Silas swallowed and said, "Do you want to know the truly infuriating thing about Aldric Ragnar? He cannot be lied to."

Marek's shadows fell away, and they climbed over the cluster of stalagmites.

"I'm quite serious. It's his soul signia. His ears itch when a lie is told. Wording is everything around him. The *care* that must be taken, the kernels of truth at the core of every sentence ... absolutely infuriating. But do you know what else is infuriating?" Silas bared his fangs at the mouth of the cave. "*You.*"

Gormonger barked a laugh, streaming in with tendrils of ghost light. "You worry too much. They were already leaving. And the LOOK on your FACE!"

"Would've been the last look you ever saw if you weren't already dead. Now, where were we?"

Sephone opened her mouth, but Rose beat her to it. "Gormonger was going to answer a question for me. The best question of all." She flattened Rosadox's note on her knee. It was rather wrinkled from having been perused so many times in the past ten minutes. Or didn't you know? She'd already read it enough times to have it memorized.

(Look, just 'cause you can trust me doesn't mean I'm a reliable narrator. I'm all kinds of paradoxes—not just the time-traveling ones.)

Rose cleared her throat. "The question is ... where are the Sinner and the Saint?" She braced for Silas's rebuke about no War-related questions, but it was the ghost Warg who lost his head. Gormonger worked himself into such a fury at the words, frothing and snarling, that it popped off

307

his body and hung from the ceiling, impaled by a stalactite.

In the end, it was Silas who answered. "The Sinner and the Saint? Might've mentioned it sooner. You just missed them."

ENTRY 30

AUTHOR(S) INTERLUDE PART 4

Disclaimer: This is for the Reader Name Here _____ who skipped ahead. ~1532 A.S.

For shame, Reader Name Here _____. ~1527 A.S.

And we had such faith in you! ~1530 A.S.

Welp, your loss. Guess you missed the part where dragons take over the asylum. ~1529 A.S.

Yeah, and the ghosts turn out to be a hoax. ~1526 A.S.

And Malachy turns into a werewalrus! ~1527 A.S.

A ... werewalrus? ~1526 A.S.

Well, he does have the beard for it. ~1532 A.S.

Not the teeth, though. Walruses have huge *teeth.* ~1527 A.S.

Tusks, Little Me. They're called tusks. ~1529 A.S.

Whatever. Point is, Reader Name Here ____ missed it because they skipped ahead, didn't they? They also missed the part where we wake up from a dream and realize Heartstone Asylum isn't real at all, that our friends—Marek, Cade, Malachy, Sephone, Aiden—are just figments of our imagination to cope with the fact that we've actually been in an asylum all our lives. Didn't they? ~1527 A.S.

... ... ~1530 A.S.

... ... ~1532 A.S.

... did 1527 just spoil a future plot?! ~1526 A.S.

No comment. ~1530 A.S.

Moving on with the story. ~1532 A.S.

But—
~1526 A.S.

No buts. Reader Name Here _____ has learned their lesson. No more skipping ahead, you hear, Reader Name Here _____? It spoils stories. Case in point. Now carry on. ~1532 A.S.

Ugh. Fine. ~1526 A.S.

ENTRY 31

SECRETS IN THE ATTIC

The Sinner and the Saint. Leaders of the War o' the Wargs. Not dead like their armies. *Alive.*

Malachy. His way with dogs. Malachy. His unicorns. Malachy. His crinkle-eyed smile. Malachy. Sinner.

Malachy the Sinner. Ragnar the Saint.

(DID YOU REALLY WONDER WHICH WAS WHICH?)

Deep inside, Stormy was heavy with condensation. It got that way sometimes when Rose was really upset, weighing her down and making her skin clammy. She rubbed her chest, humming a lullaby Amber used to sing, and pulled the blanket of her storyteller's chair tighter around her shoulders. Marek was near enough to touch, sitting on the lip of the dais, knees pulled up to his chest. Beta sat next to him like a gargoyle, solemn and watchful.

Last night, they hadn't said a word about the revelation. They didn't need to. Their thoughts were the same. Their feelings were the same. Their shoulders were sharing the same burden. Talking was a formality—like chewing applesauce—but today, in the stillness of the library, it felt right.

"Remember what he said after Story Hour?" Rose's voice crackled from disuse. Or pent-up lightning? "About Caelix. 'Some things you don't come back from.' " She'd seen the history books. The War o' the Wargs. Towns decimated. Houses chewed to kibble. Families torn apart.

"Makes you want to scrub it all away, doesn't it?" Marek said softly. "Make it clean again. Make it better."

"Why d'you think it happened? The War. All Malachy and the Wargs were trying to do was get Warg-riding tournaments reinstated so the Wargs wouldn't starve. How could he let it turn into ..." Bloodshed. Pain. Pointless, endless fighting, growling, snapping, bones breaking, *screaming*—

"Wars begin over the smallest things," Marek murmured, "but they're always at the heart of something much bigger. Hatred. Fear. Misunderstanding. It's amazing how easy it is to go wrong even while fighting for what's right."

Rose nodded mutely. What else had Malachy said about Caelix? *He either spent the rest of his life trying to make up for his mistakes, or he ended it.* Malachy knew. He knew the weight of his mistakes and was trying to make up for them. But what must that burden feel like, to know, no matter how hard you try, you'll never outweigh the evil you've done?

Her storm cloud groaned with heaviness. It was too much, too much to hold. Condensation leaked from the corners of her eyes, and Rose wiped her cheeks. "What do we do now?" Rosadox would know. What she wouldn't give to write a letter to the future ...

"You don't need letters anymore, silly," her future self would say. *"Just talk to yourself."*

Marek breathed deeply. His shadow-blurred wings quivered. "He needs someone to believe in him, to believe that he can become more than his mistakes. So, what do we do?" Marek slapped his knees and stood. "We don't give up on him. Not for a second."

They hadn't seen Malachy once that day. According to Shadow Boy, this was typical behavior for Moonsfrost Eve, and given recent information, it made sense that neither he nor Ragnar would participate in the asylum's festivities.

Oh, wait.

***

What *are* Moonsfrost Eve festivities? Glad you asked! To start, you should have a comprehensive understanding of what Moonsfrost Eve *is*. Not knowing could leave you with a partially-caved skull and some pretty hefty welts.

Moonsfrost Eve is when Shaolandir's new year begins. Specifically, it happens when the moons eclipse at midnight, and the combined moonlight freezes into moonstones, dropping like hail from the sky and immersing the world in frozen moonlight. *Beautiful* stuff. Also dangerous as all get out. The eclipse only lasts for a minute, but if you aren't watching from the safety of your home, it could beat you black and blue.

Festive, isn't it?

The afternoon of Moonsfrost Eve is usually spent making candy moonstones: chocolate, fudge, sugar, you name it—and then everyone breaks out their costumes and dresses up as lunatics, the avid celebrators of the moons.

Next comes frost-calling. At dusk, well before the deadly stroke of midnight, flocks of lunatics go outside with little baggies and stand under their neighbors' windows chanting, "One o'clock, two o'clock, three o'clock ..." and so on until they reach twelve and everybody shouts, "Midnight! Let's eat the moonlight!" The windows open, and neighbors pelt the lunatics with candy moonstones. Once they've gathered enough to fill their baggies, they all go home to sit together at windows, munching moonstones and watching the eclipse happen while *real* balls of frozen moonlight fall from the sky.

And that's Moonsfrost Eve.

This information is brought to you by the Info-Asterisks Association. Now, back to your regularly scheduled chapter.

**

With Malachy absent and Cade distracted by her and Elektra's duties in leading the festivities, slipping off to the Topsy-Turvy Library had been easy. Per Silas's request, Rose and Marek were there by evening. Whether Team Hero would join them was yet to be seen. Last night, they hadn't exactly agreed to follow Silas's instructions. To be honest, they hadn't spoken at all, and this time it wasn't like chewing applesauce. They *needed* to talk. They needed to know whether they were in this together. Plus, there was her and Marek's status as patients at the asylum. Technically, they weren't allowed to be alone in the library without an orderly present. Sooner or later, someone would come looking for them, and if Aiden wasn't there supervising ...

"D'you think we should—" Rose began, and the door of the Topsy-Turvy Library opened. Sephone marched in like they'd had an appointment, and she was right on time. Aiden followed behind her, carrying a bowl of candy moonstones in blue wrappers.

"Got us an alibi. Told Elektra and Cade we'd rather toss candy from the library window than frost-call this year. Think they bought it." She heaved a crate onto a nearby table. "Also brought us some lunatic costumes. We have to look the part to be convincing."

Marek's response was only marginally delayed. "Well, that's ... very quick thinking. Thank you."

Sephone smirked. "Didn't think we'd come, did you?"

"There was a moment."

"Yeah, well"—she and Aiden plopped down at a table —"we didn't have much choice, did we? Have you heard anything?"

Silas's mysterious signal. "Not yet," Rose told them.

A moment passed. An awkward, silent moment. Beta sniffed Aiden's baggy pant leg and backed up, head cocked quizzically.

Aiden mirrored the canine gesture with uncanny precision. "Sephone and I were thinking about this whole 'Sinner/Saint' situation, and we had something to say. Didn't we, Seph?" He gave her a significant look.

"I don't know." Vines twisted languidly around her fingers. "Did we?"

"Yes, we *did*. We wanted to say that we're sorry about Malachy." He shuffled a kick at her under the table.

"Yeah, sorry about Malachy. That's messed up." Sephone stared off into space, brows furrowed darkly. "This whole *thing* is messed up."

The question that had been scratching at the walls of Rose's brain finally crawled out her mouth. "Do we tell anyone?"

"Not yet," Marek said before Sephone could explode in the affirmative. "Think about it. Thanks to the undead cookbook and *Blackout's Tales*, we know the revenants are going to be reanimated tonight. We know they come back every century hellbent on destroying Caelix, who murdered them, but that they'll take their revenge out on anything that crosses their path. We know they're what killed Malachy and Ragnar's armies a hundred years ago, and if they get loose, the asylum will be in serious danger."

"And since your stupid Warg friend dug up the revenants' bodies from the graveyard and *hid* them somewhere, the odds of them getting loose are very likely," Sephone interjected pointedly.

"We don't know where Silas hid the bodies or why," Marek conceded, "but we do know he has a plan. A plan that makes sure 'all safety measures have been taken to prevent any harm from coming to the asylum and its patients.' That's what he told Ragnar last night, remember? And Ragnar can't be lied to. All Silas has asked us to do is wait in the library for his signal before we tell Malachy and Ragnar what we know. Whatever's going on here, Silas knows more about it than they do. If we don't follow his instructions, we risk ruining whatever plan he has that ensures the asylum's safety. I say we follow them. Any objections?" He raised his eyebrows.

Sephone grudgingly kept her mouth shut.

"Then let's wait for his signal and go from there."

So, they waited. In silence. There were no clocks in the library. Aiden substituted by clicking his tongue.

Sephone stood abruptly. "Elektra and Cade will be in to check on us before frost-calling starts." She dumped the crate full of lunatic costumes. "Come on. We have to pretend to be having fun."

You know, halfway through, it didn't feel like pretending. Moonstone blue is the customary wardrobe hue for Moons-frost Eve, and they painted each other's faces the same color as their clothes. Marek's eyes matched to perfection. He and Aiden claimed two sock hats knitted to look like half-moons, and Sephone stenciled craters over their eyes and on their cheeks to complete the illusion. Rose found a bottle of glitter and powdered it over her and Sephone's blue faces. They sparkled like frozen moonlight. She followed up with azure blue blush, periwinkle eye shadow, and dark blue lip ink.

Sephone sorted through the lunatic clothing and passed around vests sewn with glowing moon patches. She fished out the last garment and promptly dropped it like a dead mouse. "How did *this* get in here?"

It was a poofy blue tutu, extra poof, with hazy little moons dyed in the tulle.

Rose's hand shot into the air. "Ooh! Me! I want it! I love poofs!"

Sephone threw it in disgust, and Marek snatched it from the air. "But *I* love poofs, too. Doesn't it match my eyes?"

319

Rose grabbed the tutu ferociously from his grip. "Mine," she growled and slipped it on over her pants.

Needless to say, when Cade and Elektra popped in to see if their charges were truly in the festive spirit, they were convinced. "The first group of frost callers should be at your window shortly," Cade called as they left. "Be ready! You certainly look it."

"*One o'clock, two o'clock, three o'clock—*"

"How are we supposed to hear *anything* over this racket, let alone a signal?" Sephone snapped as patients chanted outside the library's chapel window.

"*—ten o'clock, eleven o'clock, MIDNIGHT! Let's eat the moonlight!*"

Rose opened a compartment of the window and pelted the lunatics with candy. Take that! And that! How often do you get to throw things at someone and get thanked for it? Patients scrambled to collect the edible moonstones and went on their merry way.

She closed the window, waiting for the next group. It was dark now. Somewhere out there, something dead was waking from a hundred-year slumber. Why would Ragnar let his patients out on a night like tonight, anyway, especially with the ghosts behaving as unpredictably as they were? And what did the ghosts do during the eclipse? Moonstones hurt them worse than any other paramagical repellent. Did the trees protect them? Or were they out there, homeless and vulnerable, with nothing to defend themselves?

"*One o'clock, two o'clock, three o'clock—*"

"My turn." Marek grabbed the candy bowl from her hands.

A few minutes later:

"*One o'clock, two o'clock, three o'clock—*"

Aiden came swooping from a zip line. "My turn!"

Rose popped a chocolate moonstone into her mouth. "Sephone should have a turn, too."

"Yeah. It's fun! Hey, Seph!" Sephone was in the obstacle course hemisphere of the library, concentrating on hearing the mysterious signal. Aiden gestured wildly at her with his wing. "Come here!"

Sitting on the rope bridge of an upside-down book-case, she crossed her arms and shook her head. Glitter flew from her cheeks.

"Come on!" Aiden jumped up and down now, waving both wings. "Just for a minute!"

Sephone sighed. She pushed herself off the rope bridge and landed in an agile crouch. "What? We're going to miss the signal."

"Forget the signal for a second." He pushed the candy bowl into her hands. "It's Moonsfrost Eve. Have a little *fun.*"

"I don't—"

"Throwing things will make you feel better."

She rolled a sugar moonstone between her fingers and pegged him right between the eyes. "Huh. It does."

Tap, tap.

"Ooh! You're on!" Aiden nudged her to the window.

Between the darkness outside and the soft glow of the library, the images beyond the glass were fuzzy.

"What happened to the chant? Did they forget how to count?" Sephone opened the window.

There was no one there.

Tap, tap, tap.

Beta's teeth were bared in a soundless growl.

"That's not ..."

"It can't be."

"... our signal?"

Tap, tap, tap, tap.

They spread out immediately. "It's coming from the floorboards!" Sephone declared, ear pressed to the ground.

Which would be true of any room except the Topsy-Turvy Library. "It isn't the floorboards," Rose said. "This room is upside down. The floor is the ceiling, and the ceiling is the floor, which means if it were coming from the floorboards, it'd be coming from up in the obstacle course." She knelt, pressing her hand flat against the ground. "This is the ceiling. What does a ceiling have that a floor doesn't?"

Marek snapped his fingers. "An attic!"

"Look for a hatch in the floor—ceiling—*the thing we're walking on!*" Sephone's vines shot from her wrists, pushing aside tables and pulling out chairs.

With all the bookcases aboveground, there weren't

many places a hatch in the floor could hide. Tables, chairs, no rugs. Rose fluffed her tutu thoughtfully. The one defining feature of the Topsy-Turvy Library's lower hemisphere was—"My storyteller's chair!" Sitting on a heavy stone dais. What had Rosadox said yesterday about how sitting on the chair made her feel like she was on top of something very important?

It took all four of them to move the dais, inch by ear-grating inch. And beneath it? A hatch no different than the one Rose used every day to get to her bedroom. Save for the ginormous bolt locks.

Tap, tap, tap, THUMP, THUMP!

The doorframe rattled, and they scuttled back.

"Here?" Sephone croaked. Her voice grew in strength. "He hid them *here*?"

Rose swallowed. All those hours curled up on her storyteller's chair ... "We have to call Silas."

"I'm sorry—the crazy Warg who hid a horde of undead killing machines *inside the asylum*? I don't think so, New Girl. I don't care who he is right now, I'm getting Ragnar."

"Wonderful. And we'll get Silas. It'll be a happy old War reunion," Marek said cheerfully.

Sephone's eyes narrowed into spearheads. "Are you really going to fight me on this, Marek?"

Shadows poured off his wings like a riptide. "You're picking your battles, Seph."

Her lips tightened. "Keep them busy, and *don't* let

them call for the Warg," Sephone said to Aiden and made for the exit. Aiden blocked Rose and Marek's path.

"Are you going to transform now?" Marek asked him. "Lovely. Rose has been looking forward to this."

"She has?" Aiden wiped the goofy grin off his blue, cratered face. "Ahem. I mean—prepare yourselves! You have no idea the monster you've unleashed." And he pulled his shirt over his head.

Aiden stood there, bare from his half-moon sock cap to his too-big pants, staring them down. A shudder ran through his body, and he doubled over, gripping his kneecaps.

Then he threw back his head and *howled*.

ENTRY 32

THE GIRL WHO CRIED WOLF

As Aiden's howl lengthened, so did his face, shaping into a long snout tipped with a wet, black nose. Aiden's sock cap popped off his head as his ears grew upward, becoming two triangles bent in half. His carrot top curls receded, making way for the coppery red fur sprouting through his blue face paint. It was the same copper color of his wings. Aiden hunched over again, his bones making strange popping noises as they extended. Muscles bulged, thickening under his skin and adding fifty pounds to his lean body.

Funny, but those baggy pants didn't seem like a fashion statement anymore.

He froze in his crouched position, clawed fingers digging into his knees. Beta danced back and forth on his paws, teeth bared. Then Aiden straightened, a seven-foot dogman with viscous saliva drooling off his black lips. He opened his mouth, and tongues of fire came out, melting the puppy's bravery into a puddle of goo.

Holy, haloed—"Hellhound?" Rose squeaked, Beta scurrying behind her legs. "Aiden's a *hellhound*? But they're ..."

"Rare? Reviled? Punishable by law to hire on any premises?" Marek offered in quick succession.

"I *can* hear you, you know." Aiden's voice was canyon-deep and distorted like he was gargling gravel. "I have sensitive ears. And feelings."

Marek looked at Rose and smiled. "Don't you know by now that Heartstone is a home of misfits?" He stepped up to Aiden. There was a foot height difference, but Marek's bear-like frame still had him beat in the weight category. "And Aiden, you bring such life and laughter to the asylum. I'm not interested in what the law says. I'm *glad* you're here." Shadows gathered around his fist. "Remember, nothing in the next five minutes changes that."

And he landed a shadow-powered punch on Aiden's jaw.

Ever seen a bear in a dogfight? The results can be ... surprising.

Aiden flipped Marek flat on his belly and slammed onto his back.

"The window!" Marek shouted, shadows pulling at the hellhound crushing him from on top. "Get to the window!" Shadow Boy heaved to all fours and threw Aiden over his shoulders in a painful somersault. His bravery re-solidified, Beta pounced on Aiden's neck, nipping at his ears, and Rose jumped over both of them to get to the library's chapel window. She was inches away when a jet of hellhound fire licked the bottom of the window frame, melting the compartments shut.

Really, Aiden?

She yanked on a compartment. Pried it with her fingernails. Shoved it with her shoulder. Banged it with her fist. Rose wiped perspiration from her forehead, and her hand came back blue and glittery. "It's stuck!"

"Take your time." Marek twisted under the hellhound straddling his chest. He elbowed Aiden's stomach and was rewarded with a spitty growl and a stranglehold. "I—can do this—till I'm blue—in the face."

Rose eyed his blue face paint. "But you are."

"Exactly. If you could *hurry—just—a bit.*"

She tugged on a different window compartment. Outside, there were no chants from frost-callers. Apparently, they knew better than to interrupt a hellhound orderly facing down two wayward patients. "It just won't—"

About a zillion pounds of lumberjack flew through the air, hitting the window and smashing the compartment to pieces. Marek bounced painfully off the frame and landed back in the library. "There you go," he groaned from the floor.

Rose managed to stick her head out and scream, "SILAS! WOLF! SILAS!" before Aiden hauled her back. "No, don't! Don't *touch* me!"

Stormy, weak and weaker with every use, still put out a defensive spark. With Aiden's thick fur, it couldn't have been more than static shock, but instantly he put her down. "It's okay, Rose. Deep breath. I'm not going to hurt you." For all his transformation, Aiden's eyes remained their normal hazel. He was still him. Mushy poet and sidekick of Sephone Darrow.

Rose relaxed, and the lightning sucked back into her skin like a precious resource, like water in a scorching desert.

"Easy, Thunder. Easy." Marek got up gingerly, glass crunching beneath his boots. "It's over."

Was it, though? They each held their fighting stance, tense and unsure.

Tap-tap-tap-tap—THUD, THUD. Beneath their feet, the unquiet dead were getting restless.

Marek bent down slowly, brushing glass shards from his pants with the backs of his hands. He moved to his boots, where his palms overlapped, making a cup that brimmed with shadows.

Rose understood what he was asking as if his thoughts were her own. Blind faith in Marek was her specialty.

But she could do leaps, too.

She lunged, stepping into his cupped palms, and he launched her high over Aiden's head. Shadows propelling her, tutu puffed in flight, Rose opened her wings to carry the momentum and collided with the library door. Aiden growled, bounding in her direction, but was sideswiped by Beta. His big, hellhound feet (when had he lost his shoes?) stumbled, and Marek took the opportunity to jump on his back. They both crashed bodily to the floor.

Rose left them to Bear vs. Dogfight: The Continuing Saga and hurried to Ragnar's office. When she arrived, panting, the door was slightly ajar. Inside, the room was dark but not empty. The sprawling world map behind Ragnar's desk was rolled up, revealing a hidden safe stocked with weapons, which Sephone was rooting through. Rose gave the door a soft knock.

Sephone whipped around, her blue, glittery face dazzling in the moonlight. "Sweet *magic*, you're like a splinter I can't get rid of."

Rose stepped into the office. "Thorn, actually. In the side. Foot. Preferably not butt."

There were noises from Ragnar's living quarters in the next room. Quiet voices. Clinking glasses. The Sinner and the Saint spending the anniversary of their War's end chatting like old friends.

"Don't try to stop me." Sephone returned her attention to the weapons supply. "It's too dangerous not to tell them."

"Go ahead. We already called for Silas, and he said we could tell Malachy and Ragnar after that, anyway."

"Just as soon as I find something to stab them with," Sephone muttered under her breath.

She ran her fingers lovingly over a spear, hesitated,

and pulled out a sword in its scabbard. "Here." She held out a familiar, rose-shaped pommel.

"T.K.!" Rose slid her beloved birthday present from its sheathe. "Oh, I missed you, missed you, missed you!" She kissed the blade up and down. "Thank you!"

Sephone watched, tongue between her teeth. "Don't mention it. Or this. To anyone."

Rose sheathed her sword tenderly and belted it over her tutu. "But why? Why are you giving this to me?"

She turned indifferently to the weapons safe. "Heard about your magic. I know Malachy's still trying to ..." His name made them both swallow. "Anyway, if we're going to be fighting revenants, don't waste it. No one should lose their soul signia." Sephone picked out a spear and spun it experimentally. Vines knotted the shaft to her wrist. Nodding curtly to herself, she made for the door to Ragnar's living quarters.

"Just *what* do you think you're doing?" Rose blocked her path, arms crossed in amusement.

Sephone stopped, arms crossed in aggression. "Telling Ragnar about the revenants."

She rolled her eyes. "I know *that*. I mean, what are you doing just *walking* through the door?"

"Do you expect me to knock?"

Silly, silly hero. "*Nooo.* I expect you to wait for an entry sentence."

Sephone's vines wound irritably around her spear. "A what?"

This girl. Zippo imagination. "An entry sentence," Rose repeated. "It's like … okay, you know in stories when the heroes are all gathered together making plans to defeat the Big Bad, and all of a sudden—*boom*. The villain strolls in with this super snazzy way of twisting their last sentence into a dramatic entrance? How d'you think they do that? How d'you think they nail it *every time*?"

"… by crouching outside the door to listen?"

"Exactly! An entry sentence. You'll know it when you hear it."

Sephone frowned suspiciously. "Are you sure this isn't you coming up with an excuse to stall?"

"No, this is me making up for my lousy entrance with the window yesterday." Rose squatted by Ragnar's door. "Come on! You're gonna miss it."

Sephone huffed and crouched next to her. The voices were hard to distinguish at first—one, because of the solid door, and two, because of the distinctive slur.

Oh, you've *got* to be kidding.

Sephone was stepping in the same puddle of realization. The puddle became a tidal wave of fury, and she rose to her feet, vines grasping at the doorknob.

Rose yanked on her sleeve. "That wasn't an entry sentence! You can't even hear them!"

"Of course I can't!" she hissed. "They're *drunk*."

"All the more reason to shock them to their senses."

Sephone grimaced and laid her ear back on the door.

"… take her soul outta her body." Malachy's drawl was

thicker than butter. "I mean, what am I s'posta do with that? How d'ya fix somethin' that requires ya to take someone's *soul* outta their *body*?"

"It *is* ... a conundrum," Ragnar agreed with sage lethargy.

Rose's hand reached past her tutu and clutched instinctively at the unicorn cupcake paperweight in her pocket. Magic. They were talking about her magic.

"All I'm *sayin'* is 'at ... couple more uses of magic and *bam*—her soul signia's gone. And where'll 'at leave her? No magic. No storm cloud. No reason to be in an asylum."

"What are you suggesting?"

"Look, I—I like her well enough, Ace, but we gotta be practical 'bout this. She ain't qualified for the work we do. The work you *brought* her here to do. So, let her get that last bit o' magic outta her system. Then send her home. No harm done."

Stormy was filling up again, pressing heavily on her lungs. Like paper under a paperweight. Rose gripped Malachy's unicorn so tight the horn left a dent in her skin. It was his security deposit. His *promise*.

Marek's words played over and over. *We don't give up on him. Not for a second.*

There was the *glub-glub* of liquid sloshing from bottle to glass. "Marek wouldn't like it," Ragnar said. "You know what he would do."

"Yeah, but think of what *you* could do. This girl's gonna be a Dame Commander. That's the kinda friend in high places Heartstone could use, right? She's still an advantage. But keep her here, and she's just a waste of resources." Malachy smacked the table once as if that settled the matter.

Ragnar's silence was meditative, and Rose pictured him pensively sipping his drink. "You went every week with Marek to their meeting spot. You watched her grow up. You worked as hard and as faithfully as anyone to get her here. I don't believe your sudden apathy."

"Ace. Is my apathy *ever* sudden? I wanted her here because I was promised a girl with a soul of storms. The parlor trick is bad enough, but without her magic, she's useless to me. Simple as that."

Simple as that. No magic, and he didn't want her. No magic, and she was useless to him.

Deep in her pocket, the unicorn horn punctured Rose's palm.

"Hey." Sephone touched her wing. She looked deeply uncomfortable, but there was a fierceness in her expression. "He's the Sinner, Rose. He's the *Sinner.*"

Somehow that only succeeded in making her storm cloud heavier. Condensation gathered at the corners of her eyes, but Rose blinked it away. Every raindrop cried was a drop closer to giving Malachy what he wanted and losing Stormy forever.

We don't give up on him. Not for a second.

A single tear slipped through.

"No," Ragnar said finally. "Rose needs our help. *That* is

what Heartstone Asylum stands for. She cannot lose her soul signia. It's wrong. It's unhealthy. I cannot condone standing idly by and letting it happen."

"No, you're right," Malachy fired back. "Let's stand idly by while she's reunited with her family. Let's stand idly by while she gets back to that sister she loves so much. Think about it. It'd be like bringing her back from the *dead*. There's no sin in taking her home."

Sephone's face lit up like dynamite. She threw the door open with a bang, a wraith of glitter and righteous indignation. "Well, you'd know all about the difference between a Sinner and a Saint, wouldn't you? And she's not the only thing coming back from the dead."

*

Her dramatic entrance? Stellar. Flawless. A star pupil! How effortlessly Sephone paved the way for a dramatic explanation. Which consisted of, "Revenants. Library attic. Grave Dancer." Verbatim.

They'd work on those next.

Armed with her spear, Sephone took the lead to the library, her stride one of bold, unswerving purpose. A runaway train would have careened out of her path. Rose trotted to keep up, her arms full of a variety of weapons: two swords (not including T.K.), a two-bit axe, and a flail with heavy chains attached to three spiked balls that looked like lethal baby hedgehogs. The flail was the hardest to carry, those poky hedgehogs snagging her tutu. Sephone refused to give Malachy and Ragnar their weapons till they could walk a straight line. Behind them —*far* behind them—the legendary Sinner and Saint staggered, bumping wings to keep each other balanced.

It wasn't their finest moment.

Sephone rounded the corner where Bear vs. Dogfight: The Continuing Saga had now moved into the hallway. She gave a sharp whistle, and Marek, Beta, and Aiden broke apart, rolling to all fours.

"You were *supposed* to stay in the library," she said, one hand on hip, the other dangerously on her spear.

"What? We are in the ..." Aiden looked around. "Where *are* we?"

Marek, smudged face paint aside, was unruffled. He helped Aiden to his big, furry feet and straightened Beta's goggles. "What's our plan?"

"Weapons!" Rose lifted her armload unnecessarily. Shadow Boy reached for her heaviest burden, the flail.

(*YES, I WAS EXPECTING HIM TO TAKE THE AXE. YES, IT'S BECAUSE HE'S A LUMBERJACK. YES, I WAS STEREOTYPING. YES, LOOK ON ME IN SHAME.*)

"Hoggers! Oh, I've missed you, missed you, missed you!" He kissed his weapon up and down.

Sephone blinked. "Okay, is this like a *thing* with you two?"

Rose giggled. "Hoggers?"

"Because they look like hedgehogs." Marek bumped the spiked balls together. "Don't you think?"

Sometimes she wondered if Marek wasn't the other half of her brain.

Sephone held a sword out to Aiden. "Take this. You need a ranged weapon."

He looked at the proffered handle with distaste. "The pen is mightier than the sword."

"One drop of revenant blood, and they'll kill you stone dead. What's your pen going to do, then? Squirt ink in their eyes?"

Aiden placed a hand delicately over his furry chest. "Though I be a lover, not a fighter, yet I will fight for what I love." He took the sword. "I thought you went to get Ragnar? Where is he?"

"Gentlemen," Rose began with a dramatic sweep of her arm.

(*Note to selves: teach Sephone dramatic arm sweep.*)

"The cavalry has arrived." Malachy and Ragnar stumbled around the corner.

Aiden's black nose twitched. "Are they ... ?"

"Yes."

"Well, that ... isn't ideal."

Understatement of the century.

"Leave them. They'll make it eventually." Sephone

took the lead again and marched them to the familiar plaque.

The Topsy-Turvy Library
Because bookworms need exercise, too.

The door was closed. Rose opened it, fully expecting to be met with a caramel-furred Warg and a battle plan.

Instead, they were greeted by the sight of a gaping maw in the upside-down ceiling.

The attic was open.

ENTRY 33

BROKEN GLASS, MIND YOUR FEET

I magine, if you will, the thrill of hide-and-seek meeting the terror of looking for monsters under your bed, and you have a glimpse of what it felt like peeking inside the attic.

What they found was scariest of all.

It was empty.

While Marek, Sephone, and Aiden spread out in a cautious, methodical sweep of the library, Rose ventured to her storyteller's chair, Beta at her heels. Situated on the cushion was a letter addressed in familiar handwriting. Propped next to it was a scarlet umbrella.

She opened the letter without hesitation.

 Hi, Little Me!

I know I told you that you didn't have to write

letters anymore to reach me. You just have to talk to yourself.

"You didn't say that! I *thought* you saying that!" Rose whispered.

 Exactly.

"As in, in my head."

 Well, where else would I be saying it? Look, you'll know more about our mechanics of communication by the end of the book—I mean, tomorrow night. It'll all make sense then. Meanwhile, there's no harm babying you with a few more letters from the future, baby girl. I know you're in a funk, but you can do this! The revenants aren't in the asylum anymore. I made sure of that. Take the umbrella, and don't open it until you truly need it. Prepare for any scenario, remember?

Don't forget what I said yesterday about Sephone (even though I personally won't be saying it for another two years—time travel, am I right?).

Love you, Little Me.
Rosadox

P.S. I see you found the tutu I stashed in the lunatic costumes. You're welcome.

Rose patted her poofy skirt and smiled.

"Look who finally decided to show up." Sephone grabbed the weapons off the table Rose had set them on and shoved the sword into Ragnar's chest—

(NOT THE POINTY END, IT SHOULD BE NOTED)

—and the two-bit axe into Malachy's. "Here. Impale your foot, I don't care. They're gone."

Malachy blinked bloodshot eyes. "What?"

"The revenants. They were in the attic, and now they're gone. We think they got out through the window."

Fumbling to attach his sword to his belt, Ragnar crossed to the Marek-shaped hole in the window. Malachy crouched by the mouth of the attic, inspecting the inside. He didn't look up—not at Rose or Marek.

Rose knew what she was feeling. Hurt, obviously. Betrayal. A healthy dose of anger. But what must *Malachy* be feeling? How many years did he spend trying to put his sins as the Sinner behind him? And here they were being thrown in his face. How long did it take to build a new life out of the second chance Ragnar must have given him? And here it was being torn apart. He probably felt like his mistakes were doomed to repeat themselves, like he could never get away. Like nothing good would ever last because he ruined his life the day the War began.

Rose was hurt, betrayed, angry ... and aching. Her heart ached because somehow, *somehow*, she still cared. She cared about whatever was making Malachy's jaw clench and his eyes harden. He was putting on armor inside, armor he hadn't touched in a hundred years, and Rose *cared*. She cared, and she didn't want to stop.

Shadows brushed her hand, and one look at Marek's face was all she needed to know their thoughts were the same. *We don't give up on him. Not for a second.*

"If this is some sort of elaborate prank ..." Ragnar said.

"You'd know if we were lying," Sephone scoffed. "Your soul signia? Yeah, we know about that, too."

"Well, aren't you just a veritable wellspring of knowledge today," Malachy exhaled.

Ragnar traced the edges of the broken window, looking troubled. Then he brightened. "Oh, this could be much, much worse!"

Sephone stared at him. "*Really?*"

"Yes. It looks like the damage is only to one pane. We'll have this window fixed in two shakes of a Warg's tail!"

If glares could dismember, the third shake of a Warg's tail would find Ragnar limbless.

He cleared his throat sheepishly. "It just seems we've been replacing quite a few windows lately."

CRASH! The second windowpane ruptured into a thousand pieces as a large, caramel-furred force barreled in with a flying leap. Silas landed with grace, his fur glistening glass shards.

Whoa. That was—"Sephone, are you taking notes?"

Sephone's mouth formed the faintest o. "Yes."

How long had Silas waited for *that* entry sentence?

Malachy and Ragnar's delayed reaction—Ragnar staggering back, patting around for his sword, which he'd put on the wrong side, and Malachy falling backwards on his haunches, dropping his axe to steady himself—was as comical as it was disheartening. If this was the state they were in when the revenants attacked …

"Love the lunatic costumes," Silas remarked, judging them up and down. He didn't bat an eye at Aiden's hellhound form. "Apologies for the delay. I was rounding up a few friends." His tail flicked towards the window.

Outside, behind the courtyard's wrought iron fence, an army of ghosts had gathered. Two armies, to be precise. The Sinner's and the Saint's.

"What is the meaning of this, Grave Dancer?" Ragnar demanded.

Malachy joined him by the broken window. "Silas, what's going on?"

"Don't presume to call me by my familiar, Sinner," Silas growled. "There are but two in this room who are so privileged." His candlelight eyes flickered to Rose and Marek.

Malachy wheeled on the Warg, teetering only slightly. "Just whose side are you *on*?"

"The side of justice. And you have done your soldiers a great *in*justice. They followed you to the death, and you have denied them their rest. They are trapped in this world while you have the means necessary to free them. A hundred years they've waited, but you have become comfortable with your new lives. You forget them and the debt you owe for their service to you."

"We didn't ask them to come back," Malachy said lowly.

Silas shook his fur, spraying glass shards.

(Quick, Reader Name Here _____! Cover your eyes or you'll be picking glass out of your imagination for a week!)

"But they did. Out of loyalty. And now, beneath your feet, are the very enemies that destroyed them, and they will destroy you, too, if you do not accept our help and every term and condition that comes with it."

"Uh," said Rose, "about that."

*

"After everything we've done for you, to feed you, to give you a home, *this* is how you repay us?" Ragnar paced, *almost* in a straight line.

"Feed him?" Marek echoed. "He was starving. A Warg needs more than a few steaks and wild berries to live. You

343

should know." He locked eyes with Malachy. "You fought a war over it."

Malachy preferred to look at Silas, taking in his sleek coat and fuller frame. "So, these are the little nuisances packing on your pounds."

Rose wrapped her arms firmly around Silas's neck. "Yes."

"You've been using them to—" Ragnar's outrage was cut short by Marek.

"He hasn't been using us at all. We give to him of our own free will. Screaming doesn't have to be from pain or terror, or did you forget that during the War?"

Ragnar stilled, if only for a moment. "But you know who this Warg is? You *know* what he—?"

"We know who he is. We know what he did during the War. And it matters. But not in the way you think." Rose sought Malachy's gaze, hugging Silas tighter. For a second, Malachy's armor slipped, and she could see his brown eyes full of pain. Then he turned his back to her and stood in front of the third, unbroken windowpane.

Ragnar pinched the bridge of his nose and shook his head. "This is getting out of hand. Marek, Aiden, fetch Cade and Elektra and bring all the patients indoors. Round them up in the Dining Hall and lock every door and window."

Marek and Aiden didn't need telling twice. They hopped out of the two generous-sized holes in the window.

"I myself, along with Malachy, will search every nook and cranny of the asylum before deeming it safe," Ragnar continued. "Sephone, Rose, you will stay here with Grave Dancer until we return."

"You cannot hope to defeat the revenants without the ghosts of your soldiers," Silas persisted. "You know this."

Ragnar shared a glance with Malachy. "You have put my entire asylum at risk, Grave Dancer. The safety of my patients comes first. Only then will we consider your proposal."

"You're making a mistake." Sephone's voice was dead of emotion. "The revenants aren't in the asylum. Search the forest first."

"I agree with Sephone," Rose put in quickly.

Sephone, while surprised, was bolstered by her endorsement. "Marek and Aiden would've seen a horde of revenants sneaking by. They must've left the library through the window and gone into the forest. And if you waste time searching the asylum, they might make it *out* of the forest before we can stop them. What if someone gets killed? What if someone gets killed and someone *else* comes poking around Heartstone Asylum looking for answers? You don't want someone dead, and you *really* don't want someone poking around Heartstone Asylum, do you?"

"The Petrified Forest is not so easily navigated," Ragnar dismissed. "We have time."

They say a watched pot never boils—

—but have you ever done it anyway? You stare and stare and stare, and the water seems so calm, so unperturbed, but just when you're about to walk away and leave it to its business, tiny bubbles start fizzing at the bottom of the pot. They're small, inconsequential, and hopeless for cooking noodles, but you know what they mean.

The boiling has begun.

"No, we *don't* have time," Sephone spouted, the sparkles on her face paint reminiscent of those tiny, fizzing bubbles, "but you're going bankrupt trying to buy some because you're scared. You're *scared*, aren't you? You don't want to search the forest because you *will* find the revenants, and you don't want to! The *great* Sinner and Saint—no, you know what? We're not even going to *address* that insanity right now. We have bigger things to worry about. The asylum doesn't need the Sinner and the Saint. We need Aldric Ragnar and Malachy Thaynwood, but since they're both too *tipsy* to do their job, I'll just search the forest myself!"

"Sephone ..." Ragnar sighed.

"I can help," Rose offered.

"Ah, yes, the sparkly lunatic brigade come to save the day!" Silas said with feeling.

Sephone ignored him. "Help? Oh, yes, you can *help*. By staying in the Dining Hall. The last thing I need is a tagalong getting in the way. I know what I'm doing."

Rose unsheathed T.K, posturing indignantly. "I'll have you know, I'm trained as a knight!"

Silas stamped a paw. "Tutu to the rescue!"

"*No.*" Sephone was in a rolling boil now. "Malachy's right. You aren't qualified for this work. Without magic, you're useless."

Oooh. That tongue, Seph. Watch where you point that thing. Rose lowered her sword, biting hard on her lip to keep the wobbling in check.

Still facing the window, Malachy's wings bristled. "You heard that?"

Silence was her answer.

"Rose ..." Ragnar's eyes were soft and sorrowful.

"It's like Sephone said"—ugh, why did Stormy have to make her voice so rain-soaked and husky?—"we have bigger things to worry about."

Malachy punched the window so abruptly that Beta scrambled under a chair. Glass rained down on the ever-growing pile of fragments on the floor.

"We're searching the asylum," he snarled. "You three stay put or there'll be hell to pay. Sinner's word." He stalked out of the library, knuckles dripping red. Ragnar grimaced apologetically, shot a doleful glance at the broken windowpanes, and followed.

Thirty seconds. For thirty seconds, they managed to do as they were told. Rose rocked back and forth on her feet, crunching the glass beneath into powder. Silas swept fragments away with his tail, Beta chewed contently on a chair leg, and Sephone, arms crossed and spear clenched, didn't move a muscle.

At thirty-one, she stepped towards the broken window.

Rose jumped for the scarlet umbrella on her storyteller's chair and hooked the curved handle under Sephone's arm. "Where are you going? Ragnar said—"

Sephone's vines twisted around the umbrella and wrenched it from her hands. "Ragnar said! Ragnar said!" she mimicked, sounding on the verge of hysteria. "Ragnar says a *lot* of things. I'm going to find the revenants and destroy them before someone gets hurt."

Rose considered herself something of an expert in heads that weren't screwed on right, and at present, Sephone's was as crooked as they come. "By yourself? Two whole armies couldn't take them down! They only have a fighting chance now because they're *dead*! You said it yourself, one drop of revenant blood, and you'll turn to stone. You can't do it alone. It's impossible!"

"Well, that's what I'm supposed to do, isn't it? The impossible. 'Save the worlds, Sephone! It's your destiny!' If you knew the *half* of what goes on here—"

"More than half," Rose muttered, rubbing her nose. Blegh. Hero allergies.

"—you'd know that every crisis, every disaster, it always comes down to *me*." Sephone touched the notch in her lip. "Me and my stupid scar." She turned back to the window just as Rose covered a sneeze. "Just this once, I thought Ragnar was going to handle it. I *wanted* him to handle it. But then we got to his office and ..."

An image flashed in Rose's mind: Rosadox cupping Sephone's face, brushing a thumb against her scar. *Look at me ... You are not the Chosen One ... You're a valuable member of a team ... The weight of the world does not rest on your shoulders, and whoever put it there was dead wrong ... We do this together.* The words rang clear as day, etched in the crystal clarity of her memory.

"*Pu-lease,*" snorted a voice in her head. "*You don't remember half of what I said. I'm doing a voiceover.*"

Oh, hush.

"Look at me," Rose instructed, copying her older self. "Sephone, look."

Sephone obeyed, sans enthusiasm. Her scowl was cracked, bleeding utter exhaustion. Even her vines, her soul signia, were flopping like earthworms. Body and soul, she was spent.

Rose couldn't stop herself from reaching for her. Cradling her face was her first instinct, an instinct she would follow through on in half a decade or so, but for now, her hands settled on Sephone's shoulders. "You're strong, Sephone. Really strong. But these shoulders? They weren't made for the weight of the worlds. No one's are. If you do this, I'm going with you, and there's nothing you can do to stop me."

Sephone's jaw clenched. Then a vine wrapped around

Rose's wrist, giving a gentle squeeze. She nodded once, sharp and decisive.

"This is all very touching," Silas said, "but who says I'm letting either of you go?"

"We need to talk." Rose dragged him aside by the ruff. "You have a *lot* of explaining to do, mister. Yesterday, you told Ragnar you put safety measures in place to keep anything bad from happening to the asylum and its patients tonight. Please explain to me how hiding a murderous horde of the dead *inside the asylum* is a safety measure! Marek and I stuck our necks out for you, Silas! How are we s'posta convince anyone you aren't the bad guy when all you've done so far is invite *more* bad guys into our home? We care about you, but we can't stand here and let you put hundreds of innocent patients in danger. You have to know that."

"Of course I do. I expect no less from you." Silas let out a quiet whine. "I'm not the villain, Rose. The revenants were *never* meant to escape. Hiding them here in the library *was* a safety measure because it would ensure that Malachy and Ragnar would do exactly what I asked, and in return, I would give them what they need to keep the asylum safe: the protection of their armies."

"And what is it you want from them?"

He sighed heavily. "Freedom. For their soldiers. These ghosts, both my enemies and my brothers and sisters, have suffered enough. I feel their pain, their desire to be free from this world. A hundred years is too long to wait for eternity, particularly when Malachy and Ragnar have the means necessary to help them move on. What they needed was a fire kindled beneath them—hiding the revenants here in the asylum was that fire."

Rose nodded slowly. "Is that why the ghosts have been coming so close to the asylum? They've been waiting for the revenants to wake up?"

"The dead can be surprisingly impatient."

This conversation was gobbling up precious time—

(AND NOW I'M PICTURING A TIME-TRAVELING TURKEY.)

—but she had one more question to ask. An important one. "What are these 'means' that Malachy and Ragnar have to help the ghosts move on?"

"Wargs, if you'll remember, are proficient at necromancy," Silas answered. "We were once spirit guides to the dead, leading them to the eternal realm after death. Sometimes, if a spirit became trapped in this world and their window into eternity closed, Wargs would have to find a way to create another one. They fashioned a ritual known as the Calling Howl, which opens a portal to the eternal realm and allows ghosts to pass through freely. It is a painful and, at times, costly ritual that will require Malachy and Ragnar's full cooperation to succeed."

Her stomach squirmed at the words *painful* and *costly*. "Are you sure they'll do it?"

"Despite their shortcomings, they are men of honor. They will do what is necessary."

Rose nodded again, chewing her lip. "I agree that we should help the ghosts move on. I *don't* agree with how you're forcing Malachy and Ragnar's hands to do it. But you did it, it's done, and now we have a bigger problem: stopping the revenants from making it out of the forest." The fractals of a plan were casting a shape in her mind. "I need you to do something for me. Let Sephone and me track down the revenants."

All traces of Silas's earlier humor were gone. "And sign your death certificates?" he growled.

"Did you not just hear me make a very moving speech about teamwork? I literally just said it. We're not gonna take the revenants on by ourselves. We have to work together—the living *and* the dead."

Silas shook his great head. "The ghosts won't help until Malachy and Ragnar have agreed to perform the ritual."

"I know," she said. "But I know one ghost that will. Find Marek and Aiden and tell them to meet us at the graveyard. Oh, and bring shovels."

"Why?"

Rose tapped his nose with the flat of her sword. "Because I have an idea."

ENTRY 34

THE SCENIC ROUTE

"This is a terrible idea."

They crunched through the snow, Beta leading the way with his paramagical-sensitive nose. Up in the sky, the moons inched closer together. Uncomfortably close. Moonlight reflected off the mounds of snow, lighting the world from the ground up. Barring cloud coverage, Moonsfrost Eve is usually the brightest night of the year, which is an advantage when hunting down a horde of the undead in a haunted forest.

Rose knocked Sephone's shoulder. "D'you have a better one, Miss Let's-Rush-In-Swords-Glinting-With-No-Plan-At-All? This is a wonderful idea."

Sephone knocked her back. "It's terrible. Revenants aren't mindless zombies. We read it in the cookbook! They're ghosts animating their dead bodies, operating with the same intelligence they had when they were alive. And you think you can trick them?"

"I'm tricking them *because* they're intelligent. They'd be much harder to predict if they were stupid. Try leading mindless zombies into a trap."

They were quiet again, keeping an ear out for moans, a nose out for rotting flesh, and an eye out for footprints. Nothing.

"What do you think they want?" Rose asked softly. "The revenants. Blackout says they're out seeking revenge on Caelix, but he's been dead for centuries. What now?"

"You saw what they did to the armies. Look at the trees. Their *blood* did that. They just want to destroy everything that comes across their path." Sephone gripped her spear, kindly refraining from adding, *And we're next. Yay us.*

The muscles in Beta's neck were tense, his fur raised but for no obvious reason. If the revenants had been here, there'd be signs. Staggering footprints, a most distinguishing smell. But nope. Just still air and the muted chill of snow.

"I've been thinking about that," Rose continued. "Now that we know the graveyard was for the revenants, where are the bodies of the soldiers?"

"I think I know." Sephone paused, rolling words around her tongue like peppermints. "There's a place beneath the asylum where we keep ... well ..."

"Things like the giant snake you were sneaking through Ragnar's window my first night here?"

"Yeah." Sephone scratched absently at her lip scar. The notch was even more pronounced than usual with the blue lip ink of her lunatic costume. She caught Rose staring. "You're wondering how I got it, right? I don't remember. It's just a scar, but Ragnar thinks it makes me special. The 'savior of all their problems.' "

"Seems like a lotta pressure for one little scar."

She laughed, short but genuine. "You're telling me."

Say what you will about the powers of imagination—

(AND FROM YOU, IT SHOULD BE ALL GOOD THINGS, OR WE WOULDN'T BE HAVING THIS CONVERSATION.)

—but take a hike through the Petrified Forest at night, and you start seeing things. Stone leaves that haven't moved in a century seem to sway in the breeze. Tree limbs begin to look like *actual* limbs—an arm here, a leg there, each carved from stone.

Rose reached for Amber's necklace tucked under her shirt. The outline of the key pendant pressed against the fabric, and she pushed her finger through the key's heart-shaped bow. It was a conduit of her sister's presence, making her braver.

Beta halted in his tracks, teeth bared, a soundless growl building in his chest. Rose knelt beside him. "What is it, boy? Whatja find?" His nose pointed upward, and she froze. "Uh, Sephone? Remember how I said the revenants were smart enough to trap?"

Sephone leaned on her spear, sounding resigned. "Yes?"

"They're also smart enough to trap *us*."

Figures dropped from the stone Scalpo trees like scalplums, forming a circle around them. To be fair, it was easy to see *why* the revenants had been so difficult to detect. You think "ghosts operating their dead bodies," you assume that they're shambling, smelly corpses, correct? Then you, like your darling narrator and her reluctant companion, would be forgetting one important detail. These revenants were the Wingless Ones of *Blackout's Tales*, cursed in life by Dimidia with hearts of stone. And their curse, as predicted by *Cooking Up a Scare: The Necromancer's Guide to Undead Recipes*, had tripled its potency in their afterlife.

The revenants' bodies were remarkably preserved in a grayish, scaly, crackling layer, like they were turning to stone from the outside in.

"Someone forgot to moisturize," Rose murmured.

(*Note to selves: undead spa idea?*

Is your skin flaking, graying, or falling off in chunks? Do you suffer from dry bones? Necrosis? Are you dead on your feet? Book your weekend at The

The revenants' skin troubles didn't end there. Their bodies were ravaged by blade marks and battle wounds, some from the War o' the Wargs, and others, perhaps, as old as the deathblows of Caelix himself. Every slice in their skin was clotted by a crusty black scab, evil and oozing. The revenants' faces were petrifying—in more ways than one. Mouths twisted, jaws gaping, their grotesque expressions were hardened in place, frozen in rage and pain.

But despite their profusion of physical deformities, it was their lack of wings that unnerved Rose most of all.

"Pick up Beta," Sephone commanded, quiet and firm. "When I count to three, grab onto me and don't let go."

Grab onto her? But that—that was like hugging. And hugging was dangerous. "But I—"

"No buts. One." Something was happening to Sephone's skin. Her russet complexion hardened, darkening like it had in the library the day before. "Two." Ridges appeared and dark knots like birthmarks. *Bark.* Her skin was turning into tree bark! The vines that

357

reminded Rose of veins popped through, sporting small green leaves, and her rich dark hair split into thousands upon thousands of fine roots.

This was Sephone's soul signia in its fullest glory. And it was very weirdly beautiful.

"Three!"

Rose threw her arms around the scratchy bark that was Sephone's neck, crushing Beta between them. Vines shot from Sephone's wrist, wrapping around a stone tree branch outside the circle of the undead. She secured an arm around Rose's waist—it really *was* an almost-hug— and swung the three of them over the revenants' heads. The treetops were too low for flight, but Sephone opened her wings, using their momentum to glide. They hit the ground, and the almost-hug was over.

Rose kinda missed it.

"Smooth move!" She slapped Sephone a high five and immediately regretted the splinters. The revenants hadn't moved from their spot. They stared from a distance, still as statues, as if their curse had reached the muscles in their legs. "Think they'll catch up?"

The revenants made a sound like rocks grinding in a landslide and broke into a very un-statue-like run.

"Yep." Sephone dragged Rose up by the armpits. "Time to execute your terrible idea."

(*WEIGH IN ON SOMETHING, READER NAME HERE* _____: *DID*

Running through water is hard. Running through *solid* water? Possibly worse. "Shoulda—brought—snowshoes!" Rose panted. It didn't help that she was carting an umbrella or that she was wearing Marek's oversized cloak because hers was *still* missing. Beside her, Sephone's expression was unyielding (hard to avoid when your face is made of bark), but her breathing was short and ragged. At this rate, the revenants would catch up with them long before they reached the graveyard.

Unless.

Unless they took the scenic route.

"Have—idea!" Rose gasped.

"Terrible," Sephone wheezed.

"Wonderful," Rose wheezed back and took the lead. Beta bounded alongside her in the snow, the only one not losing steam. Good. She needed his help for what came next. How'd Marek's directions go again? *Follow the path to the fork, make a right off the trail, another right at the broken branch, go straight till the moss-covered boulder, another left, and,* "Yes!"

Ragnar's ramshackle old cottage came into view. Rose barreled past the iron gate and into the half-destroyed home. Without Gormonger's ghostly presence lurking, Beta followed her in without hesitation. It was Sephone who was reluctant to cross the threshold.

"Get in!" Rose pulled her inside and shoved the unhinged door over the entrance.

"What are we doing in here?" Sephone hissed.

"Slowing down the revenants."

"How? According to your *terrible* idea, the revenants should be able to make it past the iron fence."

Rose had a theory about the revenants. A very *logical* theory, mind you. Iron is a strong repellent of ghosts; Malachy and Ragnar had built the iron fence around the graveyard for that purpose, as a precaution to keep the revenants contained. Sounds reasonable. But revenants aren't *just* ghosts. They're ghosts covered in dead bodies. What if their flesh provided enough of a barrier to let them pass through normal paramagical repellents?

"Yes, but *they* don't know we know that. They think that we think that we're safe in here." Rose looked around fondly at the crumbling cottage. "Didja know Gor tried to decapitate me with a footstool in this very spot?"

"What I wouldn't give for that footstool," Sephone muttered.

Rose pressed her eye against a crack in the wall. Outside, the revenants were testing her theory. One of them stood in the middle of the gate, clawing at the invisible paramagical barrier. He looked like he was swimming through tar. With a final butterfly stroke, he stumbled forward, past the barrier, and into the iron-fenced yard.

She stepped away from the wall. "They're through.

Climb out the back window, and when I tell you to cover your ears, cover them."

They hopped the chasm in the floor caused by Beta's growl several weeks ago. When they passed the specter-glass, unmoved since Gormonger last pushed it, Rose couldn't resist. "Hey, Sephone? Ever read 'Legend of the Ghost Who Lost His Eyepiece'?"

Sephone glowered at her. "What do you think?"

Rose hoisted Beta out the broken window and climbed after him. They crouched outside, waiting for the revenants to burst through the broken door. And burst they did, flooding the room like a colony of ants.

Yanking Sephone back from the window, Rose shouted, "Cover your ears!" and spoke the one command forbidden to all Sonorific Husky dogs. "Beta ... SPEAK!"

"WOOOOOOOOOOOOOOOOOF!"

His sonic bark knocked them off their feet, and Ragnar's cottage—his poor cottage—survivor of a deso-lating attack by a patient with unstable magic, years haunted by a cooped-up Gormonger, and a growl by a Sonorific Husky puppy that shook its foundation to the core, gave a sigh of release and collapsed. The revenants were crushed by an avalanche of plaster and mortar.

Rose raised an eyebrow at Sephone. "Terrible?"

"Wonderful," she admitted. A scaly, gray hand shot out of the wreckage. "Let's keep it that way," she said, and they ran for the graveyard.

They jumped the iron fence, dodging headstones and

leaping over open graves. The graves' dirty innards were scattered about, pits wallowing in darkness. Certain gravediggers had been busy. Rose slowed to a stop outside Silas's cave, breathing hard, and tied Beta's leash to a stalagmite inside. "Stay, Beta. *Stay.*" The last thing she wanted to see was her precious pup turn into a garden statue from an encounter with revenant blood.

Sephone pinched her lightly. "Look. Round Two."

The revenants, slightly dustier and far more annoyed, congregated by the graveyard's arched iron gate. Experience had taught them well. They didn't shove their way through the paramagical barrier but selected a scout from their numbers, an undead Wingless One with intersecting scabs on his cheeks like black *X*s.

X-Factor stuck his arms into the thick, invisible paramagical barrier and performed a beautiful breaststroke that sent him headfirst into the graveyard. He righted himself on his stony legs, heedful of the open graves, and set his sights on Rose and Sephone. The revenant charged, hurdling over dirt mounds and the gaping holes in the earth.

Sephone's wings flared, and she twisted her spear. "Keep him as far away from you as possible. Avoid any bloody wounds. We have to make this clean or we're dead."

Rose cleared her sword of its sheath, crisscrossing it with her closed umbrella. Lightning buzzed on her tongue, and she crushed it against the roof of her mouth.

Now was not the time to lose a single drop of magic. Got that, subconscious? Not a drop.

The revenant was almost on them, his frozen face positively murderous.

"You're head, I'm feet!" Sephone shouted and skidded into a slide. The shaft of her spear whacked the revenant's legs, and he tripped forward, the perfect height for Rose to slice cleanly through his neck with T.K.'s mighty blade. Only it wasn't clean. It was *stuck*. She wrenched it free and struck again. And again. And again. "Oh, you've *gotta* be kidding me!" Toxic, black blood dripped from the wound in the revenant's neck, and Rose jumped away. "Their bones are made of stone!"

Thwack went Sephone's spear, and the undead Wingless One was on the ground, belly-up. The too-big sleeves of Marek's cloak had unrolled at least a foot past Rose's hands, and the too-long hem was coming untucked from the belt. She pushed back the loose fabric and lifted T.K. high like an executioner's axe, bringing it down on the revenant's neck with all her strength. There was a resounding *crack*, and the head rolled away from its body.

And that, lords and ladies, is how you kill a revenant.

"Duck!" Sephone yelled, and Rose instinctively hunched over as a forked stone branch whizzed overhead. The revenants were making their landslide noises again, furious and throwing whatever they could get their hands on. But they made no move to enter the graveyard.

Well, that simply wouldn't do.

Rose took a step towards the revenants, dropping Marek's cumbersome cloak from her shoulders. She stood there, a girl in a tutu facing down a horde of the undead.

(AND IF THAT ISN'T A SENTENCE YOU'VE ALWAYS WANTED TO READ, THEN YOU, DEAR READER NAME HERE _____, FRANKLY HAVEN'T READ ENOUGH.)

Behind her was the unmistakable *fump* of a gravestone tipping over, and a brush of cold breath kissed her neck. Her shoulders relaxed.

"Ohhh, you want to *throw* things. I'm game." Rose caught Sephone's eye and grinned, nodding at the forked branch and the revenant's severed head. "Let's play!"

Scooping the head up with the branch, Sephone tossed it in the air, and Rose, converting the flat of her blade into a bat, hit it as it sank. The connection was solid; it flew the length of the graveyard and landed at the revenants' feet.

They gawked at the head. Then at Rose and Sephone. Then the head again.

The moment of indecision was over. With a cry like a grinding stone, the revenants piled through the iron gate, flashing full tilt across the graveyard, and the world shattered with shadows and growls as a hellhound, a ghost Warg, and a Shadow Boy lunged from the open graves.

ENTRY 35

STONE COLD

Fight scenes. A pain to visualize, aren't they? They're all, "and so-and-so got punched in the face" and "so-and-so did something funky with her sword" and "so-and-so did a mega-awesome mid-flip kick backwards on tiptoes and knocked the weapon out of other so-and-so's hand." What does that even *look* like? Ridiculous. For your convenience, and to avoid unnecessary strain on the imagination, your narrator is proud to present a simplified version of the following sequence, namely the *sounds* of a fight scene. You may fill in imagery however you see fit.

Without further ado, the Sounds of the Battlefield:

Snick.
Whump.
"Blegh!"

And it's variants:

Snick.
Whump.
"Gross!"

And:

Snick!
Crunch.
"Oops. There went your modeling career."

Battling the revenants had turned into a game. *Bury Your Dead*, Rose called it. The objective? Shoving revenants into open graves and locking them inside their old coffins. The rules? No skin-to-skin contact with the undead. Must capture revenants in four moves or less. Less means more points. Tripping acceptable. Every fresh wound inflicted on a revenant equals points lost (and, you know, the likelihood of your mortality rate spiking). Revenant death by beheading, while occasionally required for survival, resets points to zero.

Rose was up three points. Gormonger had boasted the lead—lucky dog didn't have to worry about one drop of revenant blood turning his ghostly self to stone—till he'd stopped to dig more graves, and she quickly ended his winning streak. Keeping her own was a challenge. Sweet *magic*, she was tired. Ottis's worst training sessions hadn't been this bad. How long had they been fighting? Twenty minutes? An hour? *All night*? No, that was impossible. It wasn't even midnight. The twelve moons were overlapping in the sky, bathing the world in blue. A couple more minutes, and they'd have to retreat to Silas's cave or be pelted to a pulp by the eclipse's moonstones.

Duking it out with the revenants by the light of glow-worms? Not a pleasant thought. Out here with the snow and the moons, it was almost as light as day. Gormonger lapped up the moonlight like a bowl of milk. The ghosts would be strong tonight, drawing their energy from the moons. Ironic that the balls of concentrated moonlight, which would be falling from the sky in ten minutes' time, would also rip through their manifestations like rocks through paper.

(*Paper doesn't beat rock. It just doesn't. Forget rock, paper, scissors for making important decisions. Decisions should be logic-based. Thumb wars are far more rational.*)

Silas *promised* Malachy and Ragnar would agree to their role in whatever ritual the ghosts needed to move on if it meant saving the asylum. But what if Malachy and Ragnar didn't wanna do it? Or what if they did, and they arrived at the graveyard just as the clock struck twelve and a shower of moonstones tore their armies to spectral shreds?

Fwoop!

Whump.

—zap!

It happened faster than Rose could think. One moment she was bombarding a revenant with her patented umbrella-lunge sidestep—the next, that revenant was lunging for her throat. Her muscles seized with fatigue. She couldn't bring her sword arm up fast enough, and that was when a super-charged bolt of lightning shot down her umbrella arm, bursting from the tip and striking the revenant square in the chest. The revenant stumbled back towards an open grave—four-point lead, here she comes!—and a sneaky shadow wrapped around its ankle, yanking it off its feet and sending it headfirst into the hole. There was the crack of a coffin lid slamming shut. "My point!" Marek cheered.

"Cheap shot," Rose grumbled.

"Easy mark. Now go catch your breath a minute."

"But—"

"But nothing." He loosed a mighty swing of his flail, and the receiving revenant crashed backwards into one of its friends. They spun away, a tumbleweed of arms and legs. "Pace yourself. You're of no use tripping into a grave from exhaustion."

That, and he didn't want her using her magic. Using it and losing it. Already Stormy felt smaller in her chest, like that one discharge of lightning had shrunk it to half its size. "You just wanna steal my winning streak."

"Exactly. And if you stay, I'll keep taking your points."

Rose huffed. "Point taken." Dodging Sephone's vines, Aiden's fire breath, Gormonger's fountains of grave dirt, and the rampant pandemonium of the undead, she trotted to a tree at the edge of the graveyard and collapsed behind it, completely out of breath. No one else was gasping for air. No one else needed a sit-down break. Maybe there was something to this "pace yourself" thing.

Massaging her sword arm, Rose watched the battle from behind her tree. Aiden was impressive, Gormonger in his element, but Marek and Sephone were mesmerizing. They didn't just fight. They poured their *souls* into it. Sephone's soul signia, in all her tree-girl glory, shot vines right and left and recruited the help of the Scalpo trees, so that stone roots erupted from the ground, capturing revenants in unbreakable nets. Marek's soul signia burst from his wings, cyclones of shadows catching the undead in whirls of darkness and throwing them bodily into graves or stone tree trunks. This wasn't unstable magic Rose was witnessing. These were finite minds tapped into the infinite magic of the subconscious. They fought like they'd trained for this, like fighting monsters was something they did every other weekend.

And maybe it was.

Even so, three asylum patients, a hellhound, and a ghost Warg weren't gonna beat what two armies couldn't,

369

and Rose never expected them to. All they had to do was keep the revenants busy till reinforcements arrived. That would be any minute now.

Any minute.

Any.

Minute.

Around the world, the countdown to the eclipse was starting. Rose had to call for a retreat. Cupping her hands around her mouth, she shouted, "Cave! Get to the cave!"

All across the graveyard, her companions looked up at the sky where the moons overlapped, forming a long oval. Sephone quickly spun a web of vines between two trees, and Aiden set fire to her handiwork, creating a flaming barrier that allowed them to beat a hasty retreat. Gormonger followed, a speedy ball of ghost light.

Marek had a longer sprint to the cave. Shadows spilled from his wings like twin waterfalls, knocking the revenants off their feet. He gestured wildly at Rose. Ha! If he thought for one *second* that she'd retreat without him, he needed to get his head checked. Which, being an asylum patient, was pretty routine, actually.

Shadow Boy kept coming, flattening everything in his path. He was a rolling boulder, an invincible rock that nothing could chip, nothing could harm, nothing could—

He was close now. Close enough for her to see the panic written all over his face like a toddler's messy scribble.

Swathes of shadows plowed full steam ahead, slamming into Rose with a hug like a freight train. She flew back from the tree, and her skull banged against the ground.

Black spots. Black spots everywhere.

Marek stood over her, arms out, wings flared protectively, and his face ... his face was *covered* in black spots. Rose blinked to clear her vision, and the spots disappeared, soaking into his skin, changing its color from brown to gray. In the tree above, a revenant ran a sharp stone leaf across its scaly forearm. Black blood poured freely from the self-inflicted wounds and onto Marek's head.

His sweet, sweet head that was already a lifeless visage of stone.

ENTRY 36

ROCK OF AGES

The moons eclipsed.

Dropping her sword and umbrella, Rose took cover in the shadow of Marek's now shadow-less wing as thousands of moonstones fell from the sky. They were blue. Blue like his eyes. The night was crying for Shadow Boy, blue, glittery tears spilling from its face, drowning her in a sea of sorrow. Tearing off her glove, she reached into the downpour. Two moonstones landed in her palm. She cradled them and her hand, throbbing with grape-sized welts, to her chest.

Rat-a-tat-tat. Rat-a-tat-tat. Frozen moonlight bouncing off a statue.

Rose squeezed her eyes shut. Her face pressed against stone feathers. She was cold. So very cold without Marek's cloak.

Moonstones piled past her ankles. She counted to

sixty in her head, and just like that, the *rat-a-tat-tats* ceased, and the frozen moonlight dissolved at her feet.

The eclipse was over. The new year had begun.

That's the magic of moonstones. The moment the eclipse is finished, they melt into puddles of moonlight, sinking into the snow and making it glow for days. If you want to keep a moonstone, you have to catch it as it falls, catch it with your bare hands. That's why they're so rare. No one wants to pay the price.

She brought her hand, swollen and bleeding, to her lips and kissed the moonstones inside. Then she stepped away from the stone wing that had given her shelter and looked her guardian angel in the eyes. They were wrong. All wrong. Dull and gray and nothing like moonstones. His face was wrong, too. Marek was never meant to be a garden statue. He was too—too—

Rose stood on tiptoe and ran her fingers over his squat nose, his caterpillar eyebrows, his broad, square cheeks.

Good lords, he was the ugliest garden statue on the face of the planet. A *pigeon* wouldn't perch on him.

But for all the wrong, there was a single right: Marek's posture. His bulk was on display, wings splayed, arms straight out and hands up to say, "You want her? You have to get through me first." He was a monument to guardian angels everywhere.

"I'd do it," she choked. "I'd put you in my garden. You take good care of roses."

"And I always will. See? You've finally found the perfect pet

rock," he'd say and laugh. His full, rumbling laugh. The most wonderful sound in the world.

A sound she'd never—that she'd never hear—

Her storm cloud was so heavy in her chest that she tipped forward, grabbing Marek's waist for support. You know what the saddest thing was? This was the closest she'd come to hugging Marek in *two years*. Rain gushed from her eyes, draining grief and magic.

"*Shhh, Thunder Rose. It's okay. It's okay.*"

"No, it's *not* okay!" Rose sobbed. "You're *gone*! You're *gone*, do you hear me? *GONE!*"

"*Rosy?*" Another voice in her head. "*Snap out of it, Rosy! He does hear. He does. That's his voice! Listen to me! Listen to yourself think. He's still here.*"

Rosadox. How could Rose have been so blind? In the library, her future self had made it sound like she and Marek were in this together, both of them time travelers, Paradoxes, *whatever they were*, living out adventures side-by-side. But if that were true, where was Marek's future self that night? Why wasn't *he* at Rosadox's side?

Because on Moonsfrost Eve 1525, six years earlier, he die—

"*No!*" Rosadox's voice cracked like thunder. "*Think about it. We write the letters from the future, but who makes the carvings that come with the letters? Who?*"

The carvings. The carvings on Marek's mobile. The empty coffin with its clinking spades and the four hands piled on top of each other. They had Shadow Boy's finger-prints all over them.

"Yes! And how could he have made them if he was dead? Listen to me, Rosy. Look up. Look up!"

Rose lifted her head. Time stood still.

Not like the expression when something amazing or terrible happens and your brain is working overtime trying to absorb every detail so that it *feels* like time has stopped. Time had *actually* stopped. The revenant from the tree was suspended in the air, mid-fall from the lowest branch. In the mouth of the cave, Sephone was on her knees, restraining a stock-still Beta. Aiden huddled around them, arms bracing Sephone's shoulders, paws locking over Beta's chest. Gormonger had his head thrown back in a miserable howl.

Not one of them moved.

"Did ..." There was no *way* she had, but ... "Did I do this?"

"Well," said a familiar voice, "sort of." A girl stepped out from behind the tree. She was different than the girl from the library. Same curls, same chubby cheeks, but the coyness was gone. There was nothing subtle about her laughing eyes, just giggles and glee. Giddiness rolled off her feathers like perfume, and she walked like someone was tickling her feet, every step a wiggle and a dance. The girl was young. Hardly older than Rose was now. She had a sword in one hand and a scarlet umbrella in the other.

And still no storm cloud.

"Wow. I just—wow." Rosadox circled her, biting her lower lip like Rose did when she was pinning down a squeal. "Look at you, with your tutu and everything! I could just—*uhn!*" An abrupt shake of her head. "Sorry. I've never been on this side of the equation before. It's exciting!" She turned to Marek, and her face sobered. She placed a hand against his cheek. "Hey, Boulder Brain."

A voice reverberated in Rose's head. *"I heard that!"*

Rosadox seemed to shudder with amusement. "Of course you did!"

Rose rubbed her temples. "How is this—?"

Her (slightly) older self pulled her hands away from her head. "Don't think about it. You'll give us a headache. It gets explained, don't worry, but that one's not on me. My job's to save Boulder Brain from a lifetime of scaring pigeons. But before I do, I have to give you something extremely important." Rosadox stared at Rose very seriously. Then she enveloped her in a crushing hug.

Rose squirmed against herself, wings fighting to break free, but Rosadox held on tighter. "Shh. Shh, Rosy. You need this." She stroked her curls. "You need this."

Rose hadn't been hugged in *years*. It felt ... weird and wrong and warm and wonderful. Her body gave in, slumping against the identical one embracing her. Tears pricked her eyes.

"There." Rosadox pushed her back but kept her hands on her shoulders. "Hugging is extremely important."

Rose sniffed and swiped at her cheeks. "How do we save Marek?"

Rosadox chewed her lip, pretending to ponder. "D'you remember when we first met Marek, and we saw his eyes? What did we think about them?"

That was easy. "That we should scoop 'em out and add them to our gem, button, and assorted shiny objects collection. Because they looked like moonstones."

"And what do you have in your hand?"

The two blue balls of frozen moonlight were cold in her palm.

"Eyes are the windows to the soul," Rosadox said, pressing the tip of her blade into one of Marek's stone eyeballs, "and his are all blocked up. Let's give his soul something to shine through, shall we?" And with that, she drove her sword into her best friend's eye socket.

Well, okay then. Rose stuck her own T.K. into Marek's other eyeball and began chipping. The going was slow—or maybe it wasn't. Hard to gauge when time's standing still. Soon (whenever that was), Shadow Boy's eyes were nothing more than shards of gray on the glowing snow, his sockets scooped clean. Rose pressed the moonstones into the empty holes. Perfect fit.

Rosadox stepped back to admire their work. "That should do it." She gave another one of her jiggles like someone was running a feather down her spine. Or she really had to pee.

"Is that it?" Rose asked. "Is that all we do?"

"No. One more thing. I have to give you something extremely important."

Rose rolled her eyes and tackled her future self in a hug. Rosadox giggled, hugging her back. "You're adorable. But I have something else, too." She hooked a finger under the chain around Rose's neck and pulled out Amber's sister necklace. Pinching the key pendant, Rosadox produced a small, gray stone from her pocket. It had a distinct mottled pattern, dark dots at the center of hexagons, and it was shaped like a heart. The same exact shape as the key's heart-shaped bow. "It's called a petoskey stone. Very special, very rare." She clicked the stone into the pendant. Another perfect fit. "Amber says these necklaces are 'the keys to each other's hearts.' " She undid the top button of Marek's flannel shirt, a non-magical item that hadn't turned to stone, and tugged it down on his right side over his heart.

(WHAT? YOUR HEART'S ON YOUR RIGHT SIDE, TOO, ISN'T IT?)

"Our sissy is smarter than she knows. C'mere."

Rose moved closer, and a warm sensation pierced her shirt. Her necklace's new stone had changed, blue light pulsing from the dots in the petoskey stone's hexagons.

"Shine it over his heartstone." Rosadox was bouncing on the balls of her feet.

Rose waved the key pendant over Marek's smooth, hard skin, and in the flashes of blue light she saw

—"Marek got a *tattoo*? And didn't *tell* me?" It was a stunning piece of artwork: the face of a clock set over his heart with all the cogs and gears spilling out the sides. Rose withdrew the pendant's light, and the clock vanished from his skin. "Wait, he got a tattoo with *invisible ink*?" She inspected it further. The clock's hands pointed to twelve o' two. The exact time Rosadox had *stopped* time. And where most hands join at the center of a clock, this one had a keyhole.

A *keyhole*? She needed to have a word with Marek's tattoo artist about the drawbacks of invisible ink and putting *holes* in their patrons. It was literally notched into Shadow Boy's skin. She could stuff her pinky into it except—ew.

A keyhole. Huh. Rose rubbed a thumb over her necklace. She wasn't supposed to ...?

Rosadox rested a chin on her shoulder. "It's a keyhole. You're holding a key. What d'you think?"

Rose held the pendant up to the hole. The third perfect fit of the night. If she jammed this into Marek's chest, it would drill right into his heart. "Is this gonna hur—?"

Rosadox slammed her hand on top of Rose's, inserting the key deep into Marek's chest. "Not a bit," she chirped.

Rose shook out her stinging hand.

"Now, turn the key." Just turn the key, and her best friend's heart would start beating again. Or maybe it wouldn't. Turn the key, and her world would fall apart. Or fall into place.

Rose had seen this scene before. She was Caelix. She was the Heartbreaker on his knees, begging a statue to come to life, to reach down and fix his broken heart. Praying for Dimidia to save him.

Click. She turned the key with its pulsing blue light ... and prayed.

The pulsing stopped. The dots of light flickered and went dull. There was a low moan, the sound of tectonic plates scraping together, of an earthquake splitting the ground. A hand touched her shoulder, and Rose looked up.

"It never ceases to amaze me," Marek said through barely moving lips, "what a girl in a tutu can accomplish."

*

He could've doubled as a revenant.

From a distance, anyway. Up close, Marek's skin was encased in a layer of stone that splintered with movement, revealing the normal brown beneath. And his *eyes*. His eyes were so, so alive, blue, if no longer moonstones. The gems had transformed into regular eyeballs, which was a bit disappointing, to be honest.

"Why? Because now you can't scoop them out and add them to your gem, button, and assorted shiny objects collection?" Marek raised his eyebrows. A poof of stone dust, and three rifts appeared in his forehead.

Lightning tingled at Rose's fingertips, and it took every ounce of self-control not to hug him. "You're reading my mind. He's reading my mind!"

"I know." Rosadox's fingers tapped manically at her side. "Isn't it great?"

"How—"

She tsked. "*Patience.* I came to save Boulder Brain, remember? Not explain *how* I saved him or anything else." Rosadox stood on tiptoe and knocked on Marek's head. "Hm. Still boulder-y. Welp, did my best." She wiggled her nose against his stony one, and Marek's cheeks cracked with a smile. "How're you feeling, Shadow Boy?"

He groaned, rolling his shoulders with a series of cracks. "Stiff."

"You, sir, have a date with a bubble bath and a pumice stone. You'll be good as new." Rosadox twisted the key in his chest and jerked it out of the lock.

Marek winced, touching the spot of the now-invisible clock tattoo. "That felt ... "

"Not as weird as you were expecting?" She held the key up by its chain and swung it back and forth in front of Rose's eyes. Pfft, you can't hypnotize *yourself.* Can you? "Put this on." Rosadox pulled an identical necklace from around her neck. "See? I never leave home without it. Or this." She picked up Rose's fallen umbrella. "Remember what I say in the letter. Don't open the umbrella until you truly need it."

Rose accepted the necklace and umbrella dutifully. "Yes, m'lady."

Her older self nodded in satisfaction. "My work here is do—AH!" She gave a sudden whoop and sprung into the air, wings flapping frenziedly. "Stop it! Stop! That *tickles!*" Landing sideways, she laughed breathlessly and shook out her feathers. "That's it! I can't hold it any longer."

"Maybe you shoulda gone before you came," Rose suggested.

"I do *not* have to pee!" Rosadox's glare was electrified even as she crossed her legs and wobbled. "I just have to go—*not like that*. 'Go' as in I'm leaving."

"Wait. Before you go—as in leave—do you have any advice for defeating the revenants?" Marek asked.

She squeezed her eyes shut in great concentration to hold *something* in. "Sure. Close your eyes and turn around. No peeking! Are you ready?"

"Yes!" they chorused. No answer. They waited, listening. Something shifted in the atmosphere. A stillness became active. There was wind and falling snowflakes and an army of the dead groaning. Time had resumed. Rosadox was gone.

And in the distance? The war howls and battle cries of their salvation on the horizon.

Better late than never.

ENTRY 37

PAYING THE PRICE

The ghosts were magnificent.

There they were, sworn enemies in life, comrades in death, led as a single army by the Sinner and the Saint. They charged through the haunted grove just outside the graveyard, the ghosts' iridescent edges flickering as they soaked in the moons' glorious light. Their manifestations were so strong they looked almost solid. But when they reached the iron gate, it took Malachy riding Silas to smash it apart, destroying the paramagical barrier. The ghosts poured through the opening like water through a broken dam, submerging the revenants in ghost light.

The fighting began.

"Should we help?" Rose asked uncertainly.

"Yes," said Marek. "By getting out of the way."

Moving to the cave was a chore. Never mind the icy

shock of walking through an unsuspecting spirit or deflecting sprays of dirt from ghosts digging fresh graves or dodging the occasional flying revenant limb—Marek's body was still ninety-five percent encased in stone. He staggered, each step a concerted effort to lift his legs. Aiden spotted them from the cave, and he and Sephone rushed to help.

"What *happened* to you?" Sephone grunted, hoisting Marek's stone arm over her shoulders.

"Oh, I died for a few minutes," he said. "Nothing too traumatic."

They collapsed in the mouth of the cave where Gormonger lay with his head on his ethereal paws. He watched the battle wage with a grumpy expression.

"Gor!" Rose exclaimed. "Your army's out there fighting for their afterlives, and you're sitting on the sidelines? What gives?"

He grumbled something and nestled his snout deeper between his paws. "Just don't FEEL like it."

"You? Don't feel like getting into an out-and-out brawl?" Marek dragged himself painfully to Gormonger's side and sat. Rose took his other side just like they did during sessions. Only now, instead of a haunted mirror between them, it was a warhorse-sized ghost wolf. "All right, big guy. Talk to us. What's going on?"

Gormonger blew a snort of misty ghost breath. "Aren't YOU the ones always telling ME that fighting for fighting's sake only lowers my opinion of my own self-worth and the worth of those around me?"

"Ye-e-s," Rose said.

"And aren't YOU the ones always telling me that just 'cause I'm BIG doesn't mean fighting is all I'm good for, that I'm more than just some MEATHEAD?"

"Also, yes," Marek said.

Gormonger sat up suddenly, towering over both of them. "Then WHY would I go pick a fight for someone who doesn't even WANT me there?"

Rose was silent, observing the maelstrom of ghosts and revenants outside the cave. It was chaos out there—noise and light and showers of grave dirt as the ghosts played Bury Your Dead, unearthing coffins and forcing the revenants inside. "Look at 'em, Gor. It's a mess out there. They need help. And who's better at cleaning up messes than you?"

"They locked me up. They HATE me."

"They need you." Marek picked up her thread. "They need you to be the bigger wolf here—and you are by far the *biggest* wolf here. Just look at the size of those paws! And those legs. You could dig those graves faster than five Wargs combined."

Gormonger stretched one of his impressive legs and scratched absently at an ear.

"And during the War, wasn't yours the only voice that could carry across the battlefield? I see Malachy and

Ragnar shouting a lot of orders that no one seems to be hearing."

It was true. Not even Malachy's dog whistle, the one he used with the Sonorific Huskies, was carrying over the noise. Rose drove it home. "You're the strongest soldier they have. You're a—a *tide* turner! Why else d'you think the ghosts tricked you into being trapped inside that cottage? They know you're a fighter. But we know you're *more* than a fighter. This time you aren't fighting for fighting's sake. You're fighting *for* someone. For them."

Gormonger licked his teeth over and over, contemplating. "I won't fight for them. But there is someone I WILL fight for." And he covered their cheeks in spectral slobber and barreled into the fray bellowing, "MORONS! He's saying pull to the RIGHT! Not pull up in FLIGHT!"

You'd think a fight to the undeath would last an eternity—

(HA!)

—but the ghosts attacked with a vengeance. It was the Battle of the Petrified Forest all over again, and they'd had a hundred years to re-imagine its ending. They fought with power and purpose, but none more than Malachy and Silas. Seeing him ride the only living Warg in the graveyard, it was easy to picture Malachy in his glory days before the War. Back when the Sinner was known only as the most celebrated, undefeated Warg rider of all time. Gripping Silas's ruff in one hand and wielding his axe in the other, Malachy was the paradigm of ballerina balance and executioner's grace.

And who better than a ballerina executioner to end the battle?

The butt of his axe rammed the last revenant in the chest. The undead Wingless One tripped towards an empty grave, and Silas swiped a paw, completing the action. The slam of the final coffin lid was drowned out by the ruckus of an army vindicated. A bark from Beta wouldn't have broken the noise.

And then, one by one, their clamor ceased.

Ragnar sheathed his sword like it weighed a hundred pounds. "What an honor it has been," he said, "to fight with you this day. Never before have I been prouder to raise my sword at your side. But now ..."

"Now it is time to fulfill your word," Silas finished. "We have done all you asked of us. The battle is won. The price must be paid."

Malachy dismounted slowly.

"Price?" Rose said. The price of the ritual to open a portal to the eternal realm? She waded through the sea of spirits, Marek close behind. "What's the price?"

"We have your word, Saint. A bond not easily broken." Silas looked pointedly at Ragnar.

Ragnar bowed his head. "I will keep my word, Grave Dancer. I always have."

"And he always will." Malachy clapped him on the back. "Time to put our troops to rest."

"How?" Marek asked. His question went unanswered. Malachy was still gung-ho on pretending they didn't exist.

"Before we do, there is something I must say." Ragnar cleared his throat. "Malachy, you have always been my most worthy adversary. You are also my oldest friend. And ... I confess, you are more adept with a razor than I could ever hope to be."

"Ah, Ace." Malachy grazed a thumb over his expertly trimmed beard. "I know."

Hold up. Ragnar was *willingly* forfeiting the Battle of the Beards? But—but they'd been at it for decades! We're talking a century-old tradition here, and Ragnar just up and broke it? What could *possibly* provoke him to—

"What's the price?" Little fissures appeared in Marek's stone wings, shadows whistling through the cracks. "The price to send the ghosts home. What is it?"

Malachy refused to look at them.

The whistling in Shadow Boy's wings reached a painful pitch. "Malachy, look at me. What's the price? Tell us!"

Malachy met their eyes for the first time, and Rose understood even as Marek's wings shattered with shadows.

The price was the Sinner's death. They were going to kill him.

"No," she breathed. "Silas, you can't. You *can't!*"

The Warg lowered his head. "I will speak with you alone." He led her and Marek away from the army and said in a low voice, "To open a portal into the eternal realm, I must use a ritual known as the Cowl—the Calling Howl. It is performed in a graveyard and requires two participants: the Screamer and the Cowler. The Screamer must be something other than a Warg, as we cannot ingest our own screams. The Cowler, on the other hand, *must* be a Warg to perform the ritual. Our magic is contained in our venom, and so the Cowler injects the Screamer through biting and swallows their screams. The Cowler then bites himself with his own venom to establish the magical connection. Once this is done, the Cowler must absorb the necromantic energies of the graveyard by ... dancing on the graves."

"Grave Dancer," Rose whispered and touched the bite mark scars beneath his caramel fur. "You're a Cowler?"

"It was my duty during the War." His candlelight eyes reflected an ancient sadness. "We would open a portal to the eternal realm and call the ghosts of our fallen soldiers to aid us in our fight. To complete the ritual, the Cowler uses the energy of the graveyard to regurgitate the Screamer's screams and convert them into the Calling Howl. The Cowl then transforms the mind of the Screamer into a portal and calls to the dead."

"Transforms the mind?" Marek repeated questioningly.

"Yes. The ghosts enter through the Screamer's thoughts."

"Bit unnerving, isn't it?"

"And not uncommon. Be wary what thoughts you let into your mind. It may be something evil using it as a backdoor into reality."

(BRRR. WAS THAT A DRAFT? READER NAME HERE _____, DID YOU LEAVE THE WINDOW CRACKED?)

"What happens next?" Rose prompted, rubbing her arms.

"The Cowler and the Screamer strive to keep the portal open until the ghosts finish whatever purpose they were called for. The ghosts are then safely returned to the eternal realm, the portal is closed, and the Cowler and Screamer take time to recover."

Wait, but that meant—"The Screamer doesn't die?" Rose said hopefully.

"Not ..." Silas ground his claws into the earth. "... not unless they're an angel. Your species is unique in using the mind as a storehouse for magic. Particularly the storage of excess in the subconscious. When the Calling Howl is used to transform your mind into a portal, it destroys the dam that separates your mind's magic from your subconscious mind's magic. Which means ..."

An image flashed in Rose's head of Malachy's magic blackboard and his diagram of the circle with the line

391

separating *Sub.* from *Con.* When he removed the line that kept them apart and knocked on the board ... "Our heads would explode!" She gaped at the Warg. "Then what good is using an angel for a Screamer?"

"Your mind does not have enough room for the magic stored in your subconscious, but it will still try to accommodate it. It may take hours, sometimes days for ... the inevitable to happen."

"The inevitable being *an exploding head!* And you want to do this to *Malachy?*" Malachy, lying in bed for hours, *days*, in agony, his mind stretching, breaking until—

"I have *never* used the Cowl on an angel before," Silas said vehemently. "*Never*. And if there were any other way, I wouldn't be doing so now. But the ghosts have been imprisoned here a hundred years. They have served their sentence. They have paid for their sins. They followed Malachy into the War o' the Wargs, and now it is his responsibility to lead them out of it. This is the Sinner's price to pay. And it *must* be paid."

Rose fingered the unicorn cupcake paperweight in the pants pocket beneath her tutu. It represented something from Malachy's heart—kindness. Compassion. A willingness to help. The very same things that had inspired him to take up the Wargs' cause in the first place when they were starving to death because of the angelic communities' discrimination. Or had Silas forgotten that?

"You said the Cowl destroys the dam between the mind's magic and the subconscious mind's magic. That's why our head explodes—because all that subconscious magic comes rushing in with nowhere to go. But what if ..." Stormy stirred inside her. "... what if there wasn't any magic left in the subconscious?"

Shadows intertwined her fingers.

"What do you mean?" The Warg's brow furrowed.

"I mean, what if an angel didn't have subconscious magic? What if it all leaked out somehow, and now there's nothing left to flood their mind if the dam breaks? Their head wouldn't explode, would it?"

"Rose ..." Marek said softly. "You know what it would mean, don't you? Once that dam is broken, you could never get your magic back. Even if we found a way to untie the knots in your soul, the moment it starts making magic again—"

"My head could explode. I know." Tears pricked her eyes. "I'll lose my storm cloud for good. But it's worth it, isn't it? Malachy won't die. The ghosts can go home."

Silas growled. "What are you two talking about?"

Rain pouring freely down her cheeks, Rose held her umbrella in both hands. Rosadox said not to open it until she truly needed it. Well, she needed it now. In fact, it might be the last time she ever did. She popped it open, and a letter fell out. Rose knelt to pick it up and unfolded it.

The paper was blank.

Blank because she already knew what she was gonna do, and her future selves did, too.

"I'll pay it." Rose sniffed, straightening. "Malachy's price. I'll pay it."

"What?" Silas barked.

"I'll be the Screamer. I don't have any subconscious magic. Use my mind for the portal. Break the dam, it won't hurt me."

He backed up, shaking his head furiously. "No. I won't do it to you."

"I'm on my last dregs of magic. My soul won't make any more. It's safe."

"It's not *safe!*" he snarled. "The Screamer is a victim! The venom of a Warg is specifically designed to make the most of every meal. The pain is unbearable. Even if your head doesn't explode, it will hurt you. *I* will hurt you." He continued to back away. "I won't do it. I *can't.*"

"Silas." Rose reached for him. "Please." She pressed her face against his fuzzy forehead. "*Please.* He's worth saving. Trust me."

A sigh. Then a warm, sandpaper tongue licking her chin. "I shouldn't be surprised. You see the best in everyone, bringing it to the surface when no one else can. Sinners, Wargs, killers ... you're astonishing, the both of you. Marek, you have nothing to say to this?"

"Just one thing." Marek braced Rose's shoulders with his stony fingers and crouched to her level. His eyes were a bittersweet tonic of sorrow and pride. "That you have the most beautiful soul of anyone I've ever known. I've seen it.

Soul signia or not, I've always seen it. And I *will* always see it, even when dawn breaks and the clouds pass away."

Thunder choked her throat, and Rose smiled, wiping her tears with his shadows.

"Are you ready?" Silas asked quietly.

Fear coiled in her stomach and lurched up her throat. She nodded. He approached her contritely, tail between his legs, and nuzzled her cheek. Rose clutched the unicorn paperweight in her fist and kissed it firmly. She looked up at Marek. "We don't give up on him," she said. "Not for a second."

"Forgive me," Silas murmured and sunk his teeth into her shoulder.

ENTRY 38

SEEKING: LEGEND SEEKER, PAST EXPERIENCE PREFERABLE

(Not gonna lie, what happened next is hard to write. Nay, as the horses say, impossible. You'll just have to fill in the blanks yourself. [Nothing you aren't used to, eh, Reader Name Here _____?] We shall pick up our story eight hours later when—

What? What's this? You're filing a complaint? For what? "Negligent narrating" and "withholding information"! Of all the—I was incapacitated by Warg venom, my mind was being used as a portal for the dead, the dam between my conscious magic and subconscious magic was shattering to pieces, and you expect me to remember what happened?

Snippets. That's all I've got. Snippets. Take 'em or leave 'em.)

There'd been pain, of course. Something like lava clogging her veins. Screaming. So much screaming. Not all of it was hers—there was Malachy's voice, desperate and dangerous, "She's a kid! *A kid!* Silas, what have you done?"

She must've fallen at some point because Marek was cradling her on the ground. A wall of shadows had encircled them, blocking out everyone else.

Then ... then ... oh, that was the other thing! Silas was a *really* good dancer. He'd stomped the graves like those ladies stomp grapes, only instead of grape juice squirting between his toes, it was a strange, milky ghost fog. He inhaled it like steam from hot cocoa, and for a second—a split second—the pain from the venom had ebbed, and she'd stopped screaming. Then Silas arched his back and made the *weirdest* noise. It was like all her screams mixed together, messy and overlapping and funneled through a howl. His breath came out with all the milky ghost fog, and then—well, then things got fuzzy again because her head felt like it was splitting down the middle. That was probably the portal opening, breaking the dam between her magics.

After that, she didn't think of much. Just Marek rocking her and the little fizzles of lightning erupting across her skin. Oh yeah—Stormy had been acting up. Using that last bit of magic to defend her. But the enemy wasn't *outside* her body. It was in the fire and the magic and the venom blazing through her veins.

She hadn't thought to stop it, to save her storm cloud from spending itself. Instead, she thought of ghosts. She thought of ghosts the way you think of ghosts when walking through a graveyard at night: compulsively. There they were, drifting through her head, so *many* of them ... and the last face she saw was Gormonger.

She never got to say goodbye.

Her last memory was the clearest. The tears. Streaming down her face. They hadn't tasted right. Too salty, less metallic. More saltwater than rain. The ratio was usually equal, but now ... now her storm cloud was leaving her. It was going. Fading. Draining the last of her magic.

The panic had wrought a scream from her ragged throat—a scream that brought with it a small gust of condensed water vapor. A cloud, no bigger than a pincushion. Frail. Wispy. Barely holding together.

"Bye," she'd whispered, touching it with the tips of her fingers. "Bye, you."

Stormy had given the tiniest spark, blowing her a kiss, and the action caused its molecules to disperse in the air.

Her soul signia was gone.

Everything went black.

*

Rose dreamed of sweat pouring through her lunatic face paint, rivers of blue melting her face off. She dreamed it was so hot she was shivering, and someone had the genius idea to throw her in a bathtub of ice water, which only made the shivers worse. Duh. Then she dreamed she was a caterpillar with a flaming torch held under her cocoon, squirming and boiling to death from the inside out when someone ripped off her covers and threw her into the icy bath. Again. Rose dreamed a lot of different scenarios, but they all seemed to end with her wet and shivering in a tub.

She woke with sunlight tangling her lashes and a hollowness in her chest. The only thing cold and wet was a compress on her forehead. Or was it Stormy? Yes, that was it. Her little storm cloud kissing away the sweat and heat of her fever. That's why she couldn't feel it inside anymore. Because it was outside, taking care of her.

It was nice to pretend. For a minute.

Rose opened her eyes. The Lollypop Tower had changed its décor from bunnies to beautiful sunrises. Hopeful colors splashed across the pictures on the walls, and the lampstand on the end table was of a woman holding the sun.

Cade sat at her feet on the Lollypop Tower's comfiest couch, focused on a bundle of black material in her lap. A needle pierced the fabric again and again, up and down, up and down, in and out, in and out, pulling a silver thread.

"Cade?" Her voice, not even a whisper, cracked pitifully.

Cade's concentration broke. "Rosy?" She immediately put aside the sewing project and moved to Rose's side. "Shh, don't strain your voice. It's all right." Taking Rose's wrist, she checked her pulse. Pushed back her lids to peer at her eyeballs. Removed the compress to feel her fever. "You're recovering remarkably well. Grave Dancer said you would be unconscious for at least a day, but it's only been eight hours."

"Cade?" Rose tried again.

Cade went on as if she hadn't spoken. "Your body has eliminated most of the toxins, and your fever is greatly improved!" She freshened the compress in a bowl of water, moving swiftly and efficiently. "In fact, I daresay—" her cheerful voice broke. She closed her eyes briefly and continued. "I daresay the venom will have completely left your system by tonight." A tear streaked down her cheek, but her movements were steady and calculated as she whipped out a syringe and flicked it expertly. "This is to relax your muscles so they'll release the last of the toxins. Just lie still."

"*Cade.*" Rose grabbed her wrist, full skin-to-skin contact, and for once, it was Cade who jolted. Their eyes met, and Rose did the unthinkable. She wound their fingers together.

Cade smiled then, wet-eyed and wobbly. "My girl. My

brave, beautiful girl." She brushed sweaty curls from Rose's forehead. "How are you feeling?"

Let's see: Her throat was a mess. Her body ached all over. Her shoulder felt exactly how you'd expect a shoulder to feel after a Warg bite (to his credit, though, Silas barely broke the skin). And deep in her chest where her storm cloud made its home ... "Empty. I lost it. My soul signia."

"I know. I'm so sorry."

Rose played with Cade's perfectly manicured fingers. "It's not *all* bad." She looked up with a glimmer of mischief. " 'Cause now I can do this." Summoning every ounce of strength from her tortured muscles, she lunged across the couch and threw her arms around her purple-haired nurse.

Hugging involved a lot more elbows than Rose remembered, but Cade hugged her back, elbows and all, laughing wetly into her curls. "You had us scared to death!"

A sound like a boulder hurtling down a mountainside broke them apart. "Cade, is she awake?" It was Marek, stumbling out of the bathroom, and he was—

Have you ever had an image, an image so funny and absurd that your brain takes a snapshot and tucks it away in a special, mental scrapbook, one that magically flips open when you least expect it and makes you grin all over again?

This was one of those images.

Marek was in a damp, pink bathrobe, hair pulled back in a fishnet, his cheeks and neck smeared with one of Cade's green, moisturizing clay masks. The fresh, new face of the Manly Spa Movement. He dropped to his knees in front of Rose, and she threw her arms around him, too.

(*Practice makes perfect.*)

He smelled like wet stone and soap.

"Thunder Rose," Marek sighed a laugh. "Thunder, Thunder Rose."

"Not Thunder anymore." She buried her nose in his velvety feathers. "Just Rose."

He pulled back. "You'll always be Thunder to me. Thunder Rose, soul of storms. That hasn't changed. Not one bit." He booped her nose, leaving a gritty smear.

"Let's see the arm." Cade rolled back the sleeve of Marek's bathrobe. His skin was—okay, it was pretty hideous: a layer of gravelly grime shedding like scales, but it was progress. Patches of brown showed through. "Back in the tub," Cade instructed. "Keep soaking and use the pumice stone!"

"I will, I will, but have you given it to her yet? I just want to see her face when you give it to her."

"Give me what?" Rose asked.

"I was just finishing the stitching. Forgive me for borrowing your cloak without permission, Rose, but I needed it as a pattern," Cade shook out her sewing project, the bundle of black material, "so I could make this."

A black cloak. White lining. Silver names embedded in the sleeves. Rose stared at it in awe. "You made me a Corner Cloak? Does that—does that mean—?"

"Master Ragnar wants to speak with you as soon as you're well enough to meet him." Cade draped the cloak over Rose's arm. "Try it on. Let me know if it needs any adjustments."

Like anything Cade did ever needed adjusting. "You *made* this?"

"Made it? She *created* it," Marek said proudly. "Cade is the greatest inventor this side of the multiverse."

The greatest inventor this side of the multiverse blushed modestly. "Well, I don't know about—"

She was interrupted by the front door opening and a puppy bursting through. "Hey, Cade, I brought Beta up for —" Malachy stopped short at the sight of Rose. "Oh. She's awake."

He stood there, alive, whole, an unexploded head on his shoulders, and the empty space inside her chest filled a little. A smile came without prompting. "Malachy—"

"I'm gonna take the dogs for a walk," he said abruptly, and the door slammed shut behind him.

Ouch.

Cade touched her shoulder, and Rose didn't flinch. "He's not angry with you, dear. He's angry with himself."

Somehow that failed to take away the sting.

Malachy didn't come back once that day. By evening, the shot of muscle relaxant combined with gentle massaging had relieved the last of the venom from Rose's system. She was achy but eager for her talk with Ragnar about *you know what.*

(HINT: IT RHYMES WITH "PHEASANT KEEPERS". UM. SORT OF.)

And on the way to his office, who was she to run into but Team Hero.

"I wrote a poem for you." Aiden was less hairy now and back to his baggy pants. "To commemorate what happened. I call it, 'The Sacrificial Rose.'" He cleared his throat meaningfully.

"T'was midnight on the hour
The night the rose lost her power
Thorns stripped for Sinner's sake
To save him from a grisly fate
Petals crushed, their fragrance sweet
For Sinner's life, his soul to keep
She gave her own to save his head
If not for her, then he'd be dead

"What can be said of such sacrifice?
What lines of poetry would suffice?
What tongue of angel dare endeavor?
For I could go on forever and ev—"

"Yeah, yeah, yeah, she gets the point," Sephone cut him off. "And the point is this." A sunny yellow flower sprouted in the center of her palm.

A yellow rose. For friendship.

Aiden picked it up and threaded it shyly through Rose's curls. "There. Looks good on you."

Well, shucks. She went ahead and hugged them both —with significantly less elbows, she might add. And when Ragnar opened the door to his office, Rose hugged him, too.

He laughed in surprise and patted her back. "It's good to see you up and about!" He ushered her inside. "Tell me how you're feeling, and no minimizing."

"I'm tired," she admitted. "Really sore. And just kinda ... icky."

"Warg venom will do that to you."

Rose moved to sit in the chair in front of the desk, but Ragnar stopped her. "No, please." He guided her to the high back chair behind his desk. "I have not earned the right to sit here for this conversation."

They sat. Ragnar attempted to strike his traditional pose of steepled fingers with elbows on desk, realized he fell about a foot short, and scooted his chair forward with a few ungainly squeaks. "Ahem. Rose, I must begin with a series of apologies concerning yesterday. What you witnessed between Malachy and myself was an absolute disgrace. I've promised a safe and peaceful environment at Heartstone Asylum, and last night I failed my duty. I bear full responsibility and will do everything in my power to rectify this mistake. My actions have consequences, and my deepest regret is that they've fallen on you. What you did for Malachy ..."

"Have you seen him?" Rose asked tentatively.

"Yes. He came by earlier." Ragnar regarded her with sympathy. "He needs time, Rose. He's not angry with you, he's—"

"—angry with himself, I know. But if anyone should be angry with him, it's me, and if *I'm* not angry, then he shouldn't be either!"

"Malachy is a complicated man."

"Yeah," she huffed, "two-fifths oxy and three-fifths moron. He's hard to add up."

Ragnar chuckled once and became serious. "Malachy cares about you, Rose. He was determined to find a solution to save your soul signia. Having you lose it for his sake is, to him, unforgivable."

"I don't think he cares that much. I heard your conversation." Rose's cheeks filled with heat, and she looked down at the cherry wood desk. How was it possible to sit in this imposing, high back chair and still feel so small? "He wanted to send me home."

"It should interest you to know that he wasn't being entirely truthful." Ragnar scratched at one of his ears. "I felt it. Malachy may hide behind his pretense of indifference, but I have never met anyone who will go to greater lengths for the ones he loves. After Warg-riding tournaments were banned, he was the only one who cared that the Wargs were starving. They were like family to him. He took on their impossible cause because that is who he is."

Rose played with the unicorn cupcake paperweight in her pocket. He'd taken on her impossible cause, too.

"Malachy and I both made horrendous mistakes during the War, but the War wouldn't have happened if I'd had one ounce of his compassion for the forgotten and the despised. Still, he allows his passion to rule his reason from time to time, and no one regrets this more than him." Ragnar sighed deeply. "When we knew we had to agree to the Calling Howl in order to gain our armies' assistance, he volunteered to be the sacrifice immediately."

Rose let this sink in. "I'm glad I took his place. Even ... even if it meant losing my soul signia. But whether he meant it or not, it's just like Malachy said during your conversation: I don't have unstable magic anymore. I don't have *any* magic. No more reason to be in an asylum. Are you gonna send me home?"

"You have to understand, that was a hypothetical discussion. I was *never* going to send you home."

"Not even if it meant having a Dame Commander for a friend?"

"My priority is to the patients of my asylum," he said with conviction. "You are my patient, and I want to do what's best for you as an individual. Sending you home is *an* option, though not a wise one. Your father is going to be in a lot of hot water if his daughter miraculously returns home from an asylum. He could be accused of misusing his authority, and there's no saying Blackthorn Asylum won't be called again to take you away. And this time, Heartstone won't be in any position to intercept. There are *other* options, however. Heartstone Asylum will always be a home to you if, despite what you've seen, you'll still have it." Ragnar leaned forward in his seat. "And if you choose to stay, there is another option still."

Now they were talking. "Yes?" Rose encouraged.

"As you know from your first night here, there is more to this asylum than meets the eye."

She sat forward in her chair. "Yes?"

"Something lurking beneath the surface. A mysterious operation of sorts. The secret at the heart of Heartstone."

"*Yes?*"

"And now"—Ragnar's eyes gleamed with anticipation — "*you're* going to tell me all about it." He laughed at her expression. "Don't give me that face, Rose Skylar! You're far too clever to sit there and pretend like you haven't figured it all out. You've known for some time, haven't you?"

Ooh. Busted. "What gave it away?"

"You don't ask questions. One who doesn't ask questions either lacks in curiosity or already knows the answers."

"What if I'm just not curious?"

"Then your favorite book wouldn't be *Blackout's Tales*." Ragnar sat back in his chair and managed his steepled-finger thing with his elbows on the armrests. "So, tell me. What is the secret of Heartstone Asylum?"

The words were sweet on her tongue, and they tasted sweeter the longer they stayed. Finally, *finally*, Rose spoke. "That you're like me. Legend seekers. My guess is, after you were attacked by the Wingless Ones, you realized the legends of *Blackout's Tales* are true. You started tracking them down, didn't you? You and Malachy, to keep what happened to your soldiers from happening to anyone else. Then you found Heartstone Asylum, the *real* Heartstone Asylum, and decided to make it a safe place for angels with unstable magic ... but also a place to train more legend seekers. If you could harness unstable magic, tame it, you'd have enough power to tackle anything. Every monster, every myth. Right?"

Ragnar just smiled and motioned for her to follow him to the other room, his humble living quarters, where the original *Blackout's Tales* sat on the pedestal at the end of his bed. "We call ourselves Blackouts," he said, "after the great legend seeker himself. We use his book as a guide, the original with all his notes. It helps us find what legends we can and bring them here for safekeeping. Our facilities are below. Would you care to see?" Ragnar placed his hand over the glass display case and magic rumbled as the pedestal scraped across the floor. Beneath was a yawn in the floorboards, a steep ladder leading to its depths.

Rose stuck her head down the manhole. "Whoa!" The tunnel stretched like the gullet of an enormous snake. Way, waaaaay at the bottom was a small coin of light.

Ragnar pulled her back gently. "Understand this, Rose. Heartstone Asylum is first and foremost an asylum: a place of protection and rehabilitation for patients with unstable magic. Life as a Blackout is entirely your choice, and you may choose to leave it behind at any time. But what say you? From one legend seeker to another"—he held out his hand— "shall we join forces?"

She took it and almost shook his arm out of its socket. Then she swung to a halt. "What about what Malachy said? During the, you know ... your conversation." There went the blush again. Dang it. "Malachy didn't think I'd make much of a Blackout without my magic." His exact words were *useless* and *waste of resources,* but why add insult to injury? She had plenty of both to go around.

"It will be harder for you, yes. But an angel's power does not come from their soul signia. It comes from their *soul.* We'll train you in other areas. It may take longer, but you'll make a fine Blackout yet." Ragnar nodded confidently. "Now, down you go."

Rose climbed into the manhole. "Aren't you coming?"

"I've arranged a guide for you. You'll meet at the bottom."

She was halfway down the never-ending ladder when her sore muscles begged for a rest. "Where is this taking me?" she called up.

Ragnar looked down at her from above. "To church," he said.

ENTRY 39

GO'N TO THE CHAPEL AND WE'RE – GONNA SMASH SOME W-I-I-I-NDOWS

I t really did feel like slithering down a snake's throat—even the walls were slimy—but the ladder did not end in the belly of a beast. When Rose hopped the last rung, wiped her hands on her pants and turned, she found herself in a small chapel. The walls and pews were made of stone, carved and smooth. A crimson runner rolled down the aisle all the way to the rock-hewn pulpit. Behind it, a single stained-glass window lit the room with a mysterious light.

In the very front row at the end of the pew sat a man, head bowed. "So, you think you've got what it takes to be a Blackout." He chuckled softly. "We'll see about that." Malachy stood, a sledgehammer propped on his shoulder. "Welcome to the Chapel of Legends, sweetheart."

Rose closed her mouth before her tongue dried out. *"You're* my guide?"

He shrugged with the shoulder supporting the hammer. "Wasn't a volunteer position." Translation: *Ragnar's making me do this. I don't wanna be here at all. Fact, I'd rather bash my skull in with this sledgehammer than spend another second in your company, but we all gotta pay our dues.* "So? What'll it be? Your first legend—what d'ya wanna see?"

"Oh. Um ..." Here it was, the most exciting moment of her life, and she couldn't even focus. "How 'bout the giant snake Elektra's team brought in? The Leviathan from 'Legend of the Perilous Fishing Trip.' "

"Interesting choice," he said in a tone that wasn't interested in the least. He walked up to the stained-glass window and stood about a foot away, studying it. There wasn't much to see. It was a mosaic of colors with no real image in mind. Malachy chewed his thumbnail. "Let's see ..."

The panels shuffled like a deck of cards and rapidly rearranged themselves in the shape of a giant snake looming from the sea, its spiked tail coiled around an unfortunate fishing boat.

Rose approached the magical glass in wonder. "It's *beautiful.*"

"Yup." Malachy handed her the sledgehammer. "Now break it."

"Break it?" She hefted the hammer uncertainly. Something tingled in her fingertips. Not lightning—*excitement.* Malachy gave a terse nod of approval, and Rose swung for the stained-glass window. BAM! It shattered in a rainbow of shards.

"Are you *sure* this is okay?" she questioned.

(*Bit late for that.*)

"You know how Master Ragnar feels about broken windows," she added. Malachy's right hand was bandaged thickly where he'd punched the window in the library after he found out she'd overhead his less-than-flattering conversation with Ragnar. "How are your knuckles?"

"Fine," he said shortly and climbed through the broken window. He stuck out a hand to help her over. Once she was through, he let go like she'd electrocuted him. Which hurt, actually. Hurt a lot.

The broken window opened into a rectangular, stone-walled chamber smelling of saltwater and seaweed. They stood on a rope bridge that stretched over what could only be described as a humungous indoor aquarium. Below them, water lapped at a large grate skimming the surface of the pool. A long, coy shape undulated beneath the placid waves.

Have you ever dipped your toes in a nice, cool creek when—gasp! You see a shape moving with the waves and shriek, pulling your piggy toes from what is surely the mouth of a hungry water snake?

Only it isn't a water snake. Just a log in cahoots with a trick of light.

So, how do you tell the difference between a slithery reptile that'll nibble your toes to soggy nubs and a harmless (if conniving) piece of wood?

Basic criteria:

1) Logs don't typically lunge at you when you pass by.

2) They don't spray you with water as they lash at the bars of their cage, because who the heck cages a log?

3) Unless they're about to spontaneously combust, logs —lacking suitable vocal cords—don't hiss.

The criteria had spoken. Rose was standing over a giant water snake.

"Whoa!" She leaned over the bridge, peering at the violent waves below. "This thing is *huge*. No wonder Sephone had trouble getting it through the window! I wondered where you guys were hiding it. I kept thinking, maybe the plumbing? So, I gave our toilet a listening ear." The Leviathan flashed its magnificent fangs, chomping at the bars, and Rose leaned over further.

"Hey, hey, not so far!" Malachy pulled her back by the wing and released her just as fast. "You'll, uh, you'll lose your flower."

She reached for the yellow rose in her hair. "Thanks. Sephone made it for me."

"Did she, now? Huh. Usually takes her years to give so much as a thistle, and that's if she likes you. How'd you manage to weasel into her affections so quickly?"

He made her sound like some sorta parasite or—or garden grub. Or really persistent weed. "I'm a Rose.

Sephone likes flowers. Change your name to Daffodil, and she might give you one, too." Gazing down at the Leviathan, she asked casually, "So, how long has Sephone been at Heartstone?"

"Since she was little. Seven or eight, I think," Malachy said.

"And how old was she when she became a Blackout?"

"She's what, fifteen now? I'd say eleven. Few years after Aiden and his mom moved here."

"Has Master Ragnar always ..." Rose searched for the word, "*required* so much from her?"

Malachy ran a hand through his shaggy hair. "Not at first, but Ace has his own ideas about who Sephone is."

"The Chosen One."

"Yeah."

It begged the question, "Chosen for what?"

"To save the worlds from whatever gave her that scar, apparently. It's coming back one of these days, whatever it is. And when it does, Ace wants her to be ready for it. That's why he trains her so hard. He's doing what he thinks is best for her."

"But you don't agree?"

"He also thinks becoming a Blackout is what's best for you." Malachy turned without looking at her and headed for the broken window.

Rose stared at his retreating back. This was getting plain ridiculous. He could be all standoffish and "look at me, I can swagger away from any conversation I want," but he couldn't avoid *certain subjects* forever. She caught up with him. "I know what I wanna see next."

"Something gruesome? Something grotesque? Something that'll give ya an eyeful of the fun you're in for?" Malachy vaulted the broken window and offered a hand.

She didn't take it. She climbed through herself, nicking her palms on the jagged edges. "They aren't *legends*, exactly. But they were killed by one."

His wings stiffened.

"Sephone thought they'd be down here," she continued quickly. "I wanna see them. Please. I saved them."

"And what, you think that *entitles* you to something?" Malachy's careful mask of indifference was slipping. "Saving someone gives you *no* rights to them—especially when they didn't ask you to! They owe you *nothing*."

Cade and Ragnar were wrong, you know. Malachy might be angry with himself, but he sure as heck was angry with her, too. "I know," Rose said quietly. "But I still wanna see them."

The mask was back in place. He gestured mockingly to the shattered window. "Be my guest." At the wave of his arm, the glass shards on the floor sucked back into the frame like a window breaking in reverse.

Rose stepped up to the stained glass. How'd this go? Did she just stand there and visualize what she wanted to see? She closed her eyes, concentrating. There was the sound of shuffling cards, and when she opened, the panels had rearranged themselves as the image in her mind.

Something tingled in her fingertips. Not excitement, not lightning. *Dread.* Rose swung the sledgehammer, and the window broke, revealing a different chamber. What was inside made her throat tighten. "You don't have to come in," she said. "Not if you don't want to."

When someone says something's *in stone*, they mean it can't be changed. Walking amongst the statues of soldiers, Rose would say the Battle of the Petrified Forest was *in stone*. What happened to the Saint's men and the Sinner's Wargs couldn't be changed. They were dead. Their bodies were petrified, splattered by revenant blood a hundred years before.

But their spirits were free.

She roamed the statues, touching armored hands and stony faces. Their expressions were terrible, twisted by pain and fear. "I'm sorry," she whispered. "I'm so sorry." She sensed Malachy's presence behind her. "For a while, we thought the graveyard was where the soldiers were buried. Then we realized it was the graveyard of the Wingless Ones. Why didn't you keep them down here like the rest of the legends?"

"Thought it'd be safer to keep them outside the asylum," he said.

Rose gave a half-smile. "Got that bit right. How come you ..." she trailed off. In a forgotten corner of the chamber, there was a statue unlike any other statue. Most of the soldiers had turned to stone while fighting. Their bodies were frozen in impressive poses: weapons held aloft or brought down in mighty swings. Some had died mid-charge, their legs stretched in eternal leaps. But the statue in the corner did not strike an impressive pose. The Warg solider was in a heap. One might even say he'd died lying down.

Something this particular Warg wouldn't be caught *dead* doing.

Her feet carried her in a daze. She crouched by the fallen soldier.

Gormonger had died with a sword rammed through the roof of his mouth, penetrating the top of his skull. He must've been killed before the revenants arrived, when it was just the armies going at it. "You and your big mouth," Rose laughed, pressing her face against his forehead. Tears splashed on his furry stone cheeks. "I miss you."

Malachy cleared his throat. "I come down here sometimes. To remember my mistakes. To apologize. I want ya to know that I didn't—that *we* didn't—" He sighed roughly. "That Ace and I didn't want our soldiers to suffer. We knew their ghosts were trapped here, and we did what we could to make 'em comfortable. But they're dead 'cause the legends from *Blackout's Tales* are real. And we had to make the choice to focus on the living we could still save. That's why the Blackouts exist."

"You stop this from happening to anyone else." She kissed Gormonger between the eyes and stood. Malachy thought she was useless without her magic. Well, when she was most useless to him, she'd saved his life. And she'd do it again in a heartbeat. "I wanna do that, too. I wanna be a Blackout. I know you think I'm just a waste of resources but—"

"I do *not* think you're a waste of resources. That whole conversation you heard was just me being—"

"Truthful?"

"An absolute *idiot*." He leaned his back against a statue and slid a hand tiredly down his face. "I don't know how to fix this, Rosebud."

She loved that nickname. "I might." Rose reached automatically for her pocket. "I have something for you. Something very special to me. I take it everywhere, but I think you should have it back now." She held out the cupcake unicorn paperweight.

Malachy looked at it. "I can't take that," he said flatly.

"I want you to."

"I can't."

"Yes, you can."

"No, I *can't*."

"I *want* you to. Just take it, Malachy. Please, I want you to take it!"

Malachy grabbed the paperweight and hurled it against Gormonger's thick skull. The cupcake broke into three large pieces. "I *can't*! Don't you get it? I gave that to you till I could find a way to fix your magic. Now your magic's gone, and there's nothing I can do about it! I *failed* you, Rose."

The broken paperweight glittered on the floor. Rose's bottom lip trembled, and she sucked it in. Brave face. C'mon. Brave face.

The fight left him. "Sweetheart." Malachy put his hands on her shoulders, but they slipped off like they'd met an ice patch. He hunched against the statue again and was quiet for a long time. "Why'd you do it?"

Did he really not know? "Because I think you're worth saving."

Feathers quivering, Malachy held his head in his hands. When he pulled back, he glared at the two appendages as if he'd like nothing more than to hack them off with his axe. "These hands break everything they touch. You shouldn't have saved me. I deserved it. I deserved to die. You lost *everything* 'cause of me. And here I was trying so hard to—" He stopped himself with a bitter laugh. "Ya wanna know why I was trying to get Ace to send you home? I was afraid. I was afraid if ya stuck around long enough, I'd end up hurting you somehow." He blew air out of his cheeks. "Bit late for that now, I guess."

Malachy stooped, picking up pieces of the paperweight. "Ya know, this wasn't my favorite unicorn till a li'l girl smashed a cupcake in my face?" He met Rose's eyes and hesitantly brushed his bandaged knuckles against her cheek. "Reminds me of you."

She wasn't gonna cry. Nope. Nuh-uh. Those weren't tears leaking from her eyes. They were just—just … rain?

No. Not rain. Not anymore.

Malachy swiped at her cheeks with his thumb. "My *gosh*, you're like a leaky faucet." Somewhere her wet giggles became full-blown sobs, and Rose tackled him in a hug. Sixth one that day. They were *addicting*.

There was always the danger of Malachy transforming into Malachy the Cacti, all stiff and prickly, but it was worth the risk when he hugged her back, wrapping his wings around her. "Hey, hey, hey." He rocked her side-to-side. "Rough couple days, huh, cupcake?"

Cupcake. That was a new one. She nodded, burrowing under his chin.

"You know," Malachy said after a moment, "when you said they were gonna name a mixed magical arts move after your hugs, I was expecting something a bit more punchy."

Rose jerked her head up, knocking his chin, and he laughed through a grunt of pain. "That's better."

"Malachy?" Gosh, her nose was stuffy. "I'm really glad I saved you."

A pause. Then, "I'm glad you saved me, too."

ENTRY 40

YOU HAD ME AT GOODBYE

Getting to sleep that night would be a waking nightmare.

Rose put it off as long as she could, telling stories, asking for stories, challenging anything that moved to a game of checkers.

(THE COFFEE TABLE POLITELY DECLINED—I'D BUMPED IT WITH MY FOOT BY ACCIDENT.)

She even made mugs of warm milk with a touch of maple syrup—Marek's recipe—for everyone in the Lollypop Tower, but after Cade and Malachy went to bed and Marek's eyes were getting bloodshot, she was running out of ideas.

Then Marek suggested a campout in the den, which was the best idea ever. Rose hurried to grab pillows from her room and saw something on her dresser. It was Malachy's paperweight. All the pieces of the cupcake and unicorn were glued together again. The same hands that broke it had fixed it, too.

She smiled.

Downstairs, she piled the couch with pillows, and Marek made a bed on the floor. It was better with him close by, but nothing changed the fact that when she closed her eyes, she still had that awful feeling to face.

The emptiness in her chest.

"Thunder?" Marek hoisted up on his elbows to look at her. "It's going to be okay."

Rose blinked the not-rain tears away and looked reproachfully over her pillow. "Promise?"

He held up a solemn pinky. "Pinky promise." And Marek *never* broke a pinky promise.

(*Reference entry 2 for proof.*)

She fell asleep with his finger linked through hers.

*

Rose woke up screaming.

Is there any other way to wake when you're dreaming of your best friend's death? Marek's pinky wasn't linked through hers anymore, and for a horrible moment, the dream was real.

But his hands were on her shoulders, anchoring her to reality, and she gripped his wrists like a lifeline. Around them, the pictures on the walls had transformed into images of weather-beaten statues in graveyards.

"Just a dream, Rose. Just a dream." Marek sat on the edge of the couch. A patch of stone surrounded his right eye, the remnant of his sculptural state. No matter how hard he scrubbed, it just wouldn't leave. She traced the jagged circle. "You died for me." The words were heavier than boulders on her heart.

He laughed, gentle with mirth. "I'm your guardian angel. It's my job description." A shadow tugged on one of her curls.

Something—questions, anger—bubbled up for no reason. "Is that why you brought me to Heartstone? Is that why you went to our meeting spot every week for two years? Because it was your *job description*?"

Shadow Boy's playfulness retracted. "What's this about, now?"

What *was* this about? Her thoughts felt as unstable as her magic used to be. "I just, I—I don't wanna be like some goldfish someone got you that you didn't really want, but now you're obligated to take care of because you're not a monster and you won't flush it down a toilet!"

"I never thought I'd need to say this, but I would never flush you down a toilet."

"That's my *point!* You're too good, too *noble* to do something like that. So, if you died for me out of some stupid sense of duty or responsibility or—or *why are you smiling?*"

"Because I have something to show you." He got up off the couch. "Get your cloak. It's nippy out there."

*

What remained of Ragnar's old cottage couldn't be called ruins any more than a skeleton can be called a corpse. After Beta's sonic-bark, the structure had collapsed completely, leaving nothing but a pile of dusty rubble.

Rose gripped the iron pickets of the fence surrounding the cottage, red umbrella hooked over her wrist. "*This* is what you wanted to show me?"

Marek smiled nostalgically at the wreckage as if greeting an old friend. "Have I ever told you the story of what happened to this cottage?"

"About the patient who destroyed it?"

"About *why* they destroyed it." He opened the iron gate and went inside. "This is where Master Ragnar gave me his welcome speech my first night at Heartstone. Later, this is where he asked me to become a Blackout. And this is where I agreed—under two conditions. One, that once a week, he would let me visit a special friend of mine, a legend seeker herself, at the border of Pandrum and Faberland. And two, that when the time was right, he would help me bring that friend to Heartstone Asylum to become a Blackout.

"Ragnar was all for it. Until he found out you were first in line to be a Dame Commander. Then he invited me to this cottage and tried to change our agreement. Well, not *change*—Ragnar would never break his word—but *modify* it. Basically, he wanted to bring you to Heartstone ... but not for many, many years. First, he wanted to see how long you could last without being suspected of unstable magic."

"Because if I made it to Dame Commander, that's the sort of friend in high places Heartstone could use," Rose finished. It was the same argument Malachy had employed to try and convince Ragnar to send her home.

Marek nodded. "I, of course, told him this was unacceptable, that we had a deal, and he was going back on it, but he kept insisting and insisting, and finally, he pushed just a smidge too far."

A tiny smile formed on her lips. "And you brought down the house."

He brushed a wisp of shadow from his sleeve. "Honestly, he should've known better. You don't push an angel with unstable magic. He must've thought I'd do the same to the asylum because he changed his mind rather quickly. Said we should bring you to Heartstone the moment you were old enough. On your very birthday, even." He glanced at Rose from the corner of his eye. "Still think I brought you here out of obligation?"

"I ..." She went quiet.

"Look at it, Thunder." He took her by the shoulders from behind. "Really look at it. Why did I tear this house down?"

"Because you had a promise to keep."

"Look harder."

"Because you didn't want me to hurt."

"You're not seeing it."

"Because ... because you missed me."

Marek pressed his chin against her head. "Now you see."

But she didn't. She *didn't* see, and it was the most frustrating thing on the planet. "It's one thing to tear down a house, but Marek, you *died*. You died for me."

"And you still think it was out of duty."

Rose's shoulders slumped.

"Fair enough. Let's try a different angle." He moved to her side. "Why did you lose your soul signia for Malachy? Why did you take the bite for him?"

"You know why."

"Tell me. Did it make you feel important, having his life in your hands? Is that why you did it?"

She rubbed her nose. "Of course not."

"Did you do it so he would owe you? That's a mighty favor to repay. Or perhaps you were swept up by a mysterious wave of 'do the right thing' and sacrificed everything for the sake of your conscience."

"*No.*" Rose wiped her rapidly dripping nose on the hanky Rosadox had given her.

Marek continued. "But maybe I'm overcomplicating things. Maybe it was as simple as you wanting to be the hero."

She sneezed violently. "You take that—" she sneezed again, "*back!* You take that back—" another sneeze, "right—" and another, "*now!*" She blew her nose furiously.

He waited patiently for her to stop impersonating a foghorn. "Then why did you save him?" he asked.

"Because I *care* about him!"

Shadow Boy raised his eyebrows.

Oh.

Ohhh.

Casually folding his arms, he turned back to the cottage. "But if you still think me saving you was some sort of heroic sacrifice out of devotion to my own personal goodness, let me ask you one simple question. When I died ..." he glanced at her sidelong, "why didn't you sneeze?"

Rose stared at the sopping hanky in her hand. " 'Cause you weren't trying to be a hero," she said. "You were just being ... you."

And she hugged him.

She looked past the shadows steaming from Marek's feathers at the rubble of Ragnar's cottage and beamed up at him. "You really destroyed a whole house for me?" Her beam dimmed. "Gor woulda loved that."

"Pity it happened during the day. He probably didn't even notice." Marek sighed, giving Rose a final squeeze. "I miss him already." They let go.

In the utter desolation of the cottage, a single item remained upright. The specterglass from "Legend of the Ghost Who Lost his Eyepiece." "Guess that's stuck out here now," she said. "No ghosts left to move it."

The specterglass moved an inch.

They blinked. "Did that just—?" Marek began, and the specterglass toppled with a crash.

"*BOO!*" The roar echoed in the stone trees behind them.

There was only *one* voice that could reach that volume in a single syllable. Rose whirled around. "Gor?"

A giant, wolfish silhouette appeared, hazy and see-through. "In the ectoplasm."

"Gor!" She and Marek barreled forward, arms outstretched. Their hugs went straight through Gormonger's feeble outline.

"Yeah," he rumbled, sheepish, "sorry about the lousy manifestation. All this STUPID iron."

"You're alive! I mean—you're not gone! How are you here?" Rose had *seen* him enter her thoughts when the portal was open. She'd *seen* him go through!

"Well ..." his face was too blurry to hold detail, but he had to be full-tooth grinning, "there I was, halfway through the portal, when I thought, 'What am I DOING? I spent a hundred years stuck in a COTTAGE, and now there's a whole FOREST out there with no cranky BROTHERS and SISTERS to keep me out of it!' So, I came back."

"But that was your only chance to move on," Marek said.

Gormonger shrugged. "I know. But there isn't anyone waiting for me on the other side. And I knew there was someone waiting for me here. You and Bedhead."

Aww. "Gor, we—"

"Nah, enough mush. I got me a FOREST to explore! Thanks for leaving the gate open!" Rearing on his hind legs, Gormonger charged the gate, bursting through it in a blur of ghost light. His howl of joy reverberated through the Petrified Forest.

Marek crossed his arms with a smile. "Silas is going to be over the moons about this, isn't he?"

The iron gate swung in the ghost Warg's spectral breeze. "Question," Rose said. "If Gor can't open the gate himself ... who closed him in?"

They turned to the remains of the cottage. Something

431

rustled in the rubble. Perhaps a family of raccoons had moved in? Or—

Two winged figures exploded from the wreckage, broadcasting debris in all directions.

Her and Marek's combined scream could've fed Silas for a week. The figures landed in a roll, covered from wingtips to toes in powdery plaster, and they were ... laughing? They were rolling on the floor, *laughing*?

"Your—faces!" Rosadox gasped, pounding her fist in hysterics. "Your—*faces!*" She gave a particularly thunderous snort and stiffened. "Ahem. Anyway." Her companion helped her rigidly to her feet.

Rose stared at him.

"Well!" said Marek affably to the newcomer. "I was wondering when you'd be popping by. It's good to see you." He offered a hand.

"And you," said his future self, taking it. They shook. Kept shaking. Marek looked at their firmly gripped hands. "May I challenge you to an arm-wrestling match?"

"You may," he laughed, "but it won't end well for you, Little Me."

Calling Marek a "little" anything was a stretch, but next to his older self, it was true. Maradox was bigger still. Bigger and stronger and different but the same. He had a short beard on his chin. His right eye was encircled by a ring of stone. That wasn't going away, then. It would always be there, a permanent reminder of his sacrifice.

Maradox caught her staring and winked. "So, Rose

isn't impressed by our grand gesture, this beautiful monument to our friendship?" He spread his arms wide at the demolished cottage.

"Monument?" Rosadox snorted. "It's a pile of rubble!"

"Yes, but a pile of rubble *in your honor*," Marek pointed out. "Isn't that right, Rose?"

But Rose didn't answer. It made sense now why Marek had been silent the night he first met Rosadox. Like him, Rose was busy studying her best friend's future self, inferring as much as possible. Was he happy? Healthy? Did he stand up straight? Were those laughter lines or frown lines? Both? What had caused them?

She didn't even notice he was moving till he was standing right in front of her, bending so they were face to face. Rose blinked. Shadows tucked her curls behind her ears. "Hi, Thunder," said Maradox, and all her questions went away.

She did the first thing she thought to do—lean forward and wiggle her nose against his. He smiled a Marek-smile.

"Aren't we adorable?" Rosadox looped her arm through Marek's. She was different than the Rosadox who'd saved him from his stony fate. Older, for sure, and less *bouncy*. No, not less. The *antonym* of bouncy. She moved like she'd just got out of a pub brawl, but there wasn't a bruise on her. "To business!" she declared and pulled a folded piece of paper gingerly from her pocket. "We have a grocery list of things to go over. You want

answers? We got 'em. But first things first. The umbrella."
Rosadox pointed to the one dangling from Rose's wrist and made a squeezing motion. "Gimme."

Rose popped the umbrella protectively. "Why?"

"Because it's mine!"

"Doesn't that make it mine, too?"

"No. Go make your own. First thing on the list, see? 'Have Little Me make her own umbrella.' So, hand it over."

Rose blew air out of her cheeks. "Fine."

Rosadox took the umbrella and twirled it lovingly over her shoulder. "I didn't even wanna give it up, but my Rosadox pulled rank. Now, second thing on the list. 'Eggs.' Eggs?"

Maradox peered over her shoulder. "Ah. That's part of our *actual* grocery list. We're out."

"Already?"

"I've been experimenting with soufflés."

"Right. We'll pick some up in our own time. Unless your recipe calls for three-year-old eggs." They laughed. Rosadox doubled over suddenly like she had a bad cramp. "Oof. Better speed this up. Third on the list is ... 'Telepathy.' We can skip 'Telepathy,' right?"

Say *what* now? "Uh, no. No, you cannot. What about telepathy?" Rose demanded.

"*Oh, just one of the perks of being a Paradox,*" Maradox's voice sounded in her mind. "*It gets tricky, communicating with multiple versions of yourself. Telepathy makes it easier.*"

Rose tugged on Marek's sleeve. "Are you hearing this?"

"Of course he is," said Rosadox. *"As Paradoxes, you're connected. Really, telepathy's nothing new to you. You just don't realize it. During Story Hour, remember how Marek's shadow puppets seemed to act out your thoughts as you were thinking them? Or how about when Marek was a statue and you heard his voice inside your head?"*

"It's mostly instinctual right now, but you'll start getting the hang of it consciously, too," Maradox encouraged. *"Just practice, practice, practice!"*

How do you *practice* hearing voices in your head?

"With skill and meditation."

Hey! Wasn't talking to you.

Maradox chuckled.

"Telepathy isn't the only way we communicate with ourselves, though," Rosadox said audibly. "Last thing on the list ... 'The diary.' "

Maradox produced a leather-bound book inlaid with a mottled stone at the top of the cover. "This is for you. Your first time traveler's diary. Every time traveler needs a diary to keep track of their time traveling so that events happen in the right order, timelines don't tangle, worlds don't collide, and life as we know it doesn't become completely unwritten. I'm sure you can handle it."

Rose took the book, running her fingers over the stone. "Isn't this a petoskey stone? The same kind you put in Amber's necklace to bring Marek back to life?"

"Noticed that, didja?" Rosadox nodded approvingly.

"Petoskey stones are crucial to time travel. When the stone starts blinking, that means the power's on. It'll reach out to whichever of your older selves are involved in the story, and their diaries will start blinking, too. The stone creates a special timeline so we can talk with each other through the pages, even if we're years apart. And we're not the only ones." She looked at Marek. "When the stone's blinking red, it's the Roses turn with the diary. But when it's blinking blue ..."

"It's our turn," Maradox said. "Though we tend to prefer illustrations to words."

Marek took the book from Rose's hands, thumbing through the blank pages. "Full-page illustrations?"

"Are there any other kind to draw?"

"But how does it all work?" Rose asked. "Petoskey stones, Paradoxes, time travel—"

Rosadox hunched forward as if experiencing a sudden shiver. "We'd love to open the floor to questions, but that's all the time we have today, folks!" she said through a grimace. "Bub-bye now!"

"Wait!" Rose grabbed her arm. "What about your shoelaces?"

Rosadox glanced at her feet. "What about them?"

"Back in the library. You were wearing a shoelace around your wrist. You called me and Marek 'gumshoes with our laces tied together' and said you'd explain it later."

"Shoelaces." Her brow furrowed. "And where one shoe

goes, the other's gonna follow.' " Rosadox's face lit up, and Rose swore she saw sparks fly from her eyes. "Shoelaces! Little Me, you're a genius! Genius, genius, genius!" She kissed her forehead with a loud smack. "*Shoelaces*, Shadow Boy! How could we have missed it? We gotta go! Wait." Rosadox stopped herself. "Wait, wait, wait. There's something I need to give you, Rosy."

Yes! An eighth hug was on the horizon, Rose could *feel* it! She opened her arms expectantly, but Rosadox stuck out her hand. As in, for a handshake. Well, that was ... weirdly formal. Rose gripped her older self's hand and gave it an uncertain jerk. Closing her eyes, Rosadox took in one of those meditation-type breaths. All the stiffness and tension seemed to leave her body, and when she exhaled, a warm buzzing filled Rose's palm.

A single bolt of lightning wound up her arm and crackled through her curls.

Rosadox let go with a wink. "See you soon."

Rose grinned so wide her head threatened to split. "See you later."

"See you sooner or later!" Marek and his older self chorused.

She and Marek watched them leave, babbling about shoelaces. "I'm sure we'll understand one day," he mused and flipped the book over in his hand. "So, these time-traveling diaries of ours. What should we call them?"

Rose thought for a moment. *Professional legend seeker. Part-time ghost hunter. Time traveler.* Those were the things she'd wanted to be when she grew up. And somehow, all it took was being committed to an asylum to become all three.

This wasn't the end. A storm was coming. She could feel it in the tingling of her arm, in the hope in her chest where Stormy used to be. When it would arrive—who knew? But she'd be waiting for it. Watching and waiting. "I was thinking ... how about *The Stormwatch Diaries*?"

ENTRY 41

AUTHOR(S) INTERLUDE PART 5

Annnd that's a wrap! Credits, please! ~1532 A.S.

The role of library Rosadox, master of dramatic entrances, was played by ... ~1526 A.S.

Me! Everyone's favorite grouchy-but-loveable Rosadox was played by ... ~1532 A.S.

Me! And the Rosadox of questionable bladder control was played by ... ~1529 A.S.

I did NOT have to PEE! Just because I'm not as good at holding in YOU-KNOW-WHO as you are does NOT mean I will be remembered as the Rosadox who had to pee! ~1527 A.S.

Too late. ~1529 A.S.

What about 1530? ~1526 A.S.

Oh, 1530 is the unsung hero of this story. (Even if she did STEAL my umbrella.) ~1529 A.S.

Well, sing away. Don't let me stop you. ~1530 A.S.

She's the one who delivered all letters from past to future and vice versa. Also, she totally kicked the revenants' butts out of the library back in Entry 32. Major kudos, 1530. ~1532 A.S.

Just doing my part. My very daring, essential-to-the-story part. You're welcome. ~1530 A.S.

And this, Reader Name Here _____, is where we part ways. I hope you loved reading our story as much as I loved telling it. You've been the best Reader Name Here _____ I could ask for, and I—I'm really gonna miss you. Oh, gosh, I think I'm gonna cry ... ~1526 A.S.

Book ends are the worst. But then, book ends are like bookends, you know? A start and a finish. A first and a last. They're what's needed to contain a story. A book can't stand without them. ~1527 A.S.

Whoa. ~1526 A.S.

That's like ... ~1530 A.S.

Deep. ~1532 A.S.

Yeah. ~1529 A.S.

Since we're feeling philosophical, I have a question. Books never end with The End anymore. Why is that? ~1527 A.S.

Because it's so final. Feels like you'll never see each other again. ~1532 A.S.

Then how should I end THIS book? I get to do that, right? Write the last sentence? ~1526 A.S.

How to Write a Time Traveler's Diary, Lesson Eight: Narrator gets the final word. You're the narrator of this diary. But seeing how this isn't really The End, may I suggest: Until Next Time? ~1530 A.S.

No! It has to start with "the" or it doesn't sound important enough. ~1527 A.S.

Fine. The Farewell? The Bub-Bye? The See You Soon? ~1529 A.S.

Ooh! Or we could end with the word "finish" in some obscure foreign language. ~1526 A.S.

... do you know any obscure foreign languages? ~1529 A.S.

Well, no. But I could learn cursive. Wait! I've got it! The perfect ending for the book! I'll say ... ~1526 A.S.

Yes? ~1532 A.S.

Let the moment build, would you? I'll say ... ~1526 A.S.

Does it have a "the"? It has to have a "the". ~1527 A.S.

I'll say ... ~1526 A.S.

This is it, lords and ladies. The big finish. ~1530 A.S.

I'll say ... ~1526 A.S.

Spit it out! ~1529 A.S.

The Toodles. ~1526 A.S.

ACKNOWLEDGMENTS

Hi, Reader Name Here _____! Rose again. So, apparently I have an author—I know, I'm as shocked by this as you are. But in lieu of an existential crisis, I have agreed to write her acknowledgements page.

My author would like to thank, in no particular order:

(OH, WHO AM I KIDDING? WE BOTH KNOW WHO COMES FIRST IN THESE THINGS.)

- Her darling momma, Samantha, for her boundless creativity and shameless mom-promotion of *Legend of the Storm Sneezer* + the tireless hours of support, "Buck up, Bucko" speeches, brainstorming sessions, and faith-filled encouragement.
  - Her darling father, Marius, for his countless pep

talks, unwavering confidence, and his ... um ... *avant-garde* marketing schemes.

- Her dearest sister, Kaiti, for reading early drafts, offering thoughtful critiques at great personal risk, and for her endless sisterly support and enthusiasm.

(My author would also like me to add that you've picked out all the boys Kristiana was supposed to marry, and in turn, she's picked out all the books you were supposed to read. Which turned out better? Inquiring minds would like to know.)

- Her dearest brother, Kaleb, for his unfailing tech support, willingness to talk forever about time travel in its many forms and paradoxes, and for being the best big brother a girl could ask for.

- Her brother-in-law, Mike, for his kindness and genuine excitement.

- Her niece and nephews, Scarlett, Sawyer, and Liam —her favorite kids and future readers.

- Her Gramma, who didn't get to read *Legend of the Storm Sneezer* this side of heaven but was unconditionally supportive of her creative projects—from fridge artwork to heartfelt fanmail—through her whole childhood.

- Her writing bestie, April Clausen, for being the best friend, CP, and cheerleader any author could ever hope for on their writing journey. Truly, you are one of Kristiana's greatest blessings.

(ALSO, MY AUTHOR NEVER SHUTS UP ABOUT YOUR CHARACTERS, AND I THINK I'D GET ALONG WITH THEM SPLENDIDLY! I CAN'T WAIT TO SEE THEM FIND THEIR OWN PUBLISHING HOMES.)

- Jim Doran for being a steady friend and invaluable critique partner.
- Her agents, Hope Bolinger and Cyle Young, for taking a chance on *Legend of the Storm Sneezer* and championing it with gusto. Special thanks to Hope for her friendship, guidance, innumerable emails, CHOCOLATE, and shared joy in reading, writing, and publishing.
- Her agency sistas and fellow members of #TeamHope, Tara K. Ross, Dianne Bright, and Alyssa Roat, for their friendship and support.
- Her Storm Sneezer Squad—

(OKAY, THAT'S THE BEST NAME EVER. DO YOU GUYS HAVE, LIKE, MONOGRAMED HANDKERCHIEFS OR SOMETHING? 'CAUSE IF YOU DON'T, YOU NEED TO PETITION FOR THOSE ASAP.)

—and her writing community: Amberly Kristen Clowe, Bonnie Lovelace, Cassidy Eubanks, Chad Pettit, Christina Dwivedi, Christi J. Whitney, Cody Nowack, Jacob Krivsky, Jordan Thompson, Kenzi Melody, Kevin E. Jackson, Laura A. Grace, Mackenzie Flohr, Paige Gilbert, The Storiers, Suzanne Jacobs Lipshaw, Teresa Crumpton, and Vanessa Burton.

- Stephanie Burgis for her kind advice, encouragement, and wonderful stories.

- Derek Landy and Jonathan Stroud. Chances are you'll never read her books, but Kristiana has sure as heck read yours, and on behalf of her teenage self, she would like to thank you for all the amazing memories and for teaching her the basics of banter, BrOTPS, and how to balance horror with the perfect amount of humor.

- Sue Rowland for being one of *Legend of the Storm Sneezer*'s first beta readers and for her priceless exuberance and generosity.

- Lorena Bassett for introducing Kristiana to *Harry Potter* and jumpstarting her love for middle grade fiction and for all of her incredible thoughtfulness and wholehearted enthusiasm.

- Mr. M for being the best driver's training instructor in all the worlds and for being the inspiration behind Malachy's magnificent teaching style. It breaks Kristiana's heart that she'll never get to thank you face-to-face, but she still hears your voice in her head whenever she gets behind the wheel, and she hopes the skies of heaven are crowded with pterodactyls. Your outspoken faith in the most ordinary of jobs is a constant inspiration to this day.

- Cammie Larsen and Mary Gray for their keen editorial eyes, humorous emails, abundant encouragement, and unparalleled passion for *Legend of the Storm Sneezer*.

(NO PUBLISHER HAS EVER BELIEVED IN ME LIKE YOU TWO, AND

YOU KNOW WHAT? I'M GLAD THEY DIDN'T. 'CAUSE THEN I WOULD NEVER HAVE FOUND MY HOME WITH YOU!)

- The whole Monster Ivy family for their love, faith, and unshakeable support of each other.

(AND NOW, THE LAST NAME ON THE LIST, WHICH EVERYONE KNOWS IS THE MOST IMPORTANT ...)

- Her own Author, Jesus, for telling the best stories.

ABOUT THE AUTHOR

Kristiana Sfirlea knows what it means to get in character. She spent five years as a historical reenactor trying her best not to catch her skirts on fire as a colonial girl from the 1700s. Working at a haunted house attraction, she played a jumping werewolf statue, a goblin in a two-way mirror, and a wall-scratcher—so if she's standing very still, growling, checking her reflection, or filing her nails on your wall, be alarmed. Those are hard habits to break.

Kristiana's speculative flash fiction has been published by Havok, and her debut novel is a spooky MG fantasy. She dreams of the day she can run her own mobile bookstore.

Or haunted house attraction. Or both. Look out, world—
here comes a haunted bookmobile! (And this is precisely
why writers should never become Uber drivers.) She loves
Jesus, her family, and imaginary life with her characters.

CPSIA information can be obtained
at www.ICGtesting.com
Printed in the USA
LVHW082005180620
658457LV00012B/229/J